# "Don't look so I'm really not such an ogre as I've been making out."

Tilda stood helpless as those long fingers drifted along the line of her jaw, a light, compelling tracery on her soft skin. Eyes wide, she trembled, unable to break away. His feathery touch held her as surely as iron chains.

She swallowed. "Really, Your Grace…" If only he wasn't so appallingly handsome.

He drew an audible breath. "And I have another crime to confess to you."

Another crime?

"You thought I knew something of your past, your marriage. I did not until my mother explained matters to me."

Tilda felt a strange shiver pass through her. Without thinking she said softly, "I am free now, free to live as I please, make my own choices…."

"Free to choose your own husband, for example."

\* \* \*

***The Unruly Chaperon***
**Harlequin Historical #745—March 2005**

# ELIZABETH ROLLS

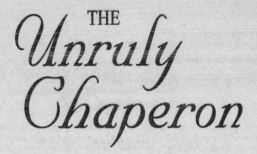

## THE Unruly Chaperon

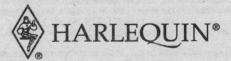

## HARLEQUIN®

TORONTO • NEW YORK • LONDON
AMSTERDAM • PARIS • SYDNEY • HAMBURG
STOCKHOLM • ATHENS • TOKYO • MILAN • MADRID
PRAGUE • WARSAW • BUDAPEST • AUCKLAND

ISBN 0-373-29345-3

THE UNRULY CHAPERON

Copyright © 2003 by Elizabeth Rolls

First North American Publication 2005

www.eHarlequin.com

**Printed in U.S.A.**

Please address questions and book requests to:
Harlequin Reader Service
U.S.: 3010 Walden Ave., P.O. Box 1325, Buffalo, NY 14269
Canadian: P.O. Box 609, Fort Erie, Ont. L2A 5X3

# Chapter One

'Uncle Roger, let me be quite certain I have understood you correctly.' Lady Winter stood in the drawing room of her uncle's house, Broughton Place, carefully drawing off her York tan gloves, having dutifully kissed Lord Pemberton on the cheek.

'Aunt Pemberton wrote to me, asking me to come and stay with her during her approaching confinement, but now you tell me she wishes me to act as chaperon to Milly. At some house party.' Lady Winter's tone did not suggest that she viewed this disposal of her time at all charitably.

Tall and elegant in her rich brown, twill carriage dress, nothing in her dignified air or posture called to mind the rather gawky and shy Miss Matilda Arnold who had married Viscount Winter some seven years earlier. Her uncle, however, saw no difference.

'Now, see here, Miss—' Lord Pemberton began to bluster.

Lady Winter broke in. 'Surely Aunt Casterfield was chaperoning Milly this past Season? What has become of her? I should have thought that you would regard her as far more suitable than my poor self.'

The unarguable truth of this last remark did little to placate Lord Pemberton. He swelled dangerously. 'Now, see here...'

'Some fearsome scandal has made her unwillingly, or unfit, to continue her duties, perchance?' mused Lady Winter hopefully. 'Or have Milly's suitors shocked her so much that she must retire from the lists?'

'Her mother-in-law!' snapped Lord Pemberton, plainly goaded beyond endurance.

Lady Winter raised incredulous eyebrows. '*Old* Lady Casterfield has caused a scandal? Goodness me! How very shocking. Do you know, at eighty-eight, I should have thought she would be more up to snuff.'

'She's dying!' Lord Pemberton ground out.

Lady Winter affected surprise. 'Dying? There's nothing scandalous in that.'

Lord Pemberton practically had a seizure. 'My sister,' he snarled, 'very properly feels that, in such a situation, her mother-in-law's claim rates more highly than Milly's.'

Lady Winter gave this due consideration, and finally pronounced, 'Very proper indeed. But I still don't see quite where I come into your calculations. And, if I do, why I was not even consulted.'

Teeth audibly grinding, Lord Pemberton began. 'Your aunts and I do not see that it makes the least difference to *you*, where you are—'

His undutiful niece interrupted in tones of calm indifference, 'Very likely not, sir. But I am not to blame for your lack of percipience. You tell me that you have committed me to attend a house party, as Milly's chaperon, without even the courtesy of asking me?'

Lord Pemberton glared at her and attempted to assert his authority. 'You're our niece and ward, miss, and you'll do your duty!'

Lady Winter smiled sweetly. 'I fear you are mistaken sir. I'm no longer your ward, but rather Jonathan's widow. And my *duty* is to our daughter. Furthermore I am five and twenty and my own mistress. While naturally I have every sympathy for Aunt Casterfield's dilemma, so far as I am concerned the decision as to whether or not I attend this house party is entirely mine. And at the moment I am not at all inclined to do so.' She smiled even more sweetly. 'No doubt you will inform me of the venue, the hostess, and what arrangements have been made for my daughter, in your own good time so that I may make a final decision. Now I am weary and should like to retire for a rest before dinner. You may tell me all about it later.'

She dropped her uncle a slight curtsy and glided from the room, leaving a stunned and furious peer behind her. Lord Pemberton had seen little of his niece in the years since her marriage. Lady Pemberton had seen even less. Very much occupied with her own lyings-in, she took little notice of a niece that she actively disliked, and had not even attended on Lady Winter when her only child, Anthea, was born.

Having presented her husband with a son first, Lady Pemberton had safely dismissed the birth of the Honourable Anthea Cavendish as a matter of little consequence.

'How like that undutiful girl to have a daughter first,' had been her comment when the news arrived and she gave it no more thought, beyond directing her eldest daughter, Miss Amelia, to write to her cousin and say as little as was proper.

Lord Pemberton fumed and fulminated on his misfortune in having been forced to house such a girl as he poured himself a generous tot of brandy. Here was Amelia set to make the catch of the year—of the decade! And Miss Matilda—humph, *Lady Winter*—thought she could overset all their plans. Not a doubt but what widowhood had gone to her head. So she thought she could ride roughshod over them all, did she? Not while he had breath in his body!

He paced back and forth in front of the fireplace, recalling all the means he had used in the past to enforce his intransigent niece's obedience. Grimly he pondered. He'd even brought her to heel over her marriage to Viscount Winter. The same methods should work now.

Lady Winter, holding on to the rags of her dignity and temper with difficulty, ascended the main staircase of her ancestral home and headed straight for the best spare bed-chamber. Not unsurprisingly she discovered it to be inno-cent of her own baggage and that of her daughter. She smiled, consideringly, and tugged at the bell pull imperi-ously.

Five minutes later the startled housekeeper came in. 'What in the...oh! It's *you*, Miss Tilda!'

Lady Winter nodded and said, 'That's right, Mrs Penny. Has my luggage not yet been brought up?' Bright interest sheathed this artless question.

Mrs Penny blinked. 'Well, of course it has, Miss Tilda!' She encountered a haughty gaze and amended, 'My...my lady. The mistress gave orders that it was to be put in Miss Amelia's room, like always.'

Feigning innocence, Lady Winter stared in well-simulated astonishment, a mobile brow rising in haughty inquiry. 'And what use do you imagine Miss Amelia has for my belongings? Have them brought here, if you please. And precisely where is Miss Anthea?'

Floored by this defiance from one who had never said so much as boo to a goose, let alone defied her aunt, Mrs Penny opened and closed her mouth several times. 'Miss Anthea is in the nursery...with...with the other children.'

Lady Winter seemed to consider that. 'Oh. Visiting her cousins. Very well. But she may sleep here in the dressing room. Please see to all that, Mrs Penny. And I should very much like a cup of tea. Thank you.'

Somehow Mrs Penny found herself outside the door without quite knowing how she had got there. She shook her head in amazement. Marriage had certainly changed Miss Tilda, that it had!

As soon as the door shut behind Mrs Penny, Lady Winter, *née* Matilda Arnold, sank into a chair and breathed a sigh of relief. Really, this business of being assertive and sticking up for herself was exhausting. It *was* fun, though. Never had she imagined just how put out her uncle would be. Let alone poor Penny! Still, it wasn't over. She had yet to encounter her aunt.

She set her jaw mulishly. She was damned if she was going to run in their harness ever again. Certainly not for any plot to catch Amelia a rich husband. No, she would stay to assist her aunt, or if, as seemed likely, that affecting plea for support had been merely a ploy to lure her into their net, she could always leave for Leicestershire tomorrow. Well, maybe the day after, since the horses needed resting.

Her luggage and Anthea's arrived within fifteen minutes along with her maid, Sarah.

Barely had the door closed behind the footman who had brought the trunks than Sarah shot an amused glance at her mistress. 'I take it ye're set on puttin' 'em all on end, milady?'

Tilda simply grinned and said, 'Why not? Being polite and submissive never worked, so…'

The door opened again and a slender child of five, clutching a doll, came in.

'Mama, am I to sleep in the nursery? Great-Aunt Pemberton says that I must be there at all times and that I must sleep with Cousin Maria.' Worried hazel-brown eyes pleaded for a stay of execution.

Tilda laughed and held out her arms. 'You will need to be in the nursery with the other children when I cannot be with you, but you are to sleep in the dressing room here.'

A relieved sigh broke from Anthea. She flew across the

room and hugged her mother. 'Oh, good. Cousin Maria wanted to have Susan in *her* bed!'

'And what did you say to that?' asked Tilda, dropping a kiss on the brown curls so like her own. She cast a warning glance at Sarah.

*Later.* She didn't want Anthea caught up in the bitterness between herself and the Pembertons.

'I said she couldn't,' and came to find you,' said Anthea, snuggling closer.

'Good girl,' said Tilda. 'Let's unpack and get everything sorted out, then we can have a story before you go back to the nursery for supper. I'll come up and put you to bed between courses.'

By the time she went down to dinner, Tilda had her plan of action worked out. It was simple, guaranteed to be effective, and, most importantly, would infuriate her family. She smiled into the looking glass and observed the stranger there with relief.

She *had* changed. Beyond colouring, there was little resemblance between the gangling, dowdy girl of seven years ago and the elegant matron who gazed back at her. Of course she was still far too tall, but at least she no longer tripped over her own shadow. Instead of the very plain scraped-back styles her aunt had insisted on for her, glossy brown curls were piled high on her head and confident golden brown eyes stared from under delicately arched brows.

She might not be a beauty, but she had improved. She had filled out for one thing, so the gown of deep green satin clung and shifted against her generous, yet slender curves in a most satisfactory way. It was cut quite discreetly over her bosom, but she could not think it at all a suitable gown for the chaperon of a young girl.

A fact which Lady Pemberton was at pains to point out the moment she set foot in the drawing room.

Resplendent in puce satin, she stared in outrage at the elegant creation swathing her niece's graceful figure. 'Good heavens, girl! That's not the sort of gown a chaperon wears!'

Tilda stepped back mentally to make way for Lady Winter, who raised one eyebrow, the same one that had annihilated Mrs Penny, and said languidly, 'No, it's not. How clever of you to notice. Good evening, ma'am. I trust you are well. My uncle said you were resting when I arrived so I didn't disturb you.'

Ignoring this greeting, Lady Pemberton said, 'And I understand you've set yourself up in the best spare bedchamber. Well, you may stay there for the night, but in the morning you must move back to your cousin's chamber. The guest chamber is for our guests!'

Lady Winter disposed herself gracefully in a *bergère*. 'Really? I had no idea that you were planning to entertain so close to your confinement, ma'am.' She cast a surprised glance at her aunt's very swollen belly. And smiled gently. 'You know, I cannot think that Amelia will welcome both her cousins in her room.'

Lady Pemberton frowned. 'What is this nonsense? Your daughter, Matilda, may stay in the nursery where she belongs. I'll have no spoiling.'

More than a hint of steel crept into Lady Winter's voice. 'I beg your pardon, ma'am, but I will order Anthea's life as *I* see fit. Naturally she will be with the other children during the day, but she is used to being within call of me at night.'

At this inopportune moment his lordship came in. Lady Pemberton enlisted his support at once.

'My lord! I must insist! Here is your niece, quite the grand lady! She has the insolence to insist on the best spare chamber!'

Her spouse immediately bent a threatening glare upon his niece and unleashed a hectoring tirade that would have reduced Miss Matilda Arnold to tearful obedience seven years earlier. He raged at her impudence, her undutiful behaviour, her ingratitude and finally said, 'You'll go the same way as your mother! Mark my words!'

Lady Winter sat back and listened with no more than bright-eyed interest. Even his final taunt failed to bring a blush to her cheeks. She commented merely, 'In that case, I'm stunned that you consider me a suitable chaperon for Amelia. If you've thought better of it, I'll remove my polluting presence from Broughton Place as soon as my horses are rested.' A faint smile curved her lips. 'In the meantime, I shall remain where I am.'

Lord Pemberton pulled up short and stared in disbelief. He was prevented from any further explosions by the entrance of his eldest daughter, Amelia, and his eldest son, Thomas.

A glance was enough to inform anyone that the pair were brother and sister. Both had dark curly hair and the bright blue eyes that in Lady Pemberton had faded somewhat. But whereas Amelia had inherited her mother's petite daintiness, Tom had favoured his father's height.

Turning to greet her cousins, Tilda thought that the years had not reneged on the early promise of beauty Amelia had shown. The rippling dark curls and vivid blue eyes were as startling as ever. Her figure was perfection. Small, yet beautifully proportioned, with just that hint of fragility that so many gentlemen seemed to appreciate.

For an instant she felt a gangling, awkward girl again, constantly being compared unfavourably with her far prettier cousin. But the stunned look of admiration on Tom's face as he surged forward to greet her swept all her nerves aside.

'Tilda!' He took her in a bear hug. 'I swear I wouldn't have recognised you!' He held her away at arm's length. 'You look famously. That green suits you. They'd better not send *you* to chaperon Milly. His Grace might decide he prefers you!'

A delighted chuckle broke from her. One that very few besides her daughter and eldest cousin had ever heard. 'Oh, Tom! What a Banbury story! As though anyone would prefer me to Milly.' She turned to Amelia and said sincerely, 'You look lovely, Milly. I need not ask how *you* go on!'

Amelia sniffed and said, 'I really prefer to be called Amelia now that I am out and grown up. Milly sounds so childish!'

'Oh stubble it, Milly,' recommended Tom with brotherly candour. 'Why, here's Tilda, looking as fine as five pence, a Viscountess to boot, and she don't fuss about her name!'

He turned back to his cousin. 'Tell me. Are those capital bays in the stables yours? And the grey mare?'

Tilda nodded, a faint twinkle in her eyes. 'Oh, yes. But I fear Frosty won't be quite up to your weight!'

Tom sighed. 'More's the pity, but those bays! Complete to a shade!'

The boyish longing in his tones made her smile. 'If you wish and my uncle permits, they may be harnessed to a phaeton or curricle tomorrow and you may try their paces.' She paused and added meaningfully, 'Once I am persuaded that you can handle them!'

Tom blushed and grinned self-deprecatingly, but his father stared. 'And pray tell, who is to make the decision as to whether Tom is able to handle this pair?'

Calm hazel eyes met his glare. 'I thought I made that clear, sir. I will.'

'Not in any carriage of mine, you won't!' pronounced Lord Pemberton awfully. 'Damned if I'll have a chit of a girl overturning my sporting carriages! You'll let Tom try those horses and there's an end of it.'

Tom flushed scarlet and shot an apologetic look at Tilda as though expecting to see her wilting under his father's fire.

She raised her brows and said bluntly, 'I'm afraid not, sir. They are my horses, and, since I've had no opportunity to see Tom drive since he overturned me in a mere gig eight years ago, I must decline to allow him to drive them alone until I am sure he is able to handle them.'

'Good God!' Lady Pemberton was scandalised. 'Do you set yourself up to know better than your uncle?'

'No, ma'am,' responded Tilda. 'But I certainly know my own horses better than he does. I will risk neither their knees nor Tom's neck. And do tell me, what does one have to do to be offered a drink?'

Tom laughed and said, 'You've done it, Tilda. What can I offer you? Ratafia?'

She shuddered artistically. 'No, I thank you. Jonathan was very particular in educating me. I would prefer Madeira.'

Pemberton's frown was darkling. 'In *my* day, a young woman—'

Mocking hazel eyes tilted up at him. 'Dear sir, don't say that. Why, anyone would imagine you were old enough… to…well, to be my husband!'

A stunned silence greeted this pointed reference to the fact that the late Lord Winter had been some thirty-five years his eighteen-year-old bride's senior. It was broken by Lady Pemberton.

She bridled and said, 'You were lucky to receive *that* offer!'

'I'm sure I was,' agreed Lady Winter pensively. 'Now, tell me all about Amelia's season. Your second season, is it not, Amelia? My! And not yet betrothed? Why, I was snapped up after merely *half* a season. Was I not, ma'am? Dear Jonathan positively beating a track to the door. Ah, thank you, Tom.' She directed a charming smile at her cousin and sipped the Madeira thoughtfully.

Amelia drew an angry breath. 'I see how it is. You're

jealous because I'm prettier. Because I have received more offers than you—'

She was gently interrupted. 'Not at all, Amelia. You are to be felicitated. And how many offers have you received?'

Before Lady Pemberton could frown her into silence, Amelia blurted out, 'Four! Five if you count his Grace!'

'Four!' Lady Winter smiled. 'You are indeed fortunate to have your choice. And here was I, thinking that the men in London must be blind that you are still unwed. You see, I thought it was imperative to accept the *first* offer in order that money might be hoarded for the next girl's come-out.'

'Oh, but that was Lord Walmisley!' protested Amelia. 'He is far too old. Why, he must be forty if he's a day!'

'Forty!' marvelled Lady Winter. 'That *is* quite an age. Dear me, I'm surprised poor Jonathan managed the walk back down the aisle.' She paused thoughtfully. 'Let alone the wedding night.'

Shrieking silence followed this, to be broken by Lady Winter who appeared to have lunched on shrapnel.

'And may one know which Duke Amelia has on a string?' inquired Lady Winter in dulcet tones. 'I collect it *is* a Duke that she has in her sights, and not a widowed Archbishop. You did say *his Grace*, did you not, Tom?'

Her dazed cousin nodded. 'Er, yes. St Ormond.'

There was an infinitesimal pause. 'Dear me,' said Lady Winter brightly. 'That *is* quite a conquest. Well worth passing over poor old Walmisley for. And just think; his Grace cannot be a day over six and thirty.'

At this point Providence took pity on Lord and Lady Pemberton by permitting their butler to announce dinner.

Dinner was not a success. Lord Pemberton's attempts to bring his niece to a sense of her iniquities were thoroughly hampered by the presence of the servants, while Lady Winter's barbed tongue appeared to run on wheels. She said nothing indiscreet, but it was plain that she was taking the greatest pleasure in mercilessly baiting her uncle and aunt.

By the time the ladies withdrew, Lady Pemberton was stiff with fury. Barely had the drawing room door closed behind them than she launched into a comprehensive condemnation of Tilda's manners and style.

Lady Winter sat back and listened with seeming attention. Only at the end, when Lady Pemberton paused to gauge the effect of her attack, did she speak. And then rather absent-mindedly.

'I do beg your pardon, ma'am. My mind was wandering. Could you repeat that? Oh, not all of it,' as Lady Pemberton gasped in disbelief. 'Perish the thought! Just the last little bit. You know, the bit about my not being fit to chaperon anyone. That *did* command my attention.'

Milly's gasp of amazement at her cousin's temerity was interrupted by the timely entrance of her father and brother.

His lordship came straight to the point. Directing a threatening frown at his niece, he said, 'I hope you have come to your senses and realise that your place is to do as you are told and abide by our judgement.'

'But of course, sir,' said Lady Winter with a mocking smile. 'My aunt has just informed me that I am unfit to chaperon anyone. I am more than happy to abide by that judgement.'

For a moment it seemed likely that Pemberton would fall victim to an apoplectic fit. His eyes bulged and his face went an unbecoming shade of purple.

Lady Winter took advantage of his momentary incapacity to press her advantage. She spoke in a soft, but deadly, tone. 'You see, my lord, I am no longer a chit of a girl, dependent upon you for anything. Frankly, I neither desire nor need your goodwill. Unbeknownst to yourselves, you set me free by forcing my marriage to Jonathan. I am an independently wealthy woman and I can do as *I* damn well please.'

She paused for breath and continued in a chilly voice, 'I came, not because you ordered it, but because I felt that the request made for my assistance during my aunt's lying-in was perfectly reasonable, and that I ought not, as a woman, refuse… And—' her voice shook slightly '—because I thought that you might at long last have discovered some slight affection for me. But I will not submit to being bullied or manipulated. If that is how you mean to go on, then Anthea and I will be leaving almost immediately.'

Lord Pemberton gave a scornful bark of laughter. 'Wealthy! You may choose to think your jointure wealth, but I can assure you that it will not go far if you continue to waste the ready on your back the way you must be.' His eyes raked the green satin gown, the expensive reticule and dainty satin slippers.

Lady Winter stared back incredulously. 'You really didn't know? You paid so little attention to the man you married me to, that you knew nothing of his capacity to support me?'

Her uncle shrugged. 'Everyone knew that Winter's estates were well enough. But you can't tell me that after providing for his daughter, he was able to leave you much. And tied up against your *possible* remarriage, no doubt.' His tone suggested that he saw such an eventuality as exceedingly remote.

Genuine amusement crept into Lady Winter's mocking smile, which deepened as she spoke. 'You really shouldn't let appearances blind you, sir. Despite the lack of ostentatious display to impress people whose opinion he couldn't have cared less about, Jonathan was extremely wealthy. That little jaunt to India in his youth was rather profitable, apparently, and quite independent of the title and estate, of course. He left half of it to me, whether or not I remarry.'

Tom was the first to recover his breath. 'Is this true, Tilda? You're not bamming us?' His voice held sincere, unalloyed delight.

She nodded.

'You're a wealthy widow?'

She nodded again, still with that faintly mocking smile lifting the corner of her delicately cut mouth. 'Shockingly wealthy, Tom.'

Savagely, Lord Pemberton broke in. 'No doubt you'll run through it in no time!'

She shook her head. 'Oh, no. Jonathan made quite sure I learnt how to manage my investments. And, until I am thirty-five, his heir is my principal trustee. He considered it…likely, shall we say…that he would predecease me. He always took his responsibilities very seriously. I am entirely capable of looking after myself.'

Her next shot was deadly. 'So, you see, asking me to chaperon Amelia is not at all a good idea. After all, even had my looks not improved slightly in seven years, I am now wealthy enough to give the most exacting of men a case of…selective blindness…to go with their…er… selective deafness, you know.'

Lady Pemberton gritted her teeth. Audibly. 'Then you intend to remarry?'

Lady Winter put her head on one side. A considering look crept into the golden eyes. 'I suppose I might. But really, I don't see the need.' One dark brow lifted suggestively. 'After all, the possibilities as a widow are *far* more appealing!'

'Why, you little *slut*!' exploded Lady Pemberton.

Milly blinked.

That dark brow arched even further. 'My dear ma'am, whatever can you mean? After all, there is not the slightest need for me to tie myself up in matrimony, depriving some poor girl of a husband. Besides, I like being my *own* mistress.' She smiled cheerfully, apparently impervious to the atmosphere of scandalised resentment. 'Anyway, enough of all this. I am a trifle fagged and will go up now. Good-night.'

She left the field littered with dead and dying. Four pairs of eyes watched her go—two full of furious resentment, one of dazed wonder…and one laden with confusion.

Oddly enough, her signal victory over her family did not occupy Tilda's thoughts for long. She checked on Anthea, soundly asleep in the dressing room, Susan clutched possessively to her breast. After bestowing a tender kiss on each, she wandered back to her bedchamber, stripped off her gown and slipped into a silken nightgown and peignoir. She wriggled her shoulders appreciatively against the soft material. After years of wearing sensible, warm nightgowns of voluminous and unattractive aspect to appease her husband's fear of her contracting a chill, it was enormous fun to wear something frivolous and daring. Something that made her feel like a seductive hussy. Even if there was no one else to appreciate it. A state of affairs that she fully intended to maintain.

She tugged the bell and waited. Some ten minutes later Sarah came in.

'Here y'are, m'lady,' Sarah frowned. 'Lor', if I haven't told ye over an' over! I'm supposed to help you undress!' Bustling forward, she swept up the discarded gown and shook it out lovingly.

'Oh, stop that, Sarah!' said Tilda. 'For heaven's sake, you know I can manage for myself. Just tell me what they're saying in the servants' hall.'

Sarah sat down uninvited on the daybed, the gown cradled in her lap. 'All of a flutter at the difference in you, for starters. Most of 'em reckon it's a good thing.' Mildly, she commented, 'Must be quite a difference. Not havin' known you afore your marriage, I did just wonder.' Faint curiosity tinged her voice.

Tilda grimaced. 'I was the most browbeaten, pathetic excuse for a female that can be imagined. Not to mention the most gawky of Long Megs. I was used to trip over everything and everyone.' She chuckled wryly. 'I daresay *Lady Winter* is quite a shock to them all. Amazing what a difference clothes can make. Good. Now, what about this Duke? St Ormond, I'm led to believe.' She said the name lightly enough, but was conscious of the very slightest tightening in her throat.

Sarah grinned. 'Seems to me the announcement ought to 've been in the papers already, the way they're talkin'. Miss Pemberton's invited to a house party given by the Dowager Duchess. Word is that it's a chance for his Grace to get to know her before makin' an offer. They reckon as how he was courtin' her in town. Dancin' at the balls, walkin' in the park. Even came to see your uncle.'

Tilda considered. 'Very well. They want me to chaperon her at this house party. Naturally my aunt cannot do so. And had they asked me, rather than trying to bully me into it, then I just might have consented. As it is, I rather think we will be going home in a few days. Thank you, Sarah. Go to bed. I'll ring for you in the morning.'

Sarah heaved herself to her feet and favoured her mistress with a grim smile. 'A Long Meg, eh? Don't sit up too late!' After placing the silken gown tenderly in a closet, she was gone, leaving Tilda to her thoughts.

Restlessly she paced up and down, the silken skirts of her nightgown whispering around her ankles. St Ormond. The name blazed in her mind. Seven years, and the name could still conjure up that churning feeling of affronted hurt, of anger and wounded pride. Seven years, and the very name still had the same power over her, to enthral and captivate.

Damn it! She was Lady Winter now! A wealthy and passably attractive widow. Not the clumsy and painfully shy débutante she had been. So why did the memory of a childish fancy still affect her so deeply? A fantastical dream that she had never taken seriously, even in her wildest maiden fancies. It had not needed his Grace's unwitting cruelty for her to realise that her path and his would not lie together, that he would never accord her a second glance. And that his first and only glance had left him unimpressed.

And she was not going to this beastly house party anyway, she thought, as she sat down on the chaise and curled her legs up under her night gown. So why was she shaking so much? Almost against her will, her memory drifted back to that dreadful night at the Seftons' ball... His Grace, as elegant as ever, in a superbly cut coat of blue superfine...she could still see the bright gold of its buttons...the diamond pin nestling in his elegantly tied cravat...powerful thighs encased in immaculate inexpressibles. Well over six foot, he towered over every man in the room, one of the very few she wouldn't have to stoop to dance with. His chestnut locks glowed with bronze lights and wicked green eyes narrowed as he laughed with a friend, the embodiment of a lonely and friendless maiden's dreams. The *parfait et gentil chevalier* of her imaginings.

She looked back at her younger self with gentle mockery, remembering how she had watched him from afar throughout the first weeks of her season, seeing him sought after, courted, flattered. Once he had reached down a book for her at Hatchard's; three nights before that he had actually stood up with her...

His intended partner, the lovely and graceful Lady Diana Kempsey, had been overcome by faintness at the start of their dance. He had returned her to her mama, and Tilda, with her usual half-full dance card, had been standing nearby with her aunt.

With his customary charm he turned and begged her to indulge him with a dance. 'Not the most flattering invitation you will ever receive, Miss Arnold, but I do beg you will accept!'

Accept? She smiled wryly as she remembered how she floated out to dance. He even knew her name! Speechlessly she placed her hand in his and felt the long fingers clasp

hers. Unbelievably, it was a waltz. The scandalous dance
had recently gained the approval of Almack's haughty pa-
tronesses, but due to her height, all five foot eleven of it,
she was rarely solicited for the honour.

When she was, it became a species of musical torture.
She could not fit her stride, her exuberant joy in the music,
to the rather sedate young men with whom she danced.
Invariably she stumbled, trod on their toes, bumped their
shins, and her embarrassment made matters worse. So terrified was she that she could not even converse rationally.

With St Ormond she found her perfect partner. She felt
it the moment his arms closed about her; a sense of right-
ness, of inevitability. His height suited her to perfection;
she glided and twirled effortlessly in his embrace. And it
went beyond physical comfort. She could even chat to him,
responding to his banter and questions happily. She actually
found herself telling him about her pet cat, Toby, raised by
her from extreme infancy. St Ormond seemed to find her
caustic description of raising an orphaned kitten in her bed
hilarious, and had countered with a tale of raising an orphaned foal, now his favourite mare.

'Not that I raised her in my bed, of course. Mama would
not hear of that. But I did spend a great many nights bedded
down in her stall!'

All too soon the dance ended and his Grace returned her
to Lady Pemberton, with a laughing injunction to be mentioned to Toby. And she responded in kind, asking him to
give Sirene a carrot for her.

Lady Pemberton frowned mightily upon this exchange,
calling her to order in a vicious undertone, telling her what
a cake she was making of herself. That, in setting her cap
at St Ormond, merely because he was too polite to snub
her, she was shaming her family.

Tilda tripped over her next partner's feet and had to be
taken home with a bloodied nose.

Three nights later Lady Pemberton relented from her

avowal never to take Tilda to another ball. Her lord's saner counsel had prevailed. How the devil were they to get the chit off their hands if she wasn't seen? And old Lady Pemberton was insisting that the girl be given a season—to silence the gossips. So she consented to take Tilda to the Seftons' ball.

His Grace of St Ormond was there, of course, but Tilda came nowhere near him until after supper, when she managed to withdraw to the retiring room for a few minutes to recover from a particularly gruesome dance with Lord Winter who was several inches shorter than she, and who had been painfully gracious about her assault on his toes.

Emerging from the retiring room when it filled with giggling young ladies, she slipped back to the ballroom and took refuge behind a potted palm. St Ormond had strolled by with his brother-in-law, Lord Hastings.

Their cheerful conversation still burnt in her memory.

'Really, Cris, here you have every charming débutante just itching to retrieve your handkerchief, and you tell me that not *one*, not even *one*, takes your fancy! You are becoming entirely too picky, my boy!' Lord Hastings twitted his friend with gentle sarcasm.

St Ormond shrugged and said, 'Take a closer look, James. There's really very little there. In most of them, anyway. Most of 'em aren't even interesting to dance with! All far too young! Now, take Miss Arnold for example! There's a chit who shouldn't have even been let loose in London...' The pair had moved away and the rest of his Grace's remarks were lost.

Thankfully lost. Seven years later she could still flush with humiliation for the naïve dreamer the eighteen-year-old girl had been, still remember the hurt. She'd come out from behind the palm, so white and shaking that even Lady Jersey, avidly gossiping nearby, noticed and took her to Lady Pemberton immediately. Somehow Tilda had made it through the rest of the evening, forcing herself to honour the few gentlemen on her dance card, forcing herself to respond to Lord Winter's kindly gallantry. Telling herself that St Ormond's thoughtless cruelty did not matter, that she had always known her dreams were insubstantial.

But it did matter, she found, when she finally buried her face in her pillow that night. In the cold light of his brutal assessment she could no longer indulge in the comfort of her daydreams, no longer lose herself in the fantasy where they wandered hand in hand in Arcadian delight. Instead of going to sleep dreaming of him, she cried herself to sleep, her dreams shattered into pathetic fragments. It might have been a hopeless dream, but at least it had been a comfort.

The next day her uncle had informed her that Lord Winter, a man thirty-five years her senior, had offered for her and that she was to marry him in three weeks, just as fast as the banns could be called. She had tried to rebel, terrified, revolted by the thought of marriage to a man she scarcely knew, a man slightly older than her uncle. Despairingly she saw herself trapped into a life even worse than the one she knew. Her uncle's tyranny replaced by the far more intimate tyranny of a husband.

Her rebellion had been doomed from the start. Unlike her mother, she had no one to take her side and, short of refusing to make her vows at the very altar, she could see no avenue of escape. Several beatings for impertinence had resolved her that, regardless of what the marriage bed involved, Lord Winter could be no worse than Lord and Lady Pemberton.

So she had married. And discovered that Jonathan Cavendish, Viscount Winter, was as kindly a man as ever lived. He treated his terrified bride with consideration and if her marital duties were initially extremely painful, at least with time they became merely boring.

Lord Winter was indulgent and, above all, treated her

with affectionate respect. She came in return to have a very real affection for him.

He had died some fifteen months ago, leaving her a very wealthy widow, with an equally wealthy four-year-old daughter. The estate and title had gone to his cousin, who had made it quite clear that he was only too delighted to have the Dowager Lady Winter quartered at the Dower House.

'Really, Tilda! Of course you must stay!' Max had expostulated when she had suggested that he and his wife might prefer her elsewhere once the period of her strict mourning was over. 'Jon practically ordered me to keep an eye on you, and Cassie and I would miss you dreadfully!'

She could not doubt the insincerity of their affection and so followed her own inclinations and stayed. At Winter Chase she was happy and protected. The people knew her and respected her. She had enough money to live in comfort, in luxury if she chose. And she had not the least use for society, or most of her family. Tom, the only one of her cousins to whom she had ever been close, was up at Oxford and spent the vacations with various friends. So the half-hearted commands to return to the bosom of her family were treated with the contempt they deserved. She strongly suspected that they had every intention of turning her into a drudge and very carefully kept the truth about her financial circumstances to herself.

That her marriage had turned out a blessing was due to no care of theirs. Indeed, in her more cynical moments the Dowager Lady Winter was inclined to wonder if they would have countenanced her marriage had they known the truth about the reclusive Lord Winter's wealth.

With a sigh she returned to the present. Nothing had changed. When the letter had come, requesting her to assist with the household during her aunt's tenth lying-in, she had felt it her duty to agree. She had been through one childbed herself and, despite her dislike for her aunt, could feel only sympathy for any woman facing her tenth.

Besides now that her period of strict mourning was over, she was beginning to find herself pestered by any number of men who plainly thought a generously dowered widow was just the thing to boost their sagging fortunes. And Tilda had absolutely no intention of ever marrying again.

The only problem was that she felt restless, confined— as though her safe, comfortable life was slowly choking her. Oh, she had Anthea and her independence—riches enough for any woman, even without the fortune Jonathan had left her. But what should she do with her independence? What use was it if she didn't use it?

So she had come, vowing that the confidence she had learnt over the years of her marriage should not desert her, that she would not become again the cowed and crippled creature she had been.

She had almost persuaded herself that this was a chance to heal the rift. To soften the loathing engendered by her mother's elopement with a young man of great charm and no fortune rather than marry a wealthy man twice her age. Since she had still been underage at the time, her marriage was only two months old when her baby was born. Her family had cast her off in disgrace and it had been with great reluctance that Lord Pemberton had received the orphaned five-year-old Matilda into his home. Indeed he had only done so because several of his sister's old friends, influential hostesses all, had kept on enquiring after the child.

Now, faced with the inescapable conclusion that she was to be manipulated and bullied into submission, Tilda had decided to hurl down the gauntlet. As far as she could see, Lady Winter was in an unassailable position. Even without the wealth Jonathan had left her, she was independent and did not need her family. Max and Cassie Winter considered her one of their closest friends. She was as happy as a grig.

So why on earth was she feeling so shaken up at the idea that she had been invited, however vicariously, to a house party hosted by his Grace the Duke of St Ormond?

A soft scratching at the door interrupted her singularly unavailing attempt to find an answer to this perplexing question.

## Chapter Two

'Come in.' A puzzled glance at the clock on the chimneypiece confirmed that it was well after midnight. Who on earth would want to speak to her now? Unless, of course, her uncle wished to utter some specific threats...

Amelia's face, appearing hesitantly around the door, put this unpleasant thought to flight.

'Milly! I...I mean, Amelia...what...?'

'Oh, don't call me that!' begged her cousin, coming fully into the room. 'I still hate it, but Mama is so insistent that I must be *Amelia* now. Tilda, is what you said true? That they forced you to have only half a season to save the money for me?'

Tilda flushed. She should not have said that in front of Milly. There was no vice in the chit, she was merely spoiled.

'No, Milly,' she said quietly. 'They didn't do it because of that.'

'But they did cut your season short? As soon as Lord Winter offered?' Milly's upset was evident.

'Yes.'

'But, why?'

Grimly Tilda faced the truth—the real reason her season had been curtailed. Oh, Lord and Lady Pemberton had said openly that they did not wish to waste money on a clumsy Long Meg, who had miraculously secured a respectable offer, money that could be better put aside for little Amelia and the other girls. So she had lashed out, hiding her grief at the truth. But the real reason was far more painful than that. A reason that had eaten at her heart for years before her season. One that she had dimly realised but had never put into words. Until the day her uncle told her that, whether she accepted Lord Winter or not, her season was over.

Incredulously she had stared at them. 'You hate me, don't you? All the discipline and...scoldings...it's not because you want to make sure I don't behave like Mama! It's because you hate me! Isn't it? *Isn't it?*' Rage at the injustice had flamed through her.

'Really, Matilda! Such intemperate language, such excessive emotion is to be deplored in a lady!' Her aunt's chilly rebuke had seared deep into her very soul. They had not even bothered to deny it.

At that moment she had made up her mind to marry Lord Winter. At least she would escape her family. He seemed kind enough. Nothing could be worse than this. And, besides, Lord Winter was over fifty. At untouched eighteen that ranked as extreme old age. The chances were that she would be a widow very soon and free to live her own life within the bounds set by society.

And so she had married, with widowhood as her aim.

She couldn't tell Milly all that. She knew that Lady Pemberton was genuinely fond of her children; that, despite Milly's irritation, she loved her mama. Tilda was not prepared to hurt by that means. It would be despicable.

'They don't like me, Milly,' she said gently. 'Because of my mother. They have always been afraid that I would take after her, disgrace them. So when Jonathan offered for me they...they insisted I accept...to...ensure nothing went wrong.'

'You didn't love him, did you?' It wasn't really a question.

'Not as you mean,' said Tilda. 'I did come to…care for him, in a friendly sort of way. He was very kind and considerate, you know.' She repressed a shudder at the memory of her wedding night, the awkwardness, her embarrassment, her revulsion at what was expected of her. No good could come of telling Milly any of that. With a younger man she was attracted to, or even in love with, things would doubtless be very different.

'Now, tell me all about St Ormond.' Somehow she forced her voice to remain light. 'I danced a waltz with him once, you know!'

'Did you?' asked Milly. 'Dancing the waltz with him is ghastly. He's so tall that I just can't keep up. And if he shortens his stride he treads on my toes!'

Tilda blinked. 'Poor man,' she said. It had never occurred to her that someone as elegant as St Ormond might be afflicted by his height in the same way she was. Milly *was* very small!

Her stare suggested that she thought Tilda had lost her mind. 'What about my toes?'

'They'll recover,' said Tilda with a faint grin. 'Try thinking about *his* mortification. How would you feel if your positions were reversed? If you were always feeling like a clumsy oaf with him?'

'Oh,' said Milly. Patently she had never exercised her imagination in this way before. 'I suppose you're right. Which brings me to what I came to say, to ask you. I have been speaking to Tom, and he said I must. Please, Tilda, will you come to this house party with me? Tom says you will know just how I should go on. That if I don't behave like a spoiled brat, you might agree.'

Tilda was aghast. 'Milly—'

'Please? I'm terrified. Apart from St Ormond, his mama, the Dowager, will be there and lots of other grand people.'

As Tilda shook her head, Milly bit her lip. 'Tom said Mama and Papa had set your back up so that you were liable to go straight home.'

'They did,' said her cousin drily. But that wasn't the real reason she quaked at the thought of attending this house party.

'Well, I'm apologising for them,' said Milly. 'And for being a brat at times,' she added generously. 'Please come with me.'

Tilda swore mentally. Aloud she asked, 'Do you like St Ormond?'

Milly flushed. 'Oh, yes. He's charming. And so handsome! He's the biggest catch of the season.'

'And how does he make you feel? When you're chatting? When he...touches you...?' Tilda had no idea if St Ormond would have attempted to kiss Milly yet, so she kept her questions general.

Milly blushed. 'He...he did try to kiss me once. I...I didn't like it at all. He scared me. I don't think he meant to, but he's so big!'

Tilda raged inwardly, *Oh, hell and the devil!*

Milly continued. 'And when we talk, well, I don't always quite catch his meaning, when he jokes. So I feel very uncomfortable. But he's very nice about it.'

Tilda nearly groaned aloud. *Worse and worse. At least I was never scared of Jonathan precisely. And I always understood him. In fact, he told me that was why he liked me. Oh, drat it! I'll have to go to this beastly party. Blast them all for landing Milly in this mess. And double blast St Ormond!*

Crispin Anthony Malvern, Duke of St Ormond, was pacing the Great Hall of Ormsby Park, his principal country residence, in a very unducal manner. His restlessness was due not so much to impatience at the tardiness of his intended bride, but to a powerful desire to be somewhere, anywhere, else. Hanging around the house on a bright summer's day was not his notion of fun. And he had been caught here all day as guests arrived.

True, they were family and did not expect him to do the pretty. Most of them had given him a cheery greeting and wandered off about their own pursuits, quite happy to make themselves at home. The Dowager, however, had insisted that he should be about all day to greet them. To his utter disgust, the carriage that must be bearing Miss Pemberton and her aunt had been spotted far down the avenue just after he handed his own Aunt Seraphina out of her antiquated and distinctly lopsided travelling coach.

'Damned thing's got a lean like a drunken sailor!' sniffed Lady Hollow. 'Have one of your people see to it, m'boy.' She had stalked up the shallow front steps, mightily resenting his supportive hand under her elbow. 'Not in m'grave yet!'

Crispin gritted his teeth, reminding himself that, had he not done so, she would have waxed lyrical over the omission, and decided that he'd done the right thing. After all, if the old girl took a tumble down the stairs she'd be quartered there for weeks. Politely he assured his aunt that her carriage would be seen to as a matter of urgency.

And now Miss Pemberton's carriage had been seen, rendering it useless to head back to the billiard room where his younger cousin Guy and his brother-in-law Hastings awaited him. He groaned as he paced up and down. Miss Pemberton was well enough, but her Aunt Casterfield was worse than Aunt Seraphina. At least the latter had a sense of humour.

Lady Casterfield, who had chaperoned her niece's second season, had very nearly put him off the whole idea of offering for Miss Pemberton. She was a holy terror, without the least leavening of humour in the lump. And she had made it perfectly plain that she did not consider his high degree or vast wealth in any way atoned for the scandalous reputation as a rake he had acquired over the years.

No doubt she would be playing her role of chaperon to the hilt. Making it impossible for him to have any opportunity to become better acquainted with Miss Pemberton. Just as she had all season in London. Damn it—he was intending to offer for the girl, had actually spoken to her father; and still he thought of the chit as *Miss Pemberton*! Surely it was about time he called her Amelia and she called him Crispin. Though doubtless Lady Casterfield would encourage her to use his title in bed. He shuddered to think of the likely result if she explained the duties of the marriage bed to her niece.

He could hear the carriage drawing up at the steps. Steeling himself to his fate, he went out under the portico to greet his guests of honour. His gaze narrowed, focused fully on the pair of sweating bays harnessed to the equipage. They were a far cry from the usual showy peacocks Lord Casterfield favoured. And they certainly weren't job horses. Blinking slightly, he switched his attention to the elegant grey mare hitched behind the chaise and the little grey Welsh gelding beside her. Good God! Surely Miss Pemberton—dash it all! *Amelia*—knew he could mount her perfectly satisfactorily? And what was the pony for? A dogcart? He probably even had one of those collecting dust and spiders somewhere.

As his footman let down the steps of the chaise, Crispin affixed a welcoming smile to his face and waited for Lady Casterfield to descend.

To his utter stupefaction a small girl with a wealth of dark brown curls scrambled out and smiled sunnily up at the equally startled footman.

'Thank you,' piped the child. About five or so. Crispin assessed her dazedly. He'd seen enough of his sister's brood to hazard a reasonably accurate guess.

She was followed by a goddess. Or at least a very tall,

elegantly dressed woman, no doubt her mama, since there was a striking resemblance between them. Dark brows arched delicately over huge liquid golden eyes in a serenely lovely face framed with silken brown curls. Her figure, admirably displayed by the well-cut carriage dress, was an elegant combination of graceful lines and voluptuous curves. All in all, she looked nothing like Lady Casterfield. A fact that he assimilated with great approbation.

Just as he was thanking whatever gods had taken mercy on him, the likely truth of the matter dawned on Crispin. They must have the wrong house. Possibly, as his mind ran over which of his neighbours might be expecting visitors, the wrong county.

The descent from the chaise of Miss Amelia Pemberton disabused him of this misapprehension.

She stared at him in obvious surprise. 'Oh! Your...your Grace. I didn't expect *you* to be here!'

Crispin managed to choke back a moan of despair at this singularly witless remark and said merely, 'I live here. Remember?'

He encountered a glare from the goddess that rocked him to his toes. Wildly, he tried to remember which of the Greek deities had been able to slay with a look. Whichever one it was, she had been reincarnated right here on his doorstep.

'What my cousin means is that she did not expect to find your Grace adorning the front steps.' Her voice was divine too; warm and husky, but with a hint of hauteur. And a hint of familiarity—surely he'd heard it before?

'Oh...er...ah....' Crispin floundered. 'I was just greeting my aunt. We saw your carriage so I...er...waited. No point going back to the billiard room.'

He was stunned to hear himself sounding so totally at sea.

The goddess, however, judging by the faint smile,

deigned to be amused at his expense. Her next words confirmed it.

'How romantically eager. So charming, your Grace.' The curve of her lips deepened. And his Grace wondered what they tasted like. Peaches, he'd bet, or possibly strawberries...something sweet, anyway...and probably hot.

Shocked at the direction of his thoughts, Crispin pulled himself together. Who in Hades was this woman?

'Perhaps you would be so good as to introduce your companion, Amelia,' he suggested as he accompanied them up the steps. 'While naturally delighted to welcome you both, I was expecting Lady Casterfield.' Encountering an indignant glance from his youngest guest, awaiting her elders with every indication of impatience at the top of the steps, he amended, 'I beg your pardon. I am delighted to welcome *all* of you.'

Amelia blinked up at him, patently surprised. 'This...this is my cousin, of course, your Grace. Mama wrote to you!'

'I beg to differ, Amelia,' he said very politely. 'Lady Pemberton wrote to *my* mother. Don't assume that I have been enlightened. All Mama saw fit to tell me was that you would arrive today.'

'Oh.' Amelia looked thoroughly flustered. 'Well, this is Tilda, I...I mean Lady Winter. She's my cousin.'

Crispin was conscious again of an odd feeling of recognition as he turned to Lady Winter. Somewhere, bone deep, he was sure he had met her before. That she had made an impression on him. The hazel eyes teased at his memory—beckoning...tugging... He shook his head slightly to clear it. He *couldn't* have met her before. The impression she was making on him now was not one he was likely to forget. Ever.

She was watching him, he realised. Calmly, but with a definite challenge in her bright eyes.

'The *Dowager* Lady Winter,' she added helpfully. It didn't help in the least. Because all his speculations about the taste of her lips suddenly stopped being academic. Given that this was almost entirely a family party, he'd been wondering just how he was to entertain his admittedly baser instincts. An unrelated widow had distinct possibilities...especially one this alluring.

Good God! Had his wits gone begging? Was he seriously contemplating the seduction of Amelia's *chaperon*? Imagining what it would be like to have her writhing under him, their limbs entwined, hearing her soft moans as he made love to her? He shook his head again, frantic to get some sense into it.

He forced himself to speak normally. 'And this, I take it, Lady Winter, is your daughter?' He smiled encouragingly at the child.

She smiled back. 'I'm Anthea,' she offered. 'And that—' indicating the pony behind the chaise '—is Henry. He's mine.' All the pride of ownership rang in her voice.

Crispin, who could remember the joy of his own first pony, responded promptly. Turning, he subjected the little grey to a searching appraisal, before saying, 'He's a beauty. Just the right stamp for a lady. Can he jump?'

Anthea looked a bit self-conscious. 'Well, *he* can, but Mama says I'm too little yet. But I'm getting bigger!'

Obviously a contentious issue, thought Crispin. He adopted guileful tact. Usually a safe bet with the ladies. 'I'm sure your mama will be the first to notice when you *are* big enough. In the meantime, come indoors. Henry will be well cared for, I assure you.'

Reeling from shock, he bowed them over the threshold, wondering just what else his mother might have concealed from him. He distinctly recalled making a number of pithy observances about Lady Casterfield only this morning. So why on earth had Mama neglected to mention the change of chaperon? On further reflection the reason was fairly plain. *His* Dowager had a streak of mischief a mile wide.

He was only surprised she hadn't managed to be on hand to witness his shock.

'Ah! We're all here, then. How simply lovely.'

Crispin bit his lip to hold back a laugh. The Dowager Duchess of St Ormond stood just inside the front door, a lilting smile on her face.

'Amelia, how pretty you look! And, Lady Winter, I'm delighted to see you and your daughter. You look so much like poor Sylvia! I knew your mama very well.'

The goddess turned to marble. 'Did you, ma'am? I'm afraid you have the advantage of me then.' Shards of ice formed on her voice—the hint of hauteur deepened. 'I scarcely remember her.'

Coolly she turned to Crispin. 'Perhaps, your Grace, we might be shown to our rooms.'

Rigid with anger, Crispin beckoned to his butler, hovering close by. 'Bebbington. Have Lady Winter, Miss Pemberton and Miss…Miss Anthea, shown to their rooms, please. No doubt they will wish to refresh themselves.'

Jaw clenched, he watched them go. Let Lady Winter try that with his mother again and she'd learn a lesson she'd never forget! His jaw set like granite, he watched with narrowed eyes as Lady Winter mounted the stairs, hips swaying provocatively, the luscious curves of her bottom lovingly outlined by the elegantly cut carriage dress. Heat roared through him as he imagined those curves filling his hands, heating, squirming against him as he… Damn it! She needed lessons in civility—not bed sports!

A light hand on his sleeve recalled him. Glancing down, he saw his mother twinkling up at him.

'Dear Cris! Don't go tilting at windmills on my account.' She seemed quite unperturbed.

He stared at her. 'Mama, she was atrociously rude! Scarcely a suitable chaperon, I'd have thought!'

She chuckled. 'Would you prefer Lady Casterfield? You

leave Lady Winter to me, Cris. I was, after all, appallingly tactless.'

Crispin drew a deep breath and counted to ten—slowly. 'I don't suppose you'd care to elaborate on that?' he asked.

She smiled and shook her head. 'No, dear. Not at the moment.' Five sweet chimes rang out. 'Great heavens! It's nearly dinnertime. I must change.'

A flurry of silken skirts and the Dowager was gone, flitting up the stairs with a lithe grace that thoroughly belied her fifty-six summers.

Crispin narrowed his eyes. He was damned if he could see how it was tactless to tell a woman you remembered her mother. His mother's calm acceptance of Lady Winter's rudeness notwithstanding, he fully intended to try a tilt with her ladyship. And when he was finished, she'd know that it didn't pay to cross swords with St Ormond! He'd teach her a lesson in civility; if he managed to teach her a few other things along the way, then that would suit him down to the ground.

# Chapter Three

By the time she reached her room, Tilda fully regretted her instinctive reaction to Lady St Ormond's remark that she had known Sylvia Pemberton. Too often, during her first and only season, had matrons to whom she was presented remarked that they had known her mama. Such references had always been edged with disdain, a supercilious curling of lips. An all-but-explicit intimation that as the daughter of such a woman, she was herself suspect.

In denying that she remembered her mother she had lied. She remembered her sad and lovely mother extremely well. It was not a memory she had ever shared with anyone. There had never been anyone to share it with. Even Jonathan, kind as he had been, had found the subject of her mother's disgrace excessively embarrassing.

She had discovered that when, in an unavailing attempt to persuade him to withdraw his offer, she suggested that she might prove as headstrong. He had been scandalised, but the kindly way he took her to task for cheapening herself had helped reconcile her to the match.

Now she had been monumentally rude to Milly's prospective mother-in-law and mortally offended his Grace. So she would have to apologise—to the Dowager, anyway, for Milly's sake. With this in mind she rushed through her toilette in a fashion that made Sarah shake her head in disapproval.

Still, the result, when she examined it in a looking glass, would pass. Her gown of old gold silk suited her tall, graceful figure, its colour a perfect match for her hazel eyes. The narrow cut of the skirts gave her a willowy elegance and the neckline, while discreet, was cut to follow the contours of her bosom with tantalising faithfulness. She might not have Milly's beauty, but at least she put the ghost of Miss Arnold to rest.

'Humph,' was all Sarah would say when Tilda grinned at her mischievously in the glass.

'Humph yourself, Sarah!' said Tilda. 'Now, don't wait up for me, for heaven's sake. I should much rather you stayed by Miss Anthea.'

Sarah nodded reluctantly. 'Oh, aye. I'll do that. Not but what she's as happy as a grig. Would you believe that his Grace sent up a message to her that Henry was settling in and had eaten all his dinner?'

Tilda stared. '*Did* he? Whatever for?'

Sarah shrugged. 'I dare say he was hungry. Long run he had today.'

'His *Grace*! Not Henry!'

'Oh.' Sarah considered. 'No idea. Still, he did seem to take a liking to Miss Anthea. Maybe he just likes children.'

Tilda gave this her consideration as she went downstairs. It seemed odd to her. More likely he was trying to turn her up sweet, she thought cynically. As Milly's chaperon she had, she realised belatedly, a certain amount of power. The thought was a novel one. Naturally one would not abuse it, but it could do no harm to enjoy its existence, meditate upon its possibilities.

She had been uncomfortably conscious upon seeing him again that St Ormond was just as lethally handsome, just as disgustingly attractive as ever. Even more annoying was the fact that her stomach still turned over at the sight of him. And he hadn't even recognised her!

She was not entirely sure if that was a compliment or otherwise.

Sternly, she vowed that he should never realise the peculiar power he wielded over her. No doubt most women reacted like this to him. Instead, she would make him aware of her power. If she wasn't convinced it would be a happy marriage for Milly, then she would stop it if she could.

She entered the Blue Salon a good ten minutes early and, to her relief, found it empty. Good. With a little bit of luck the next person down should be the Dowager and she could get her embarrassing apology over and done with.

Sure enough, five minutes later the door opened and in sailed Lady St Ormond, regal in midnight blue, the famed St Ormond diamonds ablaze at her throat and ears. She stopped dead on the threshold.

'Goodness! Am I late? I'm so sorry, my dear. Did you ring for Bebbington? Should you care for a glass of ratafia? Or Madeira?'

Tilda blushed scarlet. Here she had come down early to make sure of finding Lady St Ormond alone in order to offer her an apology and the tables were reversed! A thought struck her. What if she had misinterpreted Lady St Ormond's remark?

Plunging in, she said desperately, 'Ma'am, I came down early to find you. To...to apologise for my rudeness—'

'Oh, no!' Lady St Ormond interrupted her at once. 'I should not have been so tactless. You could not have possibly known how fond I was of Sylvia. You have her eyes, you know. Just for a moment...I thought...well...it was foolish of me. And you were so small, it is little wonder you have no memory of her. Or of me.' Her lovely smile deepened as Tilda's eyes widened in consternation.

'That's right, my dear. I remember you as a little girl. Sylvia always brought you when she called on me. She loved you very much and she was so proud of you. You used to sit in the corner and play with my cat.'

Memory stirred. An image of a very large formal room came to Tilda. A very patient tabby cat and a lady who had always had some special toy ready for her to play with. But the woman's face was lost to her—it must have been Lady St Ormond. Very few had received her disgraced mother. And she had snubbed one of the few who had.

'I...I beg your pardon...I don't really remember...not properly.' Tilda blushed scarlet. 'I...I do remember Mama, but sometimes people...' Her voice trailed off. What excuse could she offer for rudeness?

'No, no, my dear!' Lady St Ormond was patently horrified. 'I told you only to explain my seeming tactlessness. You must not apologise. I dare say there have been many who have not scrupled to throw Sylvia's misfortunes up in your face. Now—' she smiled brightly '—where is Milly?'

Tilda's jaw dropped in ludicrous dismay. She had completely forgotten to escort Milly downstairs. And she was meant to be chaperoning the girl. Horrorstruck, she gazed at her hostess and wondered just how much worse this visit could get.

The Dowager simply collapsed laughing. When she could, she spluttered, 'You poor girl! Don't give it a moment's thought! She can't come to much harm here, you know. All the guests are family, so unless she gets lost she is perfectly safe.'

The door opened again to admit a tall young man whose attire proclaimed him a budding dandy. His intricately tied cravat was enormous, his shirt points dizzying and his cherry-striped waistcoat blinding. Tilda blinked at all this sartorial magnificence, but the Dowager merely raised her brows.

'Dear me, Guy, poor Crispin will feel quite put in the shade. Lady Winter, may I present my nephew, Guy Malvern. Dear boy, be an angel and go up to the pink guest chamber and escort Miss Pemberton down. Here is poor Lady Winter, so unused to the role of chaperon she has forgot her charge.'

The elegant Mr Malvern grinned engagingly. 'I should think you might, ma'am. You don't look like any chaperon *I've* ever been cursed by. Regular fusty mugs, most of 'em! Very well, Aunt Marianne, I'll fetch her down. As long as *you* explain to m'father why I'm down late!'

As he left, Lady St Ormond turned to Tilda again and said, 'You will find us all quite informal, but I dare say you are used to that. As I recall, Jonathan had never much taste for pomp.'

'Did you know my husband?' Tilda asked without thinking. Belatedly she thought that Lady St Ormond was probably not much younger than Lord Winter would have been if he were still alive.

'Yes, indeed I did,' said Lady St Ormond. 'He was friendly with my elder brother and often spent holidays with us as children. Now do tell me, is your little girl comfortable in her rooms? I put her in the old nursery because all Cris and Georgiana's toys are still there. But if you would be happier with her nearer to you, then we can shift her tomorrow. And you must not be thinking that she cannot join in with some of our entertainments. I know Cris wishes to have a riding picnic in a day or so if the weather holds fine. I will probably come in the gig so she could come with me, you know. Unfortunately Georgie has left her younger brood with her sister-in-law. A pity, but I am sure we can find plenty for the child to do.'

A rush of emotion flooded Tilda. She had been in terror that Lady St Ormond would resent Anthea's presence but she had not been able to face leaving the child with the Pembertons or sending her home alone. This kindness, this acceptance of Anthea's presence as perfectly natural, was quite unlooked for.

Her tangled thanks were lost in a gust of conversation as the door opened and several more people trooped in.

'Marianne!' A tall, military-looking man with iron-grey hair came forward and bussed the Dowager heartily. 'And who's this?' He cast an appreciative glance at Tilda.

'Lady Winter, may I present my brother-in-law, Lord John Malvern?'

Tilda curtsied gracefully as they exchanged greetings. So this was St Ormond's uncle. She could see a resemblance.

He glanced about him and frowned. 'Where the devil's that cub of mine? Boy ought to be down by now! Dare say he's still fussing over his cravat! In my day—'

'Dear John,' the Dowager broke in on what promised to be a scathing condemnation of modern youth, 'Guy is very kindly undertaking an errand for me. So helpful!'

She winked at Tilda, who choked back a laugh.

Lord John looked very slightly mollified. 'And so he should be!'

The next few moments passed in a whirl of introduction, under cover of which Milly slipped into the room with her escort.

She came at once to Tilda, who said, 'I'm dreadfully sorry, Milly. I should have come to your room to collect you.'

Milly smiled radiantly. 'It doesn't matter. Mr Malvern came for me. And he knows all about the house and has promised to show me around.'

Tilda felt it encumbent upon her to remind Milly of why she was here. 'Perhaps St Ormond would like to show you his home himself.'

Milly's crestfallen face suggested that this idea did not have anything like the cachet of Mr Malvern's offer to do the honours. Tilda couldn't blame her, but it would be the outside of enough for her to countenance Milly being shown the house by her prospective husband's young cousin.

'He might be too busy,' said Milly hopefully.

At this juncture Mr Malvern himself came up with a pretty young girl, whose height and chestnut locks proclaimed her a Malvern connection at once.

'Lady Winter, may I presume on Aunt Marianne's hasty introduction and present my cousin, Miss Hastings? Louisa, this is Lady Winter and her cousin, Miss Pemberton.'

Miss Hastings curtsied and said, 'I'm so glad you're here. Usually at these family parties, I'm the only girl. It will be nice to have company.'

Rapidly Tilda worked out that this was the eldest daughter of St Ormond's sister, Georgiana, Lady Hastings. Listening to her chatter with Amelia, it transpired that Louisa would be presented the following year, since she had only just turned seventeen.

'I'm out for family parties, but nothing else,' said Miss Hastings. 'Which makes no difference here, since Aunt Marianne always let us younger ones join in a bit. Why, Uncle Cris taught me to dance when I was ten!'

From which Tilda gathered that informal family fun was very much a way of life for the Malverns. It contrasted sharply with the rigid formality of the Pembertons' household where children were on occasion seen but most certainly not heard.

The door opened again to admit St Ormond. Tilda, in her position directly opposite, had a perfect view as he entered. To her great delight her stomach remained completely unmoved by the vision of understated elegance he presented. Plainly he studied to follow the dictates of Mr Brummel. His coat was a marvel of discreet black moulded to shoulders that filled the doorway, his cravat a monument to skilful patience. Unlike his younger cousin, who sported several fobs and rings, the only jewellery he wore was a single pearl in his cravat and a heavy signet ring.

Not a single flutter, she thought proudly. No doubt it was

just the shock of seeing him again for the first time in so long. Then she realised that he was making straight for her.

To her immense disgust, her stomach did a great deal more than flutter at his fluid, lethally graceful approach. Despite his height and powerful build, he moved with all the elegance and purpose of a large cat. Which would have been fine, she loved cats. But not when she felt like the mouse.

'Good evening Lady Winter, Amelia.' He bowed gracefully and his voice was positively arctic. 'I do hope my people are looking after you.'

Lady Winter smiled graciously. 'Everything is very comfortable, thank you, your Grace.' She couldn't blame him for the chill. After all, she felt just as savage towards those who sneered at *her* mother.

He nodded and turned to his niece. 'Hullo, Louisa. They tell me you're out now!'

Louisa nodded gleefully. 'Yes, Mama says I may be seen at family gatherings now. And she will take me to Bath this winter, so that I shall know how to go on next year in London.'

'God help us all!' said St Ormond in heartfelt accents. 'I shall have to go to ground for the season. Oh Lord, there's Great-Aunt Seraphina glaring at me. Excuse me, Lady Winter, *you* may have no complaints, but I can assure you, Lady Hollow will have several!'

Tilda viewed his departure with some relief. His ease of manner and fondness for his niece were disarming, but she was *not* going to succumb to the folly of permitting a childish fancy for a handsome face to cut up her peace!

Finding herself seated next to St Ormond at dinner annoyed her considerably. Someone, she thought crossly, had it in for her. Naturally she acquitted St Ormond of fell intent. On reflection, since she was the highest-ranking lady present after the Dowager, it would have been the height of rudeness to place her anywhere else but on his right. At least for tonight. But as far as she could tell, with the exceptions of herself and Amelia, all the guests were family. Surely in those circumstances they would not be starchily formal about rank and precedence?

'Lady Winter?'

Belatedly she realised that his Grace had addressed several remarks to her and was awaiting a response. With no idea of what he had said, she stared at him helplessly.

'I...I beg your pardon, your Grace...I didn't quite follow.' He would think her witless, but that was better than thinking her rude.

'I merely wondered if you would care for some wine.' His cool tone told her clearly that he was perfectly aware she had been wool-gathering—and that he was not used to being ignored by anyone and probably considered it a further example of bad manners.

Despite herself, she flushed miserably. Heavens! She might not have wanted to be a chaperon, but she had agreed to do it. Surely she could do better than this.

'I...no thank you, your Grace.' She lifted her chin defiantly and met his faintly mocking gaze. 'My wits are scrambled enough after our journey. I dare say a glass of wine would have me asleep at the table, not merely daydreaming.' If he disliked her, then it would be all the easier to keep her dangerous attraction to him under strict control.

His brows lifted sceptically. 'A tiresome journey, Lady Winter? But Broughton Place is no more than fifty miles, I believe.' Even as he spoke he reached for a jug. 'Water only, Lady Winter.' He filled her glass.

She snorted. 'I suggest you try travelling fifty miles with a five-year-old who has to be rested every hour, lest she succumb to carriage sickness! Not to mention regulating your speed to allow her pony to keep up with the chaise!'

Sipping his wine, his Grace thought about that. 'Hmm. You should have sent the pony over in advance, of course.

Or written to me, rather than to my very absent-minded mother! I would have been delighted to mount Miss Anthea. As for her travel sickness: use a coach with a driver, not postilions. Then she may travel on the box.'

Stunned at his response, Tilda stared open-mouthed. 'Travel on the box?'

He nodded. 'It worked with me as a child. In fact, that's how I learnt to drive. You cannot conceive of my father's horror when he discovered that he had been driven halfway to London one year by, as he put it, a scrubby school boy of eight.'

The vision thus conjured up, of an apoplectic Duke and his unrepentant heir, drew an unwilling smile from her. Somehow she gained the distinct impression that the present Duke's father had not been at all unsympathetic to his heir's infirmity. She grimaced inwardly as she recalled the journeys of *her* childhood. Any vestige of travel sickness had been treated as a premeditated crime and punished accordingly. Certainly no one had ever suggested that she travel on the box.

Without thinking she said, 'You are fortunate, your Grace.'

He blinked. 'What? In having suffered travel sickness as a child?'

'No. In that your parents were sympathetic towards it.' She kept her tone light, but it was laced with bitterness.

A forkful of beef stopped halfway to his lips. His expression was arrested. 'I think rather, Lady Winter, that you have been *un*fortunate.'

At the mere hint of sympathy in his voice, she froze. Pity was not acceptable! Angrily she lashed herself for allowing anything of her feelings to show.

To her vast relief he turned his attention to Lady Hastings at his left and she finished her duckling and green peas in relative peace.

'Should you care for some lobster?'

She turned and smiled at Guy Malvern, seated to her right. 'Thank you. I would love some.'

He provided her with a generous portion, based, she suspected, on his own abilities as a trencherman rather than any knowledge of hers. Rather daunted, she gazed at the massive helping, smothered in a cheese sauce.

'Aunt Marianne orders them from Bristol. No need to hold back,' he assured her cheerfully. 'There's plenty!'

There was indeed. On her plate!

Lady Hastings, seated directly opposite, caught her eye. Unmistakably she winked, before turning to respond to Sir Richard Benton, a local magistrate who had plainly been invited to entertain old Lady Hollow.

Much encouraged, Tilda embarked upon the lobster.

'I'm Cris's cousin, you know,' explained Guy. 'I must say, I was surprised to find you and Miss Pemberton here. Thought it was just a family party. Cris doesn't bother much about big house parties. He says he can think of much better ways to waste his blunt than entertaining a horde of hangers-on he doesn't like above half!'

Tilda murmured something about her mama having been a friend of Lady St Ormond. If his Grace had not seen fit to inform all his family of his intentions towards Milly, then it was certainly not her place to do so.

Guy did not seem to find her explanation at all unlikely. He nodded. 'Do you ride? Cris always has famous riding parties. Shooting too, later on.'

Her reply was lost as Sir Richard broke in. 'Shooting? Hah! There'll be precious little of that if St Ormond don't do something about these damned poachers! Not a bird left if the rascals have their way!'

St Ormond looked up from the head of the table. 'Poachers, Sir Richard? What do you imagine I can do about your poachers?' He did not seem at all shocked that Sir Richard was so informal as to have spoken across the table.

'You can stop encouraging them, that's what!' barked

Sir Richard. 'It's open knowledge that your keepers are lax about catching them! Should sack the lot, m'boy!'

One brow quirked and a flash of amusement lurked in his green eyes as St Ormond said mildly, 'Providing the country with yet another starving family and yet more poachers. Who would, of course, know my preserves so well that they'd strip them!'

Sir Richard glared at him. 'Do you tell me, St Ormond, that you are encouraging this menace? This…this criminal activity? Damn it all! If you don't do something I'll have to use the road when I dine with Whittlesea. One of the rascals will probably shoot me on that right of way of yours one night!'

'I trust not, Sir Richard.' St Ormond smiled. 'And I am not encouraging *criminal activity.* I am merely telling you that how I choose to manage my preserves is my concern. Frankly, times are hard. With the Corn Laws, the people are literally starving. I'd rather lose a few birds and a rabbit or two, than have my tenants turning to crime!'

'Poaching *is* a crime!' expostulated Sir Richard, quite patently shocked by this heresy.

St Ormond shrugged. 'Not if it's not bothering me it isn't,' he said calmly.

Sir Richard goggled. 'Just encouraging lawlessness,' he spluttered. 'These fellows should be laid by the heels and transported! Made an example of!'

'Leaving their children starving, turning to crime and ending on the gallows or being transported themselves?' St Ormond's voice suddenly lost its geniality. 'Tell me, Sir Richard, do you find the idea of a starving child of six or seven being condemned to the gallows for stealing his breakfast repugnant? Because I do! And I would far rather his father helped himself to a few of my rabbits!'

Tilda shuddered. A child of six! Anthea was nearly six…she felt ill at the very thought.

Sir Richard glanced at her. 'Here, I say, St Ormond!

Distressing the ladies! Can't expect them to listen to this over their dinner!'

Tilda's nausea disappeared in a blaze of anger at this well-meant, but ill-judged, gallantry. She was fully aware that the entire party had stilled, was listening to the exchange, but she weighed in regardless. 'I beg to differ, Sir Richard. Since you raised the subject, I must assume that you did consider it, with all its ramifications, a fit subject for discussion by all present. In what way is St Ormond, in tacitly permitting his tenants to have the occasional rabbit, doing anything wrong? Would it be wrong if he went out and shot a dozen rabbits a day to hand out to them? Why should they not catch their own dinners and save him the effort?'

'My dear Lady Winter,' he said patronisingly, 'your feelings do credit to your tender heart, but as a female, we cannot expect you to understand the legal implications of what you are saying!'

'So explain it,' she said dangerously. 'In simple layman's terms. If I don't understand, I'll ask a question. Or two.' Unconsciously her fist clenched on the table.

Plainly nettled by the challenge in her tone. Sir Richard responded bluntly. 'Put simply, Lady Winter, it is a criminal offence for anyone except a squire, or squire's eldest son, to kill game. Therefore St Ormond has no right to take such a lax attitude to the business. The law is the law, and must be obeyed by all.'

'Bravo!' St Ormond clapped lazily. 'Lady Winter, was that beyond your capacity to understand?'

She shot him a look that made him blink. 'Not at all, your Grace. But I do have a question.'

To her shock, he reached out and covered her clenched fist with his hand. A shiver ran through her, leaving her dizzy and breathless, scarcely able to concentrate on his next words. 'You will have to excuse her, Sir Richard. If I have learnt one thing about women in my thirty-six years, it is that they always have a question. Or three.' He smiled encouragingly at Tilda. 'Ask your question, Lady Winter.'

Desperately trying to ignore the light pressure of his fingers, she asked, 'Have you sons, Sir Richard?'

He frowned. 'Three. Though what that has to say to anything…'

Trying very hard to ignore the warmth stealing through her whole body at the touch of St Ormond's hand, Tilda asked sweetly, 'Then, can one assume that you forbid your *younger* sons permission to shoot on your land? After all, technically they are poaching, are they not? Guilty of a criminal offence, in fact. Dear me! What a hotbed of crime your average shooting party must be! Or does the host make sure all his guests are legally permitted to accept his invitation? I can tell you right now that my husband certainly never did anything of the sort!'

A stunned silence fell over the table at this. Tilda assumed that she had shocked the company with her outspokenness. She couldn't have cared less, and waited with flashing eyes for Sir Richard's reply.

Sir Richard turned an interesting shade of purple. 'Well, naturally…of course…one cannot…' He floundered hopelessly.

'One cannot condemn, say, the youngest son of a duke?' pressed Tilda. 'Then you are saying that the law is the law and must be obeyed by some? While others may break it at will, merely because of unearned aristocratic privilege? Hardly justice, Sir Richard.'

'And that,' said St Ormond placidly, 'really does spell the end of the subject. Even if Sir Richard could find a decent argument to counter Lady Winter, he has, of course, been brought up never to contradict a lady. Even one with revoluntionary tendencies!' The note of authority in his voice was not to be brooked. A babble of conversations broke out, none of which mentioned anything to do with poaching, crime or aristocratic privilege, unearned or otherwise.

Calmly, St Ormond reached for the claret jug and filled Tilda's glass.

'Your Grace...I...' Meeting his amused gaze, her voice trailed off.

'I don't think you're in any danger of falling asleep, Lady Winter,' he murmured, under cover of the general conversation that had sprung up. 'If anything, I should be plying you with wine just to blunt your blade.' He shot a glance at Sir Richard, fulminating to Lady Hollow. 'But you know, I can really fight my own battles.'

She glared at him. 'You may rest assured, your Grace, I did not speak out in your defence! It was...merely... that...you spoke of children...' Her voice faltered. She could not even frame the words. She had wanted babies so much...to hear of children being sent to their deaths in the name of justice... Her stomach clenched.

'Young children...going to the gallows?' His voice was hard.

She nodded.

'It happens, Lady Winter.' Hard and uncompromising, his voice bit into her.

'It should not,' was all she could manage.

'No, but what do you propose to do about it?'

Her eyes widened. Do about it? What on earth could she do about it? She could not stand for parliament and oppose the sentencing laws. She could not even vote. Most men did not have the right to vote. Yet his tone had not been mocking. Challenging, yes, but not mocking. Something deep within her responded.

'I have no idea, your Grace,' she said quietly and saw cynical amusement flicker in the green. Still more quietly she added, 'As yet.'

Surprise flared and a brow quirked. 'Lady Winter, your

blade is as keen as ever. I shudder to think what else you may be able to slip past a man's guard!'

The gentlemen did not linger over their port for long after the ladies withdrew. St Ormond, conscious that he really ought to make an effort to dance attendance on his prospective bride, brought the usual round of chat to a swift end. Sir Richard had not opened fire again, but was looking thoroughly disgruntled, not even responding to cheerful attempts by Lord John to engage him in conversation.

As they passed from the dining room, Lord Hastings drew his brother-in-law aside and murmured, 'Lady Winter dealt a knockout blow there, Cris!'

Crispin nodded. 'She did, didn't she?' He said no more. All his rock-hard certainties about Lady Winter had been shaken to their foundations. He had started the dinner determined to teach her a few lessons in the civility due to his mother. Now he was completely at sea. He'd thought her an arrogant, ill-mannered upstart, in serious need of a set-down. She'd shown herself, under the fashionable veneer, to have the tender heart of any decent mother, and the swift wits of a politician.

He frowned as he led the way to the drawing room. However much of an enigma Lady Winter might be, she had still been appallingly rude to the Dowager. And no matter what the Dowager might think, he was determined to put her ladyship right on that subject. Besides, it might take his mind off a few other things he'd like to teach her. On reflection, seducing his intended bride's chaperon would be in highly dubious taste.

Pondering how to put her in her place, he entered the drawing room.

To discover the subject of his thoughts chatting animatedly with his mother and sister. By all appearances the three of them were entirely happy with their company and scarcely glanced up as the gentlemen entered.

He glared. Damn the woman! She had an uncanny ability to wrong-foot him. He'd spent enough time on her anyway. A quick survey of the room revealed Amelia gossiping happily with Louisa. Suppressing a grimace at the girlish prattle he would have to endure, he made for them. It was time to become properly acquainted with Amelia.

On the surface she had every qualification he required in his duchess. Pretty, malleable, brought up in the right circles. She was young enough that he could mould her as he pleased. She would not be likely to cause him any worry whatsoever and he would be free to pursue his own life of untrammelled freedom while doing his duty in providing an heir in the direct line.

But as he sat down with his young niece and Amelia he was conscious of the effort he had to make to attune his conversation to their level. He frowned inwardly. He had never before felt chatting with Louisa to be onerous. He normally enjoyed her youthful enthusiasm, was happy to chat about female fashions, without ever betraying just how he happened to know so much. Suddenly, he knew that it was not something he would care to do all the time—that to forever have to guard his conversation, so that his wife was neither hurt nor shocked, would be a penance.

With a jolt he realised that if he sat discussing bonnets with Lady Winter, those bright eyes would widen, a dark brow would lift in unspoken, cynical understanding... He forced his mind back to the innocent talk of hats, and noted that while his niece was perfectly at ease with him, Amelia was not.

'I say, Miss Pemberton, your cousin's game, isn't she? Taking on old Benton like that!' Crispin looked up. Guy had joined them, a teacup in each hand. He grinned ingenuously at his cousin. 'Aunt Marianne asked me to hand the cups around. One for you, Cris?' He handed cups to Louisa and Amelia.

'Don't trouble yourself, Guy,' said Crispin lazily. 'Tea doesn't really thrill my soul at any hour.'

They chatted on. Amelia, Crispin noted, had relaxed substantially. Good. No doubt she was just feeling a bit shy, plunged into a family party, and not having seen him for some weeks. It was, after all, a very difficult situation for a young girl. Perhaps she felt herself to be on trial as it were.

He thought about that as he settled down in his very large bed later that night. He had not intended this party to be a trial for Amelia. Not really. Just a chance for her to see what she was taking on before he made a formal offer for her hand. He would have to reassure her that *his* mind was made up.

He wriggled his shoulders into the soft down. And turned over. Several times. After a few minutes he swore vigorously, sat up and relit the lamp beside his bed. He'd read for a bit. The bed was not really cold. He'd seen his valet, Stubbs, remove the copper warming pan. It was just his overactive, libidinous imagination creating that impression. Which, given that he was contemplating a permanent remedy for the problem, should not have worried him.

And it would not have, had the subject of his lurid imaginings been Miss Pemberton... As it was, her chaperon's lush curves threatened to inflict a sleepless night and headache on him. Not to mention an ache in an altogether different part of his anatomy.

In the next corridor Tilda tossed and turned. Why on earth should St Ormond have clasped her hand like that at dinner? It was as though he had thought they were in some sort of alliance! And why the devil should she worry about it? Why did her hand still burn at the memory of those powerful fingers? And why, oh why, did her body have to remember those same fingers lightly clasping her waist seven years ago? Why, when she closed her eyes, did she feel herself whirling down that wretched ballroom in his embrace?

Thoroughly frustrated in her attempts to sleep, Tilda sat up and hugged her knees. St Ormond's challenge haunted her. *What do you propose to do about it?*

Very well. What *could* she do about it? She was an independent lady of means. If she really wanted to do something to help, then she could. All she had to do was think of something. Something that she could help with in a practical way. Just giving money was too easy. She wanted to be involved.

She had always thought that with Anthea and her independence she could be content. Rapidly she was discovering that she could not. She had so much. And others had so little. At times the contrast made her feel guilty.

So, since she could not stand for parliament and join the reform movement, what could she do? The answer was probably to stop the children ever getting as far as having to steal their breakfasts. Which meant helping orphans, unmarried mothers and helping children old enough to find decent trades. She thought about that. It was plenty to be going on with and would do for now. Perhaps she should write to the Vicar at home. He would know what was needed.

She fell asleep still pondering the problem, but with a warm certainty that she had hit on the answer to St Ormond's challenge. Not that she was going to tell him, of course—but she sent a silent thanks winging his way. He'd forced her to think of something that would help others and lessen her guilty feeling of having far more than she deserved.

# Chapter Four

A week later Crispin paced up and down his library in considerable irritation. On the surface his house party was perfectly successful. Everyone was having an agreeable time with rides, picnics and boating on the lake. The weather was superb from their point of view, although he knew the farmers would welcome a little more rain. If it didn't come now, it was bound to come just as they were harvesting.

Unfortunately Lady Winter was proving as big a bugbear as her predecessor Lady Casterfield. Worse, in fact. He'd never been conscious of the least desire to creep into *her* room at night, get into *her* bed and ravish *her*.

Furious at the well-travelled direction his thoughts were taking, Crispin reined in his imagination and concentrated on his legitimate complaint against Lady Winter, which was that she was altogether too conscientious a chaperon. He'd had scarcely a chance to see Amelia alone; the wretched chit, despite his hint that he'd like to be on less ceremonious terms with her, persisted in calling him *your Grace*. And on the occasions that he had taken her arm she had stiffened up like a poker!

Granted, she had never been more than accepting of his suit, but now it was as though his addresses had actually become distasteful to her. And he suspected that the reason was not far to seek—Lady Winter. The damned woman must be influencing Amelia against him. She had been content to receive his addresses before coming here and the only thing he could think likely to have changed her mind was her chaperon.

Lady Winter obviously disliked him. She had begun her visit by being very reserved and formal with everyone. Now she was on far easier terms with the entire party, including his Great-Aunt Seraphina. She was especially friendly with Guy. The pair of them had struck up a firm friendship and it irritated the hell out of him.

She liked everyone, in fact, except himself. With him she was completely reserved, addressing him only by his title—if she addressed him at all, and never, since that first evening, had she permitted him to see anything of her feelings.

It was plain to the meanest intelligence that Lady Winter disapproved of his suit. On what grounds, beyond her own dislike, he could not imagine. He was disgustingly wealthy, possessed of an old and proud title, loathed gambling so was unlikely to lose his fortune, kept his mistresses discreetly in the background and had every intention of indulging his wife. What her picky ladyship could cavil at in all *that* was beyond his comprehension!

*What a coxcomb you sound like!* He could almost hear Hastings saying it. He laughed. James had been thoroughly amused when he had confided his plans for Amelia. *If you intend tying yourself up in matrimony, at least let me be granted the blissful sight of you courting the girl! Good luck, and remember, the terms you offer a mistress won't do for a wife!*

So he'd invited Amelia down for the annual family gathering, thinking that it would give them a chance to see more of each other in a less formal setting, become acquainted. But Lady Winter had other ideas.

Feminine laughter rippled through the doors opening on to the terrace. He cocked his head... Louisa, by the sound of it...and...yes! Amelia! Excellent. It shouldn't be too hard to fob off Louisa.

He stepped out on to the terrace. 'Good morning, Louisa, Amelia.' He smiled approvingly. They really looked very pretty in those pale muslins. Just the thing for very young ladies.

'And where is Lady Winter this morning?' No point in getting rid of Louisa if her ladyship were about to appear and spike his guns yet again.

Amelia replied in all innocence, 'Oh, Tilda is teaching Anthea for an hour. She does so every morning just after breakfast and then takes her for a walk, you know.'

Crispin nearly choked. He certainly *hadn't* known that. Typical Lady Winter! She knew perfectly well that he handled estate matters for about two hours each morning, so she had timed her daughter's educational needs to suit. Of course, in all charity, it was the most convenient time for all concerned, but still!

'And what is Miss Anthea learning this morning?' he asked idly.

Amelia grimaced. 'French conversation.'

'An accomplished young lady, then!' said Crispin. 'Like her aunt.' He waited confidently for the self-conscious blush at his neat compliment.

Eventually Amelia looked up and found him watching her. 'Do you mean *me*? But I'm her cousin, really—even if Tilda and I were brought up together like sisters.' She pondered this. 'I don't feel *nearly* old enough to be an aunt or uncle.'

Very drily Crispin said, 'I can assure you at least that you will never attain the latter distinction.'

'Uncle Cris,' broke in Louisa. 'Have you any idea where Guy might be?'

He shook his head. 'No, but you put me in mind of the

fact that I need to speak to him. Would you mind very much finding him for me?' He knew a slight twinge of conscience. He'd spoken nothing but the truth when he denied knowledge of Guy's whereabouts, but he *had* seen him heading for the stables some time ago.

'Of course not,' said Louisa obligingly. 'Shall I send him to the library?'

'Or here on the terrace,' said Crispin. 'I shall keep Miss Pemberton company while you are gone.'

The look of dismay on Amelia's face was ludicrous, and, since Louisa was standing slightly behind her, seen only by Crispin.

Very naturally seeing no impropriety in leaving her friend unattended with her uncle, Louisa disappeared on her errand.

Crispin heaved an audible sigh of relief. He turned to Amelia and found her regarding him as she might an escaped lion. He smiled and said, 'Now we may be comfortable, my dear.'

'Oh, er…yes…of course, your Grace.' She didn't sound or look convinced. Her feet shifted nervously.

'Crispin,' he corrected her.

She stared.

'It's my name,' he reminded her.

Wordlessly she nodded. Then, 'Should we find Tilda, do you think? I…I mean…after all…'

Crispin sighed and gave up temporarily. 'Why don't we go and find my mama? No need to disturb Lady Winter.' Yet. But as soon as Miss Anthea Cavendish had done enough French conversation for the morning, he was going to have a long-overdue chat with her mama about the duties of a chaperon.

Tilda received his Grace's summons with outward composure. 'Thank you, Bebbington. Please assure his Grace that I will join him in the drawing room in about twenty minutes.' She certainly wasn't going to skimp on Anthea's education just to suit him.

Twenty minutes later, having sent Anthea off to change her shoes in readiness for their walk, she made her way to the drawing room. Her host was awaiting her, standing by the windows, a heavy frown upon his face.

Rapidly she searched her memory for any crime Anthea might have committed, but could think of none. 'Good morning, your Grace. Can I help you in some way?'

His Grace did not bother with any conventional greeting. He went straight to the point. 'You may clarify several things for me, Lady Winter. For a start, I should like very much to know what grounds you have for disapproving of my suit. And, secondly, I should like to know why, when her parents approve, you have taken it upon yourself to discourage Amelia from accepting!'

Tilda stood stock-still, blank amazement on her face. How on earth did *he* know that she disapproved? She hadn't said a thing! Certainly not to Milly!

Playing for time, she asked, 'What makes you think I disapprove?'

He snorted derisively. 'Oh, for heaven's sake, woman! Don't fence with me! It's moderately obvious that you dislike me. You make quite sure I never have a chance to converse with her privately. And, furthermore, it is evident that since I saw Amelia in town, she has become very nervous of me. *Someone* must have given her a reason!'

Sheer outrage took Tilda's breath away for a moment. A moment in which her fury crystallised. 'Are you suggesting, St Ormond, that *I* have traduced your character to my cousin?' Her voice dripped icy scorn.

Quite undeterred, he repeated his original question. 'I wish to know what you have against me as a suitor for Amelia. And what right you feel you have to influence her in this way. After all, you have benefited handsomely from marriage. Why discourage your cousin from making a good match?'

Had he punched her in the stomach she could not have been more shocked. He dared throw her marriage in her face!

'You arrogant beast!' she exploded. 'I should have thought my story would be enough to tell you exactly what my objection is! But since you have neither the wit nor sensitivity to think of it for yourself, I'll tell you! I think it iniquitous to force a young girl into marriage with a man she scarcely knows, well nigh old enough to be her father! You ought to be ashamed of yourself! Is it any wonder that Milly should feel nervous? Had she expressed the least desire to have time alone to come to know you, then I would have been the most compliant of chaperons!'

St Ormond was glaring back at her. 'You dare to suggest that *I* make Milly nervous? Then why the devil did she agree to receive my addresses? Why come to this house party specifically to meet my family, if she viewed my suit with distaste?' He paused for a moment. 'And I am not old enough to be her father!'

'She is eighteen!' Tilda pointed out. 'You, I believe, are thirty-six? I'm tolerably certain your Grace is just as capable of doing that piece of subtraction as I am. There are nearly twenty years between you. And since she has come here, she views you as the uncle of her friend Louisa! With respect and liking, but she cannot imagine you as her husband, her lover.'

'She has said all of this to you?' Cold and hard. The anger in his voice pierced through her.

'No! Of course not!' Tilda was indignant. 'I would never have blurted out something like that told me in confidence!'

'Then this is all your very vivid imagination, Lady Winter.' The vibrant anger has been replaced with scorn.

Hazel eyes flashing sparks, she riposted, 'Imagination has very little to do with it, St Ormond! Put it down to experience and cynicism having engendered a dislike of May and December marriages! But of one thing you may rest assured: I have said nothing to Milly, you are quite out there! I will do nothing to influence her one way or another. If she wishes to be with you at any time and ultimately to accept your offer, then I will wish her happy with all my heart! Now, if your Grace will excuse me, I will take my daughter for her walk. Good day!'

And she spun on her heel violently and marched from the room, her head held high, presenting Crispin with a thoroughly distracting view of her bottom shifting vigorously beneath her thin muslin morning gown.

The door shut with a snap on this enticing vision. It was not precisely a bang, but there was every indication that only severe restraint had prevented it from being one. What on earth had happened to the cool and cynically collected Lady Winter?

Crispin fumed impotently. The damned cheek of the woman! To infer that he was pressing an unwanted suit on a girl young enough to be his daughter! There were only eighteen years between them. Very well! His birthday was next month—nearly nineteen! But still!

He mulled over what she had said. She had let something slip about her own marriage. Had claimed to know what she was talking about when she explained Amelia's feelings. What on earth had she meant? Winter…Winter…the only Lord Winter he could remember had been a man somewhat younger than himself. A mild enough fellow, he'd died in some accident. And, oddly enough he still couldn't recall where he'd met Lady Winter before. Yet the feeling persisted that he had.

Who would know about her marriage that he could ask without making a complete fool of himself and setting tongues wagging?

The answer came to him almost immediately, but he

fought against it for several moments before humbling his pride and bowing to the inevitable.

'Mama? Are you too busy to answer a couple of questions?'

The Dowager looked up from her menus. 'No, dear. I think the green goose will round off the second course quite nicely, Simmy. And do ask Marcel if we might have that delicious tart again! The one with the pears and the almonds. Thank you, Simmy.' She smiled graciously at the housekeeper, who curtsied and gathered up her lists.

Crispin leapt to hold the door for her. 'You may add my pleas for the tart to her Grace's, Simmy. Good morning.'

Closing the door behind her, he turned back to his mother and said simply, 'Help!'

She burst out laughing. 'Whatever has happened? You look quite distracted.'

Crispin bit his tongue on the ready answer. No self-respecting rake admitted to his mother when he had been distracted by a lady's bottom.

Instead he asked, 'Mama, if I asked you for some very personal information about someone, and promised not to reveal it to a soul, would you give it me?'

Marianne St Ormond frowned. 'That would depend, dear, on the someone, what the information was, and whether or not I had been asked not to reveal it. And on why you wished to know.'

Crispin came to sit beside her on the chaise. 'Can you tell me about Lady Winter? Her marriage? Her husband? I think I have just planted my foot in my mouth.'

She blinked. 'But you were on the town when it happened. Indeed, you knew Lord Winter!'

Crispin shrugged. 'Only slightly, Mama. He was a few years younger than I, and I'm damned if I can recall anything about him that would make his widow so dead set against her cousin's marriage to me!'

'Oh.' The Dowager's tone suggested that she did. 'Tilda Arnold was not married to the man you recall. She married his heir.'

*Arnold.* The name stirred in his memory but he repressed it and said, 'Go on.'

Marianne sighed. 'To fully understand what happened...well, even I do not know the whole. After her mother's death, I believe Sir Roger only took the child in to still the gossip if he did not. It was plain enough, when Lady Pemberton brought Tilda out, that their only idea was to marry her off to the first man that offered, regardless of his character or fortune. Or his age.'

Sick understanding dawned. 'How old was he?'

His mother grimaced. 'Jonathan? He was fifty-three when he married Tilda.'

'*Fifty-three?* Mama, that is utterly appalling!'' He felt completely revolted. 'How old was she, for God's sake?'

'Just eighteen. It was seven years ago. The Pembertons ended Tilda's first and only season the minute Jonathan Cavendish offered for her. They were married four weeks later.'

Crispin was silent. A short engagement was not unusual. But he was perfectly capable of doing the arithmetic necessary to work out the age difference. Lord Pemberton had forced his niece to marry a man thirty-five years her senior. Eighteen! It was nothing short of criminal.

He reined in his disgust. 'You said Jonathan Cavendish. Wasn't he a friend of Uncle Ned's?'

'Yes, dear. He never expected to inherit the title, so when his first wife died he didn't remarry, but his nephew died out hunting and poor Jonathan had no idea who the next heir was after himself. So he decided it was his duty to marry. And to marry a girl young enough to give him several heirs.'

'Good God!' Crispin could hardly sit still. 'Then she was forced into this marriage?'

'I should imagine so,' said the Dowager soberly. 'But don't cast poor Jonathan as the villain of the piece. He was very kind and very understanding. He retired to Leicestershire with his bride after the marriage, so I saw nothing of them, but I have often wondered if he offered for Tilda partly to rescue her. Of course his choices were limited; not many parents will marry off their daughters to a man so much older. Especially since Jonathan went to some pains to keep his wealth hidden. He had made a fortune in India as a young man, but he lived very simply and only those of us who knew him well realised just how wealthy he was.'

Crispin absorbed this slowly. And realised he had still a few more questions. Why had Lady Winter needed rescuing from her own family? Why had Lord Pemberton disliked his niece? 'What happened to Tilda's mother? Can you tell me?'

'That's no secret,' she replied sadly. 'She was Lord Pemberton's younger sister and he, as her guardian, attempted to force her marriage to a man over twice her age.' She sighed. 'Sylvia was very lovely and very foolish. Instead of holding out until she came of age, she eloped with David Arnold to escape what she described as her brother's persecution. Tilda was born about two months after she married on her twenty-first birthday, Pemberton having refused his consent to the marriage. David Arnold was killed in a street accident a year or so later and Sylvia died when Tilda was about five.'

'So her uncle took her in...'

'To quell the inevitable gossip if he did not. Sylvia had been popular, you see. And although very few would receive her after her disgrace, when she died, opinion swung around. Your father and I felt sorry for her and I made it quite plain that she had my support, but you know what society can be like. It wasn't until she had died that other people began to say, openly, how stupidly Pemberton had behaved.' She sighed. 'I wrote and offered to have Tilda to stay several times when she was a child, but the answer was always that they believed it was of the first importance that she be brought up according to the strictest guidelines for her own safety.'

'For which read, they were determined that she should never have any joy or pleasure,' said Crispin savagely. 'Good God, Mama! I owe Lady Winter the most grovelling apology and how I am to make it without revealing what you have told me, I don't know.'

'None of it is a secret, dear,' she pointed out. 'Merely forgotten. Personally I should opt for openness with Tilda. She values that, you know.'

He smiled. 'You've become very fond of her, haven't you, Mama?'

Her nod was emphatic. 'Yes, Cris. I was fond of her as a tiny girl and somehow, despite what has happened to her, she is a very lovely person. A little cynical and wary perhaps, but a woman in her position needs a few defences.'

Her words haunted him as he went off to find out where Lady Winter might have gone. Just what sort of defences would a woman need after what his mother had described? An air of cool indifference? She had that right enough. Pride? That too was there. Courage? Determination? Both were present in large quantities. She had responded to his accusations with all the fury of a lioness.

And that puzzled him. Had it not been for her response to Sir Richard at dinner that first night, he would have said that Lady Winter did not indulge in emotions.

Anyway, emotions or not, he would now have to apologise. So where was she?

Bebbington gave him the clue. 'They went out the side door, your Grace. With a bag of bread. Miss Anthea was talking about the ducks.'

Crispin nodded. 'The lake, then. Thank you, Bebbington.'

* * *

Alone, it would have taken Tilda no more than fifteen minutes to reach the lake. With Anthea dashing aside to admire every flower and gaze enraptured at every deer or peacock in the park, it took close to half an hour to get within a hundred yards of it.

The prospect was lovely. The lake lay in a sheltered hollow, grassy slopes leading down to it. On the far side the ground looked marshy and yellow flag irises blazed among the reeds. Willow trees nodded gracefully to their shimmering reflections and water lilies spread over much of the surface near the edge. Between the lily pads, ducks paddled on the reflected clouds floating in the blue.

Tilda heaved a sigh of pleasure at such peaceful loveliness. It was just what she needed after her turn up with St Ormond. It would be beautifully cool under the willows too, a relief from the oppressive heat of the day. And she'd be able to think about the very enthusiastic response she had received from the Vicar at home. He'd sent her a six-page reply, franked by Cousin Max, detailing the number of orphans and unmarried mothers who would currently benefit by such a scheme in their parish. From what he said, it would barely make a dent in her very large income.

A letter from Cassie had accompanied it, full of her delight and determination to assist in the practical aspects of the plan.

*Max is simply delighted. He has been thinking along these lines for some time and when the Vicar mentioned your idea, he was all for it...*

A house would be needed, mused Tilda. And they would have to consider the sort of training to give the children and girls. And then people would need to be found to provide the training. Perhaps some of the local gentry would take extra staff to train—for those that wished to go into service eventually...

A faint shout behind them interrupted her thoughts. Calling to Anthea, now rushing ahead, to wait, she swung around. The tall figure striding towards her with such leonine grace was unmistakable.

St Ormond. Her eyes narrowed and her jaw hardened mulishly. What did he want now? An apology? When hell froze over!

She waited with her head held high and a defiant blaze in her eyes. When he came up she did not give him a chance to speak. 'If you have any more insults, your Grace, might I suggest that you air them privately, and not where my daughter will hear them. At the moment I am busy!'

He held up a cloth bag. 'More bread. I thought she might like to feed the carp in the lake as well as the ducks. They'll take it from her hands. There's a boat moored there under that nearest willow. If I push her off and tie the rope to a root she can feed them quite safely. Then I can apologise in peace. And you can tell me exactly what you think of me without fear of interruption.'

Stunned didn't begin to describe Tilda's reaction to his masterly speech. Every gun had been spiked. Every avenue of retreat sealed off. He'd completely rolled her up. All she could do was stare at him with her mouth open in disbelief.

Lightly, he placed a finger beneath her chin, pressing upwards. 'Don't look so shocked, my dear. I'm not really such an ogre as I've been making out.'

She stood helpless as those long fingers drifted along the line of her jaw, a light, compelling tracery on her soft skin. Eyes wide, she trembled, unable to break away. His feathery touch held her as surely as iron chains.

And his eyes. The friendly, teasing glance had blazed into a searing intensity that pierced her soul, sought out every secret she kept hidden. She knew the urge to step closer, closer into the heat she could feel pouring from him, feel that heat surround her, in his arms, his body, in the touch of his lips. She swayed, her weight shifted.

He stepped back abruptly, turning his head. 'Good morning, Anthea. I brought some extra bread for you to feed my fish from the boat. Would you like that?'

'*Oui, Monsieur le Duc. Je voudrais bien manger votre poisson! Merci beaucoup.*'

The twitching ducal lip suggested that Monsieur le Duc had caught the slip, but would not dream of correcting it.

Tilda was made of sterner stuff. 'No, dear, *nourrir* not *manger*! You would very much like to feed the fish, not eat them!'

'Oh.' Anthea blushed.

'There's a line in the boat,' said Crispin with a grin. 'If you can catch one, you can eat it. But I give you fair warning, a big carp will put up a big fight!'

'Ugh!' said Anthea. 'And they're so horridly slimy! But feeding them would be fun.' She cast a glance at her mother. 'Er...I mean...'

Tilda sighed. 'Never mind, pet. Let's declare today a holiday. You may speak English.'

Five minutes later Anthea had been safely deposited in the boat with all the bread, told very sternly by her host that she was on no account to stand up, and pushed off. Tilda watched St Ormond tie the end of the painter to an exposed root with a very secure knot. She told herself that she was merely checking that Anthea was safe, but in truth she was utterly fascinated by the deft action of his fingers as he made the line fast, and mesmerised by the ripple of muscles under his coat as he shoved the little boat away from the bank.

He straightened up and came back to her. 'I told her she could push off further with the oar over the stern. She'll be quite safe. If, God forbid, she does fall in, it's not deep. I can just wade in and grab her.'

'Did you happen to tell her which bit is stern?' asked Tilda, smiling faintly.

'Yes, my dear. I did!' He stood before her with a disarming grin and shrugged out of his coat.

The ripple of muscles under his shirt sleeves and waist-coat was even more riveting, Tilda discovered. Her lungs certainly thought so. Air was suddenly in very short supply.

He spread the coat on the grass. 'There you are. Sorry there's no seat, but that should save your gown.'

She started. 'Don't be silly! Your valet will have a fit!'

His voice took on a crisp tone of command. 'Sit, girl! I have an apology to make and I'm damned if I'll do it staring up at you. Sit!'

She had obeyed before she even realised, curling her legs and muslin gown under her to keep the delicate material off the grass. Resentfully she shot him a glare as he stretched out on the sward beside her. 'I am *not* one of your spaniel bitches, to be ordered around!'

He smiled. 'Put it on the list. I'll apologise for that too. Don't worry about my coat, I was taking it off anyway. It's far too hot.'

She swallowed. 'Really, your Grace…' If only he wasn't so appallingly handsome. And if only he wasn't reclining there beside her in this attitude of friendly intimacy under the protective willow. Just propped up on one elbow, long powerful legs in their immaculate leathers and boots stretched out before him.

'Crispin,' he said firmly. 'If you call me Crispin or even Cris, then Amelia might follow your lead.'

'But…' she tore her mind from the contemplation of his legs.

'Crispin, then,' he compromised.

'And how do you propose to address me?' she asked. She promptly wished she hadn't. He'd already called her *my dear* twice, and she'd rather liked it.

His smile left her breathless. 'Hmm. Matilda, isn't it? Pretty, but a trifle formal. I don't like Mattie, nothing in the least doormattish about you. Tillie? No. Rhymes with Milly. Not to mention filly. Too tempting to think up rude verses.' He quirked a brow at her uncontrollable laugh.

'Tilda. Very nice. And Mama calls you Tilda, I've discovered. As does Amelia, of course.'

'You wish to call me Tilda?' Why did her voice have to wobble like a blancmange, just because he wished to use her pet name? Or did that smile have something to do with it?

'Only if you will permit it,' he said with a twinkle.

She humphed. 'I'll save my breath for more important matters.'

'Excellent.' His direct green gaze held hers. 'Now that we have that settled; Tilda, I most sincerely beg your pardon for upsetting you, for imputing scheming motives to your actions and for being generally arrogant and overbearing…'

'Your Grace…' She met his challenging look. 'Oh, very well! *Crispin!* You need not abase yourself. I was not very civil either, so —'

'Civility was not deserved after the way I spoke to you and the interference I accused you of,' he said. 'It was unwarranted and unfair. Whatever your circumstances.' He drew an audible breath. 'And I have another crime to confess to you.'

Another crime? What was he talking about?

'You thought that I knew something of your past, your marriage. I did not. I had assumed you were the widow of a man I knew very slightly, a man some years younger than myself. My mother explained matters to me. I am afraid I have been prying into your personal affairs. But she told me nothing that had not once been common knowledge.'

Tilda felt a strange shiver pass through her. There would be very little that Lady St Ormond did not know. She had been intimate with her mama, she had known Jonathan. There was no point in blaming Crispin. She had assumed he knew her story, that even though he had said nothing, he remembered who she was, had been. She could not blame him for finding out.

'It doesn't matter,' she said at last. 'After all, it was a very long time ago.' She went on softly, 'I am free now, free to live as I please, make my own choices…'

'Free to choose your own husband, for example.' His voice was idle.

She gave vent to a cynical snort. 'What on earth for? Why would I saddle myself with a husband?'

Crispin blinked. 'There are a few advantages to us, aren't there?'

'Not that I can call to mind, no.' She smiled mockingly. 'It may be a universal truth, as Miss Austen would have it, that "…a single man in possession of a good fortune, must be in want of a wife…" but I can assure you that a single woman in possession of a good fortune would have to be a confirmed ninnyhammer to marry! I, for one, don't call it an advantage to lose all control of my fortune.' Certainly not now that she had thought of something worthwhile to do with it!

He grinned. 'Surely this is mere…er…*prejudice* on your part, my dear?' His choice of phrase and the twinkle in his eye told her that he'd recognised and appreciated the source of her cynical comment.

She glared at him. He'd said he wanted to call her *Tilda*. Just what was he about, using that infuriating endearment?

She continued smoothly, 'Not to mention losing the guardianship of my child. Neither do I call it an advantage to be the chattel of any man. I am my own mistress now and intend to stay that way. I can think of nothing a husband can offer me that I do not have already.' Except more babies and she'd dealt with that, albeit vicariously.

A wickedly lifted brow inferred that Crispin could think of at least one other thing, intimately connected with babies. And she doubted that there would be anything vicarious in his methods.

She blushed and suppressed a grimace of distaste. He *would* think of that. Didn't men ever think of anything else?

Upon reflection, probably not. Well, it certainly didn't interest her!

Lifting her head, she said defiantly, 'Even that. I am a widow, not a young innocent. If I choose to conduct a discreet liaison, no one will censure me. In fact, if you think about it, a mistress gets far better terms than a wife! She is not legally and morally bound to submit to his…desires. And she can give him his *congé* whenever she wishes.'

She viewed his startled gaze with relish. She sincerely hoped she'd shocked him witless.

Whatever Crispin might have said was lost.

'Mama! Your Grace! Look! They're eating out of my hands!'

Anthea was leaning perilously over the side of the boat, pandering to the shamelessly greedy appetites of half a dozen ducks, who quacked and squabbled over the largesse of the ducal kitchens.

'And the fish ate out of my hands too! One was *enormous*!' She spread her arms to an improbable stretch.

'That's Bede,' called Crispin. 'Be very polite. He's probably even older than I am!'

Anthea plunged back to the other side of the boat, searching for the venerable Bede.

The exchange reminded Tilda of one bit of incivility for which she certainly owed an apology. And a change of subject was definitely called for.

'I'm sorry I compared your affection for Milly to my own experience,' she said. 'My arithmetic is not that bad. There…there can be no comparison. And if you care for Milly…then…well, I came to be very…attached to Jonathan, so I dare say…' she tried to ignore the explicable sensation that the words were choking her.

He stared at her, an arrested look on his face, 'But I…' He stopped. 'Perhaps we should be reeling her in now. It must be nearly lunchtime. Getting hot too. There'll be a thunderstorm tonight.'

The walk back to the house was enlivened by Anthea's chatter about the fish, the ducks and the boat. Tilda was very quiet and tried to force her mind to concentrate on the letters she planned to write to her cousins and the Vicar. Her host, she noted, had a set, hard look to his jaw and appeared to be annoyed about something. Probably her outspoken remarks on the institution of marriage had disgusted him.

A fact which she assured herself bothered her not one little bit.

No doubt he found such attitudes highly convenient, but disliked hearing them voiced by a gently bred female. She grimaced. If he had inveigled her mother's story out of Lady St Ormond, he might not, in fact, consider her gently bred.

After lunch Crispin excused himself and retreated to his library, ostensibly to finish his correspondence. In reality he needed time to sort out the confusion of emotions surging through his blood with unbridled enthusiasm, before facing his family again. And Lady Winter…damn it! Tilda! He'd had to exercise the greatest self-discipline on the walk back to the house not to openly admire the lady's walk, the graceful swaying of her hips and the temptingly long legs… He stopped his train of thought right there.

In itself, admiring her would have been harmless enough. What infuriated him was the unpalatable knowledge that he might not be able to resist the temptation to sample one or all of those enticing curves. He was barely in control of his passions.

He glared ferociously at an inoffensive bust of Plato, which only survived the experience unscathed since it was already made of marble.

He had a sinking feeling that insisting on Christian names would prove a serious tactical error. Not that he feared *she* would develop encroaching habits and take advantage, but that *he* would! Naturally one knew that widows were fair game. Especially one with her family history.

Also, she was perfectly right in her assessment that, if she were discreet, no one would be censorious if she took a lover. Certainly no one would censure the man who took her as his mistress.

Except himself. The mere thought of another taking advantage of her situation and shocking views made his hackles rise.

Which was utterly outrageous, because he could think of nothing he would like more than to take shameless advantage of her. Several times. Right now. And make sure that fleeting expression of distaste never crossed her face again by proving that not all men were such liabilities in bed as her husband must have been.

Which led him to the unpleasant conclusion that he was behaving in a very ungentlemanly, dog-in-the-mangerish sort of way. He really couldn't attend to Lady Winter's education himself. Seducing his intended bride's cousin, let alone her chaperon, would not be at all acceptable. So why on earth should he cavil at her very logical appraisal of her situation? Why should the idea of another man attending to the matter make him feel like issuing challenges in advance?

And why, in the name of all that was holy, did her very accurate, if cynical, view of the respective merits of marriage versus whoredom shock him? He had, on occasion, uttered very similar sentiments himself, and certainly had no qualms about using such mores to his advantage. Maybe Amelia was right…he must be getting old.

# Chapter Five

Given the oppressive heat of the day, most of the ladies, including Milly, cried off the afternoon's proposed riding party. Milly, indeed, succumbed to a headache after lunch and retired to her bedchamber at Tilda's behest.

'Oh, Tilda, I do feel so rude, going off like this,' she wailed as her cousin tucked her up on the chaise. 'Do you think anyone minded?'

'Why should they?' asked Tilda. 'It's a horridly hot day. You rest here and you'll feel much more the thing by this evening. And remember—there is the ball tomorrow night. You want to be fully recovered by then. I'll be about the house or in the shadiest part of the garden with Anthea. Go to sleep, love. Everyone gets a headache occasionally!'

She handed Milly a steaming cup of herbal tea. 'Drink this. I got it from Mrs Simms. Yarrow and feverfew. It should relieve your poor head.'

Milly took the cup and sipped obediently, pulling a wry face at the bitter concoction. 'I hope it works better than it tastes!' she said.

Tilda chuckled. Milly always complained about medicine. She was about to leave when Milly spoke.

'Er, Tilda? Do you like Mr Malvern?'

For a moment Tilda was at a loss. 'Mr...oh, you mean Guy. Yes, very much. Don't you?'

The telltale blush that spread over Milly's cheeks was answer enough. She liked him far more than a young lady should if she were contemplating matrimony with another.

'Oh, yes.' Milly looked away and said, 'He seems very much taken by you.'

'Guy?' Tilda thought rapidly. 'Is he?'

Milly met her eyes squarely. 'Yes. He flirts with you all the time. And you flirt with him.'

Tilda improvised. 'You know Milly, being a widow has certain advantages. Young men are much more inclined to flirt outrageously because there is not the same expectation of marriage attached to a widow. We have had our turn at the marriage stakes.'

'Oh.' Milly digested that.

Tilda waited a moment and went on, 'I might add that a sensible young man should always be awake to the benefits of buttering up the chaperon of any young lady in whom he is interested!'

Milly stared. 'But...but I have to marry St Ormond.' She didn't sound happy at the prospect.

'Says who?' asked Tilda. She thrust away the knowledge that her behaviour was shocking. No respectable chaperon gave her charge this sort of advice.

'Well, Mama. And Papa, of course,' answered Milly.

'You can always refuse,' Tilda pointed out. 'That's why it's called an offer of marriage, rather than an order.' She comforted herself with the thought that she had, after all, given her uncle and aunt plenty of indication that she was most unsuited to the task laid on her.

'*You* didn't.'

Tilda flushed. She could hardly tell Milly that she would have accepted an offer from the devil himself to escape Lord Pemberton. She swallowed convulsively as the memory of his visit to her chamber the night before her capitulation seared her.

'Tilda?'

Milly's voice called her back out of her pain.

'I had no other choice, Milly. You do. And your mama and papa are much fonder of you than they are of me. So drink up that revolting tisane and shut your eyes.'

Milly obeyed and Tilda tiptoed from the room, tolerably certain that her cousin would be asleep in minutes. She needed time to think. She had done exactly what St Ormond had accused her of doing. Oh, not exactly perhaps. She had not *traduced his character*. But she had given Milly every encouragement to refuse his offer.

She met Crispin on the stairs and blushed furiously.

'Is she better?' he asked. 'Should I send for a doctor?'

'Good heavens, no!' said Tilda, rather touched at his concern. It also racked her with guilt. None of this was his fault. 'It is just the heat. I have given her a tisane and left her to sleep. I am sure she will be better this evening.'

He nodded. 'Mama thought we might have a little musical entertainment. Louisa plays well, as does Georgie. Guy even has a tolerable voice. And then maybe a few round games. We can go out on the terrace for dinner. There will be a thunderstorm later, I'm sure, but not that early.'

Tilda nodded and excused herself. Since Milly did not need her, she would spend the afternoon with Anthea. And she'd borrow that little travelling writing desk from Lady St Ormond and write to the Vicar at home about her orphans. She smiled to herself. She'd taken to thinking of those as yet faceless and nameless unfortunates as very much hers.

And she had better think very carefully about how she intended to handle Milly and Guy Malvern. If he married her, good. But if he didn't and Milly had conceived a *tendre* for him and married his cousin…disaster. Tilda shuddered.

Had she been horribly irresponsible? Should she warn Milly of the dangerous path she trod?

The evening was stifling. Even on the terrace the air scarcely moved and although she was much recovered, Milly ate very little. The seating had been contrived to place her next to Crispin, who exerted himself to entertain her in as light a vein as possible.

From further down the table Tilda could see that Milly was more relaxed with him, less nervous. But the smiles in response to his jokes and witticisms were rather automatic, she thought. More as if Milly perceived from his tone that he had made a joke, than as if she had really understood it.

He was simply too sophisticated for Milly, Tilda realised as she sipped at her hock. His age was not the problem. It was the trend of his mind. Subtle, witty. He would be the wrong man for Milly even were he ten years younger.

She was still frowning over this as she went to bed, bed hangings, curtains and casements wide open. Sarah had left, muttering her disapproval and predicting all sorts of gruesome disorders attendant upon the noxious night vapours, but Tilda ignored her. She'd rather risk the night air than succumb to a thumping headache herself.

What to do about Milly and St Ormond?

Or Crispin, rather. So far Milly had not followed her cousin's lead. She had stared, shocked, when she heard Tilda tentatively use his Christian name. On the other hand she was on very easy terms with Guy Malvern, who had hovered about them after dinner, bringing cool drinks and keeping them both in a ripple of laughter with his inconsequent chatter.

Tilda grimaced as she sank back on her pillows. There was nothing automatic about the beaming smiles Milly accorded Guy. Oh, dear! Should she warn Milly that it would be very foolish to allow herself to form a *tendre* for her prospective husband's cousin?

She had not the least doubt that Lady Pemberton would roundly condemn the advice she had given Milly and would be furious if she ever found out what a dressing down her niece had given St Ormond. Tilda shuddered to think of her reaction should she ever find out her niece was on Christian name terms with him and had spent a peaceful and happy half-hour in his company under a willow.

Her own reaction to Crispin was more worrying. Far more so than her girlish fancy for him. Then she had merely seen him as a figure of fantasy, an improbable character in her daydreams. The flesh-and-blood man was far more lethal.

He constantly slipped past her guard; making her lose her temper, inducing her to say things that would have been much better left unsaid. To wit, her outrageous avowal that she would never remarry. That in itself was perfectly acceptable, but to have told him her reasons and declare that she would rather take a lover smacked of insanity. She could only wonder what maggot had got into her head to make her reveal such thoughts to anyone, let alone a man renowned for his amorous conquests.

Luckily he didn't find her attractive. Otherwise she'd be fending off his advances. At least she hoped that she'd fend them off. But he didn't seem to find her at all interesting in that way. Indeed, if he wanted Milly, then his preference was for small dainty women who could look up to him. Not great beanpoles who could nearly stare him in the eye! He'd almost said as much all those years ago. No doubt she hadn't changed that much.

Sighing, she blew out her candle and snuggled down. Tomorrow she would concentrate really hard on playing propriety. And she would see what she could do to encourage Milly. After all, if Crispin wanted her, he would make a charming husband.

\* \* \*

She awoke with a start several hours later to a crash of thunder. Another one followed almost immediately and a flash of lightning lit the room. Sullen rumbles echoed on and the wind could be heard whining around the chimney pots.

Tilda flung back her covers and leapt out of bed. Swiftly, she lit a small lamp, grabbed the robe on the end of her bed and headed for the door. Anthea was terrified of thunderstorms and in a strange house... Sarah slept like the dead and Anthea would never call out for the maid who was in the old nurse's room...she was deeply ashamed of her fear.

Nearly running, Tilda made her way along the corridor to the gallery that led to the stairs up to the nurseries. She should have thought of this and moved Anthea down to her room for the night. Crispin had said a storm was likely...if only she hadn't been so taken up with his concerns and Milly!

She slipped into Anthea's room to find the child sitting bolt upright in bed, clutching Susan and telling the doll in a high voice that she mustn't be scared, Mama was coming very soon...

'I'm here, dearest,' said Tilda. She crossed the room swiftly and got on to the tiny bed, taking Anthea in her arms.

'G...good,' said Anthea. 'S...Susan was getting very scared...I...I couldn't...'

A crack of thunder drowned her voice and with a squeal she buried her face in Tilda's breast. Tilda held her and murmured words of comfort, drawn from her own childhood terrors. After her mother's death she had always been left to deal with them alone, whatever they were.

So she sat with Anthea huddled in her arms and whispered nonsense to her, making a story of the storm as she always did. Last time the angels had been playing battledore and shuttlecock. Tonight they were moving house.

'They are shifting all the furniture about, dearest... Listen! Wasn't that a big crash! What do you imagine it might be?'

'A…a big desk?' quavered Anthea. 'Like…like that one in the library at home.'

'Good idea,' said Tilda at once. 'I wonder what angels use a desk for.'

'Counting up all the good people,' suggested Anthea. 'Like Papa. Maybe they like to know who's coming so they have enough sets of wings.'

'Maybe they do,' agreed Tilda. Another crash rumbled.

'I…I know what that is!' said Anthea at once. 'It's God telling the angels that they are too noisy, they are keeping us awake!'

And so it went on until the thunder finally died away in the distance. By then Anthea was half-asleep and so was Tilda. Tired, she lay Anthea down in the bed and settled beside her. She might as well stay until she was sure the storm had completely gone. Rain was drumming down steadily now. She could hear it beating gustily against the window panes…a pattering rattle…constant, comforting.

She awoke, stiff and cramped in the grey dawn, the lamp long since gone out. Anthea was sleeping soundly, smiling faintly. Tilda felt her heart contract sharply as she gazed down at the small, flushed face. It seemed so recent, yet so long ago, that she had been a tiny, helpless baby, then a chubby little toddling thing…and now she was a little girl who could greet 'Monsieur le Duc' with perfect aplomb. All too soon she would be growing up, making her come-out…finding a husband…

'I should be glad,' Tilda whispered to herself. 'She will have her choice of husbands, not be forced into marriage with the first man to offer. She will be happy, I'll make sure of that…' Defiantly she thrust away the thought that she could only do so much to protect her child.

…She shook her head to clear it of the crowding thoughts.

It was time to slip back to her own bed. Later today she'd speak to Lady St Ormond about having a truckle bed in her dressing room for Anthea in case of another storm. Somehow Tilda was sure that she would not see it as spoiling, that she would understand.

Yawning, she made her way back downstairs and along the gallery. She had not had a tinder box upstairs so she had left her unlit lamp behind and the gallery was very dim, since the curtains across the big windows at the end were drawn. To her absolute horror she felt something strike her elbow, wobble and fall.

To Tilda's shocked senses, the ensuing crash was worth all of the angels' best efforts overnight.

'Oh hell and the devil!' she muttered. It was that Grecian-looking marble pedestal with the little marble statue of Cupid and Psyche perched on top. From the muffled nature of the thuds, the wretched things had landed on carpet at least, but it still sounded deafening.

Cursing softly, she knelt down and tried to lift the pedestal. It was quite heavy and Tilda wondered crossly as she struggled, just how such a glancing blow could have toppled it. Of course it would be easier if she were using both hands and not modestly clutching her robe about her. After all, there was no one to view the shocking sight. She let go of the robe, grabbed the column with both hands and stood astride it. Ah! That was much better.

A faint click was followed by a flare of light.

'Just what do you think you are doing?' Crispin's voice held only mild curiosity, as if females astride Grecian pedestals, their robes revealing far too much, were an everyday part of his existence. He stood calmly watching by the light of a lamp, in a gorgeously embroidered silken robe that did nothing to disguise the blatantly masculine form it shrouded.

She dropped the pedestal with another resounding thud. It was followed by an equally resounding curse. 'Blast!'

said Tilda vigorously. She glared at him. 'What do you *think* I'm doing, St Ormond?'

He raised one eyebrow, set the lamp down on a console table by his door and strolled over with an almost offensively casual grace.

'All sorts of things come to mind,' he said pensively. 'But I feel sure that none of them are at all consistent with a virtuous widow.'

He bent down and started to pick up the pedestal effortlessly, one-handed.

Tilda, from her vantage point astride the pedestal, had a literally breathtaking view of a broad expanse of muscular hairy chest flexing powerfully as the pedestal was lifted. St Ormond, she realised dizzily, did not bother with a nightshirt on hot nights. At least, she rapidly reviewed the guests, she assumed that was the reason for his scandalous attire. Or lack thereof. She backed up hurriedly as he raised the pedestal, practically tripping in her rush to get out of the way.

Paying no attention to the flurry of silken skirts, he set the pedestal back closer to the wall than it had been. 'So inconsiderate of me to leave it lying around.' Bending down again, he rescued Cupid and Psyche from the floor and placed them on top. Then he turned to Tilda.

'Might I suggest, my dear, that next time you make, shall we say, different arrangements? Servants, not to mention hosts, are apt to come by all manner of strange notions when they find half-clad ladies flitting around the corridors at dawn.'

Far too dazed by the aesthetic treat she had been granted, Tilda really only made sense of the comment on her attire.

'Half-clad?!' she protested. 'You can talk! I mean…' Unfortunately this only served to focus her senses on his chest once again. She realised in shock that she was wondering what the hair on his chest would feel like under her hands…was it soft? Rough? Would it tickle her lips?

*Her lips! Where had that thought come from?*

Desperately she wrenched back control of her mind. Her knees were really not up to this sort of thing and neither were her lungs. He probably had a point. She'd have Anthea in her room if another storm threatened. 'Yes...well, next time I'll make other arrangements,' she said shortly.

His brows nearly disappeared into his hairline. 'Do, my sweet,' he said softly. 'You see, the servants will not so much as bat an eyelid if they see myself, or any other gentleman...er...flitting around the corridors.'

He paused and Tilda stared up at him in utter confusion. Where had that contemptuous, scathing note come from? Still silky soft, yet now his tones bit into her, like a velvet knife. And he was looking her up and down for all the world as though he were trying to gauge the capacity of a filly to bear his weight... Suddenly she felt a great deal *less* than half-clad, she was conscious of a scorching heat flaying her skin...of shivers racing up and down her spine... and the queerest melting sensation...

He went on. 'Neither, of course, will you have to contend with the attentions of other interested parties who may waylay you on your trip back to your chamber.'

The implications of what he was saying finally crashed in upon Tilda. He thought that she...that she...her mind lurched away from his implied accusation in, of all things, hurt. Not anger, she realised in shock. Hurt. Plain and simple. She was hurt that he could think that of her. Belatedly she remembered her avowal that she would rather take a lover than marry again...

And now what was he doing? She was completely paralysed as he advanced on her with all the sinuous grace of a large predator, stalking its prey. She should run, scream, anything rather than stand there like a rabbit hypnotised by a weasel!

For a moment he stood looking down at her, a fierce blaze in the green eyes. The next instant she was in his arms, helpless as his mouth crashed down on hers, devouring, ravishing. At first shock reigned supreme. Jonathan had *never* kissed her like this! Always gentle and considerate, his embrace had been a colourless, temperate sort of thing. Not this hot, surging riot of blinding fire, incited by savagely plundering lips and steely arms. And she had never felt even remotely excited or even vulnerable in Jonathan's arms after the first time.

And not even then as she did now. Completely and utterly vulnerable. And terrified. Not because of what he was doing, but because of what she, her body, was doing. Namely, yielding, melting in a surge of answering desire that she had never imagined. Even as the stunning realisation smote her, even as she remembered that she ought to be struggling, attempting to push him away, it was too late.

Her body had softened in his arms, was instinctively moulding feminine curves to masculine hardness. Her hands had drifted up to cling, to sink into his shoulders. The powerful muscles shifted and flickered under the silk as his arms tightened. And her mouth had opened, flowered in obedience to the demanding surge of his tongue against her lips.

With a groan that seemed to tear itself from him, he took instant and shameless advantage, plunging his tongue deep into her mouth in total possession. But even as he did so and her world rocked, she felt the tenor of his kiss change. His mouth eased on hers, gentling to match her tentative response. The surges of his tongue became a tender exploration, a seductive tasting that drew forth her very soul. With a dazed whimper of passion she realised that her own tongue was shyly stroking his, revelling in the taste and texture of his mouth.

His arms, though still locked, steel hard, around her, now cradled rather than confined as heat poured from his body through two thin layers of silk into hers, melting it bone deep until she would have fallen had he not held her up.

Molten liquid heat thrummed through her veins in time with her pounding heart, in time with the languid, tantalising surge of his tongue.

Then she felt one hand drop to her hip and slide caressingly over the smooth curve, over her rounded bottom, kneading, possessing. She sighed her pleasure into his mouth and felt the increased tension in his body, in his hand on her bottom, an instant before he jerked her closer, pressing her against the heated, rampant power of his loins. At the same moment his other hand shifted to close about one swollen breast.

She gasped as knowing fingers stroked and teased her nipple. He swallowed the sound as he thrust his arousal against the yielding softness of her belly in a slow evocative rhythm, matched by his surging tongue. Wild longing erupted within her, scalding hot. Her nipple hardened to a burning little bud of exquisite sensation. Then she felt him moving her backwards, gently but inexorably.

The small part of her brain still capable of rational thought screamed a warning. She cracked open heavy-lidded eyes to discover that she was being steadily pushed back towards his bedchamber. Her body said yes, but somehow, with her last remaining shred of sense, she baulked. Tearing her mouth from his, she forced her hands to his chest and pushed.

For a split second she felt his arms harden, saw the desire in his eyes and his mouth descending again. And she knew fear. Real fear. Because if he kissed her again, she would surrender willingly. Because she wanted him with every fibre of her enflamed body. It was only one tiny part of her brain that shrieked denial.

He released her and stepped back. Bereft of his support she staggered, her limbs still molten, unable to support her. Lightning swift, his hand shot out and gripped her wrist. Held her up. Slowly, her wide eyes never leaving his face, her breathing steadied slightly. Very slightly. She tugged at her wrist. His fingers felt like a brand encircling it.

Breathing raggedly, he let her go, saying with peculiar emphasis, 'Next time, my little wanton, I suggest you *start* with me. I think I can guarantee that you won't feel the need of anyone else's embrace once I've finished with you. And, after all, this is a family party. No matter how generous *I* may be about my preserves, I fear my sister will not be nearly so accommodating.'

She stared at him, beyond speech, conflicting emotions— desire, fright and rage—battering at her senses. And fled.

Crispin watched her disappear around the corner of the gallery, her robe fluttering behind her. His jaw was set and grim, his fists clenched with frustration. He was fully and unbelievably aroused; to the point of pain. He wanted the delectable widow in his bed. Now. At once. Five minutes ago. And there was not a damn thing he could do about it! Except go and wait for it to be a decent hour to ring his bell and request a cold bath.

With a groan he turned and went back to his chamber, slamming the door behind him and leaning back on the panels. Gradually, as his heartbeat returned to something approaching normal and his urge to follow her eased, he managed to ask himself what the hell he had thought he was doing. He had practically assaulted her. In anger, for God's sake! Only when he had felt the wondering innocence of her response, the answering fire on her lips, had he instinctively eased into seductive tenderness.

He shook inwardly at her remembered response, at the wild sweetness of her kisses, at the tangible surprise as he had plundered her mouth.

Groaning, he wondered if she would tell Guy what had happened. For of course, it must be Guy who had bedded her. He was the only other guest with a bedchamber in this direction for a start. Besides, knowing the devotion between Hastings and Georgie, and his uncle's starched-up notions, he dismissed the idea that she could possibly have been warming the beds of either of those gentlemen.

Lucky Guy! thought Crispin acidly, as he stalked back to his now chilly bed. Anger surged again, and with an almost physical shock he discovered that nearly all his anger was directed at Guy. Why couldn't the wretched boy have gone to Tilda's room? That was the accepted way to do things. Rule number one in conducting a discreet affair: don't shock the servants. They wouldn't think twice about Guy wandering about.

He discarded the dressing gown and slid between the sheets, wrapping his arms around the pillow for want of anything more responsive. What was Guy about to expose Tilda to such a risk? He was tempted to remind Guy of his obligation to protect the lady's name if he embarked upon an *affaire*.

The briefest of reflections served to convince him that this would not be well received. Guy was twenty-seven and his own master. Besides, if he mentioned the subject to Guy, he just might find himself strangling his cousin while informing him that if he couldn't do a better job of satisfying a lady, then he had no business seducing her in the first place. He should, in fact, leave it to his more experienced cousin.

Which brought him to the real problem. He was jealous. Pure and simple. His fury at Tilda had been borne of his jealous rage with Guy for having her, when he wanted her himself. And couldn't have her. Certainly not now. He could not possible poach on Guy's preserves!

And in all probability she was furious with him. Although what the damned woman expected if she was going to wander around a rake's residence in the dawn, clad in only her night rail and robe, he couldn't think. If she cared nothing for her own reputation, then she might at least consider her duty as a chaperon.

Still, he shouldn't have insulted her, let alone assaulted

her. The sensible thing to do would have been to say nothing. Well, nothing much anyway. There might have been some hope for him then. As it was… with a disgusted curse at himself and the whole situation, he resigned himself to watching helplessly as Guy furthered his liaison with Lady Winter.

The name didn't suit her at all, he thought. The reserved, icy goddess had been all clinging, melting nymph. The thought of all that unavailable, wanton delight was enough to drive a man demented! She had felt so right in his arms, so familiar, as though he had held her before…that odd niggling sensation deepened.

He had to be wrong. He couldn't have forgotten something like that, could he? And besides, where would he have met her? According to his mother she had been married off at eighteen and had lived on her husband's estate ever since. *Arnold.* Still the name nagged at him, tugging at some long-buried memory…

He punched the pillow. With a bit of luck she would not appear for breakfast this morning. He needed ample time if he were to preserve a dignified front with her, because he had made two appalling mistakes. He'd overestimated his own powers of control and seriously underestimated the lure of her body. Which was a combination guaranteed to cut up his peace.

It did. Much to his disgust he found Tilda before him at the breakfast table, chatting quietly to his mother. She accorded him her most charming, chilly smile and turned back to Lady St Ormond.

He blinked. He hadn't thought she'd be quite so brazen. Couldn't she even manage a token blush? And why on earth was *he* flushing? She was the one who'd been prancing around the corridors at dawn!

He greeted with relief the intelligence that his bailiff was in the estate room and would like a word with him. He finished his breakfast quickly and beat a hasty retreat, just as Guy entered to be greeted with Lady Winter's most spontaneous, *un*chilly smile.

Suppressing the urge to snarl, he stalked out. She was a shameless hussy, and the less he thought about her, the happier he'd be.

Rigby was waiting for him in the estate office.

'Good morning, your Grace,' he said apologetically.

Despite his annoyance Crispin smiled. 'It's all right. I had finished my breakfast.'

Rigby grinned. 'Glad to hear it. It ain't that urgent.'

'Good,' said Crispin. 'What is it?'

'You know as how your Grace told Marlowe and me as we wasn't to worry too much over the odd snare and rabbits and suchlike disappearing?'

'Yes.' Crispin nodded encouragingly. Marlowe was his head gamekeeper. He'd found the notion of turning a blind eye to poaching rather hard to swallow at first, but he'd come around when Crispin had put his arguments.

'Marlowe was saying yesterday as how there's been a lot more snares in the past week or so,' said Rigby. 'He thought as how some of the labourers might be taking advantage, so to speak, of your Grace's generosity.'

Crispin frowned. 'How do you mean, taking advantage?'

'Well, Marlowe thinks more is going than before. More than can be accounted for by a few labourers having rabbit stew once a week or so. He wondered if someone might be selling game.'

'They'd better not be!' said Crispin. 'I've already got Sir Richard breathing down my neck for flouting the game laws! If he manages to catch anyone selling game, he'll transport them. Or have them hanged!'

Rigby shuddered. It was a very moot point as to which was the worse fate. 'Yes, your Grace. Marlowe's been sniffing about quiet like, trying to find out who it is. Just to give 'em a friendly warning, as you might say.'

'Good,' said Crispin briefly. 'Tell him to come up and see me at his convenience. He can tell me what he's discovered and we'll have a think about what to do.'

He cursed fluently. This was the last thing he needed to really set up Sir Richard's back.

'When you see Marlowe, tell him to keep it quiet,' he said abruptly. 'I don't want this getting back to Sir Richard. We don't need him taking too close an interest in any local poaching. I'd rather settle it without proceeding to extremes.'

Rigby nodded. 'Surely, your Grace.'

# Chapter Six

Tilda was vastly relieved at St Ormond's early departure from the breakfast parlour. It was only with the exercise of extreme self-discipline that she could maintain her calm in front of him. Only by reciting lists of irregular French verbs could she keep her mind off his hands and mouth and the hard seductive strength of his body. She needed time to get her emotions back on an even keel.

By the time she dressed for dinner, she found that she was able to think rationally about what had occurred. About some aspects of it, anyway. For a start, she could scarcely blame St Ormond for thinking the worst: that she had gone to some gentleman's room. It was, after all, the obvious reason for her presence. And she supposed that she could hardly blame him for dallying—she choked on that slightly; it was an understatement, but she didn't feel capable of *that* much clear-sightedness—dallying with her himself if he thought her available...a loose woman, a widow enjoying the benefits of her independence.

Slipping a fine linen chemise over her head, she flushed as she thought about just what Lady St Ormond might have told him. No doubt he believed that her mother's history made it all the more likely. What was bred in the bone would out in the flesh. At least he had released her when she resisted. She forced away the memory of that dreadful moment when she had thought he was about to ignore her struggles.

Full well did she know that her resistance would have been of short duration. She resented that mightily. A frown creased her brow as Sarah passed her the elegant gown of green silk of which Lady Pemberton had so strongly disapproved. How dare he force such a shameful response from her! For he had used force initially. It was only when he felt her willingness, had thought she would not fight him, that he had been gentle with her. Hah! Well, he had learnt his mistake! She would not be seduced by him or anyone…no matter how much she wanted it.

And that definitely surprised her. Her experience of marriage had given her no hint at all of the passion St Ormond had unleashed in her. She had always wondered what on earth possessed women to take lovers. She had never understood why they would submit to something that was at best boring and at worst painful, when they didn't have to.

Now she knew. Or at least had some idea. Her whole body had responded to his touch, had melted in anticipation. And she knew what it had been anticipating. If he had pressed her, she would have surrendered totally to his passion. Just as his kisses had had nothing in common with Jonathan's beyond the bare fact of being kisses, she did not doubt that his possession of her body would be something quite different. Never before had she literally ached with empty yearning. She could feel it now, just thinking about him…maybe she should…*after all,* whispered an insidious little voice, *you're a widow now. The propriety demanded of a young girl doesn't apply to you, nor the loyalty of a wife. You could find out for yourself…*

No! She shook her head angrily. It was not possible. On several counts. For a start he was courting her cousin. She could not so betray Milly or lower herself. Or, she realised, permit him to dishonour himself. The thought shook her.

Why the devil was she so concerned about *his* honour, for goodness' sake? He'd made it plain enough *he* held such things of small account!

And besides, he thought she'd bedded with Guy as it was. At least so she assumed. He was the only guest quartered near the gallery. She should probably disabuse St Ormond of that particular error...for several reasons. She frowned, thinking about it. But her whole being revolted at the thought of going to him and assuring him that he was mistaken. For any reason. No matter how she put it, he might well think she was making known her availability. To him. And she had very little confidence in her ability to hold him off.

She flushed scarlet at the knowledge that she was, after all, the wanton he had called her. If, on the other hand, he thought she was having an *affaire* with Guy anyway, that would probably be enough to keep him out of her bed. No matter what he might think of her, he was not the man to attempt to seduce a woman with whom he thought his younger cousin was involved.

A faint frown creased her brow. She didn't like it much, but better he thought that than seduced her himself. She did him the credit to believe that he would never tell a soul what he believed. No harm would be done. And it was probably the best way to protect herself. She had absolutely no intention of putting her more cynical views into actual practice.

Very well, they were to be entertained with a ball tonight, got up for the local gentry. It would be the perfect opportunity to demonstrate to St Ormond—she refused to indulge in the intimacy of his Christian name any more— that she was entangled with Guy.

*Milly! What about Milly? She has already noticed that Guy and I are friends...*

Tilda groaned. What if Milly were becoming attached to Guy? The poor girl would be devastated if she thought her own cousin could behave so shabbily. Frowning, Tilda thought about it. She had to admit that Milly's understanding was not superior and she was very innocent. It was in the highest degree unlikely that she would suspect an affair. But even Milly must notice a flirtation obvious enough to deflect St Ormond.

Telling Milly what she was up to was out of the question. She would be thoroughly shocked. And she was far too transparent to connive at such a deception.

Tilda nibbled at one finger. Transparent. That was it. If Milly felt upset about what was going on, it would be very obvious. Especially to someone who knew her well. If that happened, then Tilda would just have to convince her that she regarded Guy as a nice boy, just as she did her cousin, Milly's elder brother, Tom.

She went down to dinner and was delighted to find herself seated between Guy and St Ormond's brother-in-law, Lord Hastings. Fully aware of the occasional glances her host shot in her direction, she set herself to charm both these gentlemen, always remembering to save her sweetest smiles for Guy, who was seated between her and Milly— who sat beside St Ormond.

Quite a number of the local gentry had joined them for dinner. The fierce Sir Richard was there again. Plainly, despite his disapproval of St Ormond's attitude towards poaching, he was a close friend of the family. Tilda liked that; clearly the Duke was not the man to resent a little plain speaking. She frowned. It was not a good idea to think of him *too* charitably just at the moment. Rather, she should concentrate on all the things she knew to his discredit. Unfortunately all those things made her heart pound erratically and shortened her breath.

'I say, Lady Winter!' Guy's voice sounded horrified. 'Have I said something shocking?'

She blinked. What was he talking about? He'd been rattling on in the most unexceptionable way about sailing. She bestowed her most ravishing smile upon him. 'Of course not! And please, must you be so formal?'

His face brightened. 'May I call you Tilda? I should like that very much! You weren't glaring at me, then?'

In point of fact she had been glaring at St Ormond without even realising it. 'Goodness, no! Now tell me, which bit of a boat is the boom? And why did you have to dodge? It sounds thrilling! I should so much like to try it.' That headed him off neatly. Odd how men always liked to feel they knew so much more than a mere female.

When the next course was laid, St Ormond, who had been chatting to Milly, turned his attention to his Great-Aunt Seraphina. Guy, with an unblushing wink at Tilda, switched his attention to Milly.

Oh dear, thought Tilda, as she turned to Lord Hastings. To find him gazing over her head with a speculative glint in his eye.

'Tell me, Lady Winter,' he said quietly, as he met her eyes, 'just how far settled are matters between…?' He gestured vaguely, but she could not mistake his meaning. He wanted to know if St Ormond had offered for Milly. And if he had, if he had been accepted.

She hesitated. It was not for her to discuss the matter with St Ormond's family. She raised her brows in what she hoped was an expression of quelling hauteur.

Lord Hastings smiled. 'Acquit me of vulgar curiosity, my dear. I merely wondered if Guy had any notion why you and Amelia were invited to what is, after all, a family party. Permit me to help you to some goose.'

She inclined her head graciously, wondering why her heart rate remained quite unaffected by Hastings calling her *my dear*. Couldn't the wretched organ work up the slightest flutter? After all, Hastings was just as handsome as St Ormond and equally as charming.

He went on. 'You may have noticed that the Malverns are, as a family, quite close. Naturally one would not care to see that disturbed. I was wondering if someone should just drop a hint in Guy's ear. Apart from Lord John, of course, which I cannot think would be at all consistent with Guy's dignity!'

Tilda stiffened. 'You think that *I* should do so, my lord?'

'Perhaps you might answer my first question,' he said gently.

She gave her attention to her dinner for a few moments, thinking hard. Finally she said, 'His Grace has spoken to my uncle, and been approved. He has not, so far as I am aware, spoken formally to Milly. They have been getting to know one another. She is, of course, aware of his intent.'

Beyond that she would not go. She could say nothing of what she believed to be Milly's doubts about the proposed match, let alone what Tilda suspected to be her growing affection for Guy Malvern.

Lord Hastings looked pensive. 'Hmm. I perceive, of course, that you are awkwardly placed. Very well. I had best take my wife's very blunt advice and keep my nose out of Crispin's affairs.' He smiled down at her. 'Do not be thinking, my dear, that we are criticising the way you are handling this business. I merely thought we should be informed so that we can be of some support to you, in the shocking event that Guy cuts Crispin out!' He grinned. 'After all, a dukedom is a mere accident of birth! It confers no common sense on the holder whatsoever. If Guy can open Crispin's eyes a trifle, so much the better!'

She could not keep her eyes from widening and he hastened to reassure her. 'I think, Lady Winter, that you want your cousin's happiness above all.'

Speechless, she nodded.

'Do you seriously think that she would be happier with St Ormond, than Guy, or someone like him?'

Without hesitation she shook her head.

He nodded. 'Precisely. She's a charming girl, Lady Winter. Well brought up, well bred. A virtuous young lady.

Everything St Ormond's bride should be. But...' he hesitated.

'But?' she prompted him.

He cocked his head on one side. 'Well, to be perfectly frank and thoroughly vulgar, Lady Winter  she ain't up to Crispin's weight!'

With which candid, if crude assessment, Tilda could only mutely agree.

Tilda had been vehemently ousted from her role as chaperon that evening by no less a person than Lady St Ormond. 'Certainly not, my dear! You'll have fun like everyone else and leave chaperoning Milly to Seraphina and myself. I dare say you'll have just as many offers to dance as she will!'

Tilda had blushed and disclaimed. But by the time she had been besieged for the first dance and had been persuaded on to the floor by one of St Ormond's neighbours, a very serious and worthy man in his early thirties, she had to admit the accuracy of the Dowager's prediction.

It was a country dance. Her partner performed it very correctly, chatting to her about the local scenery, asking her where she hailed from.

He seemed quite disappointed when she told him she lived in Leicestershire.

'Oh. Perhaps I may see you in town then,' said Mr Barnes hopefully.

She gave him to understand that she never went to town, with a smile to soften the blow. He reminded her slightly of Jonathan. So earnest, so kind...so safe.

The next dance was a waltz. Lord Hastings claimed her hand for this. Out of the corner of her eye she could see Guy leading Milly out. St Ormond was doing his duty by Lady Markfield.

'Don't give it a thought,' said Hastings, following her gaze. 'After all, the chit must dance with someone. Give rise to all sorts of gossip otherwise.' He swept her into the dance.

He was just as tall as St Ormond and Tilda had no difficulty in fitting her steps to his. Her mind swept back to that dance with St Ormond seven years ago. The dance he had totally forgotten. Perhaps it had just been the novelty of dancing with a man taller than herself, of feeling physically comfortable during a waltz, that had given rise to her fantasies...

She was enjoying this dance enormously. Hastings was delightful; charming and engaging, without once going beyond the line. And she felt comfortable. That was all. Comfortable. No doubt if she were to dance with St Ormond again she would discover that her memories were just that—memories, gilded by time and a young girl's dreams.

As they whirled around she caught a glimpse of Milly waltzing with Guy. Despite the fact that he was nearly as tall as his cousin, Milly was not having the least difficulty. Judging by the animated way she was chatting to him, she was not having to concentrate upon her steps much... perhaps she had gained some extra confidence...

The next waltz put paid to that notion. While Guy claimed Tilda's hand, she was fully aware of St Ormond, pointedly ignoring her, while he solicited Milly's hand. She bestowed it with a shy blush and seeming willingness. Tilda breathed what she assured herself was a sigh of relief and gave her attention to Guy.

He danced well and flirted with her outrageously, keeping her in a ripple of laughter. She thought that if this was how he'd been with Milly, she could well understand the sparkle in her cousin's smile as she danced with him. She said as much.

He looked startled. 'Flirt? With Milly? Oh, I wouldn't dream of such a thing!' A frown crossed his face. 'She told me she was hopeless at waltzing with tall men. So I told her what a dreadful little liar she is…but maybe she has a point…'

As he swung her about in the dance, Tilda could see precisely what he meant. Her young cousin was finding it absolutely impossible to waltz with St Ormond. It was very hard to tell who was having the more painful time. Neither looked to be enjoying the dance.

They turned again and Tilda lost sight of them.

'Tilda?' He paused.

She looked questioningly at him and waited.

'Please be honest with me. Am I making a cake of myself?' He sounded thoroughly downcast.

'Over what?' she asked, a trifle breathlessly.

He flushed. 'Milly. Is she really…? Well, I couldn't believe it. She's not at all like his usual…well, mum for that. He's never considered marriage before, but…'

'Who said…?' She couldn't believe that Lord Hastings or Georgie had said anything. He had as good as said that they would mind their own business.

He laughed ruefully. 'Who else? Great-Aunt Seraphina, of course. Mind you,' he continued with a faint grin, 'I did think she was exaggerating slightly when she informed me that in *her* day, a man like Cris would have called me out for making up to his betrothed!'

'She was definitely exaggerating!'' said Tilda firmly.

'But not by much?' suggested Guy. When she didn't respond, he smiled bitterly. 'I take your meaning. He has not yet been accepted, but I would be an arrant fool to think that my suit could stand against his.'

Tilda bit her lip. He was probably right, but she did not have the heart to say so.

They finished the dance without another word on the subject. Guy resumed his good-natured flirting, and, if it lacked his earlier spontaneity, few others would have divined the difference.

* * *

Few besides Crispin, that was. He had been far more
assiduous in keeping Tilda in sight than she had in watching him. He had known Guy since the cradle and he could
tell at once that something had upset him. He stepped on
Milly's toes for the umpteenth time and forced a smile
down at his scarlet partner.

'I beg your pardon, Amelia.' What ailed the girl? She
had danced easily enough with Guy, for heaven's sake!
Unbidden and definitely unwanted, Lady Winter's suggestion that he unwittingly intimidated Amelia reared itself.

'I hope I'm not upsetting you, Amelia.' He strove to
infuse his voice with kindly encouragement.

Her disclaimer was immediate. 'Oh, no, your Grace ! I'm
sure you don't…I mean…of course not!'

Revealing too, he thought, as she nearly tripped over. He
tightened his grip to support her, drawing her closer. And
felt her stiffen in shock as her breasts grazed his coat. She
gasped and pulled away. He eased his hold and gritted his
teeth. Never had he longed so devoutly for the end of a
dance.

Chatting lightly, he escorted her back to the Dowager
and met Tilda coming back with Guy. He eyed them narrowly. They seemed perfectly at ease together, but he could
not rid himself of the notion that something had upset Guy.
Tilda, as usual, revealed nothing except calm, good humour.

Until her gaze lit on him, that was. He had to admit, he
certainly had a talent for provoking her, one way or another. Her golden eyes glittered dangerously and when she
spoke it was as though an icicle had uttered speech.

'Ah, St Ormond! I hope you enjoyed your dance. Such
a delightful occasion.'

He returned her glare with interest. How dare she needle
him like this!

'So glad it meets your approval, Lady Winter,' he returned, hoping no one would realise he had avoided commenting on the first part of her remark.

Lady Winter's smile suggested that she had noticed. 'Oh, I am not excessively difficult to please, St Ormond,' she said sweetly.

He bowed. 'Indeed, my lady, I should have said that you were excessively easy…to please.'

The pause was just long enough for *her* to stiffen, but not long enough to be readily noticeable to anyone else. His lips curved in a triumphant smile as she lifted her chin, but then, just for a moment, he thought he saw something flicker under the ice…hurt…shame? His brows snapped together, involuntarily his hand went out.

But she recovered in a flash, if there had ever been anything there beyond chagrin.

'I shall bow to your Grace's wider knowledge,' she said, dropping him a curtsy.

'Er…Tilda?' Guy interrupted tactfully. 'Should you care for a glass of champagne? And, Milly…ratafia for you?'

Tilda turned to him with a relieved smile. 'That would be lovely, Guy. We shall come with you. Good evening, St Ormond!'

Milly smiled up at him politely. 'Thank you so much for the dance, your Grace. I'm dreadfully sorry about your toes.'

He disclaimed gallantly and heard Lady Winter say, as they went off, 'Really, Milly, you must be careful. Sometimes older gentlemen suffer from gout!'

Not for one moment did he doubt that she'd intended it for his ears. He'd declared war and she'd struck back at once. But the thought that he had actually hurt her bothered him. Crossly he shrugged it off. She was a brazen little hussy and deserved everything she got. Gout, indeed!

He was promised to Sir Richard's granddaughter for the next waltz, but when he came up to claim her, he found her sitting beside her mama looking extremely wan.

'I am so sorry, your Grace,' said Mrs Benton. 'Jane is feeling the heat rather badly. I am just about to take her to the withdrawing room.' She smiled up at him kindly. 'Perhaps you might dance with someone else.'

He shook his head gallantly. 'Certainly not. Perhaps you and Miss Benton would care to stroll on the terrace? I shall be quite happy to sit out with her.'

'Oh, no!' said Miss Benton, patently shocked at the idea of so august a personage as St Ormond sitting out with her. 'It is very kind of you, but you should dance with someone else...' She hesitated and then brightened. 'Why, here is Lady Winter with the water she offered to fetch.' She smiled up at Crispin. 'You could dance with her, could you not?'

Crispin turned to find Tilda at his elbow, her face a study in frozen civility. The urge to strip the mask from her was overwhelming. Along with more tangible items. And if he was going to be denied the pleasure of her in his arms under any other circumstances, he might as well take this opportunity.

Gracefully he removed the glass from Tilda's unresisting hand and presented it to Miss Benton with a deep bow. 'Miss Jane, I am your servant to command. I will do myself the honour of dancing with you another time.

'If Lady Winter will treat my infirmities with kindness...' His smile just short of mocking triumph, he offered his arm to Tilda, as the music started. Staring up at him wordlessly, she extended her hand and permitted him to lead her out. To his shock her hand was trembling slightly and she stumbled slightly as he swept her into the dance. He tightened his arm and drew her back into the rhythm, prepared to adjust his steps to hers. And then, to his utter amazement, her stride found his and they whirled together effortlessly. She felt so right in his arms, as though she belonged there...

And then it happened. So few women he danced with

could match his long strides easily that his memory inevitably slipped back—to another dancer whose steps had fitted his…golden eyes smiling up at him shyly. A girl he had invited to dance because…because his partner had felt faint, and she had been near by. The years fell away and he suddenly recognised the shy and awkward débutante in the gracefully mature woman.

'Tilda…' he began, not quite believing what his senses were telling him.

Bright eyes blazed. 'I should infinitely prefer that you ceased your familiarities, your Grace! Including that one!' Her chin lifted in an attitude of defiance, revealing the slender column of her throat, the soft hollow at its base.

He went on, regardless of this unintentional distraction. 'This is not the first time we have danced, my dear, is it?' He smiled down at her. 'Now I know why you have been pricking at my memory. When was it? Seven years ago? Your first and only season?'

Her gaze flashed up, surprise clearly etched in her face. She nodded.

'I remember now,' he said. 'My partner was unwell, so I asked you to dance. I doubt I ever realised your connection to the Pembertons. And you have changed so much I didn't properly recognise you again.' *Until I held you in my arms this morning…until I danced with you…*

'You flatter me, your Grace,' was the cool reply.

He winced. This was Lady Winter, chilly ramparts fully guarded. Where was Tilda? The vibrant, passionate woman he had kissed in the dim gallery? Where was the awkward débutante who had so amazingly turned into a swan in his arms? He had never really forgotten it. He had noticed the girl stumbling through her infrequent dances; he had vaguely been aware of her name and made a mental note to avoid her. Then, when he had been put in the position of having to dance with her or hurt her feelings, he had discovered that, with him, she was graceful, that their steps matched effortlessly. Just as they were doing now. Circling the floor with ease. She had felt absolutely right in his embrace…

And they had talked. He remembered that; of what, he had long forgotten. But he remembered that he had enjoyed the dance because his accidental partner had unexpectedly charmed him. That he had looked for her in vain over the next few weeks. No doubt that was when her uncle had forced her to accept Lord Winter's offer.

She had changed so much! Oh, she had filled out in all the right places, so that her tall frame was now elegant rather than gawky. She had grown into herself. But it went deeper than that. She had been a shy, yet oddly open girl. Now she was shuttered, reserved. Her social charm was delightful; but it was like a suit of armour, he thought. And she used her wit like a rapier! To protect what?

Even now as she circled with seeming ease in his arms, he was aware of the barriers she had set about herself. Her body might flow with his in the dance but some vital spark was missing. Something he knew was there, because it had fanned into a blaze when he kissed her.

'Would you accept my apology?' he heard himself ask gently. And couldn't quite believe it. Why the hell was he offering an apology to her? Surely not for forgetting a single dance…what? Seven years ago? She was the one who'd been scampering around his corridors half-clad in the early hours of the morning! She was the one who'd spent her night in bed with his cousin!

*You wouldn't have been insulting if she'd spent the night in your bed.* His conscience pointed that out with a certain sarcasm. *This is jealousy, not a sudden and uncharacteristic attack of morality. Let's be quite clear about that. You hurt her; that's why you should apologise.*

The lashes fluttered down, veiling her eyes. 'Why…why should you apologise?' Her voice shook slightly. 'You cannot be expected to remember every dance partner.' *Even if they remember you.*

They whirled through a turn. He answered very quietly. 'I owe you an apology because I had no right to treat you as I did. It is no concern of mine if you have an affair with my cousin.' He felt her flinch but continued firmly, 'I do suggest, however, that *you* should not be wandering the corridors. That will give rise to gossip, which you would not desire.'

The soft curve of her mouth twisted. 'The eleventh commandment, in fact,' she said bitterly.

He raised his brows questioningly.

Her laugh was brittle. *'Thou shalt not be found out.* Society's golden rule of hypocrisy.'

He nodded. 'For your own protection you should play the game according to the rules.' He was aware of a foul taste in his mouth as he gave this piece of worldly advice, a constriction in his throat... Suddenly it seemed wrong, ugly...

Tilda appeared to agree. Her eyes flashed fire. 'Your Grace labours under a misapprehension...' An infinitesimal pause. And then, 'When I play games, your Grace, I will play them by *my* rules. I have played by the rules of others for quite long enough.'

Sheer horror at the revenge society would exact if she flouted its rules made him protest. 'Tilda...think...your mother...'

She froze in his arms. 'You are not free to take liberties with my name!' Her gaze speared him. 'Or with my person, your Grace. As a widow I have the right to choose with whom I share my...affection.'

His arms tightened reflexively. 'And you have chosen?'

She inclined her head. 'I have chosen.'

The dance came to an end and she stepped back. For a split second he held her, unable to release her. Conscious of nothing but the desire to sweep her back into his arms and kiss the vibrant, glowing nymph of the dawn back into existence, right here in front of all his guests.

*And in doing so you would have compromised her so badly, you'd have to offer for her!*

The scales fell from his eyes with a resounding clang, just as she pulled back from his hold. His eyes cleared of the glorious vision that had blinded him, and he faced reality. Lady Winter…Tilda…stepping away from him… politely thanking him for a delightful dance. Instinctively he moved with her, escorting her back to her seat amongst the older ladies, exchanging smiles and greetings with his guests. And all the while his brain reeled at the revelation, and he wondered how the hell he had missed seeing the truth—that he loved her.

By the time he had bowed over her hand and headed for the refreshments, all the impossibilities of his situation had crashed around him. Firstly, he had been on the point of offering for her cousin, whom she was chaperoning! That circumstance would be enough to set society's tabbies purring with sly innuendo and malice—the claws would be out—and all aimed at Tilda.

Secondly, if she were having an affair with Guy, it was entirely possible that *he* intended marriage. She was a wealthy widow after all. It would not be odd if his cousin had jumped the gun a trifle! In fact, it would be perfectly understandable, thought Crispin savagely.

The last and most pertinent obstacle was simply that he had given Tilda every reason to dislike and distrust him. He swore under his breath. He could see now, apart from his physical frustration, just why she had bothered him so much…why he had not been able to place her properly. It had not been merely that nagging feeling that he already knew her; he had been falling in love with the wretched female without even knowing it!

And she had chosen someone else. Namely his own cousin.

He smiled automatically at Sir Richard Benton and gave at least part of his mind to the older man's hectoring attempt to bring him to a sense of his obligations to his order. He nodded and smiled and occasionally shook his head. All the while pondering on just *why* he had fallen in love with Tilda.

At least he assumed it was love. From all he had ever heard, love was a confoundedly uncomfortable, not to say dashed inconvenient, emotion. He could understand that now, after years of pooh-poohing the whole idea. He was now prey to two diametrically opposed urges, the one as powerful as the other. In the one breath he was conscious of the urge to go to her and, sweeping all her objections aside, ravish her, make her realise that she was his; and at the same time he wanted to protect her, even from himself.

So what the hell was he supposed to do? Marry Amelia in the sure knowledge that such a marriage would entail seeing Tilda far too often for his own comfort? And what if Guy offered for Tilda?

'So you agree with me, St Ormond?' Sir Richard's mollified tones brought him speedily back to reality. 'And you'll do something to lay these criminals by the heels?'

Good God! What had he been agreeing to? 'I'll think about it, Sir Richard,' he said diplomatically. That was true enough. He'd have to do something about the vastly increased trapping that Marlowe had reported. He was seeing the man in the morning.

Sir Richard humphed, but Crispin smiled charmingly. 'I'm always prepared to *listen*, Sir Richard. But I still have to think about it.'

'Precious little to think about,' the old man growled. 'Hah! Think I haven't heard you're losing more game than ever? These things get about, m'boy! And I tell you this! If I catch any of your rascals selling game, I'll have them ticketed for Botany Bay, before you can blink!'

Crispin grinned. 'As long as you haven't been shot for visiting Sir Matthew, of course. How is he?'

'Whittlesea?' barked Sir Richard. 'Gouty. That's how. Not here tonight, I notice. I'll get over to him in a day or so. Still likes a rubber of piquet.'

Crispin was getting into bed before it occurred to him to wonder just how Sir Richard had come by his information. He'd asked Rigby and Marlowe to keep quiet about the business. He paid his servants generously and demanded discretion in return. And if anyone going beyond the tacitly accepted limits was talking, it betokened a stupidity he could not quite comprehend. The penalties for poaching and selling game were well known and there would be nothing even he could do to protect a man taken for such an offence.

He blew out his candle and frowned into the darkness. Hopefully Marlowe would have something to report this morning. Best to scotch the affair quickly and quietly. The last thing he wanted was to see one of his men decorating a gibbet, or facing seven years' transportation, which would probably prove a death sentence anyway. He rolled over and settled down ready for sleep.

Unfortunately, blowing out the candle only served to focus his mind more clearly on Tilda. Just what was it about her that had caught him after so many years? She was, in point of fact, no lovelier than many women he had taken under his protection over the years. So he could acquit himself of falling in love with a pretty face and lovely figure. Yet he had never wanted a woman as much. Certainly he had never lost sleep over one—or not until he'd got her into his bed at all events.

He liked her intelligence, her quick wit—oddly enough, he even liked her cool reserve—now that he knew the fiery passion simmering beneath. The calm exterior was no more than skin deep, a cloak for wilder passions. He bit back a groan as he imagined just how that silken skin would heat and burn at his caress, how she'd feel beneath him—all soft and hot—wanton.

He swore—that was lust, not love. It kept sidetracking him. He was used to lust. Usually he could control it. This time it was controlling him, confusing him, preventing him from seeing clearly.

As Tilda herself did, he suddenly realised. She gave the impression of a cool, watchful cynicism. Anyone who got too close was deflected with her wit and occasionally barbed tongue. With two glaring exceptions—her daughter and his mother. Everyone else she held at arm's length, so skillfully they didn't even realise she was doing it.

That was why she had fascinated him from the start, he thought, thumping his pillow savagely. Why she continued to fascinate him—because he'd seen past her camouflage. Because he wanted to know the real Tilda. Intimately.

# Chapter Seven

Despite the late night he was up unseasonably early and conferring with Marlowe and Rigby over tankards of ale in the estate room by nine. The news was not good.

'Found ten more traps yesterday, your Grace,' reported Marlowe. 'Mainly wire snares, but two of the steel-jawed traps I'd use for foxes and badgers. If your Grace let me use 'em, that is!'

Crispin frowned. 'It doesn't make sense. Surely most poachers don't use those sort of traps! Damn it all, they're not exactly cheap and they're not useful for most game. And where on earth would they get the blasted things? We don't have any on the estate, do we?'

'No, your Grace,' confirmed Marlowe. 'I used 'em in your father's time. Him being more interested in shooting than what your Grace is, we kept the vermin down more. But when your Grace said just to leave the animals to theirselves...' Marlowe shrugged. 'I gave a lot of the stuff away to keepers on other estates.'

Crispin nodded. He had no argument with that. He knew that he was unusual in leaving his fields and coverts very much to take care of themselves, but although he enjoyed taking a gun out alone or with one or two friends for an afternoon's sport, he had no taste for the sort of ritualised mass slaughter indulged in by many landowners with their big shooting parties.

So he could see little point in trapping vermin. If they didn't keep the pheasants, rabbits and hares in check, his farmers would be cursing. Besides, having found one of his pet dogs in a steel trap years ago, he loathed the things with a passion. He could still remember the mangled leg, the terror in the brown eyes, the screaming agony of Jasper before he managed to free him. Jasper had limped for the rest of his days, and Crispin had sworn that he would never permit traps like that to be set on his land.

Still, other landowners used them, and that was their business.

'It suggests to me,' he said slowly, 'that a professional gang has moved in on us. Do either of you have any clue that some of our men are involved?'

Rigby shook his head. 'No, your Grace. I did happen to mention to one or two that you'd be main angry about the use of steel traps…' He shook his head in reluctant amusement. 'Well, if Hardy and Jem Beckett had aught to do with it, then your Grace might as well send 'em up to London and recommend 'em at Drury Lane! Right shocked they was. Beckett reckons one of the best things about working here is that he don't have to worry about one of his kids steppin' in a trap, and Hardy agreed.'

A reluctant smile curved Crispin's lips. Jem Beckett and Bill Hardy were two men who regularly supplemented their families' diets with a little poached game. They were highly unlikely to rock the boat.

'Very well. We can probably count them out. But at least they are warned. They'll pass the word around. I particularly want tenants with children warned.'

Marlowe nodded in agreement. 'Aye, your Grace. Rigby's got the right of it. An' if someone on the estate were up to summat like that, that pair would be on it immediate. There's just one thing though…' he hesitated '…I'm not so sure about a professional gang…'

Crispin raised his brows. 'Why not? Where else would the money for those steel traps come from?'

Marlowe scratched his chin. 'They're old ones, your Grace. Could have come from anywhere. But it's the *way* the traps are being set. Lordy! I could do better meself!'

The note of affront in his voice brought a crack of laughter from his noble employer. 'I dare say you could! You must know at least as much as any poacher.'

Marlowe grinned self-consciously. 'You could say that, your Grace. No, these traps was set by a rank beginner. The two steel traps wasn't dug in proper. I reckon a rabbit could have dragged one of 'em! An' the snares was set too high an' in the wrong spots. I tell you, I barely had to step off the main paths to spot 'em. Too obvious by half they are. You know as well as I do that you set traps in the little runs and trails the beasts make in the undergrowth. Not right beside a main path! Whoever it is must be a right lazy beggar. Stupid, too. Why, the number of people who use that path at all hours!'

Despite never having really given it any thought, Crispin knew precisely what he meant. Game didn't commonly hang about on the woodland paths used by humans. They had their own hidden trails and paths. A good poacher would know all about them; where the pheasants were nesting and were likely to fly; the exact position of a form, and which way the hare would leave it. He certainly wouldn't use a well-known right of way where he might be seen by anyone from the local magistrate down.

'So we have a very unskilled poacher,' he mused.

'Aye,' said Rigby. He added, with no trace of sarcasm, 'Which lets out all the usual suspects.'

'Hmm,' said Crispin. 'Very well. Leave the snares. But I want a close eye kept for any steel traps. Don't remove them, but check them daily and spring them. And I hate to say it, but you'll need to keep an eye on some of those snares you find. The ones you think aren't being set by one of our regulars. Whoever it is will have to come to check his traps. Obviously he doesn't share your expert knowledge, Marlowe. He'll be expecting to find something!'

Marlowe looked pleased. 'Aye, I'll fix 'un!'

Crispin levelled a straight glance at him. 'Like hell you will!'

Outraged, Marlowe protested. 'Master Crispin...your Grace! Lettin' a few tenants have a meal be one thing. You can't be lettin' someone get away with this!'

'Hardly!' said Crispin. 'But if you think I want some criminal taking a pot shot at you, you're vastly mistaken. Watch, see who comes to the traps. Don't let yourself be seen, and when you have identified the beggar you can come and tell me who it is.' He grinned boyishly. 'Believe me, if I see fit, I'll take all due measures. But I want to know who it is first. And I certainly don't want to be looking for a new keeper!'

Marlowe flushed and disclaimed, 'Pshaw! Plenty of keepers, your Grace! 'Tis me job—'

'Maybe,' cut in Crispin ruthlessly. 'But it took me long enough to convince you to leave the foxes alone and turn a blind eye to the odd snare. I'm damned if I want to go through that again with a stranger!'

Having breakfasted late, Tilda and Milly occupied themselves with a stroll in the shrubbery with Anthea after breakfast. French conversation was again the order of the day and, having discussed the scent of the roses on their way through the formal parterres and gardens, they were now engaged upon a discussion about how to spend the rest of the day. Anthea was firmly of the opinion that *'une promenade dans les bois'* would be just the thing to *'évoquer les esprits!'*

She giggled furiously when it was suggested that a walk

in the woods might well raise their spirits, but raising ghosts would have quite the opposite effect.

A cheerful hail from behind them heralded the appearance of Guy. Tilda noted with mixed feelings that Milly was plainly delighted, and that although Guy made no effort to single her out, it was plain that she was the main reason for his joining them. There was something about his eyes when they rested on Milly, a gentleness in his voice when he spoke to her. It was quite different from the funning banter and flirting manner he used with herself, she reflected. And it would drive her mad. She'd had quite enough of being treated like porcelain for one lifetime.

They strolled together for some time before Guy managed to draw not Milly, but Tilda apart.

He chatted on indifferent matters for a few moments but the tension investing him suggested to Tilda that he had something on his mind.

At last he came up to scratch.

'Tilda, will you tell me something?' He didn't wait for an answer to this very rhetorical question, but ploughed straight on. 'In your opinion, is Milly attached to Crispin or vice versa?'

After a moment's silence, in which her thoughts whirled and half a dozen polite disclaimers to knowledge jostled with several biting set-downs, she raised her eyes to his face and found him watching her with an expression of embarrassed sincerity on his face.

She sighed. 'Why do you ask? How will knowing the answer influence you?'

He shrugged. 'If Cris is deeply in love with Milly, or she with him, then I have my answer. I will leave as soon as may be and stay out of the way until they reach a decision.'

'That might be the best thing to do anyway,' said Tilda gently.

He shook his head. 'No. If I left now, who is to say that

Milly might not accept Cris, merely because she feels she has no other choice?'

'I cannot answer for your cousin,' said Tilda stiffly. Her body throbbed with the memory of his caresses two nights previously. How that could possibly equate with being in love with Milly, she didn't know. Unless of course he was suffering from frustration. But gentlemen were well known to have odd urges of the flesh, unconnected with any serious attachment they might feel. And she could hardly cite St Ormond's attempted seduction of herself as evidence that he was not in love with Milly!

But what to say about Milly? 'I do not think,' she said carefully, 'that Milly feels the degree of attachment to St Ormond that you are suggesting. He has charm, wealth and a title; he is exactly the sort of man she has been brought up to marry…' She paused. 'I do not know if her affection for another would be sufficient to make her defy her parents, or indeed to fly in the face of what she has been taught.'

'She's not comfortable with Crispin, is she?' said Guy bluntly.

Tilda flushed. 'I really should not say any more, Guy. You are just as observant as I. But I will say this: I think Milly and your cousin are not ideally suited. But that does not mean that they will not be tolerably happy together. Especially if Milly is given no cause to regret her choice.'

She dared not speak more directly but he caught her meaning at once. 'You may rest easy there, Tilda. I would do nothing to cause her unhappiness. Very well. I will bide my time. I suppose I should approach her father, but—'

'No!' Tilda was vehement. 'You would be forbidden to approach her. My uncle will never countenance her marriage to you while St Ormond's offer is still on the table. If he offers and she refuses…'

Guy snorted. 'And just how much pressure do you think will be brought to bear on her to accept?'

Tilda felt the blood drain from her face as she recalled the rage that her own intransigence had provoked; the abuse she had been showered with, the actual beatings. But Milly was their daughter, and they were fond of her, had always indulged her... Shaken, she replied. 'You may rest assured that she will not be unsupported if she does make a stand. And if they disown her, then she will have a home with me.'

He grasped her hand and raised it to his lips. 'You are the best of women!' he exclaimed fervently.

She smiled. 'Second best, perhaps. Now do stop trying to flummery me! I haven't said I'll do anything for you.'

Still holding her hand, he replied, 'You will support Milly. That is a very great deal. It is the devil of a coil. Cris has always been very good to me, my mentor, not just the head of the family. And he is the best of good fellows. To find myself with a *tendre* for his intended bride...well, it doesn't bear thinking about!'

Tilda could see his point. But she wished bitterly that she did not feel so confused about her role in all of this. She definitely did not think it was a good idea for Milly to marry St Ormond. But why? Was it merely because she was convinced Milly was not in love with him? Or he with her, for that matter! Or were her motives far less pure?

Was she influenced by her own tangled feelings for St Ormond? And what were those feelings? Did she merely desire to put a rub in his way by disrupting his courtship of Milly? There was one other possible motive; and it was one which she did not dare examine too closely.

Only one thing was certain. She would have to try to ascertain St Ormond's motive for courting Milly. Only by knowing that could she help Milly, by making her look at what she wanted in her marriage. And she could only see one way of finding out what St Ormond thought on the subject.

She'd have to ask him.

\* \* \*

She ran her host to ground in his library. She hesitated at the door. Faced with that imposing barrier of solid oak, her plan to ask St Ormond, not merely to make clear his intentions, but his reasons for them, seemed ludicrous. Drawing a deep breath, she screwed up her courage and knocked. After a brief pause, her gentle tap was answered by a rather muffled, 'Come in.'

Nervously she swung the enormous door open, marvelling that anything so large could move so silently. Peering around the door she discovered that the library, which she had not previously entered, was just as enormous as its door implied. And just as imposing.

It quite took her breath away. The room was a classic double cube in its proportions and it was flooded with light. In the centre of the long outer wall, a huge bay of windows, tastefully draped, looked out over the gardens and woods, and more light poured through the windowed dome high above in the centre of the heavily ornate ceiling, fracturing in the chandelier that hung directly below. A gallery ran around the wall and the sunlight glowed on the leather-bound spines of thousands of books.

At first Tilda nearly froze with fright. Then something about the room reassured her. For all its grave decorum, it was still a room for people. Comfortable sofas and chairs were arranged here and there, tables for chess and so on. The room had been designed as a place for the whole family to gather.

So caught up was she in the atmosphere of peaceful harmony, that she nearly forgot what had brought her there. Until her host's deep voice drew her back.

'Lady Winter. This is a pleasant surprise.'

She winced inwardly at the note of irony in his tones, and swung towards his voice. Just for a moment she could not locate him, but then she saw him, standing between a large leather-topped *bureau plat*, and the window, the light blazing behind him.

'Is there something I can do for you, Lady Winter?' The bored, indifferent voice rattled her momentarily.

She braced herself. In a moment he wasn't going to sound bored. He was probably going to sound thoroughly offended.

'There is something that I wish to discuss with you, your Grace.' Determinedly she forced her voice to a semblance of cool detachment, refusing to acknowledge the fluttering of myriad butterflies in her stomach. Crossly she told herself that anyone would be nervous who had come to ask what she was going to ask. That it had nothing, *absolutely nothing*, to do with the broad shoulders and generally magnificent physique of the man coming towards her.

'Perhaps you would care to be seated at my desk, Lady Winter.' He gestured towards the desk and she saw that there were a couple of chairs set in front of it.

She shook her head firmly. That would smack too much of an interview. 'I should prefer to remain standing,' she said. 'This is not a business matter.'

He lifted one brow. 'A sofa, then.' He led the way to one of them and inexorably handed her into it. She desperately tried to quell the trembling of her hand at the light touch of his long fingers. Her prepared, succinct and direct speech had vanished into the ether. She groped for it wildly, insanely aware not only of her host, smiling down at her in a distinctly cynical manner, but also the array of classical busts that stood around the walls directly beneath the gallery. In the face of all these supposedly wise and logical minds, her own fluttered like a trapped bird.

Sitting down had definitely been a mistake. St Ormond was looming over her in a very ducal sort of way... If only the wretched man would sit down! For a moment she considered the possibility of thinking of something else to say to him. And then, with an outraged mental shake at her own timidity, she plunged in.

'What I wish to ask you should not take long, but I

should perhaps warn you that it is of rather a personal, not to say intimate, nature.' She hesitated. 'I…I should not like you to think me presumptuous, but in this situation I can see no other way forward…'

One brow lifted. 'How very, shall I say, gratifying, Lady Winter.'

She blinked up at him. What on earth was he talking about? And why was he smiling in just that predatory and cynical way? And why in God's name was he sitting down…and sliding along the sofa towards her? Tilda decided that she had been seriously mistaken in wishing him to sit down. He had been far less threatening standing up!

She shut her eyes for a moment to drag her thoughts together.

Only to find that her breath, as well as her mind, seized completely as she felt a hard, masculine thigh press against hers. A powerful arm encircled her. She opened her eyes to find that he was surrounding her, with his heat, his body, his penetrating green gaze.

'I think I can guarantee, Lady Winter, that I will be only too delighted to satisfy all your…curiosity.' His lips curved enticingly as he leaned closer. 'And I promise you that I shall not think you presumptuous! No matter how…er… intimate you choose to be!'

Dazed, she stared back at him. And wondered if his face was a blur because she was dizzy or because he was getting closer and her eyes had forgotten to focus. The latter, she realised, as his lips brushed hers, gently, featherlight, melting her effortlessly. His arms closed around her, drawing her close, fitting her to his body. Instinctively her hands lifted to his shoulders, sliding over the moulded muscles that tightened under her touch…it felt so right, so wonderful…except it wasn't what she had come for…

Grasping wildly at the last shreds of her rapidly departing wits, she dragged in a sharp breath.

'Milly!' she gasped. And pushed hard on the rock-solid

wall of his chest, shoving him away and scrambling out of his reach along the sofa.

For one crazy, heartstopping moment Crispin thought she was calling *him* Milly. His heart was pounding, his blood was afire and he was again aroused to the point of pain. What the hell was she talking about Milly for?

'Why Milly?' she was saying. It didn't make sense. All he could think about was *her*! So soft and vulnerable in his arms. Her lips, about to part under his… He wanted her with a desire that rocked him to his foundations. Dear God! One kiss and he was in agony. What she'd do to him in bed didn't bear thinking about.

She repeated the question with a painful intensity in her voice.

'Why Milly?'

'Why Milly what?' His voice grated harshly even on his own ears. He saw her flinch and knew a savage twinge of satisfaction. Good! He felt rage with himself that he should want her so much, even to the point of wishing it was possible to marry her, despite knowing that she was engaged in an affair with Guy. And now she had come to offer herself to him! Doubtless she thought he had more to offer one way or another.

'What has Milly to do with what you are offering, my dear?' His voice was silky smooth and his eyes never left her face. So he saw the shock and anger that surged across it. And something else that flared momentarily in her eyes.

Then they blazed at him. 'I wish to know why you desire to marry my cousin!' she said angrily. 'Somehow I doubt, given your propensity for molesting *me*, that love enters into your calculations!'

'I should have thought, my lady,' he said bitingly, 'that such a question should be best left to her father!'

She snorted in disgust. 'All my uncle is concerned with is your wealth and title! I want to know *why* you want

Milly. Why her, and not some other attractive, well-bred virgin?'

His eyes narrowed. Just at that moment he didn't care the snap of his fingers for attractive, well-bred virgins. What *he* wanted was a statuesque, outrageous, not to mention outraged, widow! And he wanted her now! A fact that made his answer less than politic.

'Why Milly?' he mused. 'Why indeed. You have provided the answer yourself, Lady Winter. She is attractive, well bred and, perhaps I might add, biddable. Her youth is certainly an asset in that regard! And, of course, the indispensable qualification…her virginity. I need have no fear that my heir will be sired by another.' He spoke with a chilly brutality, born of the knowledge that he didn't give a damn about any of the above. That all he desired was one intransigent widow! A widow who was glaring at him as though all *she* desired was a blade with which to run him through. He wasn't entirely sure her eyes weren't going to do just that.

'Why, you arrogant, conceited *coxcomb*!' she exploded into incandescent rage, her golden eyes flaming in a flushed face. 'Why don't you just go out and buy yourself a nice little brood mare? Or an obedient little spaniel? Yes, that's more like it! A fawning, malleable puppy to roll over on her back for you!' Venom spat from her eyes. 'You don't want a woman to wife! And you certainly don't want Milly! Not even in the most basic way!'

All Crispin could do was wonder just how he could be supposed to want Milly, when all his mind and body was taken up with wanting *her*!

She continued in tones of contemptuous loathing as she sprang up from the sofa and paced furiously, every graceful, swaying line infused with quivering anger. 'Does it mean nothing to you that your bride will submit to you, give herself to you, in complete trust? May even care for you? And what have you to give in return? Your wealth and title have already bought her breeding and virginity! What have you to offer for her affection and trust? Or don't they matter to you?'

Pain shivered through her voice, pierced him. 'How will you make her happy? Do you even care about what will make a woman happy?'

He was beyond rational thought by now. There was just enough truth in her savage flaying of his motives and character to enrage him. And his well-nigh unbearable arousal combined with his anger to make a volatile mix of emotions.

She had ceased pacing and stood before him, her gaze challenging, awaiting his response.

He met her challenge with one of his own. 'And just what makes you, of all women, think that I cannot please your cousin, Lady Winter? Do you not think that I can persuade my bride to give herself willingly?'

She stiffened. 'Not if she knew what a beast you are!' she flashed.

Green glinted dangerously. 'As you do, Lady Winter?' His voice held a purring menace.

Golden sparks flew. 'Forewarned is forearmed,' she countered.

'There is that, of course,' he admitted. 'But even if armed, one must sometimes surrender to…er…superior firepower.'

Her gaze narrowed. 'I think not, St Ormond.' Cold as ice, the chilly dismissal proved the final spur to his temper.

Rising slowly to his feet he approached her. 'We shall see, shall we?'

Defiance flamed in her eyes, her stance. He could see the effort she made to hold steady against his advance, yet she stood fast, refusing to yield an inch.

She would yield a great deal more than that, he thought savagely, as he reached for her. His hands closed on her slim shoulders and he drew her closer, into the circle of his arms. She came stiffly, unwillingly. For a split second he wondered why she wasn't struggling. Then he understood. She intended to prove that whatever he did to her, she would remain unyielding.

She was about to realise her mistake.

He closed his arms around her stiff form and then slowly raised one hand to her throat. Long fingers grazed over it, teasing, tantalising. Her jaw clenched and with an inward smile, he traced it, lingering beneath her chin, his thumb rubbing over the soft lower lip. She was still rigid in his arms, but he could feel the tension, the desperate resolve her defiance was based on.

Still caressing her lip he feathered his lips over her jaw, found her ear and breathed warmly, sensuously. His reward was a definite shudder, a wildly indrawn breath. Lightly, delicately, he circled the shell-like curves of her ear with his tongue, breathing softly. And felt her gasp, felt her body ease against his.

Holding his scorching passion in check, he pressed warm kisses back along her jaw until he came to the corner of her mouth. She was still trying to hold out against him, but her eyes fluttered shut as he covered her lips with his own and ran his tongue along their soft curves. He teased and probed, requesting, demanding entrance. Still she resisted.

His lips curved in a smile even as he continued to kiss her. She was shaking in her effort to remain unmoved. Her eventual surrender would be all the greater...all the sweeter. Unhurriedly he shifted the hand on her waist to cup the gentle swell of one breast. Under the fine muslin the nipple surged and hardened in his palm. He trapped the bud between thumb and forefinger and massaged it. Mercilessly. And felt the despairing moan that rippled through her as her besieged mouth surrendered, as her lips softened and parted.

He took possession at once. Deeply and thoroughly. Claiming her, branding her. His tongue stroked hers with sensuous abandon, exploring the hot sweetness of her mouth with slow, thrusting expertise. With surges that echoed the fire in his loins, the burning need that coursed through his flesh.

Inexorably he drew her back to the sofa, drew her down on to it. When he felt her hands flutter like a protesting dove at his chest he deepened the kiss still further, distracting her while his fingers worked swiftly at the buttons securing her bodice.

It gaped before him and without breaking their kiss, he slipped his hand inside to find the ribbons of her chemise. Gently, almost reverently, he felt the silken, heated skin of her breast under his searching fingers, found the hardened peak and tortured it.

His mouth absorbed the sobs of pleasure that shook her. They mingled with harsh groans that he barely heard. His mind was awash with pleasure, aflame with the desire to taste more of her sweetness. Her head was resting, leaning back against his arm. Her body flowed like molten silk in his embrace. Completely unresisting, completely helpless to fight the spell of desire his hands and mouth were weaving.

Giddy with delight, he laid her back on the sofa, pressed her down beneath him and allowed his mouth to travel down over the soft throat. He paused to lave and suckle gently at the fluttering pulse below her ear and felt her writhe beneath him, felt her hips soften and flex against him.

A surge of triumph roared through him as he shifted his mouth to her breast and heard her whimper in shock, jerk under him as he teased and circled the tempting bud. And then to his joy he felt her hands frame his face, stroking, caressing, urging him to take her breast as he had taken her mouth.

Slowly he took the rosy tip into his mouth, grazing it with his teeth, licking and finally, as she arched and sobbed under him, suckling it, until she cried out softly and clutched at him, her hands gripping his scalp with frantic urgency.

Almost without knowing it his hand was sliding under her skirt and petticoat, following the graceful curve of her calf, her thigh, so warm and soft. Higher, to clasp her hip possessively and at last to tangle searching fingers in soft damp curls.

She tensed and he immediately suckled harder on the breast imprisoned in his mouth, flaying it with pleasure, distracting her, until he felt the muscles in her thighs soften, felt them part to yield their treasure to his wickedly knowing fingers. And for a moment he knew delight unimagined as she yielded those secrets, as she writhed and sobbed in wanton abandon while he stroked and teased.

And then he heard one coherent and devastating word. 'No.' And then two more. 'No more.' And on a fractured sob, 'Please.' Her hands were pushing at his shoulders. Hard.

He hesitated. It would be so easy to ignore her plea, to overwhelm her with pleasure, until she begged him to take her…he couldn't do it.

Even as temptation licked hotly at him, he was releasing her, lifting his weight from her trembling body, smoothing down her rumpled skirts. He tried to help her sit up, but she flinched away from him. His hand dropped and he got up from the sofa. Tried not to watch as she fumbled with the drawstring of her chemise, as her unsteady fingers struggled with the buttons of her bodice. Tried to ignore the painful intensity of his arousal, the primitive instinct which urged him to take and possess her.

Civilisation won. Just.

He searched for words of apology. There were none. Because he wished he hadn't had to stop.

Finally she stood up. Her voice was low and shaking. 'Very well, your Grace. We have established that you can please a woman. And how do you think she will feel afterwards, knowing that your *expertise*—' she laced the word with bitter scorn '—can compel not only her bodily surrender, but her heart and soul as well? How do you think she will feel to know that these commodities are of not the slightest use to you? And that the only use you have for her body is as relief for your own urges and as a vessel for your seed? That the only joy you feel in her surrendered virtue and innocence is the assurance of your paternity?'

She paused and passed a trembling hand across her face. A face which had become a pallid frame for suddenly over-bright eyes. 'I doubt happiness is what she will feel, St Ormond. And frankly, I don't give a fig for what you will feel!'

She turned away sharply. But not before he saw the bright eyes flood, spill over.

'Tilda…' His voice was ragged, compounded of passion and searing shame.

She wasn't listening. Blindly, clumsily, she was heading for the door.

Instinct spurred him on. He strode after her and caught her, swinging her to face him. The shamed fury in her eyes scorched him. Then he saw her eyes narrow with intent. An intent he'd never seen in a woman's eyes before.

Then he felt his head snap back as a tooth-rattling right hook crashed into his jaw.

'Let me go!' she raged at him. 'I have no desire to be insulted by you any longer!' Her voice shook with emotion.

'Then stay here,' he said roughly. 'I'll go. God knows who you'll meet if you leave now. And you're not in a fit state to be seen by anyone!'

He strode past her and left the library, barely able to navigate for the conflicting emotions racking him.

Dazed and trembling Tilda stared at the closed door. He had gone. Leaving her confused and…furious. Furious with him and with herself. What on earth had she been about to permit him to touch her like that? With a sob of despair she turned away from the door and found a chair by the fireplace. Sinking into it, she wondered if she had in fact completely lost her mind.

Surely only a bedlamite would have allowed—no, challenged a gazetted rake like St Ormond to attempt to seduce her. Which was what her behaviour had amounted to. She had offered a challenge. He'd accepted. She supposed that she ought to be grateful that he had drawn back when she begged him to stop.

Her body burned at the thought of what he'd been doing, that she hadn't stopped him earlier. But, in truth, she'd been so startled and enthralled by his caresses that she hadn't wanted to stop him. Jonathan had never touched her thighs like that, so that she felt all aching and melting. He certainly hadn't...hadn't caressed her...intimately...like that; hadn't made her feel all hot and wet. Empty. No, he'd just stroked her thighs a little, then pressed them apart and...

She shuddered at the realisation that Crispin hadn't had to press them apart. She'd opened them willingly. And she'd have opened them further if he'd pressed his advantage. If what she had experienced so far was anything to judge by, his possession of her body would be very different from anything she had known in her marriage. She'd *wanted* to feel him inside her, taking her... Which was why she'd reacted with such fury afterwards.

With a stab of percipience, she knew that if Crispin once possessed her body, he would have her soul as well. And she had told him that she would rather be mistress than wife...

She hadn't really meant it. When he'd challenged her assertion that the male sex had absolutely nothing to offer a woman in her circumstances, she'd had no idea of the magic his mouth and hands could invoke. She hadn't, in fact, known what she was talking about. So she'd said the first thing that came to mind, fully intending to shock him.

Now she did know what she was talking about. Or at least had an inkling, which terrified her, because she wanted to know more. And despite her scornful cynicism about the respective merits of being mistress rather than wife she had no intention of becoming a notorious widow. She very much doubted that that would give her any more pleasure than marriage in the long run. And deep down at the very bottom of her bruised heart she knew that was not what she wanted.

She did not dare to look closely at what she wanted for the simple reason that she would never have it. A tear trickled down her cheek as she stared into the empty grate. At least on the next cold day some kindly soul would come and light a fire in it.

She shook her head to clear it. That particular fire would leave her colder than ever when it finally went out. Scorched and burnt and chilled to the marrow, it would destroy her because she would be nothing to him but a casual conquest. The insidious little voice she'd heard before whispered cajolingly. *Why not take what he offers? Who will be harmed? You're being fanciful…as long as you are discreet, who would care?*

No. She'd had enough of being a toy, a pawn in a man's hands. She'd prefer to live her life on her terms. And she very much doubted that if she surrendered to St Ormond, she would be able to do that. Men had a way of enforcing their terms on a woman, even when they didn't mean to.

# Chapter Eight

Crispin's headlong flight from the library was summarily halted by a familiar voice. 'Ah, Crispin dear?'

Dazed, he stopped dead in his tracks to face his mother, standing halfway up the main stairs. 'Yes, Mama?'

'I was looking for you, dear. Are you dreadfully busy? Or could you spare me a moment?' she asked, giving no sign that the less than pristine state of his cravat and his generally distracted manner had registered.

Dear God! What if she had strolled into the library seeking him? Dragging in a deep breath, he assented. 'As many moments as you like, Mama.' It might even help him to get his emotions and urges back where they belonged, under his control. At the moment they were rioting about completely unchecked in a way that was making him slightly dizzy. Never before had he been in anything less than total control where a woman was concerned.

'Where shall we talk?' he asked as he joined her on the stairs.

'Well, I did think my sitting room,' she mused. 'No one will disturb us there.'

Which meant she had something important to say.

Part of his brain wondered just what was on her mind as he escorted her upstairs. But by far the greater part was taken up with his unprecedented loss of sangfroid. Desire was an open book to him. He'd read it from cover to cover. Frequently. But although he'd known what it was to want a woman, never before had he found himself acting against his better judgement, let alone against the dictates of his honour.

For that was what he had been doing. In trying to shame Tilda, he had shamed himself. Vaguely he realised that his mother had been speaking to him.

With a mental shake, he summoned up a smile for her and held the sitting room door open. He followed her in and said ruefully. 'I'm sorry, Mama. My mind is wandering.'

'I noticed,' she said drily. 'Do you want to tell me what is bothering you?'

'No,' he said baldly. 'I value your good opinion far too much. You tell me what is bothering you.' Hopefully he could do something about that.

Lady St Ormond sat down on a canopied sofa. 'I hope you won't think that I'm interfering,' she said slowly, and then looked up with a self-deprecating twinkle. 'Which should be enough to warn you that I'm about to be atrociously interfering!'

He smiled wanly. 'Interfere away, Mama.'

'Very well,' she said. 'It is simply this. I was wondering why you are contemplating marriage with Milly Pemberton.'

Without thinking he asked sharply, 'Has Lady Winter discussed this with you?'

She looked amused. 'No, dear. But I dare say our concerns have much in common, despite the difference in perspective. Naturally she is primarily concerned for Milly's happiness and I am concerned for yours.'

'I see,' said Crispin. 'And you think I wouldn't be.' Tilda had made it moderately plain that she held doubts for

Milly's happiness, but he didn't feel it necessary to share that with his mother.

A faint frown creased her brow. 'I think you might become a trifle bored.' She elaborated hurriedly. 'Milly is a dear, Cris. She is a good affectionate girl. Well brought up, attractive...but I wonder if she is the girl to hold your affections or give you the companionship you need. Naturally if your affections are engaged, then there is no more to be said...but they're not, are they?' A quizzical lift of her delicate brows stripped the question of all possible offence.

Ruefully he shook his head. There was no point in trying to hoax Mama. She knew him too well.

'No. They're not,' he admitted.

'So why Milly?' she pressed gently.

He shrugged. 'Why any girl? I ought to marry. For an heir if nothing else. And you yourself said that Milly is attractive, well brought up, affectionate...they seemed to me to be admirable qualities in a wife.'

'They are, of course,' concurred Lady St Ormond. 'But has she the maturity to be a companion to you?'

Crispin winced. 'You think she's too young? That I'm too old for her?'

Gently she said, 'It is not a matter of years, Cris. I think Milly will always be too young for anyone like you. Think about it, dear. I suspect it would make little difference if she were as old as Tilda. She is simply unsuited to you. And I think, you know, that she is aware of it.'

He stared.

'Oh, yes.' She nodded wisely. 'She is not really comfortable with you. But I doubt that she is fully aware of why. Just that you make her a little nervous...'

'You think I have frightened her?'

'Good God, no!' she protested. 'The last thing you, of all men, would do is frighten a woman.'

Sudden, scorching heat suffused his cheeks. Was Tilda

still in the library…still upset…still burning with shame? His shame.

He forced himself to concentrate on what the Dowager was saying.

'If you marry Milly, then I think you may become bored very rapidly. That your marriage will simply become a fashionable union, a marriage of convenience. If that is what you desire, then I have no more to say. Such marriages can, of course, prosper. Except that I think you would be better advised to wed a woman with the maturity to understand what is expected of her. Or at least capable of developing that maturity, which is probably why Tilda is concerned.'

Unable to help himself, he asked harshly, 'And did Lady Winter possess that maturity?'

She gave no hint that the question surprised her, but frowned consideringly. 'No, dear. I shouldn't think that she did. At first. But she possessed the capacity to develop that maturity. And I suspect that Jonathan was very fond of her, in a fatherly way.' She paused and then added with uncharacteristic tartness, 'Which would at least have had the charm of novelty for the poor child!'

She cast a glance at the glass-domed gilt clock on the chimney piece. 'Good gracious! Is that the time? We shall be late for lunch! Thank heavens it's only the family!'

Crispin escorted her down to the small parlour where a small, very informal luncheon was set out on a sideboard, to discover that they were indeed late and that Lady Winter appeared to be her usual calm and reserved self. Until Guy came in, apologising profusely for his tardiness and made a beeline for the empty chair beside her at the round table as soon as he had piled his plate with food. She brightened considerably as he sat down beside her and they resumed what, to Crispin's ears, sounded like a well-established flirtation.

He looked at Milly, sitting happily beside Lord John. She

did not so much as glance his way, giving him ample time to observe her. His mother had a point, he realised. She was never this relaxed with him, and it was not as though he had ever subjected *her* to any violent lovemaking. A few chaste kisses were all he'd ever pressed on her. To which she had submitted dutifully, but not at all as though she liked them.

Absently carving a second plateful of ham at the sideboard, he considered that. Along with the fact that she never really joined in a conversation with him. She had little to say beyond yes and no. And just listen to her now. Positively prattling away to Lord John about fashions! Who looked as though he didn't mind in the least. It would drive him insane!

'Here!' Guy's voice broke in on his thoughts. 'I know you're the host and all that, Cris. But you've got half the pig on your plate already.'

Startled, he looked down at the mountainous pile of ham he'd carved. 'Oh, it's not all for me!' he prevaricated wildly. 'Help yourself. And I...I thought Lady Winter might like some!'

Guy looked dubious as he speared half a dozen slices. 'You could try, but she's not very hungry. Still...' he grinned '...she might be prepared to do you a favour and help you with it! You sit beside her. I need to have a word with Hastings.'

Hell! thought Crispin. That was what came of speaking without thinking. Now he would have to go over to that vacant seat beside Tilda, when no doubt he was the last person she wanted within arm's length of her. Or even in the same room.

Steeling himself, he took the laden plate and went to her side. The only sign she gave that his presence was unwelcome was a stiffening. She went completely and utterly still. Glancing sideways at her, Crispin saw that her face was very pale, her eyes slightly reddened. Her calm was a façade. He couldn't quite believe how calm she appeared. What brand of courage did it take for a woman to appear so unmoved in this situation? Whatever it was, he could only admire it. He could think of few other women who would have put in an appearance at lunch in these circumstances.

How to apologise, without anyone else realising what he was about? 'Should you care for some ham, Lady Winter?' he asked gently. 'I do not wish to press anything on you, but I have carved far too much for myself.' He saw her eyes flash up, a guarded, shuttered expression in them. 'In fact, Lady Winter, I have bitten off more than I can chew, and I look to your generosity to assist me.'

Warily she said, 'What gives you to think that I am generous, your Grace?'

Steadily he met her gaze. Tried not to think about the way she had responded to him, surrendered to him, which was the very essence of generosity. Softly he said, 'Guy has not yet called me out.'

Burning colour flooded her cheeks. 'He has no reason to do so.'

Piling ham on her plate, he said, 'That you can say so is further proof of your generosity.' Did she value herself so cheaply? He was shocked to think so. Indeed, he was horrified to realise that his own behaviour suggested that he held her cheap. Gradually the colour receded from her face. Sad, resigned eyes lifted to his. 'Perhaps then, your Grace, you might pass me the mustard.'

He did so, desperately searching for some way to change the subject, before he said a great deal that ought to remain unsaid. She had accepted his apology. That was enough. For now.

Inspiration dawned. 'By the by, Lady Winter, if you are taking Anthea out for any more walks, keep to the paths if you enter the woods.'

She looked up, an oddly grateful expression on her face.

'I try to do that anyway. Otherwise my mending pile is vastly increased. But is there a particular reason? Will she upset your birds?'

'I don't care if she does,' he said frankly. 'But some fool has been setting steel traps on my land,' he continued. 'I don't allow them, but my keeper has reported a couple. It seems my poaching problem is getting a little out of hand and I should not like Anthea to fall foul of one.'

Surprise coloured her tone. 'If you don't permit steel traps, how on earth do you protect your game from vermin?'

Rather conscious that what he was about to say rated as heresy for most of his contemporaries, he shrugged. 'I don't. Big shooting parties bore me to death and, quite frankly I saw enough slaughter with the army on the Peninsula in the two years that I was out there before my father's death.' He said this with a bitter twist to his mouth and then continued lightly, 'I enjoy taking a gun out with a friend or two for an afternoon's sport, but I can see little need to trap foxes and badgers just to preserve a few extra grouse to ruin the crops!'

'And your hens?'

He smiled. 'Ask Mama. She deals with the hen woman. But I believe, when the necessity arises, that my keeper has been known to lie in wait for any overly bold fox with a shotgun!'

This reached the Dowager's ears. 'What's that about foxes and the hen yard? They're not really a problem. There's so much game in the woods that they rarely bother the hens.'

'Humph!' Lord John sounded disgruntled. 'In your father's day the vermin would have been properly trapped and shot! Not left to feast on grouse and pheasant to their heart's content!'

Crispin hid a smile. 'It's you then, sir! You're the rogue

setting traps and snares! Trying to make me see the error of my ways!'

'What's that?' Lord John was shocked. 'Someone setting traps? On your land? Country's going to pot!'

Mildly Crispin said, 'I thought you said I *ought* to be having traps set.'

'*You*, yes!' asserted Lord John. 'Not some other fool!'

'Thank you for that vote of confidence, Uncle John,' said Crispin drily.

'Someone has to tell you, Cris,' said Lady Hastings with sisterly candour. 'Apart from me, of course!'

Lord John snorted. 'You know what I mean, boy! Your land, your rules. I may not agree with you, but that's neither here nor there! What about your farmers? Could they be trying to rid themselves of vermin?'

'Shouldn't think so,' said Crispin. 'They know they are welcome to shoot any fox bothering their lambs or hens. And since the foxes keep the game down, they don't have grouse and pheasant destroying their crops. It's a mystery. Marlowe and Rigby are convinced that, despite my tacit acceptance of a bit of poaching to supplement several families' diets, it's not my tenants.'

Lord John looked sceptical. 'Don't know about that, m'boy. Give 'em an inch and they'll take ells, some of 'em! Still, your grandfather did the same and nothing came of it, so I dare say you're in the right of it.'

'*Did* he?' Crispin was stunned. 'I never knew that!'

The Dowager laughed. 'It nearly drove Sir Richard's father mad!' she reminisced. 'He used to harangue your grandfather without ceasing every time he dined here.'

'My, my, my!' murmured Tilda. 'How some things do run in families.'

Glancing down at her, Crispin was relieved to see that she had recovered some of her usual even good humour, lightly spiced with irony. 'I beg to differ, Lady Winter. I recall my grandfather as being a curmudgeonly old man who argued with every improvement my father suggested for the estate and was damnably hot at hand!'

'That was the gout, dear,' said Lady St Ormond. 'He was quite a rake, too, in his time,' she added, with a perfectly straight face.

Tilda met her eyes with an equally bland expression. 'Naturally, ma'am, one should only wear a cap if it fits.'

Lady St Ormond's eyes danced suddenly. 'Naturally, my dear.'

Lord Hastings smothered a laugh very unsuccessfully.

'I thought we were talking about poachers,' said Milly in some bewilderment.

Crispin groaned mentally. Mama definitely had a point. She obviously hadn't followed the thread at all, whereas Tilda had slipped her foil straight past his guard with the greatest of ease.

Guy, on the other hand, didn't seem at all put out. He smiled and patted Milly on the hand. 'Don't give it a second's thought, Milly,' he said kindly. 'Poachers are not at all the sort of thing a young girl needs to concern herself with.'

Good God! thought Crispin. He devoutly hoped his wife *would* take some interest in the things that concerned him! Otherwise, what on earth were they going to have to say to one another? While he could be frivolous quite happily, at some stage one did need to think about the basics of life! And Milly showed no sign of having the least interest in the running of large estates. Tilda had been chatting to Lord John quite happily the other night about the principles of crop rotation, even disagreeing mildly on occasion.

Grimly he thought that, apart from dutifully admiring the latest opera, the latest popular novel and the most admired paintings at the Royal Academy, he had never heard Milly utter an opinion on anything. Granted most men did not desire a wife who would argue and disagree. He had always found arguing intelligently with someone else helped him to formulate his own thoughts.

Tilda, in sharp contrast, had strongly formed ideas. He had heard her arguing during dinner with Hastings one evening on the rival merits of Sir Walter Scott and Miss Austen. And she was a staunch admirer of Beethoven, despite his admiration for Napoleon. He wondered what she thought of the marble of Cupid and Psyche that she had knocked over, it was a fine piece after all…and found that his thoughts had naturally progressed to what it would be like to wake up and find her leaning over him…naked…all warm and flushed…with his lovemaking…with the anticipation of more.

'Cris!' He jolted back to reality. Georgie was glaring at him from across the table. 'Pass the mustard, for heaven's sake! You've got plenty!'

He looked down. And wondered just how he had managed to get so much mustard on to his plate without noticing.

The following morning, instead of their usual walk, Tilda took Anthea for a ride with Georgie, Milly, Louisa, Hastings and Guy. St Ormond had excused himself on grounds of some work to do.

It was a bright, clear day and they enjoyed their ride immensely. Guy and Hastings took Anthea in hand and introduced her to the delights of jumping logs.

'Regular stitcher, that one,' commented Georgie, as Anthea sailed over a six-inch log with a gleeful whoop. 'Don't worry, Tilda. Guy and James taught all mine to ride. Along with Cris, of course. We've had a few broken bones, but nothing serious.'

Tilda grimaced. 'Am I being over-protective?'

Georgie laughed. 'Of course. We all are, but when you have several you start to get used to it. She's your only child. It would be incredible if you *didn't* worry about her.'

While the others went on for a longer ride, Tilda and Anthea turned for home after an hour. Tilda mulled over Lady Hastings's words. Georgie was right; she did fuss about Anthea too much. The last thing she wanted was to smother the child. She'd have to be careful. More children were no longer an option.

Upon their return to the stables they found St Ormond in a lively discussion with his head groom. His Grace was seated in a very unducal manner on a bale of straw, his long legs stretched out in front of him.

Without seeming to rush, he reached her mare long before any of the grooms who rushed from every corner of the stables to lift her down.

'My lady.' He inclined his head. 'May I have the honour?'

She glared down at him. It was the essence of the rhetorical question. Unless she wished to offer him a direct snub in front of a dozen servants, she had no choice.

'Thank you, your Grace,' she said sweetly. 'I would be most obliged.'

She steeled herself for the touch of his hands on her waist, telling herself that, as a widow of twenty-five, she ought to be indifferent to such things. Men lifted women down from horses every day without the sky falling in, so...

His hands closed gently on her waist, spanning it effortlessly. She was a tall woman, of Junoesque proportions, yet he made her feel little, protected, and completely and utterly vulnerable, as though he could break or seduce her with equal ease. His very gentleness only heightened the impression she had of something hot and dangerous leashed. The easy strength with which he lifted her and set her down made her swallow convulsively.

And then he had released her and was turning to Anthea. 'Good morning, Miss Cavendish. I trust Henry has no complaints about my best oats?' He ran a knowledgeable eye over the little Welsh grey. 'I must say he looks to be in rude health. And very well groomed. Did you do that yourself?'

He swung Anthea off and spun her around before setting her down.

Tilda blinked. She kept forgetting that St Ormond was an experienced uncle, entirely used to his sister's children, and from all she had observed, fond of them.

Anthea was responding happily. 'Do you mean, groom him myself? Could I?' Plainly the idea of getting thoroughly dirty and smelly in the stables appealed to her enormously. She turned to Tilda. 'Mama, please may I stay and help to groom him? Please?'

Tilda frowned. 'The men have work to do, dear. You will be very much in their way.'

Farnham, the head groom, demurred. 'Nay. She'll not be a trouble, me lady. I taught Lady George to manage her own pony. I'll keep an eye on her.'

Hesitantly Tilda said, 'You're very kind, but...'

All at once, she remembered the pony she had learnt to ride on. He had been the pony who pulled the mower—Tipsy, a very elderly, worn-out excuse for a nag, who had narrowly missed out on a trip to the hunt kennels. She had adored him and would have happily spent hours grooming and fussing over him, but had never been allowed to do so. And hadn't she just been vowing to cosset Anthea less?

She hesitated fatally and St Ormond settled the matter. 'If Farnham and his predecessor survived Lady Hastings and myself haunting the stables, he'll hardly be put out by Anthea. She'll be perfectly safe, Lady Winter. Farnham has a genius for letting a child get kicked just hard enough to learn a lesson! Perhaps you could consider it an exercise in independence.'

'Very well.' Tilda knew when she was outgunned. 'An hour, Anthea. And then you must come back up to the house. I shall be…' She paused as she considered where she should wait.

'In the library,' supplied St Ormond helpfully, offering his arm.

Belatedly she realised that, in agreeing to Anthea remaining, she had effectively robbed herself of her chaperon, that she had allowed herself to be outflanked as well as outgunned. And she had the shrubbery to get through unscathed! Unscrupulous beast! She was all the more infuriated to realise that her heart was pounding at the thought. Sheer fright, she told herself very unconvincingly. On his previous record, she'd be lucky to make it back with her honour intact! And he was still holding out his arm.

She could either take it, or offer him the cut direct in front of his servants. Again, she had no choice.

Outrage stiffening every line of her body, she laid her hand on his arm, trying not to let her fingers cling, trying to ignore the powerful muscles and taut sinews beneath the fine material. She might have succeeded had he not brought his free hand across to anchor her fingers more firmly.

Heat flashed through her at his touch—melting, softening heat. The urge to nestle closer, to lean on his arm, was overwhelming as he escorted her out of the stable yard.

Instead she glared up at him, to find his eyes on her face, a rueful smile curving his lips.

He shook his head. 'On my honour as a gentleman,' he said quietly.

She snorted. 'I was under the impression that you were merely a nobleman. With distinctly feudal tendencies.'

The rueful smile deepened. 'That, too,' he admitted. 'But I swear I'll keep all my *droit de seigneur* instincts under control.'

'For how long?' Mentally she cursed her unruly tongue and the waspish tone that suggested she also disbelieved in flying pigs. Although it *was* helping to hide her feelings.

'For as long as you wish,' he responded blandly. 'At

least, I promise to give you a few seconds' warning before they get out of control again.'

She bit her lip. He'd given plenty of warning yesterday. And she hadn't availed herself of it. After all, she had known perfectly well that he intended to kiss her, even if the other liberties he had taken had been a complete shock.

And if, as she kept trying to convince herself, she really hadn't wanted him to kiss her; why on earth hadn't she grabbed the *pot pourri* bowl on the wine table and cracked him over the head with it? Or just said *no*? He had stopped the minute she protested, so why hadn't she protested sooner? As for the episode outside his bedchamber—he'd had her halfway to his door before she'd realised and made her escape.

The answer made her even angrier. With her free hand she lifted her skirts clear of the wet grass as they walked through the shrubbery in silence. He led her into the formal part of the garden and along a box-edged path to a side door.

She risked a sideways glance at her host as he held the door open for her. He appeared perfectly calm, if a trifle distant. His face gave not the least clue to his thoughts. Clearly he was not having the least trouble with his instincts at the moment. Which was just as well, since she was having a great deal of trouble with hers. And it didn't help in the least that they had never troubled her before and were taking shameless advantage of her inexperience to run riot over her orderly, cynical detachment.

'Why do you wish me to come to the library?' she asked.

'I wanted your advice,' he replied.

She blinked. 'My advice? What on earth can you possibly want my advice on?'

He looked down at her, his gaze shuttered. 'Your cousin. You had a great deal to say yesterday. I am afraid I did not do you the courtesy of listening. I am inviting you to have your say without fear of interruption…or…other interference.'

Tilda's stomach lurched. 'I…I…no.'

'No?'

'No.'

'Why not?' His tone was cool, uncompromising.

She dragged in a deep breath. And wondered where the air had ended up. She took another breath. 'I was angry yesterday. And upset.'

He nodded. 'You had reason to be. But does that mean that you meant none of what you said?'

She didn't answer, but walked beside him to the library with an awful feeling of impending doom. This time she permitted him to escort her to one of the chairs in front of his desk. She didn't care how much like an interview it seemed. At least with that great desk between them, she was safe from any chance caresses or kisses. And any not-so-chance responses on her part. Because there was one thing that she was certainly going to take the opportunity of saying.

'There is something that I would like to make plain, your Grace,' she said as he gracefully lowered his frame into his chair.

He raised a brow and she ploughed on. 'No matter what my behaviour and my…my remarks may have led you to believe, I am not in the least interested in becoming your mistress!' She blushed as she said it, but held his suddenly arrested gaze gallantly.

'I see,' he said calmly. 'How very disappointing. But I feel I should point out that I have not asked you to do so.'

Somehow she managed to blush even more deeply, conscious of having made a complete fool of herself. Why on earth had she thought St Ormond would want a great, gangling creature like her for more than a casual tumble? She might have improved slightly, but she hadn't changed that much since the night of the Seftons' ball so long ago, when she'd heard him ridicule her to Hastings. No doubt he had far prettier and daintier women falling over their feet to receive his favours. Not to mention his intended bride, Milly.

She swallowed, and managed to say coldly, 'Good. As to our conversation yesterday—'

He interrupted her. 'Conversation?'

The amused tone flicked her lightly. 'Conversation,' she reiterated firmly. 'I may have expressed myself very badly, but…'

'Not badly,' he assured her, with a faint smile.

'Very well! Rudely!' she grated.

'That's more like it,' he said approvingly. 'You needn't waste any tact on me, you know, my dear. We had an argument. Quite a lively one.'

'Would you kindly stop interrupting?' said Tilda crossly. She was insanely aware of the urge to laugh, and she had yet to explain to him why she had spoken as she had.

He inclined his head and she drew a deep breath.

'It is not that I dislike you or think you a monster of depravity or anything of that nature…'

'Generous of you, under the circumstances,' murmured Crispin. 'That or your definition of depravity is more liberal than most.' The twinkle in his eye robbed the remark of any hurtfulness. A tremor ran through her at the note of gentleness in his voice.

'I meant to apologise properly, by the way,' he added.

She stared, completely losing the thread of her thought. 'You did?'

'Mmm. One of my rare, gentlemanly impulses,' he said. 'Don't count on me having another in the foreseeable future.'

'I won't,' she assured him. 'Well, I…I mean, I shan't mind it then. 'I…I won't give it a moment's thought. I dare say it won't happen again?' She could have kicked herself for sounding so damned uncertain. So unsure of whether that was a good thing. Of course it was a good thing!

One brow rose ironically. 'You misunderstand me. I wasn't apologising for kissing you.' A slight pause in which her eyes widened. 'Or for anything else I did, for that matter.'

'Then just what the devil *are* you apologising for?' she demanded. 'You haven't left very much!'

'Just my appalling lack of tact and the insulting excuse I used.'

'Excuse?' What on earth was he talking about? Excuse for what?

He sighed. 'Never mind. I hurt you and insulted you, for which I am deeply sorry. I'm not sorry I kissed you, because I enjoyed it. A lot. And so did you. Now, since you don't think me Blue Beard incarnate, why do you object to my marriage to Milly?'

She had to fight to clear her head enough to recall what she had been saying. He'd enjoyed kissing her. The intense light in his eyes was blinding her to all else. And her voice had deserted her.

At last she managed to say, 'It is just that I don't think that Milly would be terribly happy in the sort of marriage you envisage…that you…described to me yesterday. She doesn't have the…she wouldn't understand…she is very soft hearted…' Her voice trailed off.

'Unlike her cousin?' He was silent for a moment. 'Tell me, Lady Winter, how did you develop the necessary hardness of heart to manage in a marriage of convenience? Or did you have it already?'

Her face whitened, shocking Crispin. For a moment she did not answer and then she rose to her feet.

The soft curves of her mouth were trembling, her eyes overbright. She spoke as though the words were dragged from her. 'Whatever I developed, it is not something I would wish on any other woman. Certainly not Milly.' And left the room.

She left his Grace staring after her in remorse. For all she hadn't intended to answer his question, he'd seen the truth in her suddenly vulnerable eyes. She'd never developed that particular defence. However she'd managed, it hadn't involved hardening her heart. All her cynicism and cool façade were no more substantial than wreathing mist to sheathe her and protect the woman underneath from being seen. They were not really part of her. They would not even deflect as armour would. Her defences, her armour, were pure illusion.

Somewhere under the confident, yet reserved, Lady Winter, the shyly confiding girl was hidden. And she could still be hurt—all the more badly because very few would know she was there.

Setting his jaw, he forced himself to hope that Guy had seen through the façade to the truth. That Guy wouldn't hurt her even more than he had done.

# Chapter Nine

A week went by peacefully enough in riding parties, boating on the lake, walks in the park and enjoyable evenings during which the Malverns argued about everything under the sun with the greatest good humour. St Ormond paid no more attention to Tilda than to any of his other guests and she gradually relaxed, convinced that he had no real interest in her. A state of affairs that should have relieved her mind exceedingly.

Unfortunately, it merely gave her the opportunity to observe him without the distraction of wondering when he was going to pounce on her next. She was free to make all sorts of unhelpful observations about his person and character. Such as the regard in which he held his family. It gradually became plain to Tilda that St Ormond was head of his family in the best possible sense.

Far from being overbearing or telling anyone how to run their life, he was simply there to give advice. When requested. Overhearing part of a conversation between his Grace and Miss Hastings one evening, Tilda could not doubt this.

She did not wish to listen, but such was Louisa's youthful indignation at her parents' seeming callousness, that she had little choice since she was pinned to her seat by Lady

Hollow, who was regaling her with a great deal of forth-right advice on the rearing of daughters.

He listened to everything that Louisa had to say about the young neighbour who was showing signs of being thoroughly smitten by her. Much to Tilda's surprise, when she asked his opinion, instead of simply telling her what to do, he commented that she was behaving very sensibly in considering her options and then asked her what she thought should be done. Did she wish for a London Season before making her choice? Or did she wish to bestow her hand and heart on the young man and retire to what he dubiously referred to as domestic bliss, without having a bit of fun first?

Not labouring the point, he immediately changed the subject—to the delights of the next year's London Season and how much he looked forward to standing up with her at Almack's.

'It will convey such an aura of respectability on me,' he said with a twinkle. 'I shall be able to make the acquaintance of dozens of charming girls without anyone raising so much as an eyebrow!'

Louisa giggled and Tilda silently congratulated his Grace on a tricky situation well-handled.

He caught her eye and gracefully excused himself from Louisa's side to approach her and offer to take his aunt's teacup.

Lady Hollow snorted. 'I can manage, St Ormond. Think I'll take myself off now. Not as young as I was. Goodnight, m'dear. Don't take what I said amiss. You're doing a fine job with the girl!' Heaving herself to her feet with the aid of her stick, she added, 'And if St Ormond can keep Louisa from making a cake of herself, he'll be doing as well!'

Crispin rolled his eyes at her departing back and, lowering his voice, said teasingly, 'No words of censure to counterbalance that, my dear?'

A tinge of colour washed into her cheeks. 'I assure you that we were not listening intentionally!'

He grinned. 'Children of that age never remember that others may be able to hear.'

She raised her brows 'Do you consider Louisa a child then, your Grace? She is nearly eighteen, after all.'

It was his turn to colour, a faint flush staining the high cheekbones. '*Touché,*' he acknowledged. 'Your blade is as keen, and your aim as unerring, as ever.'

Guy came up at that moment to be greeted with a friendly smile from Tilda that drove Crispin away with a distinctly ungracious mutter He refused to acknowledge Guy's startled gaze and stalked off stiffly, fully aware that his conduct was atrocious. The knowledge did not help his mood in the least. Lady Winter had made it as clear as possible where her choice lay.

He watched them together out of the corner of his eye as he chatted to Georgie. They looked so easy together. Tilda seemed so relaxed. Grimly he realised that they were much of an age. After her experience of a much older husband that probably counted for a great deal.

Milly joined her cousin and Guy, and Crispin forced himself to turn away.

The next morning, having finished his estate business, Crispin emerged from the library to be hailed by Guy and Hastings.

'There you are, Cris! Come and pot a few balls. Papa's waiting for us in the billiard room,' urged Guy.

Crispin hesitated. He felt so utterly confused about his attitude to Guy just at the moment, that he would liefer do anything else. And that bothered him greatly. Despite the ten-year gap in their ages, they were good friends. It was very disturbing to feel like taking his insouciant cousin by the scruff of the neck and shaking him, merely because Guy was having an affair with a woman *he* wanted to marry! A

perfectly willing, widowed woman; who had stated un-
equivocally that she would prefer to take a lover than ever
enter the lists of Hymen again. Just because he was suffering from an unprecedented attack of chivalry and…very
well, damn it! Love!…was no reason to call Guy out, or
even harbour the urge to do so!

'You can't *still* have work to do!' protested Hastings.

Crispin noticed that Guy looked suddenly uncomfortable.

'Never mind,' he said. 'We'll manage.'

That brought Crispin to his senses. The last thing he
wanted was to cause a coldness between himself and Guy.
And last night Guy had looked thoroughly hurt by his behaviour.

'No. Of course I'll come,' said Crispin grinning. 'I've
been meaning to take my revenge for our last match!'

'Oho!' chuckled Hastings. 'Beat you, did he?'

'Just!' averred Crispin loftily.

'Several times!' struck in Guy.

'I was off my game,' said Crispin with an inward grin.

'Hah! We'll see about that!' Guy rose to the bait at once
and the three of them repaired to the billiard room where
they found Lord John knocking the balls about.

The match had not progressed very far when the door
opened unceremoniously and Rigby came in hurriedly.

'Your Grace! Thank Gawd I've found you!'

Crispin, having just missed a shot, handed his cue to Guy
and looked at the bailiff questioningly. 'Something urgent?'

'Aye.' Rigby flashed an apologetic glance at the others.
'Sorry to interrupt but, your Grace, Farmer Willis's sheep
were attacked last night. Five, with their throats ripped out
afore Shepherd could call his dogs to drive it off. And one
of the dogs in a bad way too. Just one dog it was, but a
damn big one, mastiff, Shepherd Hughes thought.'

'Hell!' said Crispin. 'That's all we need. Anything else?'

Rigby nodded. 'He reckoned it was fair torn about by
his dogs, since they had blood all around their mouths when

they came back after chasing it off. Thing is, it came this way. And Marlowe came in just now and told me he'd found a rabbit ripped to pieces in a snare early this morning. In the woods. He thought from the tracks that it was a dog.'

A horrified exclamation from Hastings brought Crispin's head around.

'James?'

Hastings was white. 'Lady Winter took her daughter for a walk about an hour ago. They were going to go through the woods to the village.'

Something very strange happened to Crispin's stomach. It lurched and contracted in a spasm of sheer unadulterated terror. The thought of Tilda and Anthea meeting a badly injured and savage mastiff chilled him to the marrow. He felt sick and unashamedly downright terrified.

'Which way did they go?' He rapped out the question in a harsh voice that shook very slightly.

'Around the lake, I think,' said Hastings slowly. 'Yes. Anthea was going to feed the ducks on the way.'

'Come on, Cris!' said Guy. 'They might still be there if we hurry.'

Cris stared at him. Why was Guy...? He remembered. Tilda was not his. Guy had every right to take charge... He turned to his brother-in-law. 'James, make sure the entire household is warned. Rigby, I want the grooms to warn every household on the estate.'

'Already left, your Grace,' said Rigby. 'I told Farnham when I left my horse at the stables. Three boys have gone.'

'That's it, then,' said Crispin grimly. 'Come on, Guy. We'd better hurry. We'll need guns.'

It was a lovely morning with the promise of heat to come. Anthea ran out of bread very quickly owing to the greediness of the ducal ducks. Heaving a sigh of resignation, she left them and followed Tilda on around the lake and into the shady woodland path.

Mindful of the warning St Ormond had given her a week ago about traps, Tilda kept Anthea close by, constantly pointing things out and challenging her to spot various birds and flowers.

The air was full of birdsong and the drifting scent of wildflowers and, walking slowly, they saw a willow warbler feeding three fat babies on a branch. Anthea watched entranced.

'I'm glad you didn't feed me worms, when I was a baby,' she whispered, as they moved on.

'Who says I didn't?' asked Tilda, her eyes twinkling.

'Ugh!' said Anthea. 'You didn't!' Then she caught the twinkle and swung vigorously on Tilda's hand. 'You're just teasing!'

They continued on along the twisting path until an odd sound came to their ears, a strange mixture of snarl and whimper. Instantly Tilda froze. It sounded like an injured animal, she thought. A fox, perhaps, or a badger.

'Stay beside me, Anthea,' she said very quietly and moved forward.

The source of the sound was just around the next bend, by the side of the path. A very large, yellow-brown dog with one hind leg ripped by a steel trap. It was worrying savagely at the limb, snarling and whining in a mixture of fear and rage.

Tilda stopped dead, prepared to back away. But Anthea, who had never seen an injured creature in her life, had no idea of the danger and rushed forward.

'Oh, the poor thing!'

'Anthea! *No!*' Tilda shrieked and flung herself forward instinctively, just as the dog looked up and hurled itself forward with a savage bark. Horrified, she realised that the trap was not dug in, that the brute had been able to drag it. That it was going to reach Anthea!

Frantically she caught Anthea and swung her away from the dog one-handed with a strength born of desperation, fending off the huge animal with her other arm.

'Run, Anthea!' she screamed as she felt teeth sink into her arm, ripping effortlessly through her light spencer. She staggered back under the force of the attack, but struck at the dog with her free hand, aiming for his eyes.

'Mama!'

She could hear Anthea screaming.

'Run!' she shrieked. She knew she would not be able to hold the dog off for long. It was too big and it was insane with fear and hurt. She staggered back, stumbling over a tree root. As she hit the ground she had no idea whether Anthea had obeyed or not. The dog landed on top of her, savagely biting and worrying at the upflung arm.

Crispin and Guy had no idea just how close they were behind Tilda and Anthea until they heard Tilda scream, heard the dog's bark. Exchanging a horrified look they broke into a run, and practically fell across Anthea, running for help.

'Mama,' she gasped. 'Oh, quickly, please!'

'Stay here!' ordered Crispin. They sprinted on.

And came upon a scene of horror.

Tilda was struggling weakly on the ground, desperately trying to fend the dog off, but it was snapping and snarling, trying to get past her torn and bloodstained shielding arms to her throat.

Guy instinctively raised the gun he carried to his shoulder but Crispin knocked it up as he ran forward, yelling a challenge with his gun reversed.

The dog looked up and, recognising a greater threat, sprang clumsily. Much bigger than Tilda and armed with the gun, Crispin clubbed it aside easily enough, sidestepping so that he was between it and Tilda.

For a fatal moment the dog hesitated. Crispin brought

the barrel of the gun to bear and fired at point blank range just as the brute gathered itself to spring. Full in the chest the charge struck it, and it sank to the ground, the life slowly ebbing out of it.

Crispin didn't even bother to look at the dying dog. He had spun around and dropped to his knees beside Tilda. She lay horribly still, blood pouring from the innumerable gashes in her arms. With a shudder of relief he realised that the dog had not reached her throat. Even so, she was losing too much blood.

With a stab of horror he saw the red pulsing and beating in time with her heart at one wrist. He swore savagely. The brute had torn an artery. He'd seen men die because bleeding like this was not stopped fast enough. He was aware of Guy at his side as he ripped off his cravat.

'I'll need yours too,' he said grimly. 'Give it to me and find Anthea. Don't let her come back—'

'Mama? *Mama!*' A small figure stood stricken beside them. 'She's not...?'

Crispin glanced up from his rapid bandaging. 'No, sweetheart. Just fainted. She'll be fine. Don't worry. I'll look after her.' It had to be the most stupid piece of reassurance in history, he thought, but it seemed to work. Although still obviously shaken, the wild terror left Anthea's eyes. And the effort of reassuring her seemed to steady him slightly. Steadied the frantic beating of his heart. Calmed the waves of panic washing over him.

'Cravat, Guy,' he said shortly. It was in his hand as he spoke. 'We'll need more,' he said as he wound it tightly around Tilda's mauled arm.

'My...my petticoat...' Anthea was hitching up her skirts even as she spoke.

'Good girl,' he said approvingly.

Tilda moaned as he worked at ripping up the petticoat into strips. 'Anthea...Anthea...' Her eyes fluttered open and her confused gaze fell on Crispin.

'Crispin?' Her voice was weak. She tried to struggle up but he dropped the petticoat and held her down.

'Anthea is fine. She came and found us,' he reassured her quickly. 'Look. Here she is.' He gestured Anthea to where Tilda could see her. 'See. She's quite well, sweetheart. Just let us look after you.'

'The…the dog…it attacked…'

'Dead,' he said shortly. 'Don't think about it. Just stay quiet and breathe deeply. Calm down. You're both perfectly safe with us.' He kept his voice soothing, low. The more frightened she was, the faster her heart would beat and the more blood she'd lose.

'About the only thing that you have to fuss about is the fact that your daughter just ripped off her petticoat in front of us,' he continued. 'Obviously she's going to be a complete hussy! You worry about that.' As he spoke he was tying a strip of the said petticoat loosely around her upper arm to use as a tourniquet.

'Find a…' Even as he spoke Guy handed him a short stout stick. 'Ah. Thanks.' He slipped it between the strip and her arm and twisted it. 'Excellent.'

Breathing hard, he looked at Guy. 'I'll carry her as far as the edge of the woods while you keep that arm elevated and keep the stick tight. Then you can run back and bring some sort of carriage. The gig, anything. I'll keep the tourniquet tight. Send one of the grooms for the doctor and a message up to the house.' He held the stick twisted tightly in the tourniquet.

Guy nodded. 'Let's go! Should I take Anthea with me?'

Crispin hesitated. It would be better for the child to go, but taking her would slow Guy down. He shook his head. 'She'll stay with me. You'll be quicker alone.' He glanced down at the child. 'You can talk to your mama and cheer her up. That arm must be hurting, don't you think?'

'Very well,' said Guy. He bent down and grasped the

injured arm and stick. 'We'll have you safe home in a trice, Tilda,' he said quietly.

Crispin pulled his watch out of his waistcoat pocket, unclipped the chain and gave it to Anthea. 'Can you tell the time, pet?'

She nodded.

'Good. Tell Guy when twenty minutes have gone by. Then it will be time to loosen the stick. Will you do that?'

'Yes, your Grace.'

'Why don't you just call me Uncle Cris, like my nieces and nephews?' he suggested. Hearing a five-year-old call him *your Grace*, made him feel beyond elderly.

He glanced at Guy. 'Ready?'

At Guy's affirmative nod, he swung Tilda up into his arms and began walking.

To his immense relief, by the time they reached the edge of the woods, Guy reported that the bleeding had stopped. He sounded jubilant.

'You'll be fine now, Tilda. Cris's tourniquet has stopped the bleeding. Just you stay here and I'll be back in a trice with the carriage!'

She barely responded. Just a faint smile, then her eyelids fluttered shut, as if she were too exhausted to speak.

Crispin noted worriedly that the sky had clouded over considerably and to his experienced eye it looked as though rain was on the way. And lots of it. He bit back a curse and settled down under a large oak, telling Anthea to strip his jacket off.

Casting a glance at the sky, Guy shrugged out of his and tossed it to him, saying, 'You may as well have this too.' Then he was off, sprinting for the house.

The first drops of rain fell before Guy was out of sight over the rise towards the lake. Mentally cursing, Crispin ordered Anthea into Guy's jacket and wrapped his own around Tilda. Despite the seriousness of the situation, with Tilda in his lap and Anthea snuggled against his side, he felt oddly complete. As though everything was right with his world.

Pure illusion, he told himself bitterly. And given that Guy had cheerfully allowed him to assume command and stay with Tilda, it looked as though their affair was no more to him than a transient pleasure to while away the time.

Crispin found himself desperately hoping that the woman in his arms felt the same way, that he had been wrong in thinking her cynicism was only skin deep. Because if it wasn't, the hurt Guy would deal her would bite deeper than the injuries to her arms.

Within fifteen minutes the rain was blinding, and despite the shelter of the oak, they were all drenched to the skin in half an hour. Crispin tried to protect Tilda from the worst of it, gathering her into his arms like a baby, shielding her with his body. He bent his head over the soft, damp curls, resting his cheek on them as he tried to persuade himself that he was only keeping the rain off.

He concentrated on Anthea. She had nestled against him, pretending that the thunder wasn't bothering her at all. But the way she flinched at every crash alerted Crispin to the truth.

'You're very brave, Anthea,' he said encouragingly. 'My sister Georgie, Lady Hastings, was terrified of thunder when she was your age.' Which was an outright lie, but he had his reward in Anthea's response.

'I...I don't really like it,' she said. 'But with you and Mama here...'

'If you don't like it, then that's extra brave,' he said seriously. 'Being brave means doing something you're scared of.'

'Like Mama stopping the dog attacking me?' asked Anthea with a sniff, pressing a little closer at a particularly loud crash.

'Is that what happened?' asked Crispin. A shiver, that had nothing to do with the icy water trickling down his spine, racked him as he imagined what the result might have been had the dog reached Anthea. She might well have been killed, judging by the state of Tilda's arms. On Anthea the attack would have come straight at face and throat.

He didn't have to use his imagination to know how Tilda had reacted. Sheer protective instinct would have taken over; just as it had for him. He doubted that she had even had time to feel afraid for herself; or that it would have slowed her if she had. Her fear for the child must have been overwhelming. And now, when she must be in the most appalling pain, she lay quiescent in his arms, her lower lip gripped between her teeth, only an occasional sob escaping to testify to her pain.

His arms tightened around her as he said to Anthea. 'You're a very lucky girl to have your mama. Just as lucky as she is to have you.'

Unthinkingly he turned his head and pressed a gentle kiss on Tilda's hair, breathing the soft fragrance in, enjoying the tickle of damp tendrils. A rush of tenderness shook him as he felt her sigh and snuggle closer. He wished he could hold her like this for ever. But reality, far chillier than the rain, told him he only had until the carriage arrived. And he knew deep down that the sooner it arrived, the better. Before she caught a chill. Before the sensation of soft, womanly curves impressed themselves indelibly on his heart. Before he couldn't let her go.

The carriage arrived in what had to be record time, driven by Farnham in a manner that bordered on the reckless. The pair of greys harnessed to it were steaming.

The lad who leapt down from the box said breathlessly, 'Mr Guy took Apollo and rode for the doctor, your Grace.'

Crispin nodded as he lifted Tilda into the carriage. Trust Guy, he thought. He'd done the sensible thing, taken the fastest horses available and gone himself.

There were several horse blankets in the carriage and

Crispin wrapped the nearly unconscious Tilda in them tenderly. She needed to stay warm. He could feel the chill creeping through her body. Shock, he thought, and loss of blood as well as the rain.

By the time they reached the house a warm bed was ready for Tilda. The Dowager met them in the hall. 'Take her straight up, Cris. Milly and her maid are there waiting. I'll take Anthea. A hot bath is ready for her.'

She held out her hand to the child who hesitated, glancing up at her mother, cradled in Crispin's arms.

Tilda raised her head slightly and said weakly, 'Go with her Grace, Anthea. I don't want you taking a chill. Your Uncle Cris will look after me.'

Guy arrived back with the doctor within half an hour and brought him straight up to Tilda's room. She was in bed by then. Milly and Sarah had chased Crispin out with about as much ceremony as they would have accorded a bedbug, while they changed her into a nightgown and got her between the sheets.

But the moment he knew she was safe in bed, he came back and not all Milly's polite murmurs nor Sarah's outraged protests could shift him from his position at the side of her bed. He sat there, gently holding her hand, his face strangely still, a cold, hard mask for the scorching passions beneath.

Something in the set of her jaw suggested that she was not unconscious, that she was hanging on to her self-control by a hair's-breadth. Her courage took his breath away. She hung on to her control with all the grim determination of some of the wounded soldiers he had seen in his years of war service.

When he arrived, the doctor did not appear to see anything out of the way in his presence by the bed, but nodded to him briefly before unwinding the makeshift bandages.

He swore when he saw the damage. 'Damnation! Begging your pardon, ladies, but what the devil possessed her to get in the way of the brute?'

'It attacked her five-year-old daughter,' said Crispin shortly.

The doctor nodded 'I see. Inevitable, then. Thank God she was there. This would have killed a child. Very well. The right arm is especially bad. I'll need to stitch most of that. Are you awake, Lady Winter?'

Slowly Tilda's eyes opened. Crispin felt his heart contract. There was no hint in the pain-soaked hazel that she was anywhere near unconscious. He had been right. She was in full possession of her senses but had barely made a sound.

The doctor was speaking again. 'I'm going to give you a little laudanum, Lady Winter. Just to deaden the pain a trifle while I stitch up the worst of your injuries.' He turned to Crispin. 'Even with the laudanum, I'll need someone to hold her. And someone to hold her arm as I stitch.'

Shakily Milly spoke up. 'I...I could hold her...I'm her cousin.'

Stephenson shook his head as he prepared his instruments. 'Being her cousin won't give you the strength to hold her steady, young lady.' He glanced at Crispin.

Crispin nodded. Without looking up he said, 'Milly, find Guy. We'll need him to help. She knows him and trust him.' He only hoped she extended him the same trust.

'But...'

'Milly. Find him.' The note of absolute authority in his voice sent Milly running from the room.

She was back within moments with Guy.

He came across to the bed and said, 'Isn't this a bit...?'

'We'll have to hold her down,' said Crispin. He drew a deep breath and said, 'If you would prefer, I can hold her arm, while you...' He left the sentence hanging. He couldn't bring himself to actually finish it. He knew how he would feel were their positions reversed. Savage, primitive, ready to murder the man holding her. Exactly as he did now at the mere thought of Guy holding her.

Guy was staring at him in disbelief, his jaw slack.

'For God's sake, Guy!' said Crispin. 'Take her!'

Guy shook his head numbly. 'You hold her. I...I don't think I could. I'll hold her arm.'

Crispin couldn't quite believe what he was hearing. Belatedly he remembered that Guy had never been on a battlefield, had never seen the appalling injuries inflicted by war. Nodding, he turned to the bed and lifted Tilda back into his arms. She opened her eyes again and gazed up at him, her underlip caught in her teeth.

He smiled at her tenderly. 'It's all right, I've got you.'

'I know,' she whispered and leaned her head on his chest. His heart tightened. So trusting, so helpless.

'Drink this, Lady Winter. It will ease the pain.' Stephenson held the tumbler of laudanum to her lips. Obediently she drank and very soon the bright hazel clouded over.

When she was quite limp in Crispin's arms, Stephenson turned to Guy. 'Very well, Mr Malvern. Hold her arm steady. Like so. Keep it absolutely still. The laudanum won't deaden all the pain, but it will take the edge off it and weaken her struggles. Ready, your Grace?'

Crispin nodded, suppressing a shudder. He had wrapped Tilda in his arms, holding her tightly against his body, one hand gripping her head to rest on his shoulder, the other anchored to her waist.

He knew when the doctor began work. He felt her body jerk in his arms, felt the whimpering intake of breath. Instinctively he tightened his hold. Not just to restrain—but to comfort and protect. To reassure. 'Hold on to me,' he murmured. 'It won't take long. Just breathe deeply.' He kept talking, gently, slowly. Talking nonsense, telling her how brave she was. Anything. To his amazement she didn't struggle, just clung to him desperately with her free arm, her face buried in the curve of his shoulder, muffling her cries. Sweat beaded on her brow.

He could hear soft-spoken instructions and requests from the doctor. At last he felt her slump against him and realised from the sounds that her arm was being bandaged. *Thank God.* Her trembling seared his body. He shuddered to think of how much it must have hurt. He looked around wildly and his eye lit on a damp cloth being held out by Milly.

'Good girl.' He took it and wiped the sweat from Tilda's face with a featherlight touch.

'Right. Change sides, your Grace.' Stephenson's quiet command brought a soft moan from Tilda.

Regardless of Guy's presence, Crispin dropped a gentle kiss on her hair. 'Hold tight, sweetheart. It won't be long now.'

'I've done the worst, Lady Winter,' said the doctor. 'You're a very brave woman.'

Carefully Crispin shifted across her, freeing her left arm and wrapping her bandaged right arm around him. Settling her back in his arms, he held her tightly as the torture began again. Every jolt of her body, every stifled sob tearing through him as though it was his flesh that had been lacerated. Sweat sprang out on her brow again. He could feel the tension in her jaw as whimpers of pain struggled for release. And he felt her body pressed against his in complete trust. It nearly killed him to remember that she wasn't his.

At last Stephenson was finished and Crispin lay her back on the pillows, his mouth tightening, his whole body struggling to resist the urge to lean over and kiss the soft, trembling mouth, stroke the damp curls back from her brow and caress the blanched cheek.

Grimly he forced himself to stand up and turn to face Guy. Fully expecting to meet a blazing challenge.

Guy had moved away and was standing by the end of

the bed, looking as though he were about to be sick. He met Crispin's eyes.

'I need a drink,' he stated in shaken tones.

The doctor looked up with a grim smile. 'Take him out, your Grace. Before he faints on us. She'll do well enough. When I'm finished here I'll see the child. Make sure she's not too shocked.'

Unable to think of a single excuse to stay, Crispin nodded and followed Guy who was already heading for the door. They found the Dowager right outside.

'How is she?' Lady St Ormond gripped Crispin's arm.

'Stephenson says she'll be quite all right,' said Crispin, patting her hand.

She heaved a sigh of relief. 'Thank God for that. Georgie and Louisa are looking after Anthea. They're in the drawing room. For heaven's sake go and tell the child. She's in a terrible state. I'll go in now and arrange with Milly and the maid about sitting up with Tilda tonight.'

Casting an experienced glance at her white-faced nephew and son, she added, 'And have a drink, both of you. Several, in fact. You look as though Stephenson stitched up your arms.' So saying, she opened the door and disappeared.

Guy shuddered. 'Come on, Cris. I don't know how anyone could do that for a living. I felt ill just watching.' As they walked slowly down the hallway he went on, 'Was she unconscious, do you think? I could hear her, but she barely moved at all while he was working. And it must have hurt like hell.'

Crispin knew from bitter experience just how much it had hurt. 'No. She was at least partly conscious,' he said shortly. He could still feel her clinging to him. Trusting him.

'Pluck to the backbone,' said Guy admiringly. 'Lord! I'd have been yelling blue murder.'

\* \* \*

The rest of the day passed very quietly. Once Anthea had been reassured as to her mother's safety, been examined by the doctor and taken up, clinging to Crispin's hand, to see Tilda sleeping soundly, she was packed off to bed with a very light sleeping draught.

'Just to make sure she sleeps,' said the doctor. 'Should be with her mama, but that's not possible tonight. Keep her close tomorrow, your Grace. She'll be shaky and out of sorts for a few days. As for Lady Winter, keep her in bed for a couple of days. I'll call tomorrow to see how she goes on. I've left instructions with her Grace, Miss Pemberton and the maid. They'll manage. Good day, your Grace.'

'Good day, sir,' said Crispin. 'I'm more grateful than I can say.'

Stephenson snorted. 'Thank yourself! Mr Guy told me how fast you stopped the bleeding. I'll tell you to your head: you saved her life. Just as surely as she saved the child's life.' With a brusque nod he was gone.

Crispin was left in the great hall with his thoughts. Most of them unwelcome. Although it was obvious that Guy was upset by the incident, Crispin could detect no sign that he was more upset than he would have been by an accident to any other woman he considered a friend. Certainly he was not moping around, snapping off the head of anyone foolish enough to speak to him. He betrayed no signs that he wished to be at Tilda's bedside in case she woke and needed him.

Which suggested that he was not in love at all.

This left Crispin in an unenviable dilemma; whether he should shout a paean of joy to the skies, or wring Guy's stupid, ungrateful neck. Or very possibly do both at one and the same time.

In the event he settled for moping around and snapping everyone's head off, so that by the time the tea tray was brought in after a very subdued dinner and he announced that he was going to bed early, everyone heaved a collective sigh of relief.

On her way to bed an hour or so later, Lady Hastings was moved to observe to her husband, 'Got it very badly, wouldn't you say, James?'

Hastings laughed. Never thought I'd see the day.' He scratched his head. 'Can't imagine what's holding him up though.'

Georgie snorted. 'I can. Easily. Male scruples. Silly clunch! I think it's time to bend the rules a trifle.'

Hastings eyed her dubiously. 'You're not going to interfere, are you?'

Her response was a wicked chuckle. 'You know I don't interfere. But a little nudge won't hurt matters. Trust me.'

He groaned. 'Georgie, do you have the slightest idea how much it scares me when you say that?'

'Naturally,' she purred. 'Why else would I say it?'

# Chapter Ten

The thunder, which had rumbled around in the distance for most of the evening, broke overhead in another fully fledged storm just after midnight. Crispin, who had been sleeping restlessly, his dreams haunted by enormous dogs savaging everyone he loved, jerked back to full and welcome consciousness.

He listened for a moment, wondering why the storm had disturbed him. He'd weathered so many appalling storms in the Peninsula during the two years he'd served there that he rarely awakened for mere thunder.

And then he remembered. Anthea was scared of thunder. He was out of bed in a flash, reaching for the tinder box to light a lamp, then rummaging in his chest of drawers for a nightshirt. Swiftly he dragged it on over his head and looked round for his dressing gown.

Still fumbling with the sash one-handed, he took the stairs that led to the nursery suite two at a time. Which room would she be in? He paused for a moment and then heard a high scared voice reassuring someone else. Georgie's old room, of course, with all the dolls. Gently he tapped on the door.

'Who…who is it?'

'Me,' he said, opening the door. 'Uncle Cris. Are you all right?'

She was sitting up in bed, clutching a doll, her eyes wide with fright but a familiar set about the jaw. A set he had become only too familiar with the previous day.

'I'm...I'm very well...but Susan is scared,' she said. 'Did the storm wake you, too?'

'Mmm.' He smiled at her. 'Would you like me to stay for a while? Maybe I could tell Susan a story.' Should he sit on the bed with her? Hold her? What would Tilda do?

Thunder crashed directly overhead and Anthea gasped as she clung to Susan, her face white. Crispin didn't stop to think. He was seated on the very small bed and had the child in his arms before the rumbles had died away. He could feel the small body shaking as she burrowed against him. Instinctively he cradled her closer.

'It's all right...I'm here...you're quite safe.' His hands soothed and petted, stroking the tangled curls. Gradually he felt her relax. A story, he thought. Something to distract her...

'Did Mama ever tell you the story of Cinderella?' he asked. It had been Georgie's favourite as a child. He couldn't begin to count the number of times he'd heard his mother read it. Personally, he'd preferred 'Jack the Giant Killer', but no doubt 'Cinderella' would be more to Anthea's taste.

She was nodding. 'Yes. Do...do you know it?'

'Yes. Shall I tell it to you?'

She snuggled closer. 'Yes, please. Susan likes it too.'

'That is a consideration,' he said gravely. 'Very well— once upon a time, long, long ago, there lived a beautiful little girl with golden brown eyes and bright brown curls...'

'She had blue eyes and golden hair,' corrected Anthea.

Crispin looked down at her, amused. 'Who's telling this

tale, Miss Cavendish? She was the loveliest little girl in the world and her hair and eyes were exactly as I have described them.'

'Oh,' said Anthea. 'Did she look like Mama, then?'

'That's right,' said Crispin. 'Shall I go on?'

'Uh huh.'

'She lived in a beautiful house with her mother and father who loved her very much...'

When the Dowager came softly up the stairs twenty minutes later, to her immense surprise she heard a very familiar voice, a very deep voice, using a tone she had never heard before.

'...and the fairy waved her magic wand and Cinderella turned back into the lovely princess and the prince kissed her and begged her to marry him and they lived happily ever after.'

'Do you think he knew her before she turned back into the princess?' Anthea's voice sounded very sleepy.

'I'm sure he did,' came Crispin's voice again. 'He was just so delighted and relieved to have found her at last that his voice wouldn't work at first. You always recognise people when you love them. Even if you don't know it at first.' His voice had softened and slowed, trailing off.

Stepping softly to the door and peeping in, Lady St Ormond blinked back sudden tears. In the glowing lamplight she could see her son propped up on Anthea's bed by several pillows, with Anthea and her doll held securely in his arms, his cheek resting on the soft brown curls.

She scarcely dared move lest she disturb them. Praying that he would not notice the flickering light of her candle, she backed away very quietly.

The deep, tender voice drifted after her. 'Sleep now, sweetheart. I'll stay with you...'

Holding her breath, Lady St Ormond crept away. Crispin, she thought mistily, was going to be a wonderful father.

* * *

Later that morning the Dowager came to find Crispin.

He looked up at once when she entered the library. 'How is she, Mama?'

'Improving. Still in a great deal of pain, of course, and she was very worried about Anthea last night. I'd forgotten that the poor child is afraid of storms…'

He smiled at the memory of Anthea sound asleep in his arms. 'It's all right, Mama. I knew. I went up.'

'Yes, dear.'

He stared at her and she went on, 'Tilda begged me to go up to her. You were already there. She was rather surprised when I told her.'

'Oh.' Crispin was conscious of a faint heat along his cheek bones. What the devil was his mother thinking? She had the smuggest, most devious smile that he'd ever seen on her face.

'Tilda asked me to thank you. For everything. Not just that.'

Suddenly his cravat felt far too tight. He suppressed the urge to loosen it with one finger. When he spoke it was rather sharply. 'It was nothing…no one could have left the child alone. I should have thought earlier. Put her in Louisa's room for the night. And as for the rest…I could hardly let Tilda bleed to death in front of me!'

Encountering his mother's raised brows, he groaned. 'Oh, damn it, Mama. I'm sorry. I didn't mean to snap! It's just…just…' *Just that I want to marry her and I don't know what Guy's intentions are or even if she cares for me…and what to do about Milly…*

'Just that you had a very nasty shock yourself and need some peace and quiet?' suggested his mother.

He looked at her gratefully. 'That will do to be going on with,' he said with a half-smile. 'Can she have visitors?'

'Later, perhaps,' said the Dowager. 'She's asleep again now. Have you found out where the dog came from?'

Crispin frowned. 'Not yet. Rigby and Marlowe reported

in earlier. They're making enquiries around the neighbourhood, but you'd have thought one of us would have noticed a dog like that. Shepherd Hughes identified it as the one that killed the sheep the night before. Whoever owned the brute is going to wish he'd never been born!'

At this moment Bebbington came in. 'Sir Richard is here, your Grace. Shall I ask him to wait?'

'No. Ask him to come in.' There was nothing to be gained in making Sir Richard wait. No doubt the old man wished to harangue him about the poaching again and if that damned dog had belonged to a poacher, he'd gladly see the scoundrel in Botany Bay for the term of his natural life!

Sir Richard came in with a queer set look on his face. 'St Ormond. Met your bailiff, Rigby, out riding. He…he says Lady Winter and her daughter were bitten by a dog. And that you shot it. Is that true?'

Slightly surprised, Crispin nodded.

Sir Richard's groan shocked him. 'Dear God. What sort of dog?'

'A mastiff,' said Crispin puzzled. 'Why? Do you know who owned it?'

Numb-faced, Sir Richard nodded. 'Bull.'

'I beg your pardon.' Crispin didn't know anyone of that name.

'Bull.' Sir Richard groaned again. 'Dear God what have I done? He was mine. Did you…did you have to shoot him? He wasn't really savage…'

If it hadn't been for the Dowager's hand on her son's sleeve, Sir Richard might have found himself the recipient of a leveller. As it was, Crispin had a breathing space in which to recall all the impropriety attached to assaulting a man nearly twice his age.

He drew a deep breath and spoke in tones of icy rage. 'Your dog, Sir Richard, attacked so viciously that when Dr Stephenson saw the injuries to Lady Winter, he gave it as his opinion that Anthea would have been killed had her mother not faced the attack.' He felt sick as he remembered the blood pulsing from Tilda's wrist, her white face. And the terrified screams that had alerted him to her danger—screams that had nearly stopped his heart, that he would never forget.

'But—'

Crispin interrupted. 'The dog had been caught in a steel trap that some fool set on my land. He'd dragged the trap and was ready to attack anything and anyone. I had no choice but to shoot.'

'A trap? But—'

'Did Rigby mention the sheep?' Crispin's rage was boundless, surging through him in torrents. 'The night before last, five of one of my tenant's sheep had their throats ripped out by your dog. The shepherd has identified your dog as the one responsible! So I would have been perfectly within my rights to shoot him anyway!'

Clearly dazed, Sir Richard sat down. 'I...I beg your pardon, St Ormond. Is Lady Winter...is she badly hurt?'

Crispin scarcely trusted himself to answer. 'Badly enough,' he said savagely. 'She needed a great many stitches to her arms and one artery was torn. Had my cousin and I not been close at hand she might well have bled to death!'

He noted with grim satisfaction that Sir Richard looked sick. As sick as he felt. 'Might I suggest that you keep—'

'Enough, Crispin.' His mother's voice was quiet, but for all that it stopped him. 'Go and find Anthea. She should go out for some fresh air. Just a turn around the gardens, but she will feel safer with you.'

Shaken by the sheer force of his emotions, shocked at the force of the fury surging through him, he obeyed. Nodding brusquely to Sir Richard, he left the library. His mother was right. A turn around the gardens with Anthea would calm him down a trifle.

*    *    *

When the Dowager found them half an hour later in the rose garden, he was recounting the story of how he had raised Sirene and Anthea was trying to persuade him to take her down to the stable to see her pony.

'My mama said a turn around the garden,' he said basely. 'I'll take you down after lunch if she says I may.'

'Do you still have to do as your mama says?' asked Anthea, very much surprised.

'He most certainly does,' said Lady St Ormond with a perfectly straight face. 'And right now she is telling him to take you up to see your mama. She is awake and would like to see both of you.'

Anthea squealed with pleasure and raced off towards the house.

Crispin and the Dowager followed slowly.

'I shouldn't have lost my temper, Mama,' said Crispin ruefully.

She shook her head. 'No, but never mind. He quite understood that you were upset, you know. He hadn't had the dog very long and it got away the other night when he took it out for exercise.'

'Oh.' Crispin felt the last of his fury drain from him, leaving him oddly empty. 'Does Tilda really wish to see me?'

'She wishes to thank you,' said his mother. 'You did save her life, after all. One does like to thank people who do us these little favours.'

He smiled. 'I dare say. Guy did help me, you know.'

'So Milly keeps pointing out to her,' said Lady St Ormond drily. 'But it doesn't seem to be sinking in. And Guy himself just says that you knew exactly what to do and took complete command. That all he did was follow orders.'

Crispin grunted.

He kept his visit to Tilda brief. Her pallor made his heart clench and her eyes told him clearly that she was still in pain. And he didn't trust himself not to take her in his arms, to reassure himself that she was all in one piece.

Tilda knew a singing joy in her heart as she saw who had brought Anthea to her. She owed him her life. Of that she had not the least doubt. But he looked so grim, so forbidding. She stammered her way through her thanks. 'And…and you went to Anthea last night…'

She still couldn't quite believe it, but then, as she saw the sudden, tender softening of his face, she could. He was kind. He had always been kind. He would never knowingly hurt anyone. Certainly not a clumsy, gawky débutante blinded by an impossible dream. Had he known that she had overheard his remarks he would have been mortified.

He had held her and protected her yesterday, held her while the doctor stitched her arm, comforting her terror. She knew that she could never have borne the pain and fright without him. Somehow, being in his arms had given her the courage to endure, not to struggle. He had been a very haven of safety. She had known that the moment she had heard his voice as she tried to fend off the dog. From that very instant she had known that she was safe, that he would protect her.

Anthea was speaking. 'He came up just like you did the other night, Mama. Except he told me ''Cinderella''. And his Cinderella had brown eyes and hair, just like you.'

Aware of his suddenly arrested gaze, Tilda glanced up. He was staring at her with the queerest look in his eyes. She couldn't place it until he spoke.

'That night you knocked over the statue, you'd been with Anthea.' It wasn't a question. She nodded. And flinched at the pain in his eyes. The sudden guilt and shame.

'I'm sorry.' He spoke very quietly.

She felt her cheeks burn as she realised why he was apologising. He was apologising for making an assumption in which she had encouraged him. Not only that, an assumption that her behaviour and comments had made possible. It was not his fault.

'There…there is nothing to apologise for, your Grace,' she said very sadly. She had herself given credence to his belief. She had accepted it and used it to deflect what she had mistakenly seen as his interest in her. And all because she had known that she couldn't depend on her treacherous, yearning body not to betray her.

Almost to herself she murmured, 'If the cap fits…what a fool I've been.'

She was the wanton he had called her, in thought, if not in deed, ever since her dreams had been haunted by what might have been had she not fled in the chilly dawn. Visions of what could have been, had she let him take her to his room and make love to her, teased her. She'd had her chance and she'd been too scared to take it. It might have been the sensible thing to do, but she was reasonably sure that she was going to regret it to the end of her days.

His voice, so gentle and resigned, broke in on her thoughts. 'I should be going now. You look tired. Sleep. I'll send Guy up later.' She nodded. Milly would be delighted to see him. And he might cheer her up slightly. Momentarily anyway. She didn't feel as though she would ever be truly cheerful again.

Crispin left with Anthea just as Milly came back into the room.

She smiled at him and said, 'Come back later. Tilda should have a sleep now.'

'I'll send Guy up with Anthea,' he said shortly.

Milly stared. 'Guy?'

'That would be better, I think,' he said gently. 'Look after her, Milly.'

He took Anthea down to his mother and went out for a walk, prey to bitter and gloomy thoughts. She had not been to Guy's bed that night after all. She had spent the night, or part of it, comforting Anthea.

And he... He groaned as he recalled how he had attempted to seduce her. How for a moment he had thought she was going to surrender, come to his bed. The heady, surging pleasure he'd felt. The scorching desire and the tempering awareness of her relative inexperience. Doubtless that was why she'd allowed him to get her so close to his chamber—quite possibly she hadn't realised at first what he was doing, what he wanted.

But she'd said no apology was needed. She was generous. What had she whispered? *If the cap fits...* She must feel that, since she had been to Guy's room at other times, his assumptions were well founded, if untimely. It didn't excuse his actions. And he would never be able to find the words to apologise properly without telling her how much he cared about her. How deeply he loved her.

He was rather surprised to find that he had reached the lake. That he was in the cool green shade of the very willow tree where he had first offered an apology to Tilda. The boat *Anthea* had sat in nodded to its own reflection as the waters rippled in response to a caressing breeze. He stripped off his coat and sat down on it.

He would have to attempt to sort out the muddle he had created and make it clear that he would not offer for Milly. That would be atrociously unfair to Milly and would bring him into contact with Tilda far too often.

If Guy married Tilda, then he would have to bear it. But he certainly wasn't going to make the situation any more fraught. The Pembertons would be furious, but he couldn't help that. And he was quite sure that if their anger was directed at Milly, that Tilda could be counted on to protect her cousin.

*You could, of course, just go to Tilda. Tell her you love her and beg her to marry you.* He could, of course. But she had told him point blank that she didn't want marriage. And if she were reconsidering, then it was Guy she was thinking of. He knew beyond all doubt that Tilda would never give herself lightly, despite that outward cynicism. So if she had been in Guy's bed, then it was because she loved him. After all, she had had no difficulty repulsing his own amorous advances.

He didn't want to hear her pitying refusal. He didn't want her pity. He wanted her, all of her, soft and warm and loving, in his life in his bed. She was already in his heart.

He went back up to the house much later, gloomily resigned to his fate. Bebbington greeted him and explained that nearly everyone had gone out for a ride, including the Dowager and Miss Anthea.

'Lady Hollow is resting in her bedchamber, Miss Pemberton is with Lady Winter and I believe Master Guy is in the billiard room.'

Crispin nodded. Perhaps he should go and find Guy. Subtly try to encourage him to offer for Tilda. It would nearly kill him, but he wanted her to be happy—whatever the cost to himself. It was the right thing to do, he told himself firmly.

So the sight that greeted his eyes as he quietly opened the door of the billiard room was guaranteed to send the blood surging through his veins in primitive fury.

Quite oblivious to the fact that they were no longer alone, Guy and Milly stood locked in each other's embrace, kissing passionately.

Even through his rage, a small, cynical part of Crispin's rakish mind assimilated the fact that Guy was going to develop a crick in the neck very rapidly if he didn't find something for Milly to stand on. And he noted wryly that Milly, who had been terrified at the chaste kisses he had bestowed upon her, showed nothing but enthusiasm for the far from chaste kisses Guy was pressing upon her.

The prudent course would have been a quiet retreat, but Crispin was too angry to think clearly.

'Just what the *hell* do you think you are doing, Guy?'

The pair broke apart and spun around. Milly gave a startled squeak.

Crispin had to credit Guy with the fact that, beyond simple surprise, he didn't react at all nervously. He drew Milly into the protective circle of his arm and spoke calmly.

'Kissing my betrothed, Crispin. I'm sorry if this is a shock to you, but—'

Crispin broke in, his tones biting. 'It doesn't occur to you that there may be another, with a greater claim to—?'

'No.' Guy spoke coldly. 'Milly assured me that you have never offered for her and never spoken of love to her. I will be writing to her father tonight.'

Crispin blinked slightly.

'No!' Milly clutched at Guy's arm. 'You musn't!'

Guy stared down at her. 'But, my love…'

Crispin gave a mental snort. Guy was doubtless about to discover the true meaning of the difference in their estates! The lure a title and wealth could be… He could almost feel sorry for him.

'Papa will be furious,' said Milly urgently. 'With Tilda! He'll blame her for not chaperoning me better. And she's not well enough to argue with him. You can't write yet. Tom told me what happened when Lord Winter offered for her!'

'What happened?' Crispin rapped out.

Milly flushed. 'I shouldn't have said that. Tilda doesn't even know he told me.'

'Get on with it, Milly,' said Guy. 'What did Tom tell you?'

Milly bit her lip. 'Mama and Papa aren't very fond of Tilda, because of her mama. You…you know about that?'

Crispin nodded grimly and she went on. 'Tom said that when Lord Winter offered, Tilda refused at first. So they shut her in her room and said she should stay there until she agreed. Tom says that he saw Papa come out of her room with his riding crop one night and that the next morning Tilda agreed to marry Lord Winter.' She paused. 'So you see, even though he couldn't possibly do that to her again, he might upset her. Please, Guy, wait till she's better.'

Guy looked sick. 'What do you think, Cris? Lord knows I don't want to cause trouble for Tilda…'

What Crispin was actually thinking, about Lord Pemberton, Guy and anyone else who might reasonably have been expected to protect Tilda, did not bear repeating. He dragged his wits together and said, 'Do as she says. Even knowing that Pemberton is likely to descend upon us will upset Tilda. Wait until she is recovered. And accept my congratulations.' He turned to Milly. 'You have my sincere best wishes for your future happiness, my dear. Perhaps you might excuse me now. I will speak to you later, Guy. I fancy you will need my support with Pemberton.'

He forced a smile and left the room. Before he could break Guy's neck. Retreating to his library, he flung himself into the chair behind his desk and felt it shudder at the impact.

Blast Guy to hell and back! Had it even occurred to him that Tilda might be expecting an offer? That even if she wasn't, his betrothal to her cousin would hurt her appallingly? Had his affair with Tilda been nothing more than a cover for his pursuit of Milly? And why hadn't *he* realised sooner just how well suited Guy and Milly were?

A thought struck him. Had Tilda realised the truth? Was that why she had tried to find out if *he* cared for Milly? He groaned. It was all so damned complicated.

The only certainty in the whole mess was that Lord and Lady Pemberton were going to think Guy, quite literally, a very poor substitute for himself. If they were to pull the thing off, he would need to convince them that nothing was further from his mind than an alliance with their daughter. Before they realised that his target was their despised niece.

And if they had any idea of visiting their wrath on *her*

then they would discover that they had his Grace the Duke of Ormond with whom to deal. No wonder Tilda was so cynical about marriage if she had been physically forced into hers. He couldn't blame her for never wanting to put herself in anyone's power ever again. After that experience, her independence would be past price. His mother had assured him that Lord Winter had been a kindly man, but even so...she didn't want to marry again.

He swore softly as he realised that her hurt might well put her beyond his reach forever. Unless he could find a way to heal it.

# Chapter Eleven

'Guy's offered for who?' The Dowager could hardly contain her disbelief at her daughter's news, that evening.

'Milly Pemberton,' repeated Georgie. 'You know, Mama. Small, pretty. Blue eyes. About as suitable for Cris as Louisa would be.'

The Dowager eyed her rather smug-looking daughter with something approaching awe. 'Whose idea was that?'

Georgie looked shocked. 'Guy's, of course! You must have noticed the way the pair of them were smelling of April and May.' She snorted. 'The wonder is that Cris didn't notice! But Guy was being so...so gentlemanly about it...you know, Crispin's intended bride...I'm not good enough for her...that sort of fustian, that I did give him a bit of a nudge.'

'A nudge?' repeated the Dowager, who had her own ideas as to why her usually observant son had been so uncharacteristically blind. 'And what constitutes a nudge?'

Georgie grinned. 'Commented to James in Guy's hearing that I didn't think Milly would be happy with Cris. And added something about how pushy Lord and Lady Pemberton could be and that it would be a pity if Milly felt she had to accept an offer from Cris just because nothing else offered!'

Lady St Ormond blinked. 'Well, if that's a nudge, I'd hate to see a shove!'

'It worked,' said Georgie with cheerful insouciance. 'And don't try and hoax me that you thought Milly suitable for Cris. She's a dear, but she'd bore him in a week.' She thought about that. 'Less.'

The Dowager sighed. 'Very true, my love. Well done. I was concerned, but you may trust me when I say that I very much doubt Cris would have offered for her.'

Encountering a questioning gaze from her daughter, she shook her head. 'No, dear. It's none of your business. And one other thing...' She paused for a moment and fixed Georgie with an uncharacteristically steely eye. 'Don't apply any of your *nudges* to any other interested parties. There are a few cliffs about that you aren't aware of.'

'Oh very well, Mama,' said Georgie. 'But you must admit, it worked beautifully.'

The Dowager nodded. 'It did. But leave Cris alone. I have a feeling that this *nudge* may be enough for him anyway!'


'He has asked you to marry him?!' Tilda was stunned.

Milly nodded, biting her lip. 'Yes, but...'

'Well...that's wonderful, isn't it?' said Tilda, puzzled at Milly's unhappy face.

'Yes, but—you don't understand,' said Milly miserably. 'He was so pleased when I said yes that he...it was me, too—it wasn't all Guy's fault...we...well, we were...'

'Kissing?' suggested Tilda. That, she thought, would tactfully cover a multitude of Malvern sins.

Milly nodded, blushing scarlet. 'He...he had his arms around me and...'

Tilda nodded. 'I get the idea.' If he'd still had his arms around her then things hadn't got too far out of hand. Not by Malvern standards, anyway. She went on reassuringly,

'It's all right, Milly. You are allowed to kiss him if you are betrothed. As long as you like it...?'

She allowed a faint note of query to creep in. After all, Milly had been less than enthusiastic about Crispin's kisses. Which to Tilda's mind ranked as insanity...

'Oh, it was wonderful,' Milly assured her, with a beaming smile. 'But you see, St Ormond came in and—well, he seemed very angry at first.'

Tilda whitened. How ghastly! What a truly dreadful way to find out that the girl you were about to offer for loved someone else. Even if St Ormond wasn't in love with Milly, the affront to his pride would be considerable. To be cut out by his younger cousin, especially after her scathing comments on May and December marriages, would be particularly galling.

'Oh, Milly! Was he very upset?'

'I think so,' said Milly guiltily. 'I felt awful. I never meant to hurt him. He never seemed to care that much for me—but he was always so polite and charming. I could never work out what he was thinking, but then—I thought he was angry for a moment and then he looked terribly sad. He congratulated Guy—as though he'd rather strangle him—and wished me happy...as...as though he meant it!'

'He probably does,' said Tilda wisely. 'If he cares for you, he will wish you to be happy and men are far more likely to feel rage with the man in these cases, I dare say.'

'But it was just as much my fault,' argued Milly.

'Yes, but you can hardly expect a man to take that logical view,' said Tilda, with a faint smile. 'They don't think that way.'

'Oh,' said Milly. 'Can I ask a question?'

In Tilda's experience people only prefaced a question like that when they had an absolute facer for one. She nodded and braced herself.

Milly blushed delicately. 'Are you allowed to tell me about the wedding right now?'

*Oh, dear God!* Aloud she said, 'I'm not the right person to ask, Milly.' And, seeing Milly's forming protest, went on doggedly, 'My experience of marriage was not the same as yours will be. You know I scarcely knew Lord Winter, that he was much older and that I did not love him... I know nothing of what it means to share the bed of the man who loves you and whom you love in return...'

She hesitated. That wasn't quite true. She knew to her bones that to share Crispin's bed would be wonderful, even if he didn't love her.

Slowly she continued. 'But if you enjoyed being kissed by Guy, then I think you will enjoy your wedding night. Being kissed by the man you love is wonderful.

Milly stared at her. 'Then there was someone you loved?'

Tilda nodded sadly. 'Yes. But don't waste any pity on me. I always knew it was nothing but a dream—he never even knew I cared...'

'Not...not Guy?'

Tilda looked up sharply. 'Guy?'

Milly met her eyes squarely. 'Yes. He flirts with you all the time. And you flirt with him.'

*Damn, I thought I'd scotched that.* Tilda improvised. 'Milly, while I think Guy is a dear and I applaud your choice, he is not at all the sort of man to appeal to me in that way. If you must have it, he reminds me rather of your brother, Tom.'

'*Tom?* But he's not at all like Tom!'

'Not to you, obviously,' said Tilda drily. 'Have you ever considered what a disaster it would be if we all fell in love with the same sort of man? What will do for you, Milly, would not do for me. And vice versa.'

'Oh, I see,' said Milly slowly, as if she actually did see. She brightened for a moment, then sobered again. 'But there was someone you cared about?'

Biting her lip, Tilda nodded. 'Don't mind it, Milly. It was a very long time go.'

'Are you still in love?'

'Yes.' Probably always. Tilda blinked away tears. 'But believe me, Milly, it is not Guy. Even if it were, it would make no difference. Guy loves you. Think about my fortune, dearest. Despite my wealth and Guy's affection for me, he has asked *you* to marry him. That speaks for itself.'

'Ohhh! I never thought of that,' said Milly, beaming with obvious relief. 'But you could tell me something, couldn't you? About the wedding night?'

Tilda shook her head. 'Nothing that you don't already know. Ask someone else. But don't believe anyone who tells you that a lady must not enjoy her husband's attentions.' She hesitated. If Milly asked her mother... She went on firmly, 'Ask Lady Hastings or Lady St Ormond. They both married for love, as you are doing.' She smiled ruefully. 'Would you mind very much if I had a sleep now, Milly? I'm a little tired.'

'Of course not.' Milly bent over to kiss her gently and went to the door. She turned back briefly. 'I persuaded Guy not to write to Papa until you are well again. He's going to be so angry that I thought it was better.' She smiled and left the room quietly.

Tilda heard the door shut and breathed a sigh of relief. Not having to explain herself to her uncle immediately was definitely a good thing. And Milly's questions had brought back all sorts of memories. The sort of memories that she needed to be alone with.

Her aunt's advice... *Only a whore, like your mother, would enjoy it. Your duty to your husband, as a lady, is to lie still and quiet. Otherwise you will disgust him...you must accept the pain without a murmur, it is your duty...* and so on.

By the wedding night she was terrified and Jonathan had known it. He'd been careful and after a while her duties became merely boring. At least, she had comforted herself, she was a lady. Surely that one gasp of pain didn't count…

Then she had heard other married ladies talking, giggling, over luncheon, over cups of tea. Gradually it was borne in on her that some married ladies, especially those in love with their husbands, did enjoy the marriage bed. A very great deal. And that this delighted their husbands.

So one night she'd tried to encourage Jonathan a bit, thinking it might help matters between them. He'd been scandalised at her sudden curiosity. At her suggestion that instead of merely raising the hem of her nightgown, he might like to take it right off as well as his own night rail.

After this fiasco she had concluded that she might as well accept boredom as her lot. She knew that many women would have looked for pleasure outside their marriage, but Jonathan was kind and cared for her. She could at least give him loyalty.

And always at the back of her mind was the knowledge that, despite her much improved looks, she was the…*chit who shouldn't have been let loose in London*. Why would anyone want her? She was plain, clumsy, and far too tall to please any man of discrimination. Jonathan had married her out of necessity and chivalry. He'd needed a wife and she'd needed a rescuer. He hadn't wanted her *per se*. And after he'd discovered that he had a perfectly acceptable heir in Max, he had said very kindly that there would be no further need for him to press his marital rights upon her.

She wriggled her fingers. Her injuries were abominably itchy, which no doubt meant they were healing. She only wished this other itch would go away as easily. This itch to find out, first-hand, just exactly what she had missed out on.

At the Dowager's insistence, Tilda spent two full days in bed, attended by Milly and Sarah.

For a seemingly gentle woman, the Dowager Lady St

Ormond could be positively dictatorial given due cause, reflected Tilda. All her protests about being a nuisance and having to chaperon Milly were swept aside.

'Nonsense!' Lady St Ormond had come up to sit with Tilda while Milly was out walking with Georgie and Guy. 'Seraphina, Georgie and I can chaperon Milly when she is not with you. And Cris is looking after Anthea. She may not be making much progress with her French but she is doing quite well with her riding, he tells me.'

Her smile was wicked. 'He seems to be very much taken with the idea of having a daughter one day. So far his thoughts have all been centred on sons and heirs.' Sobering slightly, she went on. 'Tell me, my dear, are your uncle and aunt going to be very much vexed by the way things have fallen out? Naturally Guy is not as wealthy as Crispin and has little chance of inheriting the title, but he is quite comfortably off and I suspect Milly will be far happier with him than with Cris.'

Tilda breathed a sigh of relief. 'You do not mind, then?'

'Good God, no,' laughed Lady St Ormond. 'Poor Milly would be quite out of her depth with Cris. He's far too old for her! Or she is too young for him. She would be too young if she were your age. Oh, not in years, but in maturity. She is the wrong woman for him. Even in a marriage of convenience, which he seems to think is what he wants.'

'Why should he want it?' asked Tilda, without thinking. She blushed. It was none of her business to be asking such a personal question.

Lady St Ormond did not take it at all amiss. She wrinkled her brow. 'Do you know? I am not sure. My marriage was a love match, of which he is perfectly well aware. But I suspect it is simply that, since he didn't meet the right girl years ago, he has become far too used to enjoying himself *out* of wedlock. His life is comfortable, hedonistic to say the least, and he thinks that a marriage which leaves him free to pursue that life will be easiest.' She considered that.

'Come to think of it, he may well be right. But easiest doesn't necessarily mean happiest.'

Tilda looked at her inquiringly.

And the Dowager elaborated. 'A happy marriage needs hard work. And compromise on both sides. And if either or both parties to it are in love, there needs to be an understanding of how dreadfully they can hurt each other.' She smiled. 'But enough of this solemnity. Tell me instead how you are feeling. Recovered? Up to coming down for dinner tonight? We miss you very much, you know!'

'Miss me?' No one, for as long as she could remember, had ever said they had missed her. On one occasion when she had come back downstairs after a bout of flu, her uncle had merely glanced at her and grunted, *Oh. It's you, is it?* Tears sprang to her eyes. Whatever was the matter with her that she should be feeling so weepy and depressed? It must be shock or something, turning her into a positive watering pot.


She had Sarah help her to dress in her very best gown of blue satin that evening. Her arms were still bandaged and she sighed as she realised that the effect of the gown was quite spoilt.

Correctly interpreting the sigh, Sarah said, 'Never you mind, milady. You still take the shine out of all of 'em.'

'Me?' Tilda laughed at her in the looking glass. 'With Milly there? Don't be silly, Sarah! Oh, I'm well enough, but who would give me a second glance with her there?'

She clasped a string of pearls about her neck and put on the matching earrings. Tilting her head to one side to view the effect, she smiled at the idea anyone would think her beautiful. Better than seven years ago, true enough—but all she saw was a too tall, admittedly slender woman, with plain brown hair and hazel eyes—with heavily bandaged arms. She frowned slightly, wishing that she could hide them.

Then inspiration dawned. Hunting through a drawer, she found a Wellington jacket in deep Turkey-red silk. Jonathan had always fussed tremendously when she came down to dinner in a light dress. She'd made this to appease him, so that he'd stop worrying about the inflammation of the lungs he was convinced she'd die of.

She had just slipped it on when there was a light tap on the door. Milly, she supposed and nodded to Sarah to open it.

'His Grace, milady,' said Sarah respectfully.

Tilda whirled and there was Crispin, waiting with an oddly shuttered look in his eyes. Every plane of his face was set and tense as though he held something under guard.

Her heart lurched. She thought she knew what that something was. He must have cared more for Milly than she had realised. Perhaps, she thought sadly, more than he had realised; until he lost her.

'Your Grace?' She felt as puzzled as she sounded. What on earth was he doing here? Shouldn't he be down in the drawing room?

'I came to escort you down to dinner.' The deep voice seemed to stroke up and down her spine in a warm caress.

He'd come to escort her down to dinner? Why? He hadn't even visited her again in the past three days while she kept to her room. Of course, had the other gentlemen in the party not come up to visit her each day, she might have put his omission down to a sense of propriety. Given, however, that Lord Hastings had come up with his wife and daughter, Lord John had visited briefly with Lady Hollow and Guy had come in with Milly, she had decided that his Grace was simply not interested.

In truth, the answer was very straightforward. His Grace had simply not dared. He had been far too afraid of his likely reaction if he found himself, by some unforeseen circumstance, left alone in a bedchamber with Tilda. He wanted her as he had never wanted any other, and he definitely didn't trust himself.

Only now, when he knew her maid to be with her, and when his visit would necessarily be of the briefest, did he dare cross that threshold. When he couldn't keep away any longer.

Tightening his grip on the reins of his self-control, he said quietly, 'You look lovely, my dear.' He noted the amazed lift of her brows. The softly parted lips and the delicate blush, like a girl receiving her first compliment.

A grunt from Sarah caught his attention. 'Humph! And so I tell her. But does she ever believe a soul? Not her!'

Tilda's blush deepened as Crispin looked back at her. Something stirred in his memory. The shy, rather plain débutante she had been, awkward and clumsy, until she'd danced with him. He was startled at how clearly he remembered that girl now, how he'd thought she needed time to bloom, like his sister, Georgie. She too had been a tall, potentially clumsy girl who had blossomed late—*It took me years to realise that I'd actually stopped being gawky and filled out in a few of the right places! And I only believed it because James kept telling me...* Georgie's laughing voice echoed in his memory.

Had Tilda never had anyone to tell her how lovely she had become? Had no one ever complimented her, loved her with words? The question leapt to his mind: loved her at all? He knew from his mother that she had received little enough love from her aunt and uncle—but how had her husband viewed her?

His mother's voice drifted through his mind: *I suspect Jonathan was very fond of her, in a fatherly sort of way...*

Slowly he said, 'Lady Winter may believe me that she is very lovely...' *And lovable, desirable and that I need her like I need to keep breathing!* He saw Tilda's eyes widen and fasten on his in startled query, knew that his own eyes were blazing and immediately added, as lightly as he could, 'And as a self-respecting rake, I never offer Spanish coin!'

With relief he saw the odd tension ease from Tilda. She raised a brow, 'May one ask, why not?'

He grinned and offered his arm. 'Far too dangerous, my dear. Besides, if I did that, the women I really wished to compliment would never believe me.'

She glared up at him as she came out and placed her hand on his arm. 'You, sir, are a cynic!'

'The pot is speaking to the kettle,' he said, closing the door behind them and trying to ignore the blaze that leapt up in him at her touch. He shuddered to imagine the effect her touch would have upon his senses were it not muted by his shirt and coat. Devastating was the only possible word. It was bad enough just thinking about it.

Tilda flushed again. No doubt he was joking, but still... 'I'm not really quite as cynical as you might have thought,' she said quietly.

He glanced down at her and she met his eyes gallantly. He looked so sad, she thought. Had he really cared for Milly? Had he pretended not to care just to guard against this sort of hurt? She wished desperately that there was something, anything, she could do to ease what must amount to a sense of betrayal.

'I know.' Crispin was conscious again of the urge to wring Guy's neck. If *he* had seen through her bright armour, surely Guy could have done so! And to offer for Milly the moment Tilda was out of the way—injured, perhaps needing his care and reassurance. She must feel betrayed. If she hadn't been cynical about men before, she certainly would be now. He longed to ease her pain, assure her that he at least truly loved her, for herself, as a woman.

'Tell me. Why do you disbelieve the evidence of your mirror?'

His question took her so much by surprise that she was startled into the truth.

A surge of bitter hurt welled up. 'And as for Miss Arnold, there's a chit who should never have been let loose in London!' Her voice flared with anger.

Patently shocked, Crispin asked, 'Who the devil said that?'

'You don't even remember, do you? Any more than you remembered me,' she said softly. 'You said it, your Grace. To Lord Hastings at a ball some days after our one and only dance.'

Memory flared. He *had* said something to James about Miss Arnold. What had he said? Strangely, he remembered the occasion. His mother had been worried that he'd shown no sign of settling down and he'd agreed to give the season's débutantes a look. He'd been grumbling about how boring they were and their unsubtle pursuit of his fortune and title. But Tilda, Miss Arnold, had been different. Clumsy and shy with everyone else, she had flowered in his arms—what on earth could he have said to James?

'Tilda, whatever I said to James was not meant to hurt you,' he began. 'And I didn't forget you. You had changed so much that I didn't properly recognise you. Yet I was sure I'd met you before. It drove me insane.' That and the raging desire that seared him whenever he laid eyes on her.

He laughed harshly. 'If you want proof that you have become a beauty, you have it there. In the fact that I did not recognise you again when I met you.' With the words, the gist of what he had said to James came floating back. 'I think you cannot have heard all of what I said to James. As far as I recall, it was along the lines that you should not have been brought out until you had a chance to blossom a little, gain a bit of confidence.' An eyebrow quirked. 'I was right.'

As simple as that, she thought. She'd overheard only part of what he'd said. And in her insecurity she had allowed it to fester—nursing it bitterly, instead of putting it aside. Because she'd loved him even then.

He made sure his voice was perfectly indifferent before he spoke again. 'Guy has written to your uncle and wishes to send it if you are feeling well enough. Milly insisted that he wait until you recovered.'

Her sigh, soft though it was, tore at him. 'Better sooner rather than later. If he ever suspects he was not told at once…it will make Guy's case worse than ever. Lord Pemberton will not be happy with any of us.'

'I had thought, under the circumstances, a little subterfuge might be acceptable,' said Crispin thoughtfully.

Tilda blinked. 'How do you define subterfuge?'

'Any deception that doesn't involve an outright lie,' replied Crispin promptly. 'Lord Pemberton has been told in the letter that you were badly bitten by a dog, and while you were in bed Guy offered for Milly. He'll think you didn't even know until you recovered, so he won't believe it was your fault.'

A sceptical snort greeted this. 'He might reasonably expect that I should have noticed something earlier and put a stop to it. Reminded Milly that she was supposed to have bigger game in her sights!' She forbore to tell him that Lord Pemberton would not require any excuse to rip up at her.

A warm husky chuckle broke from him. 'True, but you could always say that it never occurred to you that Guy was so lost to all propriety that he would do anything so outrageous as to consider proposing to any girl without her father's consent, let alone one his cousin was supposedly courting.' He hesitated and then went on, 'After all, I didn't notice. I have formed the intention of enclosing a letter with Guy's assuring Lord Pemberton that as head of the Malvern family, the match has my full support and that I merely thought the three younger members of the party, namely Miss Pemberton and my niece and cousin were gravitating together—with a bit of luck he'll assume you thought the same.'

Tilda thought her heart must break at this proposal. 'You

are...very generous.' What must it have cost him to do this? she wondered. To actively promote a match which, whatever his heart's involvement, must make him look a complete fool. She had seen enough of London society to know that his interest in Milly, and their subsequent presence at this house party, would not have escaped remark.

His shrug was indifferent. 'What else can one do? Shall we send the letters tomorrow? Are you sure you are up to it?'

They had reached the drawing room door and he held back from opening it to hear her response.

She looked up at him searchingly, but could read nothing in his eyes and the hard planes of his face. That told its own tale, she thought. She could not offer comfort—he would not want to be pitied, but she must say something, acknowledge his decency. Her heart would burst if she did not.

'"If 'twere done, 'twere best done quickly."' She smiled tremulously. 'Delay will only worsen the pain.' She would have seized the door handle and gone ahead of him, but a strong hand grasped her wrist and gently drew her back.

Before she could think, she found herself enclosed in a tender embrace, warm and safe. He held her in a grip as gentle as it was unbreakable. Featherlight, a finger caressed her cheek, drifted down the silken line of her throat to firm under her chin, lifting it to meet a kiss that melted her heart in its aching sweetness.

Instinctively she leaned into the kiss, into the hard strength of his body, softening still more as she felt his arms tighten. His mouth moved lightly on hers, and then she felt the hesitant touch of his tongue, pleading, requesting entrance. Without conscious volition her lips parted as her soul flowered in love. She felt with joy his gentle, yet passionate possession of her mouth, the erotic stroke of his tongue against hers. And sighed her pleasure as she tentatively returned the caress. Invited him deeper.

For a moment he accepted the invitation, deepening the kiss, drowning in her response until his senses whirled and every leashed demon within clamoured for release. Until the very small part of his brain left functioning rationally reminded him what a bounder he would be to take advantage of her hurt and pain in this way. She wanted comfort, not seduction.

Somehow he raised his head, breaking the kiss, shocked to find his breathing ragged and his arousal complete. And he had a drawing room full of people to face—most of them family who knew him too well for any dissembling. Added to which, the fashionable, skin-tight cut of his breeches was of no help at all. He swore mentally and met Tilda's clouded golden eyes.

'Go in. I'll…I'll join you all in a moment.' He turned away abruptly, hoping that she hadn't noticed his state, the tension in his body screaming for release. Screaming for her.

She stared after his rapidly retreating form in considerable confusion. Her fingers touched her lips in dazed awe. This kiss had been nothing like their earlier encounters. It had deepened to passion quickly but it had started so tenderly, as if he were wooing her, as if…her mind reeled at what her heart was saying…it had started as if…as if he loved…

No! It wasn't possible! She had offered comfort and he had accepted that offer. Comfort—that was all he had wanted. But his was a passionate nature and, if he were to be believed, he found her reasonably attractive. No doubt it was only natural that he should kiss her passionately. Perhaps, she found herself trembling at the idea, there was an element of frustration in his loss of Milly. She was no innocent schoolroom miss. His arousal had been immediately and thrillingly apparent to her.

She shook her head to clear it. To think about it all now was impossible. She had to face his family, who must not be allowed to guess that anything untoward had occurred. Lady Winter's bright armour must be burnished up to deflect all the kindly, prying eyes that might penetrate the shields to espy her secret.

So she summoned up a smile and opened the door, forcing her lips to curve more deeply at the babble of sincerely delighted greetings that broke out. And steeling herself to answer the Dowager's startled query as to what the devil had happened to Crispin. She had quite thought he must be escorting Tilda down to dinner.

Somehow Tilda got through the pre-dinner gathering. When Crispin appeared he seemed perfectly collected, if a trifle preoccupied. To her immense relief she was not seated by him at dinner. Her partners were the kindly, if irascible, Lord John and Lord Hastings, both of whom seemed to be delighted to have her with them again.

The chat was general, full of laughter and banter. Everyone seemed to be in a festive mood. Tilda found herself comparing it with the polite formality that had always prevailed at the Pembertons' board. When relatives had descended upon the Pembertons *en masse* like this, it had been viewed as a duty, something to be endured. The moment the unwelcome hordes had left Lady Pemberton would be complaining about the tedium of the visit and the expense.

Tilda had not the least doubt that Lady St Ormond's only regret would be her family's departure. She'd be missing them and planning the next visit almost before they cleared the carriage drive. Even the acid-tongued Lady Hollow was embraced wholeheartedly, if carefully.

Casting a surreptitious glance towards Crispin, chatting quietly to his Aunt Seraphina at the end of the table, she thought that he at least would not look back on this visit happily—but from all she had observed and heard, he was normally delighted to welcome his family and looked upon it as a pleasure, not a duty.

At the end of the second course Lady St Ormond broke into the hub-bub by tapping gently on her wine glass. Gradually silence fell and heads turned her way.

Once she had everyone's attention, she stood up.

Georgie protested. 'Mama, it's much too early for us to leave! Isn't there another course?'

'I was intending,' said Lady St Ormond mildly, 'to propose a toast.'

Crispin looked up sharply. Tilda saw the suddenly hard set of his jaw. Please, she thought, don't propose a toast to Guy and Milly. He'll be too hurt... She looked away quickly, not wishing him to think he had betrayed himself to her yet again.

Lady St Ormond raised her glass and said simply, 'To Tilda. And her recovery.'

Before anyone could respond, Crispin rose to his feet. He'd seen Tilda's swift, anguished glance, and the gallant way she'd tried to hide her pain. She must have thought a toast to Guy and Milly was in the offing. He could think of nothing else to explain her reaction. And she was so sad, so quiet. Even the cool, witty façade of Lady Winter would have been better. She must have been even more attached to Guy than he had thought.

'I'll add to that,' he said very quietly. 'To Lady Winter. The bravest woman I have ever met.' And raised his glass in salute amid a chorus of approval. As Tilda turned crimson, everyone around the table stood and drank the toast.

Completely tongue-tied, she said as they all sat down, 'Thank you. But it wasn't brave...I didn't even think...I...I just...'

'Rubbish!' asserted Hastings. 'You'd have done it even if you had thought. No matter how damn scared you were! If we say you're brave, then you are. And there's an end of it!'

'Hear, hear,' said Lord John firmly. 'Crispin's in the right of it, m'dear. Now drink up. This is something my brother laid down. Rather nice drop of burgundy.' He turned towards the end of the table and said, 'By the by, Cris. Any notion yet about these traps?'

Slowly Crispin nodded. 'I have, as a matter of fact. But my idea is so outrageous that I haven't even mentioned it to Rigby and Marlowe. So if you don't mind, Uncle John, I think I'll hold my tongue.'

'In *my* day,' intoned Lady Hollow, 'they was strung up and there was an end of 'em!'

'Yes, well,' said her undutiful nephew, 'in your day, Aunt—which, I might add, seems to be far from over— they did all sorts of things that would bring a blush to our cheeks.'

'Humph!' was the response to this. 'At least we did something!'

# Chapter Twelve

With Tilda's return downstairs the letters were sent off the following day. When no response came in the post on the third day following, Tilda and Milly prepared themselves for the worst.

'He'll be here tonight,' said Tilda. 'Now remember, Milly, let St Ormond and myself deal with it. No point in you setting his back up. He'll be furious with me anyway, so stay out of it as much as possible.'

They were strolling through the shrubbery while Anthea skipped ahead of them.

Milly swallowed hard. 'It's going to be dreadful.'

Tilda glanced at her and said, 'Probably not as bad as you think.'

Wide blue eyes stared in shock.

Tilda allowed herself a smug smile. 'You haven't considered, Milly. Instead of simply writing and ordering me to bring you home, he is coming himself. You know how conventional your paper is about matters of rank and precedence. How much would you care to wager that once he gets here and is confronted with St Ormond in his top-loftiest mood, he will find it nigh on impossible to refuse Guy's suit?' Her smile deepened. 'If he had given the matter a moment's thought, he'd have written and ordered you home. Now he will have to tell St Ormond to his face, that his cousin—and let's face it, to all intents and purposes, heir presumptive—is not good enough. And if you can see him doing *that*, then I would suggest that you have been reading too many rubbishy novels!'

The blue eyes widened even more as Milly absorbed the truth of this summing up. When at last she spoke it was in tones of awe. 'I never thought of that. Oh, Tilda! You're so clever!' Abruptly she frowned. 'But he'll still be cross with you. And surely, if he has to rein himself in with St Ormond and agree to the match, he'll be even angrier.'

Tilda shrugged. '*Plus ça change*. Nothing new in that. After all, he can only roar at me. So stop worrying about me and start thinking about your brideclothes!' So saying, she neatly diverted Milly's thoughts away from a highly unwelcome subject.

While she was confident that Lord Pemberton had manoeuvred himself into a position in which he would be completely outgunned and outflanked, she was not so sanguine about his likely rage with herself. *He can only roar at me...* Lady Winter could deal with that. She did not think he would dare to hurt her physically. But still the memories of her childhood reared before her, the pain of knowing herself unloved, unwanted, a blot on the family. And in her present mood she knew that keeping her bright shield in place would be very hard.

They strolled on, Tilda giving half an ear to Milly's musings on the merits of different carriage dresses for her going-away outfit.

She was on the fret when the hour arrived to dress for dinner, yet nothing had been heard from Lord Pemberton. Was he after all going to write in a day or so and demand Milly's return home? Would he try to stop her marriage to Guy? And how would Crispin respond to that?

* * *

'Lord Pemberton has arrived, your Grace.' Bebbington made this announcement as the party gathered for dinner.

Crispin felt a surge of triumph sweep through him. Sharply he swung around to look at Tilda. She looked completely unsurprised—even faintly smug. He snorted mentally. Her wits were rapier sharp. No doubt she had assessed the advantages of Pemberton arriving in person to retrieve his daughter. She would have interpreted the lack of a written response the same way he had.

He watched in awe as her reserve grew deeper, as the expression on her face reverted to the cool, watchful cynicism with which she had arrived. So gradually had her barriers disintegrated with his family, that he had scarcely noticed the process. Until now, when she retreated behind impenetrable calm and became again the untouchable goddess he'd first seen on the front steps.

Her chin lifted, the expression grew haughty, her lips, which had been curved in laughter at some sally of Georgie's, set in a smile that lowered the temperature considerably.

'Show Lord Pemberton in, Bebbington,' he instructed. 'Please assure him that we are *en famille*. He need not scruple to join us in his travelling dress.'

Accordingly Lord Pemberton was ushered in respectfully a moment later, to be greeted with a perfectly balanced blend of deference and easy informality by his host.

'My lord.' Crispin strolled forward to greet him. 'I do hope you haven't dined. We are just about to go in. Will you join us?'

Without awaiting a response he turned his head to the butler. 'Another place if you please, for my lord.' The impassive stare he received told him the place was either being laid or had just been laid. And that Bebbington had been butler at Ormsby Park since he, Crispin, was in short coats and certainly didn't need to be told to set an extra place for an unexpected guest.

Lord Pemberton glared. 'I'm in my travelling dress…'

'But of course you are,' said Crispin. 'No need to change. It's just the family tonight. Pray don't give it another thought!'

'Slovenly!' snapped Pemberton, evidently determined to make his presence felt.

Crispin raised a brow. 'My dear sir! I should not dream of describing a gentleman thus.' His smile verged on the dangerous, a faint hint of hauteur crept into his voice, giving Pemberton ample warning that his intransigent attitude would win no support.

He shepherded Lord Pemberton further in. It was vital that Pemberton sat down to eat with them and was forced to do the pretty. He would find it all the harder to retreat later. Especially if he were treated to a display of ducal magnificence in the meantime.

'Now, I am sure you are acquainted with everyone here, my lord,' said Crispin.

Gruffly Lord Pemberton admitted that he was. And glared around until his fulminating eye lit on Tilda.

Crispin felt the older man stiffen and followed his gaze. For an instant all his protective instincts surged. He had to restrain himself forcibly from stepping between Tilda and her uncle.

'My lord, how delightful to see you,' said Tilda. 'Do you know, I quite expected you would merely write. How nice of you to come in person. And how is my aunt?'

The best defence is a good offence, reflected Crispin. He smothered wry amusement as Tilda, in one classic move, opened hostilities and pointed out to her uncle the fatal flaw in his strategy—far too late for him to retreat and regroup. Judging by the arrested look on Pemberton's face, he had realised his error and was totally thrown by it.

'A daughter,' he growled. His tone did not suggest that he viewed this outcome with any expectation of future joy.

'Oh, how lovely,' said Tilda. 'Girls are such a comfort in one's old age! I know Jonathan thought so.'

Crispin nearly choked with suppressed laughter as he caught Hasting's eye. Little vixen! It was the first time he had heard Tilda's full battery turned on anyone but himself. Not being on the receiving end gave him a far greater appreciation of her technique. Dig a hole and let the victim trap himself. Nevertheless, he intervened firmly before the effort Lord Pemberton was making at self-control proved fatal.

'Do have a drink, my lord,' he urged. 'I'm sure it would prove restorative!'

As Lord Pemberton meditated on the excellence of the Madeira, Crispin drew Lord John forward with a lift of one brow. Better to let the two older gentlemen grumble together about the foolishness of the younger generation. He was quite sure that his uncle would do so out of ingrained habit and then cheerfully turn around and tell Pemberton, as though it were a *fait accompli*, how delighted he was that his son had chosen Milly.

If Pemberton had the bottom to buck then, they were in trouble. Otherwise the outcome was a foregone conclusion. Especially if they could puff off the betrothal before Pemberton got home to his lady!

He turned his attention to Lord John's conversation just in time. 'Humph! All of a piece with this generation. Only good thing about it is that he's chosen so well. Charming girl. Ought to be proud of her! Milly! Come here, m'girl. You too, Guy!'

Crispin swore mentally. He hadn't expected on this quite so early. He cast a worried glance at his erstwhile intended, but she had herself well in hand. As did Guy. Calm and self-assured. He had to wonder if Tilda had been giving lessons.

'Good evening, Papa. I'm so pleased to see you. Is Mama

quite well? We feel so dreadfully, dragging you away from her at such a time.'

Guy agreed. 'Indeed, yes. How do you do, my lord. It is quite some time since we met at White's. Papa has been insisting that I learn my way around managing the estates.'

Bravo! thought Crispin. Just the gentlest of reminders that the Malverns are wealthy enough to endow their younger sons very generously.

Breathing a sigh of relief, he moved away. Better to leave himself right out of it. The very last thing he wanted was to give the impression that he was eager to foist Milly on to Guy. Far more effective if he appeared indifferent. His letter to Lord Pemberton had merely been in his capacity as head of the family, to assure the Pembertons that the match had his approval.

And he was reasonably certain that the forthcoming display of ducal splendour would quite flatten any rearguard action Lord Pemberton might consider mounting.

Somewhat to Tilda's surprise when Bebbington announced dinner, her host came to her side and murmured, 'Follow my lead, my lady.'

He conducted her, all the others behind them, to the State Dining Room. She had peeped in with Anthea one rainy afternoon and been suitably stunned at the size and style of the apartment. And that had been with the room under Holland covers. Not even on the night of the ball had this room been used.

Now with the table revealed, twenty feet of highly polished mahogany supporting an array of silver and crystal calculated to make one blink in the blaze of light from innumerable wall sconces and candelabra, not to mention a chandelier that verged on the ostentatious, she realised that his Grace must also have expected her uncle to arrive.

Lord Pemberton, she reflected, was being given no chance to exercise a father's rights. He had been placed at the Dowager's right hand with Lady Hollow to his right.

Two influential ladies he would not dare to offend. And his conversation would be confined to them. Something about the very formality of the setting precluded the general easy chat that had characterised their dinners up till now.

The talk was all very polite and serious, not a frivolity to be heard, let alone a heated disagreement.

'You planned this, didn't you?' she said very quietly to Crispin.

He inclined his head. 'But of course, my dear. I learnt from Wellington that one of the cardinal rules of warfare is never to expose yourself to the enemy unnecessarily. And if your opponent is cork brained enough to do so, take full and immediate advantage.' His green gaze speared her. 'A rule you appear to be well versed in. Can it be possible that you play chess? The same rules of strategy apply there, of course.'

'Do you often use this room as a chessboard and your guests as pawns?' she enquired sweetly.

His grin was disarming, oddly out of place with the splendid surroundings. 'You should have seen the maids and footmen getting the place ready,' he confided. 'And poor old Bebbington thought I'd run mad! We haven't used it since Georgie's betrothal ball!'

Tilda laughed. 'A good omen then for Guy and Milly!'

Again the green gaze lanced into her. 'You see it that way?' His voice was deep, gravelly, laced with something indefinable.

She bit her lip. So caught up had she been by their shared amusement, that she had forgotten his pain. That he probably thought she had, at least in part, caused it.

Gently, she said, 'That…that is how it must be seen. I will admit that I came here determined to stop Milly marrying you, but I believe, had she not met Guy, that you would have made her very happy…' She could not for the life of her imagine how any sane female could not be happy with him for her life's partner. Would not be overjoyed to know that she was in his care, would be cherished and protected. And loved? Ruefully she reflected that Milly might never have known the difference, had she not met Guy.

Falteringly she met his intent gaze. 'All I ever wanted for Milly was her happiness. And to make sure that she was not pushed into a marriage she did not want.'

'You have achieved that.' His tone held no emotion whatsoever.

'Yes,' she agreed softly. 'But at what cost?' She felt his anguish as a barb in her own heart. A heart that felt all too much just at the moment. A heart that was breaking and could instinctively recognise a fellow sufferer.

Their eyes met.

'Perhaps we might test your skill at chess one day soon,' suggested Crispin.

Tilda nodded, grateful to have the conversation back to a less emotional level. She had felt that she was drowning, unable to breathe, lapped in liquid heat that cocooned her in its warmth and safety.

By the time the covers were removed Lord Pemberton had been neatly backed into a corner by Lady Hollow. And Lady St Ormond's legendary charm had so distracted and bemused him that he wasn't even aware of having been manoeuvred. He had been well wined and dined, especially the former, and he was in no position to gainsay everyone's assumption that the match between Milly and Guy had his approval.

Lady St Ormond took the final trick effortlessly. 'We are so pleased to see you, my lord. Do you know, we had imagined that a stern, paternal letter demanding your daughter's return would be forthcoming! But here you are, come to set your seal of approval on the happy event!'

Her bright voice cut through the other conversation effortlessly. Every head turned.

Crispin, deep in conversation with Georgie, held his breath. If Lord Pemberton were to baulk, he had to do it now. Crispin waited a moment, counted to five, waited again and then stood.

'Perhaps if everyone has a full glass, we might drink a toast to them,' he suggested, flicking a glance at the footmen who sprang to life. He heard Tilda's sharp intake of breath, but he couldn't help it. The chance was too good to pass up. Another rule of warfare; be prepared to take any opportunity to deliver a knockout blow. And there were always casualties. His heart ached at the knowledge that he was consciously causing her pain, but he stood firm and waited while the footmen scurried about, filling glasses.

When everyone was ready, he raised his glass. 'To Milly and Guy. May their marriage be long and happy!' A murmur of assent greeted this and the toast was drunk. Crispin remained on his feet. 'And to Lord Pemberton's *youngest* daughter. May she grow to be as lovely and charming as her elder sister and cousin. Congratulations, my lord.'

Lord Pemberton hummed and hawed. As far as he could see, the birth of another daughter was nothing to be pleased about. Still, it was very pleasant to be toasted by a duke, no doubt about it.

He was still mulling over it when he realised that Lady St Ormond and the other ladies were rising. Hurriedly he scrambled up and his eye fell on his niece, standing at St Ormond's side. All of a sudden, his chagrin at the outcome surged to the fore.

Oh, they might all be putting a good face on it! They had cornered him into giving the match his blessing, and it was a perfectly acceptable one. Guy Malvern was an only son and would have a patrimony many a nobleman would envy, but in comparison to the position Milly would have had as the Duchess of St Ormond—it was a bagatelle! And no doubt all caused by Matilda ! Undutiful, scheming wench!

He'd wager an egg at Easter she'd had something to do with it. For a start, she couldn't have been much of a chaperon not to have noticed what was afoot! She'd probably encouraged it, just to cause trouble. Well, he'd have something to say to her later on. Something she wouldn't forget in a hurry.

Savagely he noted how St Ormond's eyes followed her from the room. His gaze narrowed. She'd as good as said she'd take a lover in preference to a husband. No doubt she'd snared St Ormond, distracting his attention from Milly. Perhaps she even thought a ducal husband might be rather more to her taste. Lord Pemberton took a vicious delight in reflecting that St Ormond was far too experienced to be caught by a soiled widow.

He had no opportunity to speak privately with Tilda in the drawing room when the gentlemen joined the ladies. She was surrounded by Malverns at all times. Lady Hastings appeared to have a great liking for her and Lady St Ormond was constantly summoning her. And St Ormond himself was hanging around her—that told its own story, he thought nastily. He could think of only one thing a man of the Duke's cut would want of Lady Winter.

Tilda knew quite well that Crispin was still upset. She could see it in the rather forced cheerfulness he assumed with Guy, in the way he spoke to Milly—as though she were his niece. Gently teasing her about her approaching nuptials, referring her to various London modistes whom he guaranteed to be of the first stare.

She had to bite her lip not to laugh at Milly's innocent acceptance of his first-hand knowledge of such feminine fripperies and their cost.

She nearly drew blood when Milly said ingenuously to Crispin, 'How nice for your mama to have you take such an interest in her wardrobe!'

It was not so much Milly's unworldliness that overset her, as St Ormond's startled face as he recalled that he ought not to know of such things. And if he did, most certainly ought not to betray such knowledge to a modest maiden. With only the faintest of colour highlighting his cheekbones he murmured something about trying to be a good son, and left Milly's side as soon as he decently could.

The tea tray had just been brought in and he promptly volunteered to hand the cups around for his mother.

Unable to resist teasing him a little, Tilda raised one brow as she accepted her teacup. 'Doing it rather too brown, aren't you? Even Milly will smell a rat if you push the dutiful son image too far.'

A soft laugh escaped him. 'Trust the cynical Lady Winter to be awake on all suits! Had you responded as she did, I should have known I was being roasted. As it is...' His wicked green eyes invited her to laugh with him and she did so, even while her heart ached for the performance he was putting up.

'Milk and no sugar, isn't it?' he said.

'You remembered.' She was rather surprised. He had only passed her a teacup once before.

With a queer smile he said, 'I doubt I'll forget much about you, my dear.' Bowing slightly, he left her and returned to his mother, to be given more cups to distribute.

Tilda trembled. No doubt he meant that he'd remember her as the woman who destroyed his happiness. For a moment she felt ready to sink, but rescue came from an unexpected quarter.

'Starting to look like a ghost, that gel!' announced Lady Hollow. 'Send her up, Marianne! No need to chaperon Milly with all of us here, not to mention his lordship!'

Lady St Ormond, chatting to her son-in-law, cast a measuring look at Tilda.

'She does look pale, doesn't she, James?' said Lady St Ormond. 'Off you go, my dear. We will see you in the morning.'

Tilda blinked, but before she could demur, Crispin appeared at her side. 'Mama is right. It is time you were abed. Everything is under control. Trust me.'

There was nothing she had liefer do. She'd trust him with her life. Forever. If she were given the chance.

Bowing to the inevitable—she reflected that she had been manoeuvred just as neatly as her uncle—she bid the company good night.

Giving Milly a hug, she whispered. 'It's in the bag, love. Sweet dreams.' Her own would doubtless be much as they had been for nights past—disturbing, bittersweet and frustratingly unresolved.

Putting her thoughts aside, she went to her uncle. Far too tired to indulge in waspish remarks and far too grateful that all had gone so well, she said simply, 'Good night, sir. I will look forward to seeing you in the morning.'

He grunted and turned away.

Tilda blinked back a sudden heat in her eyes and squared her shoulders. Nothing had changed. She doubted that it ever would. If nothing else, the Malverns had shown her what family life could, and should be like.

The party broke up relatively early and went up to bed. Crispin, who had rather been hoping that someone would indulge him with a game of billiards to take his mind off his gloom, retired to his chamber and rang for his valet.

After getting into his nightshirt and settling into the very large, and very empty, ducal bed, he reached for his book. Only to recall that he had finished it last night and returned it to the library. He'd been doing rather a lot of reading in bed. It was preferable to the alternatives: to wit, lying there in a state of complete frustration waiting for two things— one which never came and one which was increasingly tardy—respectively, Tilda and sleep. And when the latter did deign to shut his eyes, he dreamed in shocking and explicit detail of the former. He didn't know which was worse—thinking about her or dreaming about her.

Swearing, he got out of bed and grabbed his dressing gown. He'd have to go down and find a book. Or three. Something guaranteed to put him to sleep. Gibbon's *Decline and Fall* might do the trick, he mused. Or possibly a volume of sermons might be better. There was even an outside chance they might give his thoughts a more proper direction. A very outside chance.

It took him quite some time in the library to select a volume of sermons exhibiting the required level of solid theological virtue, but in the end he headed back upstairs, the volume under his arm. He thought wryly, that even if they didn't send him to sleep, the effort of holding the book up in bed would certainly exhaust him.

He had gained the corridor that would lead him past Tilda's room when suddenly he heard raised voices muffled by a door. Frowning he stopped. Surely that was Tilda. He listened hard but heard Lord Pemberton's voice.

'I might have known you'd do everything you could to spoil her chances! You little whore! You even managed to distract St Ormond long enough for young Malvern to snare Amelia!'

Crispin stiffened. What the hell was Pemberton insinuating?

Tilda's voice, low and furious. He couldn't make out what she was saying.

'Oh, spare me the twaddle, girl! I've but one thing to say to you!'

A scream rang out, followed swiftly by a very masculine yell of pain.

'Get out! Don't you dare come in here again or I'll ring to have you thrown out!' This time Tilda's voice, shaking with emotion, rang loud and clear.

Crispin drew back in the shadows of a large niche and prudently blew out his candle. All his protective instincts had surged to the fore, but it sounded as though Tilda were managing by herself thus far. If he charged in now—were even seen in the vicinity of her room in his night rail—the scandal might ruin her.

The door opened and Lord Pemberton emerged hurriedly, one hand clutching a candlestick, the other clutching his head. Neither of which concerned Crispin in the least. He was hearing Milly's worried voice: *Tom says he saw Papa come out of her room with a riding crop one night...* Pemberton was carrying a riding crop.

# Chapter Thirteen

Fury blazed through Crispin's soul, igniting every nerve, scorching everything in its fiery path. It was all he could do to remain out of sight until Lord Pemberton had turned the corner into the gallery.

Except for the thump as the sermons hit the floor, he never remembered the last few strides to her door. Only opening it and seeing her whip around like lightning, as the violently opened door bounced back off the wall. Seeing the fear in her eyes, the fierce defiance, the heavy brass candlestick raised threateningly.

'Oh...I thought...'

He saw the convulsive movement of her throat, the quivering tension in every graceful line—and her eyes, clinging to his.

Slowly the tension drained from her body. He could see it as she set down the candlestick on her dressing table. She stood silent, clad only in a light silk nightgown gathered in beneath her breasts, her eyes on his face, huge and vulnerable in the soft light. And even in that light, the red welt on her bare upper arm screamed its accusation, bringing a curse to Crispin's lips.

'Damn his soul to hell,' he said in deadly quiet tones.

'I'm...I'm all right,' she managed. Her voice sounded

shaky. 'I hit back, you see…with the candlestick. It took him by surprise. I didn't do that last time, so he didn't expect it.'

*Last time.* Milly had been right.

He was across the room before he could consider the danger, the likely outcome of such a move. She was wrapped in his embrace, her warm, scented body pressed to his in complete surrender, her arms twining around his neck and her mouth lifting to his in blind supplication.

Crispin groaned and took her lips, her mouth, in a kiss of searing passion that incinerated the angry tension investing his body, only to replace it instantly with another sort of tension—urgent, hard-edged, scorching need. She was so soft, so deliciously wanton in her embrace, in the way her pliant thighs shifted against his, innocently caressing, inciting, responding to his hand, which kneaded and stroked her hip, pulling her against him.

For she was innocent, he thought wildly, as his fingers firmed around one swelling breast. She might not be a virgin, but her ardour was fresh and spontaneous, something that was an integral part of who she was under the bright armour. Something distinctly lacking in the rather jaded and world weary embrace of other widows he'd had.

On the thought, he knew where this was heading. Without even realising it, he was backing her to the bed. He tried to stop and discovered that, this time, the manoeuvre was mutual. Tilda was backing herself and taking him along with her.

His head whirling, his veins full of scalding desire and his loins ablaze, he somehow broke the kiss and stood firm. With some difficulty he removed the hand from her bottom. The one at her breast was a lost cause. Even as he rested his brow on hers and drew breath, his fingers continued to circle and adore the hardened rosy nipple peeping through the diaphanous silk.

'Tilda.' He could barely speak as he pressed kisses on

her brow, her eyes, her hair. He had to make sure she really wanted this. In fact, he should probably walk away right now, rather than take advantage of her hurt in this fashion. But there were limits to his self-control and he was nearly beyond them.

'Just kiss me,' she whispered, a shy finger stroking the corner of his mouth. The light touch nearly stopped his heart.

Raggedly, he said, 'Tilda, if I kiss you again, I won't be able to stop. Do you understand what I am saying? I'll have you on that bed, writhing under me...'

He shuddered at the image he had created.

Her next words were so soft that he barely heard them. 'I need you, Crispin. And I don't want you to stop.' Then, so softly he could not swear to it, he thought he heard her breathe, 'Ever.' She lifted her head and met his burning gaze, her golden eyes clouded with desire, her lips swollen from his kisses. Even as he watched, her tongue slipped out to sheen them.

He groaned and lowered his mouth to them, holding himself back to gently savour their trembling sweetness. One small hand trailed down his chest, his stomach, and lower to touch him with passionate curiosity. He nearly died. He would have if her tentative caress hadn't been muted by his nightshirt and dressing gown.

He was lost. Heart and soul. She needed him. Even if she only needed the comfort of his body. And now she was pressing against him in a way that told him clearly of her need.

His hand framed her jaw, cupping it, exerting subtle pressure to open her mouth, even as his tongue traced the outline of her lips in growing hunger. She flowered for him sweetly, her body softening even further as he took possession of her mouth with slow erotic surges that echoed the shift of his loins against her.

He felt the gentle tug at his shoulder and responded by

swinging her up into his arms. Effortlessly he carried her the few steps to the bed and stopped beside it. He lowered her on to the covers gently, but stopped her as she would have slipped beneath them.

'No.' His eyes were blazing. 'I've waited too long for this, my sweet. I want to see you. All of you.'

She stared up at him, dazed by the riot of sensation pouring through her body, the tingling skin, the aching nipples, the surging heat pooling in her loins. And the sheer mind numbing joy that he appeared to want her as much as she wanted him. That he was not shocked by her desire, by the fact that she had touched him intimately.

He was taking his dressing gown off. It fell unheeded to the floor and to her amazed delight he grasped the hem of his nightshirt and removed that as well. She felt a ripple of wild excitement as she gazed with unashamed curiosity. At the broad shoulders, with their smooth, muscled curves, powerful hair-dusted forearms. The wide chest covered in crisp curls, over the flat stomach to...

Her eyes widened. She'd just touched it, but only through his dressing gown...she hadn't realised. Her eyes flew to his and met them hot with desire, but with a tender understanding tempering the passion.

She swallowed. He was a much bigger man than Jonathan, after all...taller, more powerful. She risked another glance down. This time all she felt was anticipation, excitement.

'Good.' His voice was a growl of satisfaction. Belatedly she realised that her face must be revealing every thought. She blushed. And realised he was joining her on the bed.

She would have moved to make room for him, but he caught her mouth in a fierce kiss and braced himself over her, before lowering his weight on to her and rolling, with her locked gasping in his arms, to the middle of the bed. The feel of his body pressed to hers, the shifting weight, sent her senses spiralling.

They ended with Crispin half on top of her, his mouth locked to hers, one powerful thigh wedged demandingly between hers. Tilda surrendered completely. To his hands, to his mouth, to his hard, rampant flesh pressed against her hip. And to that thigh which shifted so provocatively, so enticingly, in its soft cradle.

She gave herself unreservedly to the joy of the moment, to the delight of knowing, just this once, the ecstasy of giving herself to the man she loved. Even if he had only come to comfort her and had stayed to accept the comfort of her body. She would give him everything she had. And in return she would have a night of passion that would warm her dreams in her lonely bed for the rest of her life. There would be no regrets. For this one night she would be his and count herself lucky to have had that much.

Never had he known such a total yielding to desire. Never had a woman surrendered to him so wholeheartedly. She held nothing back, there was no reserve, no barrier to her soul. He drank from her sweetness again and again, revelling in the taste and texture of her mouth as his fingers dealt expertly with the row of tiny buttons fastening her nightgown. At last her bodice was open. Lifting from her, he drew back to look, to worship his goddess. She lay beneath him, her eyes shut, face flushed, and lips rosy with his kisses.

As he watched her eyes fluttered open, passion dazed golden pools a man could drown in. Her hair, reflecting golden lights, spread in tumbled abandon on the pillow. Slowly, reverently, he drew his fingers through the soft waves, spreading them out, wondering at the silken texture, the heady fragrance of rosemary that drifted from them. He'd never forget this.

'Crispin?' Her voice wobbled.

'You're beautiful,' he murmured. Slowly he set his hand to the bodice of her gown and slid the two halves aside, one at a time, to reveal one by one her swollen, hard-peaked breasts. Scarcely able to breathe, he brushed the backs of his fingers over one rosy nipple and she arched against his caress like a cat, with a gasp that spoke eloquently of her state.

She wanted him as much as he wanted her.

He stroked her breast again, teasing the nipple with the pads of his fingers before turning his attention to its twin. Slowly, expertly, he fondled and caressed, while all the time she twisted and sobbed her pleasure with an unrestrained abandon that fired his own dangerously engaged passions.

Tilda had forgotten everything she had ever been told about the proper way a lady should behave. Dimly she was aware that the cries and gasps, the moans of delight, were hers. She couldn't believe that the body that was burning and dying under his ministrations was really hers. It had never felt anything approaching this before. Even their previous encounters had not prepared her for this. She had expected pleasure, not total ecstasy. Nothing could be better than this, surely.

And then she felt his mouth on her breast. Her body nearly exploded as he drew one nipple into the hot wetness of his mouth and suckled. She'd forgotten. Even so, their encounter in the library had been nothing compared to this. Then she'd known that she had to stop him. This time she wouldn't stop him if her life depended on it. She arched against him, her hands threaded through his hair, holding him to her.

One hand slid down over his shoulders, tracing the flexing muscles that held her so safely, adoring the broad planes of his back and around to his ridged abdomen, feeling it tense beneath her fingers. Exploring, caressing, she breathed in the musky, male scent of him. Gloried in his groans of delight, muffled against her soft breast. She sent her hand lower, to touch wonderingly, to stroke and, finally, to grasp. She marvelled at the contrasts, so hard, so hot, and yet so silken. Her body throbbed in yearning, aching emptiness.

Crispin had known from the start where she was headed. Had tried to steel himself. He was only partially successful. At least he hadn't simply lifted the hem of her gown and taken her. But he had to get the damn thing off or he'd be doing just that.

Lifting himself from her, he tugged the gown down over her shoulders and gathered it at her waist.

'Lift up,' he whispered harshly. And caught her startled gaze. The sudden tension in her body.

He stopped at once. 'Tilda?'

'What…what are you doing?' A siren's voice, husky, seductive. And innocent.

Shock tore through him. He drew a deep breath to steady himself. 'Your nightgown. You don't need it.' And he sure as hell didn't. 'I'll warm you.' All night if she'd let him.

'Oh!' A long breathed sigh of delight. Then, 'Jonathan never…we always…do you really want to take it off?'

Apart from the fact that her late husband, his undoubted kindness and chivalry aside, had been a conservative and undeserving clod, that innocent revelation ripped the scales from Crispin's eyes in another matter.

Reaching for control, he sat back. Even in his frantic state he knew he couldn't ask her point blank. But he needed to know just how careful he'd have to be. So he circled the issue, with all the skill he'd just lavished on her breasts.

'How long ago did your husband die?'

Tilda trembled. She'd given herself away completely. 'About sixteen months ago,' she said. Then, 'But he was ill for a year or so before that…' She left the sentence hanging, so that he could draw what conclusion he liked. Would he be angry about her deception? Nervously she avoided his eyes and wished he'd just start making love to her again.

A large gentle hand framed her jaw. She found herself meeting simmering emerald passion. 'And how long before that?'

Her blush mantled her breasts.

'Before…before Anthea was born.' She floundered on. 'You see, he located Max, his distant cousin and heir. Jonathan liked him and he…he didn't want to risk cutting him out…by…with an heir. And I…I think he'd been so much in love with his first wife that…he decided not to…have any more children, so…'

There was a moment's fraught silence while Crispin struggled to frame his next question.

'So you haven't…been…with a man in nearly six years?'

He didn't need to hear her soft assent. The truth was screaming from every dejected line of her body. He groaned mentally.

And took a deep breath. 'Then we'll take this slowly. Very slowly.' Suiting the action to the word he drew her back into his arms only to stop immediately as she wriggled to be free. Reluctantly he released her.

He stared in escalating desire as she sat up, whisked her nightgown over her head and flung it away. She knelt there, naked, her body softly flushed as he gazed at her.

Tilda felt that gaze as a heated caress, that scorched over her breasts, her slim arms, the curve of her waist and hip. And zeroed in on the curls at the base of her belly. Dizziness swept through her as the pent-up need surged through her blood.

Catching her breath, she said, 'I don't want to go slowly.' She wanted him to take her right now, ravish her, release the burning tension that sang and throbbed in her body.

His answering grin was devilish. 'Maybe not, my pet. But I can assure you, I do.' His gaze speared her and he said, 'I'm going to savour every single moment, every touch, every moan, thoroughly.' Her eyes widened as his words sent a surge of heat through her. Her mouth opened but nothing came out.

He nodded as if she'd spoken. And spoke even more softly. 'And when I take you, I'll enjoy every sob of pleasure, every scream.' Then he reached for her and enveloped her in a steely embrace, capturing her lips in a kiss that was inexpressibly tender.

His hands were everywhere, kneading, caressing and teasing, until she was a whirlpool of urgent need, pliant and heated. Still kneeling, she felt one hand splayed over her belly, felt the long fingers slide into the springy curls. And reach further, pressing into soft, melting heat.

Instinctively she shifted slightly, opening herself to him, inviting him to further intimacy. He accepted her invitation and she cried out wildly against his mouth, whimpering as he explored and loved her. Slowly, powerfully, tenderly. Until her body was melting, aching with the need to feel him inside her. Processing her, taking her.

And still he teased, stroked and caressed the sensitive swollen folds. Unerringly he found a place she had never even known existed. A place where the sensations speared straight through her body in a melting agony of desire. She gasped and arched, pressing herself against those wickedly knowing fingers. Pleading wordlessly. One long finger slid deep inside. She shuddered at the sensation, the shocking intimacy of such an invasion. It wasn't enough—she wanted him, all of him—now.

But his mouth was crushing hers—absorbing her cries and sobs. His tongue surged and retreated, filling her mouth, stroking sensuously, plundering her softness—and yet his hand was so gentle—it was driving her wild.

Crispin's blood was an inferno. She was so soft, so hot, so excruciatingly ready for him. And her voice—it was a siren's song, urging him on. He had to have her now. Gritting his teeth, he urged her back against the pillows, and discovered that he wasn't merely pressing her down, she was drawing him down. Opening her body to him, wildly eager, cradling him, lifting towards him as he let his weight settle on her, nudged her thighs wider. He felt her gasp of pleasure as he gently opened her with his fingers, probed and stroked the hot wetness until he heard a single coherent word.

'Please.'

And then another. 'Now.'

He had long ago lost track of who was taking whom. And it didn't matter. The taking was mutual. With that thought burning through him, he pressed against her, felt her hips tilt in wanton invitation.

He groaned. 'Lie still.' He didn't want to hurt her, and after so long, who knew. Somehow he would have to rein back the instinctive urge to ravish, to possess mercilessly. If he could. If she'd let him.

He tried. Eased inside her, slowly, carefully. Using every ounce of willpower he possessed to stay in control, he sank into her heated body, as she flowered and yielded, softening round him. Trusting him. That knowledge both humbled and elated him. It tempered the scorching passion with tenderness. A tenderness he had never known before—the urge to protect, controlling the urge to take.

Tilda lay still, stunned at the sensation that assailed her. Heat pooled in her belly as his masculine hardness slid inside her. His weight rested on her, holding her captive beneath him, yet all she felt was deliciously vulnerable. And safe. She felt safe, surrounded by his warmth, by his strength, by his tenderness.

She felt him shudder, felt the sudden tension as he drew back slightly. She cried out in protest and he took her mouth passionately, silencing her as he thrust deep, burying himself to the hilt in her body. Then a gentle hand stroked her cheek, so tenderly she felt a tear slip from under one eyelid. 'Are you all right?' Somehow she opened her eyes. He was watching her, his jaw rigid with tension, heavy-lidded eyes smouldering with passion. Then he lowered his head and kissed the tear from her cheek.

'Yes,' she breathed.

He brushed his lips across hers. 'Good. Then tilt your hips towards me a little and wrap your legs around my hips.'

She obeyed instantly and gasped as he sank even deeper. His groan of pleasure was unmistakable as he took her lips and mouth again. His tongue stroked hers in slow possessive surges and, frantic with need, she kissed him back wildly.

Slowly, almost teasingly he began to rock his hips back and forth, shifting inside her rhythmically, the crisp mat of hair on his chest rasping against aching, swollen nipples, using his whole body to love and worship her.

And she responded, catching his rhythm, tilting, lifting to meet each thrust, as he drove her steadily on, higher and higher, until she was nearly insane with need. His own body was screaming for release but he held tight to the reins of his desire as he revelled in the wanton fever he could feel within her, burning in her veins, heating her skin. All silken, heated passion, she shifted and burnt beneath him.

He watched her, enthralled, enslaved by her total surrender, her complete abandonment to the moment. All her defences, her shields were down. This was the real woman, who had revealed herself to no one else, had truly given herself to no one else. She was his; he'd never let her go now. The knowledge sent his passions blazing higher, almost beyond his breaking control. He shifted within her more urgently, deeper, harder, seeking to bind her to him, so that later, when he could finally tell her of his love, she might remember and accept the truth.

She felt the change and her senses seemed to expand, yet she was only aware of him, of his body possessing hers and being possessed in return and something else, that poured from him in waves of heat and found its match in her. Something that held her very soul spellbound.

Her body was enslaved, hungering for more. Writhing and sobbing beneath him, she cried out in protest as she felt his body lift away from hers. Frantically she clung to his shoulders as he braced himself over her. And fell back as he changed the tempo, surging into her yet more powerfully, far more deeply.

He looked down at her, spread beneath him, in thrall to his loving. The sight urged him on. Brown curls tumbled in wild abandon over the pillows, glowing with golden lights in the candle's gleam. Her face, flushed with passion and her eyes closed as she lifted to meet him, all reserve forgotten in the inferno that raged between them.

He groaned and reached for control. It was gone. She had incinerated it.

Tilda cracked open her eyes and gazed up into his face. At the passion in his eyes, etched in every line of his face. And heard his urgent whisper.

'Now. Let go. Come with me.' She felt his hand press beneath her hips, cradle her bottom and lift her to him, holding her against his loins as he thrust deeper and harder. Again and again.

And then she felt it. The coil of tension spiralling out of control, lifting her high on a crest of molten desire, hovering over the blinding abyss. He withdrew almost completely and drank in her frantic cry of need, felt her lift towards him in desperate entreaty, pleading for release. For a moment he held her there, poised on the very cusp of fulfilment. With one thrust, he sent her tumbling, flying over the edge. She screamed as she shattered beneath him, into shimmering fragments that scorched in fierce delight and then melted slowly into sated oblivion.

With a groan of delight, Crispin let his body have its way and went with her into the void of ecstasy. He gloried in a release more profound than anything he had ever known. And he gloried even more in the knowledge that her release had been as cataclysmic. He could feel it in the convulsions of her body, beneath him, around him. In the way she clung to him, sighed his name in a dazed, broken whisper.

Awash, drowning in the golden glow, he sank back down onto her and rolled, taking her with him still wrapped securely in his arms. Soothing her with tender murmurs and even more tender kisses, he settled her safely. Warm, relaxed curves snuggled against him, silken limbs entwined themselves about him.

He flicked a glance at the candle still burning on the bedside table. It was very low. It could gutter all by itself, he decided. For nothing less than an earthquake would he risk breaking the dreaming enchantment that held them. He held at bay the small part of his mind that warned him his joy was illusory, and would die as surely as the candle.

Tilda awoke in the depths of the night to find herself still wrapped safely in his embrace. He was lying half beside her, half on top of her, one powerful thigh lying between hers, as though to stake his claim. His arm, warm and heavy, encircled her, as though he couldn't bear to let her go. Rough hair rasped sensuously across the soft curve of her waist as she shifted against him.

A dream, she told herself. But dreams are to be enjoyed. Believed in while they lasted. So she snuggled even closer, pressing a kiss on his shoulder.

The dreams she'd had of what it would be like to surrender and be loved by him had disturbed her sleep night after night. They'd taunted, tantalised with their promise of delight. And they had faded to pale shadows in the blaze of the reality. Never had she imagined such exquisite ecstasy, such a burning of passion, such a complete giving.

Just as wonderful was the joy of lying here in his arms, held safely against his warm, relaxed body. Cocooned in safety. And it was real. The dream would never fade for her now. She knew that she would always hold it deep in her heart, that it would be a warmth and a comfort in the years ahead.

She nestled against him and pressed another gentle kiss on his shoulder. Only to feel his arm tighten, feel the hair-brushed thigh shift and caress her suggestively, demandingly.

Then a husky voice spoke into the velvet darkness. 'Once was never going to be enough. Not with you.' And knowing hands were drifting over her, teasing, stirring her body to urgent life. She heated under his touch and moaned as she felt him shift to take one aching nipple into his mouth.

She melted in an agony of love and surrender in the darkness as he loved and caressed her until she was crying out in her need. Until he covered her and took her again, possessing her, body and soul, so that her world began and ended with him.

The darkness heightened her senses so that she was exquisitely aware of every touch, every thrust. Aware of the sharp masculine scent of him. Aware of every small sound—groans of pleasure, the whisper of his hair roughened skin caressing her silken flesh, his murmurs of encouragement in her ear. And she was wildly aware of the taste of him, of his mouth as he sated her with languorous kisses, of his body as she pressed open-mouthed kisses over his chest and shoulders, even suckling at one of the hard, flat nipples.

Until the end came and they spilled out into the abyss locked together in the bliss of their fulfilment.

He loved her again as dawn crept into the room, bathing them in pale light. She had been dreaming and woke to find that her dream had become her reality. That he was deep within her, igniting her body, possessing her soul. She clung to him, urging him on, loving him in the only way she could. This would be the last time. When she awoke again, he would be gone. Then the memory locked in her heart would have to be enough.

Crispin finally forced himself from her bed in the sure and certain knowledge that if he didn't, one of the maids would see him leaving her room. That was the last thing he needed. For Tilda, when he offered for her, to have the least doubt of his motives.

He just hoped to God that the night he'd spent in her bed wasn't going to precipitate him into any rash action. That he'd be able to control his desperate need to possess and protect her. She needed time to come to terms with what had happened between them. She needed to accept Guy's marriage. And then she'd need time to accept his own love. He'd never rushed a woman in his life, and he had no intention of starting with her.

To his immense relief he managed to gain his own corridor before meeting one of the maids. Who merely bobbed a curtsy and wished him a good morning without batting an eyelid. She might have been a little suspicious had she been able to read the title of the massive book tucked under his arm. His Grace was not renowned for his interest in the sermons of Dr John Donne.

Crispin made it to his room and tossed the volume on to his bed with scant respect. The poetry of the youthful Jack Donne would have been far more to his taste at the moment, he thought.

Lord Pemberton had slept very badly. A rapidly burgeoning headache was not the least of his problems. He finally awakened as dawn crept through a chink in his curtains and fell on his eyes. He opened them with a groan. For the pain. And for the fact that he was going to have to explain the bruise and lump above his left eye.

Savagely meditating his revenge upon his niece, he dressed. Maybe some fresh air would help his head. He had just passed Tilda's door with a muttered malediction when he heard the soft click. Startled, he swung around. The door was opening.

Instinct took over, propelling him into a nearby embrasure, still cloaked in shadow. He pressed back, eyes widening in scandalised triumph, as his host appeared in his dressing gown and night rail, cast a swift glance around, picked up a large book lying on the floor, and set off down the corridor with a swinging stride.

Jaw dropped, Lord Pemberton savoured his victory. Fate had just dealt him an ace. If he played his cards carefully he might be able to block Amelia's marriage to young Guy and force St Ormond to wed her. Not even St Ormond would willingly face a scandal where he was accused of seducing his intended bride's chaperon and then foisting the unwanted bride on to his cousin!

As for Lady Winter; his eyes narrowed. A few discreet whispers to the servants as they'd be watching her like a hawk. It would only be a matter of time before one of them caught his Grace leaving. She was a doxy like her mother before her and he'd see her destroyed if he could.

# Chapter Fourteen

'Ah. Good morning, your Grace!' Lord Pemberton was positively wreathed in smiles. His eyes glinted with such good humour that Crispin snapped out of his mood of relaxed calm instantly. He couldn't believe that a night's sleep would have fully reconciled Pemberton to Milly's betrothal. Or even that he'd had a good night's sleep with that bump on his head. He viewed it with savage satisfaction.

Senses at the stretch, he responded politely, 'Lord Pemberton. I trust you were comfortable. But what is this?' He indicated the bump. He certainly didn't wish Pemberton to suspect his prior knowledge.

To his intense pleasure, Lord Pemberton flushed. 'Oh! Ah, just a little altercation with a bedpost! But enough of me! I do hope your Grace spent a...*satisfactory* night.'

In the act of reaching for the door to the breakfast parlour, Crispin froze. There was something about Pemberton's voice, a note of vicious triumph. He turned, exerting every nerve to control the impulse to choke the grinning life from Lord Pemberton.

'Just so, your Grace. Perhaps we might have a brief word. About marriage settlements.'

'In my library.' Crispin swore mentally. He'd have to

tread carefully here. If Tilda ever suspected he'd offered because of her uncle's threats, he'd be sunk. The man had forced her into marriage once; she'd never submit to that again.

Seating himself in a comfortable chair, Lord Pemberton's first words disabused Crispin of his initial suspicions.

'I believe, your Grace, that in light of recent developments, we might like to review the eligibility of Amelia's proposed marriage.'

Crispin stared, dumbfounded.

Lord Pemberton permitted himself an oily smile. 'Even you cannot seduce your intended bride's chaperon and then expect your cousin to marry the unwanted bride, while you pursue an affair with her cousin. If such a tale were to leak out…' This time the smile was beatific. 'Ruin, your Grace.'

It would be ruin all right and tight, thought Crispin. For Tilda. A discreet affair would be condoned. But it was plain that Lord Pemberton had other ideas. A tremor of sheer revulsion ran through Crispin. This man could contemplate destroying his niece. Pemberton had destroyed his own sister in much the same way.

Icy rage took hold. Crispin's jaw hardened, every line of his body stiffened in barely leashed fury. His voice, when he finally spoke, cut like a burning knife.

'If, my lord, one word of this is breathed, you will find that society has nothing but condemnation for a man who treated a young girl under his care as you did, and that in protecting my betrothed wife, a widow of unblemished reputation, my actions will meet with no argument! I will have no hesitation in making quite sure, Lord Pemberton, that your place in society is forfeited. Do I make myself quite plain? Perhaps you might care to go to breakfast now, before I am tempted to make my position even clearer.'

Observing that his Grace's fists were clenched, Lord Pemberton didn't even stop to apologise. His Grace's voice halted him by the door.

'Miss Pemberton's marriage to my cousin will take place as soon as the banns can be called. As will mine to Lady Winter. Any attempt by you to upset these arrangements would be most unwise!'

As the door closed hurriedly Crispin cursed vehemently. He'd have to offer for Tilda immediately. Somehow he had to persuade her to marriage without her thinking he offered under duress and without mentioning the word love. She was honest to the core. If she thought he offered his heart and she could not return his affection, she would refuse him.

There was something else—her clearly stated avowal that marriage had nothing to offer her, that she had her independence, both personally and financially, and did not care to lose either in matrimony. He would have to reassure her that she would lose neither in marrying him.

And as for her belief that marriage had nothing else to offer that was not freely available without interference of clergy! He thought, with a tender smile, that when she had said that, she had spoken in all innocence. Now she knew better. And that was the only trump in his hand as far as he could see. He would have to play that card very skilfully. He would have to convince her that as far as he was concerned, the only way she would get a repeat performance was in the marriage bed. After which he'd have to try and keep out of her bed until the wedding night.

Grimly he strode from the library. He had to get to Tilda before Lord Pemberton could announce the betrothal.

He ran across Bebbington in the hall and greeted him with relief.

'Is Lady Winter down yet, Bebbington?' The steadiness of his voice was rather a surprise to him. Inwardly he was shaking.

'Her ladyship is, I believe, breakfasting privately in her room. Shall I send a message up, your Grace?'

'No,' said Crispin and headed for the stairs. He turned

on the second step. 'And if anyone is asking for me, you haven't seen me.'

'Your Grace wishes me to lie?'

'Through your teeth,' his Grace affirmed.

Tilda had awoken just in time to hear her door shut gently. He was gone. And her body still glowed with the aftermath of their final loving, still throbbed to the rhythm of his possession. If she closed her eyes and dreamed she could still feel the weight of his body on hers, feel the strength of warm muscles surrounding her, feel him buried deep inside her.

Slowly she came to terms with what had happened. She had seduced, and been seduced by, Crispin Malvern. Deliberately. At least on her part. She had taken the pleasure, the ecstasy that was offered. In return she had given herself without reserve.

And now he was gone. When she saw him later in the day she would have to meet him as though nothing had happened. As though he had not spent the night in her bed. As though she had not spent the night writhing and sobbing in his arms like a wanton as he made love to her. Not once, but three times.

She snuggled back under her tumbled bedding. God only knows what the maids would think when they saw it, she thought sleepily. Sarah would probably be fussing after her all day, thinking she'd had a bad night when quite the opposite was the case. She fell asleep, still smiling.

Tilda had finished her breakfast—rather startled to find herself with an enormous appetite—and was handing the tray to Sarah, when there was a peremptory knock at the door.

Sarah cocked her head and glanced at her mistress.

Tilda nodded. No doubt it was Milly, come to see if she was up yet.

She was shocked to hear Crispin's deep voice requesting entrance.

Then he was in, looking impossibly handsome and rested. For a moment she wondered if she had merely dreamed that he had spent the whole night making love to her, until she saw the flare in his eyes as they rested on the tumbled bed. Saw the thoroughly wicked and knowing smile that curved his lips.

She blushed, clutching her robe tightly around her. And saw that smile deepen...with unmistakable satisfaction.

Her attention was briefly diverted by a strangled sound from Sarah. Eyes wide, Sarah was glancing from this very improper visitor to the muddle of bedding. Somehow Tilda managed to meet her gaze and saw Sarah's jaw drop. Then, to Tilda's outrage, a smile every bit as wicked and satisfied as St Ormond's lit her maid's face.

'Hmm. Well, I'd best be getting along,' she said. 'I'll leave you to it. Good morning, your Grace. Milady.' She picked up the tray and headed for the door.

Tilda was rather touched to see Crispin leap for the door and open it. How very kind of him, she thought. She rapidly revised her estimate of his chivalrous intent as she heard the lock click home.

She gulped. No matter what she'd done last night—and she'd done plenty—this surely couldn't be a good idea. One was supposed to be discreet. Wasn't one?

'Good morning, your Grace.' She managed to sound as though dukes wearing suggestive smiles visited her like this every morning. And encountered a raised brow.

'Good morning...Tilda.' His tone suggested that formality was the last thing on his mind. He had a point—it was probably a little late for that now.

'Is there...is there something I can do for you?'

The unholy grin that split his face had her wishing she hadn't phrased her question in quite that way.

His features straightened with what was obviously an effort. 'Later,' he said gravely.

She blushed hotly. Even more so since he knew just how heated that flush was making her skin, just how far it extended—and just how to make it go even further, burn even hotter. He'd demonstrated that last night.

'Tilda,' he began. 'About last night…'

She rushed into speech. 'Please, your…Crispin…there is no need. I…know you did not intend… I am just as much to blame… You need not say anything…' She nearly choked on the hard lump that rose in her throat. 'I promise I will not regard it. It was just last night…I…I quite understand that you meant only to comfort me.'

'You think I didn't mean to make love to you?' There was a queer, tight note in his voice.

She flinched. It had felt like he'd meant every burning touch, every tender caress—but if he'd truly wanted her, he'd have come before. Wouldn't he?

'I think you did not intend to make love to me before you came to my room, no,' she said shakily.

'You would wish to leave it there?' His voice was very quiet and deep.

Her eyes flashed to his. 'Is that not what you wish?'

'No.' Very short and hard. 'I can't.'

A shudder ran through her. Then he wanted a liaison. Wanted her to be his mistress. She closed her eyes to hide the pain. She had brought it on herself. He had every reason to think that she would welcome and enjoy such an arrangement. She forced her eyes to open and meet his.

He took a deep breath. 'I told you last night; once was never going to be enough with you. Nor, it seems, will one night be enough. Tilda, please, I am asking you, no, begging you to be…'

'Please, no.' She couldn't bear to hear him say it. 'You do not need to beg me. I…I accept your…offer.' She couldn't think what else to call it. Her experience did not extend that far. To her relief he seemed to accept her reply. Indeed, the joy and relief that surged into his face stunned her.

'You will?' It reverberated in his deep voice.

Desperately she forced herself to concentrate. Best find out now what he envisaged. For how long. Where. Bitterly she realised that this was the end of the joyous dream she had created with him last night. One night of passion could be cherished tenderly in the memory. But a relationship such as he now asked for would inevitably be soured by a parting. Kindly and generous on his part, no doubt. And with outward smiles to protect the broken heart on hers. Yet she could not find it in her to refuse. Her own need she might have managed to deny, but she loved him too deeply to deny his.

'What…what terms did you envisage?'

He blinked slightly. 'Well, the usual ones, I suppose.'

That didn't tell her a dratted thing. She had no idea, in specific terms, what gentlemen offered to their paramours. But she could see one overriding problem. Her home was in Leicestershire. His was here.

Perhaps he intended to remove to London where it would be possible for her to rent a house and he could visit her privately.

'Where do you wish me to live?'

He stared. 'Ah, here, of course…'

'Here?' Tilda felt the shock as a physical jolt. *'Here?'* It was unheard of. Even she knew that much after her mother's experience. Gentlemen did not live openly with their mistresses. No matter if all society knew the truth, one still played the game. The game society called discretion; the one she called hypocrisy. She gulped—obviously Crispin shared her views.

'But, naturally.' He seemed thoroughly puzzled. 'It's my home. You seem to like it here. And Guy and Milly won't be far away. So you can visit and…'

Tilda stared. He thought that she could live openly as his mistress and still visit her cousin? Surely not! Not even the Malvern arrogance could extend that far.

Another objection occurred to her. 'But your mama, Lady St Ormond—she won't be very pleased...she lives here...we can't...'

A very wicked chuckle interrupted her. 'My dearest goose! When Mama hears the news, she'll probably have my greys poled up and be straight down to the Rector to have the banns called immediately. She's been waiting for my marriage for so long that she'll positively fall on your neck!'

Only two words in this speech actually penetrated Tilda's suddenly numbed brain. *Banns,* and *marriage.*

The truth burst on her like a bombshell. He was asking her to marry him! She corrected herself sharply. No, he'd already asked her. And she'd accepted. At least, he thought she'd accepted. But how was she to explain what she'd thought? What she'd intended to accept.

Because she didn't want to marry him! At least, she did. Of course she did! But not without love on both sides. She didn't dare.

Somehow she forced her lips to frame the words. 'Crispin, why do you wish to marry me? After all...this...' she gestured wildly '...you won't feel this way forever...' Her voice trailed off. She couldn't go on. His pain would be gone one day and then he would find himself tied to her. Tied to a wife he didn't really want. She'd rather be his mistress and have him leave when he tired of her than see him trapped.

He was speaking again. 'You think not?'

To her shock she realised that his long strides had closed the distance between them. That he was kneeling on the bed beside her, reaching for her. His hands grasped her shoulders, drew her against him to lie soft and unresisting in his arms.

'I told you, Tilda. I can't leave it at just one night. I want you. More than I have ever wanted a woman.' His arms tightened.

Her brain reeled and her body melted at the heat of urgency in his voice. And she realised that he had not understood her. That he had not realised she was speaking of Milly. She heard her own voice, a queer strained shadow, say 'But you don't need to marry me for—'

He released her abruptly. 'No! Don't say it, Tilda! Let us have one thing quite clear—you will be my wife, not my mistress. I will not dishonour either of us by debauching you.'

Shock lanced through her as he stood up. 'But why me? You've had so many mistresses... I mean...why marry me?' Against all hope she yearned to hear him say he loved her, adored her, couldn't live without her.

'I haven't had that many!' he said indignantly. 'You make it sound as though I kept a harem!'

Glaring at him, she retorted, 'You've had more than I have, anyway!'

He grinned. 'I should think so! Unless your middle name is Sappho, of course.'

For a moment she didn't understand, but then she firmly suppressed a grin and said, 'I *meant* that you'd had more mistresses than I'd had lovers!'

A very tender smile played about the corner of his mouth. 'Well, that wouldn't be very difficult either,' he noted.

She ignored that. Along with the smile. 'Why? Why me?' She had to force the conversation back on track.

'Because I must,' was all the answer he gave her. She stared up at him, at the hard, set planes of his face, the lambent eyes, blazing with the force of his emotion. And she thought she knew the reason. Milly *had* hurt him. By taking her, he could drown some of his pain. And she would be the most convenient choice. She knew the truth, would not expect too much of him. He would be comfortable with her. They suited.

'We will suit very well, my dear.' She flinched at the tone of calm good sense, echoing her thoughts. 'You know that. My mother will love you as a daughter and I promise to be a good father to Anthea. I have no intention of interfering with your independence. Your fortune will remain yours. Settled upon you. I have no need of it.'

Her eyes widened in shock. 'These are not the terms you would have offered Milly,' she stated with as much composure as she could muster. 'You said yourself that you wanted a bride you could mould to your liking, who would be guided by you. Yet now you offer a completely different bargain. Why?'

Even to herself, her voice sounded cold, clinical. Crispin's mouth tightened. She almost expected one of the bursts of anger she could so easily spark off.

But he spoke gently. 'If I offered you those terms, you would throw them in my face. You are not Milly. You are older, independent and far more mature. And since I want you as you are, I would be a fool indeed to try to change or dominate you. That would end in misery for both of us. You need have no qualms.'

Except for her own peace of mind. Frantically she thought that it would indeed have been easier to be his mistress. The trap was closing about her and she could see no escape. She could not, to save her life, tell him what she had thought he was offering. Not when he had in fact offered her a marriage such as she had not thought possible; a marriage in which she would be valued as an equal.

Almost hysterically, she tried to imagine the words: *Thank you for your offer of marriage, your Grace, but, if you don't mind too much, I'd rather be your mistress.*

It couldn't be done. Not when Milly had practically jilted him for his cousin. She could not deal a blow like that to his pride and self respect.

Her own cynical mind had dug the pit into which she had fallen. Miserably she remembered thinking that any woman would be happy to give her life into his keeping and surrender herself to his tender care. She had been wrong.

To the woman who loved him it could be nothing but pain to know that he would never love her. That he had loved her cousin and had married her as a sort of second best. Because he was fond of her and she had pleased him in bed.

*You wanted to comfort him. And at least he has not offered for you because he feels that he compromised you.*

It was marginal comfort at best, but it was better than nothing.

The first person she met, upon leaving her bedchamber half an hour later, was Milly, rushing up to find her.

'Tilda! Darling Tilda! Is it true? Are you really going to marry St Ormond?'

Not entirely sure herself, Tilda yet managed to give a coherent response and submit to her cousin's delighted enthusiasm.

'I was with the Duchess, when Crispin came in to tell her,' explained Milly. 'She nearly fell on his neck! And said something about going to see the Rector at once. But St Ormond told her that since he'd managed to propose without her help, he rather thought he could see the Rector himself.'

Despite herself, Tilda chuckled.

'So that's where he's gone.'

'Gone where?'

'To see the Rector,' explained Milly. 'He was going to collect Guy and go straight down to the Rectory. If all the banns are called at once we can have a double wedding!'

Dear God! thought Tilda. He must be intent on getting it all over and done with as fast as possible.

'Now,' said Milly ingenuously, 'I understand why he has been so gloomy. It wasn't over me at all. He has been in love with you all along. And thought you wouldn't have him! Or that he'd have to offer for me, poor man.'

Tilda opened her mouth and shut it again. There was no way in which she could explain Crispin's motives for proposing marriage. Let alone hers for accepting such a proposal.

Milly looked at her oddly. 'Tilda…you're…you're not doing this for me, are you? Because you think if St Ormond marries you, Papa won't be able to try and force him to marry me?'

That aspect of the situation hadn't occurred to Tilda. Could that be part of Crispin's motivation? Briefly she tried to imagine anyone forcing Crispin to do something he didn't want to do. She failed completely.

Determinedly she manufactured a grin. 'Oh, come now, Milly! His High and Mightiness, the Duke of St Ormond, pushed into a marriage he doesn't want? By a mere baron? You must be all about in your head!'

Milly gave vent to a giggle and Tilda went on. 'We are getting married because we shall suit very well—' she swallowed and admitted part of the truth '—and we…we desire each other, so…'

'Ohhh!' Milly's eyes grew round. 'But he's quite old, Tilda. Do you think—?'

'He's not *that* old!' protested Tilda, aware that she was blushing. Memories of the night she had spent flooded through her. His Grace of St Ormond was hardly likely to find asserting his marital rights beyond his capabilities.

She couldn't say that! 'For heaven's sake, Milly! He can give your papa thirty years, and might I remind you that you have a new sister?'

Firmly, she changed the subject by asking Milly what she should wear for her wedding.

Outside the drawing room they met Lord Pemberton, who fixed his niece with a cold glare.

'I should like a word with you.' His voice bit into her.

Milly cut in blithely. 'Have you heard, Papa? St Ormond and Tilda—'

'I have indeed heard.' He gestured to Tilda. 'I believe the library to be unoccupied.'

Resigned, Tilda acquiesced. He could do nothing. Would not dare. He must know what Crispin's reaction would be.

She entered the library ahead of him and glided to the fireplace. Standing before it she faced him, her chin up defiantly, not a trace of fear evident in her bearing.

'Well, my lord?'

His lip curled. 'Congratulations. I had not thought it possible that the mighty St Ormond would fall victim to the shop-soiled charms of a scheming widow!' He laughed scornfully. 'My mistake! I thought he'd be so eager to avoid the scandal that he'd marry Milly if I told him what I'd seen. But no! He informed me that you were betrothed to him. You must have the skills of Aphrodite—or did you flaunt your fortune under his nose along with your body?'

Sick horror chilled her as the ugly words tore into her very soul. 'What you saw?' Even as she spoke, she knew what he must have seen.

His next words confirmed it. 'St Ormond leaving your chamber at dawn,' he said. 'Slut! No doubt you lured him into your bed as fast as possible on arriving here! The more fool he for marrying you. In my day a man didn't marry a whore! He had her and discarded her as is fitting. How times change! St Ormond has decided to protect you with his name. God knows why, but he has!'

Tilda scarcely heard the rest of the diatribe. Her uncle had seen Crispin leaving. He had tried to blackmail him into marrying Milly on the strength of it. She didn't have to wonder now what had motivated Crispin to come back and offer marriage. He might not love her, but he cared enough to protect her from the scandal that would ensue if Pemberton had spread the story.

He was a gentleman. He had known how inexperienced she was. So he had done the only thing a gentleman could do. Offered her the protection of his name. That knowledge scored itself into her like a brand. He had offered out of obligation—and made damned sure that she didn't realise it.

Her uncle was still speaking. 'And now I understand there's some nonsensical talk of a double wedding! I tell you to your head, girl! I'll not take part in any wedding of yours! Be damned if I will! Take that thought to bed with you tonight. I'll swallow Milly's marriage—if the chit's fool enough to think young Malvern a fair exchange for St Ormond, good luck to her! At least she's not a scheming, mercenary little whore!'

That shook her out of her daze enough for her to lash back. 'You really should try to make up your mind, sir,' said Tilda contemptuously. 'After all, my mother loved a man of no fortune and you refused your consent to the marriage. I wish to wed a man of wealth and title and I am immediately a *scheming, mercenary little whore.* Can it be that your point of view is entirely linked to your own self-interest? But you may rest assured that I have no intention of claiming your escort down the aisle a second time. Nor that I would willingly see you ever again.' She fronted him proudly, her eyes steady, no hint of the hurt he had dealt her showing in her face. Inwardly she bled.

He stared at her for a moment. She could feel his glare burning into her. Then, with a frustrated exclamation, he turned on his heel and was gone, slamming the door behind him.

How she reached a sofa without falling, Tilda never quite knew. But she did and huddled in it, sick and shaking.

He'd offered out of obligation. To save her reputation that her own uncle would have destroyed. He had not even wanted her to ease his own hurt. He didn't even want her money. She could give him nothing in return that he wanted.

*Except your body.* She shuddered at the thought. If he made love to her as he had done last night, she would never be able to hide her feelings. She would never be able to give herself like that without finally exposing her love.

Tears trickled down her nose unheeded. He'd already offered her the protection of his name. That was bad enough. She was damned if she'd accept his pity as well. She would have to call a halt to this. Before it went any further. She'd gladly marry him to save him pain—but not to save her own reputation. She loved him too deeply to permit that sacrifice.

The irony of her words to Milly struck at her like a blow. *His High and Mightiness, the Duke of St Ormond, pushed into a marriage he doesn't want? By a mere baron?*

Lord Pemberton had managed to do just that.

Half an hour later she was still sitting curled up on the sofa when the door opened to admit the Dowager.

'Ah! There you are! Milly thought I should find you here.'

Tilda didn't answer at first. Just stared in blank incomprehension.

'My dear, I'm so delighted—' She broke off. 'Tilda, dear, are you quite well? You look so pale. Is your arm hurting?'

Tilda shook her head numbly. Whatever else was hurting, it wasn't her arm that was troubling her.

The Dowager came across to her and sat down. 'Will you permit me to say how happy I am to welcome you as a daughter? That I'm glad it is you that has made Cris so happy.'

'H…happy, your Grace?' Tilda couldn't think why he

should be happy at all. He'd lost the girl he loved and been accidentally forced into marriage with her cousin.

'Very happy,' said her Grace firmly. 'I haven't seen him like that ever. Certainly not when he told me that he was contemplating marriage with Milly! And you may as well stop being so formal with me. Just call me Marianne, as Hastings does. We shall go along famously, you and I.'

'But…' Tilda searched desperately for the words to tell this kindly, affectionate woman the truth without hurting her. And realised that they didn't exist.

'But nothing,' said the Dowager. 'You and Crispin are going to be very happy together. Don't you dare to sit there feeling miserable or unworthy or whatever silly nonsense your wretched uncle has put into your head! Instead come and tell Anthea. I have put the entire household on pain of instant banishment if a word of this reaches her ears before you tell her yourself. She is in my sitting room, playing spillikins with Milly and Louisa.'

Anthea! Tilda realised that she had not even given her a thought. Probably because she had known, without Crispin's assurance, that Anthea would be treated as his own much loved daughter. And that Anthea herself would be utterly delighted to stay here with her 'Uncle Cris', whom she regarded in a light bordering on the idolatrous.

Dazed, she allowed herself to be dragged to her feet and shepherded from the room.

'Now, this double wedding idea,' said the Dowager, 'I must say I like it…' She went on happily, outlining all the advantages of the arrangement. No point in waiting about and, since most of the guests would be duplicated, it really made the best sense. Then Guy and Milly could take themselves off on a honeymoon while Tilda and Crispin remained here alone.

'If,' said Lady Ormond, with a faint twinkle, 'one can ever be alone with so many servants falling over themselves to make sure you think they are being useful! But you know what I mean.'

'But…but you'll be here…won't you?'

The Dowager blinked. 'Heavens, no! Didn't I say? I'm going to go and stay with Georgie and Hastings for a few weeks while you and Cris get to know each other.' Her grin became positively naughty. 'My role as chaperon ends after the church, you know! There is nothing more vexatious than actresses or chaperons who don't know when to make an exit! I even thought to take Anthea with me since Georgie's youngest, Jenny, is about the same age. Moore Park is only twenty miles away, so you could come over to see how she is going on as often as you liked.'

'How…how very kind of you,' achieved Tilda. And realised that she was digging the trap deeper with every word, that she was being manoeuvred by the entire Malvern family. That, unless she screamed from the rooftops right now that she would not marry his Grace, the Duke of St Ormond, she would find herself fronting the altar with him, in company with Milly and Guy, in just under three weeks.

There was nothing preventing her from doing just that; announcing that it was all a terrible mistake, that she had never intended to accept him. Nothing stopped her telling the Dowager right now—except her heart. Her foolish, aching heart which could not bear to hurt him any further—because it knew only too well how it felt to be broken.

'Give him a chance, my dear.'

Tilda trembled at the tender understanding in the Dowager's voice. 'A…a chance?'

'Yes. A chance to make you happy. To make up for the past.'

She flinched. Jonathan had once said something very similar to her—and she had accepted it. But she didn't want that from Crispin. She was not prepared to be rescued a second time.

## Chapter Fifteen

In the weeks before his marriage, Crispin occasionally wondered if he would still be quite sane on his wedding morning. All the indications were that he wouldn't be. That he would, in fact, be stark raving mad.

To his immense relief, Lord Pemberton stayed only a couple of days, returning home to escort Lady Pemberton to attend the marriage of her daughter. It appeared that Lady Pemberton was perfectly happy to leave her new daughter in the care of a wet nurse, but that she and her lord would only arrive two days before the wedding. But before Lord Pemberton's departure Crispin ensured that notices of both betrothals were sent to the papers and that the banns were called for the first time. He had no intention of cutting his lordship any slack.

The preparations were, thank God, almost completely out of his hands. His mother, sister and aunt had swung into action with terrifying efficiency. So completely did they plan every minute and seemingly irrelevant detail, that Crispin was moved to mutter to his brother-in-law that Wellington should have the lot of them on his staff.

Hastings merely grinned and murmured a few soothing platitudes, while doing nothing to hide his amusement.

But apart from all the upheaval, what really bothered him

was Tilda's subtle, but complete, withdrawal. She was avoiding any private conversation with him by hurling herself into the preparations and learning her way about the house and its ways—which would have been laudable had she allowed him to help. But she declared herself quite happy to be shown by the Dowager and Mrs Simms. And he thought he knew why—she believed that he had offered for her out of duty and honour.

Her withdrawal dated from the day of their betrothal. He had returned from the Rectory, after dutifully downing two glasses of the Rector's best sherry, to find that she was lying down upon her bed. With a headache, according to his mother, who had commented that she understood Lord Pemberton to have had an interview with Tilda in the library.

He had instantly gone up to her chamber, only to find the door locked. Ever since, he had only seen Tilda in company, except for very briefly last thing at night when he escorted her to her chamber. Even then Tilda neatly blocked every attempt he made to win her confidence and he knew that Sarah awaited her mistress within. So he kept his goodnight kiss very brief. Positively chaste. He was having quite enough trouble sleeping as it was, and saw no point in exacerbating the problem. Somehow, given her complete emotional withdrawal, he didn't think it was a good idea to suggest to Tilda that he share her bed.

During the day she was perennially caught up with fittings, for herself, for Milly, for Anthea. If she, or one of the others, wasn't in a state of half-undress, then she was with the Dowager, making endless lists, or consulting over the menu, how many bride cakes would be required. He had never realised just how busy a woman could be over a wedding.

But finally, ten days before the wedding, he came to the conclusion that enough was enough. Tonight he would try and slip through her misty armour. To which end he purposely made no attempt at dinner to inaugurate any conversation with her any more controversial than the weather and the rotation of crops. Afterwards in the drawing room he devoted himself to Aunt Seraphina.

Despite his subterfuge he had the distinct impression, as he escorted Tilda to the stairs, that she wasn't hoaxed in the least by his efforts. She was wound tighter than a watchspring.

Her composure was almost brittle and he knew, the instant he asked her point blank what was bothering her, that she wasn't going to tell him everything.

'My uncle has said that…he is not prepared to give me away again.' Her voice told him nothing, revealing in itself. Cool, devoid of emotion, but he felt her fingers tighten slightly on his arm, as if for support. Sheer incandescent rage flooded through him that Pemberton could so expose her to whispers. This, he reminded himself, was the man who had threatened to make known his niece's supposed affair. Who had actually encompassed his own sister's ruin.

He clung to the reins of his self-control with grim determination. 'A little awkward,' he commented. 'But not insuperable. Have you any ideas?'

She nodded slowly as they went up the stairs. 'I thought that perhaps, since I have been married before, it might be best if Milly and my uncle led the way down the aisle—that I could simply follow them, as if I were merely matron of honour.'

He greeted this with a snort. 'The devil you will! If you think that I'm going to have my bride trailing down the aisle like a lost puppy, you can think again!'

She glared at him, he saw with relief—at least she was actually responding to him instead of holding him at bay.

'No doubt you have a better idea!'

He was about to shake his head when inspiration struck. 'I'll escort you.'

A puzzled frown puckered her smooth brow, making him ache to kiss it away, along with whatever else was bothering her.

'Down the aisle,' he elaborated. A thoroughly wicked grin lit his eyes. 'I'm taller than your uncle. And you're taller than Milly. We'll look suitably ducal and awe-inspiring together—as though we're giving our blessing to the match. And we'll go first.'

'You can't do that!' she protested.

With a lift of one arrogant brow, he asked, 'Who's going to stop me? I'm a Duke. I can do what I damn well like.' He grinned shamelessly at her outraged stare. 'Within reason,' he amended.

'You'd escort me down the aisle?' She appeared stunned at this break from tradition.

He nodded. If nothing else it would mean that he could ensure she didn't bolt halfway. The only problem would be that blasted bit in the service about *Who giveth this woman*... Could it be left out? Tilda was a widow after all. Who *was* supposed to give widows away?

'And who do you think is going to give me away?' she asked tiredly, echoing his thought. 'Were you just going to bestow me on yourself?'

He eyed her forebodingly. 'You're mine already,' he murmured. 'If you care to recall.'

Blushing scarlet, she shot back, 'Were you going to tell the Rector that?'

Raising one brow, he said, 'He is a man of large charity, of course...'

Tilda snorted. 'He'd need to be!'

Crispin grinned and relented. 'Very well. Let's not test his limits. Give me a moment to think.'

He racked his brains. This was obviously upsetting her. Surely he could think of someone—a member of her family, someone with some responsibility for her... He had it!

'Lord Winter,' he said calmly. 'He's your principal trustee, your first husband's heir. Nothing could be more appropriate.'

Blinking, Tilda realised that he was right. Such an arrangement would cause no remark at all, especially since Lord Pemberton would be giving away his oldest daughter.

Heaving a sigh of relief, she looked up at him, all her reserve melted. 'Thank you, Crispin—that was bothering me terribly.'

'Do you want to tell me about the rest?' His voice was a velvety growl.

Her eyes widened as she froze again.

He was smiling down at her, his hand surrounding hers with a steely strength, just as his body had surrounded her—with warmth and safety. She looked up and thought she would drown in the tenderness in his eyes. The temptation to step closer, beg him to wait until Sarah had gone and tell him everything, battered at the barriers she had flung up. Barriers that were there to hold her feelings in. To keep her heart safe.

Even as she fought the temptation, he lowered his head and pressed his lips to hers, slipping his arms about her. His lips firmed, caressed gently, sending her senses spinning, calling forth the burning heat in her soul.

Madness. Even knowing that, she leaned against him, sinking into the kiss, parting her lips and returning the stroke of his tongue. Slow, possessive surges filled her mouth. His hands shifted over her body, holding her to him and she felt the sudden tension that invested his large frame. Powerful muscles tautening, hardening under her hands, against her soft curves.

Her body trembled, remembering how he had felt pressing down on her, how he had touched her and taken her so tenderly... He would come to her now if she asked him—she didn't dare.

She was sinking deeper into him, into a haze of desire and burning need. A tidal wave of emotion threatened to engulf her. If she didn't stop now, she wouldn't be able to. Exerting every ounce of her willpower, she pulled back slightly, breaking their kiss. She could feel the reluctance with which he released her. And it felt as though a part of her had been torn away as he let her go.

Desperately she held herself steady, as though her knees had not turned to jelly, as though her bones were still solid. Her entire body was aflame. More than ever, she realised in shock. And he'd only kissed her.

She had to go, before she changed her mind. Before she begged him to stay.

'Goodnight, Crispin.' She tried to say it firmly, as though she actually meant it. And came to the conclusion that she hadn't been terribly successful, since his brow lifted suggestively and a teasing smile hovered at one corner of the mouth that had been kissing her senseless.

She tried again. 'I'll see you…in the morning.' It was only with a massive surge of willpower that she didn't say *later*.

His mouth hardened. 'Very well,' he said quietly. And reached out to touch her cheek. One finger trailed lightly down in a feathery caress. She held still as fires leapt up under her skin. His fingers firmed under her chin and he bent to brush his lips over hers.

'Goodnight, my darling.' He turned swiftly and strode away down the corridor towards his own apartments. Quickly she went inside. If she watched him go, she'd be calling him back—or running after him.

Time. She needed time to get her feelings under control and make sure that she could keep her emotions hidden even as she responded to him physically. She thrust away the thought that it might prove impossible. Especially if he made a habit of calling her *darling* in just that tone of voice.

Crispin made it to his bedchamber without succumbing to the insidious little voice inside his head suggesting that he should go back to Tilda's room, dismiss her maid himself, and then behave in a manner that his feudal forebears would have applauded. To wit, drag his lady back to his own apartments and have his wicked way with her. All night. And very possibly all of the next day as well.

He swore vehemently as he slammed the door shut behind him. And encountered a startled glance from his valet. With grim amusement, Crispin imagined just how much more startled Stubbs would have been if he'd had Tilda over one shoulder and had calmly told him to leave.

The vision sent a surge of painful heat to his loins. He swore again. Frustration was going to kill him. He'd never known anything like it. In the past, desire for a woman had begun to wane almost as soon as he'd had her. He couldn't remember the last woman, if any, he'd taken three times in one night. Once, at the most twice, was generally enough. And he'd still wanted Tilda—more than ever.

Catching Stubbs's sympathetic eye, he said shortly, 'I'll undress myself. Go to bed and sleep in if you like. I'll be riding early, so I won't need you.' One thing was certain, he was going to have an appalling night's sleep and he might as well cut the torture as short as possible.

As Stubbs left, he flung himself into a chair by the fire. For a man about to marry the woman he loved, he was extremely depressed.

Would he be able to make Tilda happy? Would she come to care for him? Would it have been better to let her go? His heart cried out in protest at the thought. He shrugged fatalistically. It was far too late now.

His mouth twisted in wry self-mockery. He could force or trick nothing from her. Nothing worth having, anyway. Not her confidence, and certainly not her love. He wanted her freely—as she had given herself the other night. Only then would she truly be his.

"Tilda?'

She looked up with relief and forced a smile. The two lists she was checking were beginning to blur into one another and her eyes felt gritty after an appalling night's sleep. 'Guy. How nice. Is there something I can do for you?'

His glance took in the list of acceptances she was checking against the original list and he shook his head. 'Not likely. It strikes me that you are doing quite enough. I must make quite sure that next time I marry, my bride's cousin shares the ceremony and does all the work.'

She chuckled in genuine mirth. 'Milly, I should inform you, is busily sewing my daughter's dress for the occasion. And since Anthea is a terrible wriggler, I can only say, she's welcome to the task!'

'I…I should like very much to speak with you privately.'

The constrained tone in his voice brought her head up sharply. 'Is…is something wrong, Guy?'

'No, oh, no. Just that I…well, I want to…'

The door opened.

'Tilda, the wretchedest thing! That odious mantua maker—oh, hello, Guy!' Lady St Ormond came into the room closely followed by Georgie.

'Hello, Aunt Marianne, Georgie.' Guy coloured up hotly. 'You're obviously busy, Tilda. I won't disturb you.'

She frowned. 'It's quite all right, Guy. Your aunt and Georgie will excuse us if we leave them for a few moments and you can tell me whatever is on your mind.'

Lady St Ormond smiled. 'Of course, dears. The library is empty, I believe. I looked for Crispin there just a moment ago and he wasn't there. I called out in case he was on the gallery, but he must have gone riding, I think. He said something at breakfast about looking at those horrid traps.'

Tilda glanced around the library as they entered, half-expecting to find Crispin at his desk. Far from leaving all the work to his bailiffs and agents, he oversaw everything himself and read widely on agricultural subjects.

The desk stood in the bay window, littered with papers and piled high with books. The chair stood empty.

'Funny he's gone riding at this hour,' commented Guy. 'He nearly always works in the mornings. Unless something is bothering him. Then he likes to go for a ride to clear the cobwebs, as he says. Maybe the curst traps.'

Tilda bit her lip. She could think of something else that might be bothering him. Frustration. She could attest to that from personal experience. He had wanted her last night. As much as she had wanted him. At least she had the dubious satisfaction of having been the one to refuse the delights offered, but it hadn't helped her to gain a good night's sleep. Her pulse quickened at the memory of his mouth caressing hers, the tender warmth of his hands... If Crispin had spent anything like the dreadful night she had suffered, then she could well believe that he might have gone for a ride to clear his head. She groaned mentally. What a fool she had been. She would have to face this hurdle at some stage.

But not now. Right now Guy stood before her looking thoroughly shamefaced.

He spoke very quietly. 'Tilda, I have to apologise to you.'

'You...what? Whatever for?'

'I never thought that Milly would think...that anyone could misunderstand our friendship...she told me what she said to you. That she had thought you might...' If he hadn't looked so guilty, so worried, she might have smiled.

'Guy, you made it perfectly plain that it was Milly who had engaged your interest and affections. You even asked my advice. I'm not really that stupid, you know!' She looked at him earnestly and laid her hand gently on his arm.

He covered her hand with his, smiling down at her. 'I know that, but Milly was so surprised at the way you flirted.

She said you had never been in the least flirtatious before, and, well…'

Tilda blushed as she remembered the reason she had been flirting with him so conspicuously. Lightly enough, she said, 'Blame it on my frivolous old age and soon-to-be-revoked widowhood. All that freedom went straight to my head.' She smiled. 'Now, tell me—is Milly reassured that it is she you want, not me?'

He grinned. 'Lord, yes. She was cock-a-hoop to think that she had been preferred over your beauty and vast fortune, but she was worried that you might have…even knowing that it was Milly I love…'

'No.' She shook her head. 'You're a dear friend, Guy. No more. Even had you asked me, I would not have accepted you.'

His fingers tightened on hers. 'Really?'

'Really.' After all, she hadn't even meant to accept Crispin, and she was in love with him.

He raised her hand to his lips and kissed it. 'Then we wish each other happy? I know Cris is happy. He would never offer marriage unless he wanted to.'

Her smile wobbled a little, but she said, 'Very happy, Guy. Now, I had best return to those wretched lists. Will you excuse me?'

He smiled. 'Of course…cousin,' and bent to kiss her gently on the corner of the mouth. 'Thank you, Tilda. For everything.'

Standing on tiptoe, she returned his salute. 'You are very welcome, cousin.'

They looked at each other and smiled. Tilda holding her smile in place determinedly. Never mind that the tears she battled had nothing to do with Guy, she didn't dare let him see them in case he thought she had lied to him. She couldn't possibly explain the real reason.

'Come along,' said Guy. 'I'll escort you back to the lists.'

Hastily she demurred. 'No, since I'm here I'll just find something to read. I've finished the book I was reading. You go on.'

She heaved a sigh of relief as he left. A moment to steady herself was what she needed. Poor Guy. Had he really thought she might have fallen in love with him? She winked back a tear to think that Milly had such confidence and trust in her love that she could talk to him about something like that.

If only she had the same sort of courage. Another tear formed. This one escaped and slid down her cheek. She dragged in a deep breath and wiped the tear away. She had nothing to cry about. She was about to marry the man she loved. And everyone thought that he had wanted to marry her and that he was happy about it.

He shouldn't have had to offer for her. More tears fell, blinding her so that she stumbled slightly. If she hadn't given in to her own desires that night, to her own hurt and need, he wouldn't be in this trap. She steadied herself and found her handkerchief, blowing her nose and mopping up the tears. She couldn't go on like this, dissolving into tears at the least excuse.

Somehow she would have to summon up all Lady Winter's cool composure. Only the composure; she didn't want the bitter cynicism. Crispin didn't deserve that. He had only wanted to protect her by doing the honourable thing.

Shoving the handkerchief into her pocket, she left the library with her head held high.

As the library door shut behind Tilda, Crispin, seated in a large wingchair with its back to the gallery railing, groaned and put his head in his hands. He had ignored his mother, wanting a little privacy to sort out his confusion of emotions. Now they were even more tangled.

Guy had kissed her. Very chastely, he had to admit. But nevertheless he had kissed her. Twice if he counted kissing her hand. He ran his hands through his hair.

He ought to have told them he was there, but he hadn't even realised anyone was in the room until he'd heard Guy say that he wished to apologise. He must have dozed off for a moment. His lack of sleep was catching up with him. Thank God they had spoken softly. That was all he'd heard. But that didn't excuse his conduct in looking over the back of his chair in an attempt to hear more. If he hadn't done that he wouldn't have seen Tilda's hand resting on Guy's arm with his hand covering it.

And he wouldn't have seen him kiss her. As though in apology and farewell. What else could Guy have been apologising for other than raising false hopes in Tilda's bosom?

She had kissed him back. And she had wept after he left.

He swore. If only Pemberton had not interfered, he could have given Tilda time to recover from her disappointment and realise that he loved her. Now he would have to come to her on their wedding night knowing beyond all doubt that she loved, had wanted, another.

She wouldn't refuse him. He knew that. But she was reluctant to give herself no matter how much her body wanted him. She had refused last night. His whole body hardened in a rush as he remembered how sweetly her soft curves had yielded to his passion. Yet she had said no.

He longed to comfort her, ease her pain. His heart ached with the need to hold her and look after her. He didn't dare. He didn't trust himself. She had given herself once, needing comfort for her pain. He had taken advantage of her hurt. He couldn't do that again.

Over the next few days he observed an odd change in Tilda's demeanour. From quiet reserve she shifted almost imperceptibly to outright worry. A faint frown creased her brow and he frequently caught a puzzled look on her face, as though she were trying to remember something, something that just eluded her.

She was thoroughly distracted at times and people had to address remarks to her at least twice to gain her attention. He caught her watching him surreptitiously once and blinked when she flushed a deep crimson. The really odd thing though, he thought confusedly, was that she actually looked as though she were happy at times. She frequently had the oddest, tenderest little smile upon her face as though she nursed a precious secret.

'For heaven's sake, Anthea! Stand still. If I stick any more pins into you, you'll feel like a pincushion!' Tilda gave this exasperated advice through a mouthful of pins as she adjusted the fit of Anthea's dress one last time.

'Sorry, Mama.' Anthea stood still, at least, but plainly her mind was still whirling.

'Mama?'

'Mmm?' Tilda still had a mouthful of pins as she adjusted the hem.

'Will I have some little brothers and sisters?'

Tilda just managed to spit the pins out instead of swallowing them. 'What gave you that idea?' she spluttered.

'I thought that was what happened when people got married,' explained Anthea. 'I asked Uncle Cris when he took me riding.'

Keeping a straight face, as she imagined her betrothed's reaction to his prospective stepdaughter demanding information on that subject, was nigh on impossible.

'Did you?' Her voice only wobbled slightly. 'And what did he say?'

'He said I was enough to be going on with, but he thought it was quite a good idea,' said Anthea, obediently pirouetting as Tilda gave her a gentle push. 'And that he was looking forward to it,' she added, coming to a halt.

Tilda blushed. She wondered just what Crispin was looking forward to: having children—or begetting them? Or what she was looking forward to, for that matter.

'I see,' she managed faintly. 'Perhaps, dearest, you might save these questions for me in future. Young ladies shouldn't ask gentlemen things like that.'

'I know *that*,' said Anthea indignantly.

'Then why in heaven's name did you ask Uncle Cris?'

Anthea looked a little conscious. 'Well, I only knew after he told me. He said it was the sort of thing you'd tell me later.'

Much later. Tilda stuck in the last few pins firmly.

'Very well. Take it off carefully, sweetheart. Take it back to Milly and she will sew it up. What are you supposed to be doing now? Does Aunt Marianne have a task for you?'

Anthea shook her head. 'No. I'm helping Mrs Simms. She wants me to stuff the lavender bags while she sews them.' She wriggled back into her dress and scampered off happily.

Tilda and Sarah exchanged glances.

'How sure are ye, milady?' asked Sarah. 'Might just be late this month.'

'Two weeks?' Tilda snorted.

Sarah shrugged. 'Happens, lass—milady.'

'Not to me it doesn't,' said Tilda firmly. 'The last time I was this late, I had Anthea.'

She sneaked a careful look at Sarah. Wasn't she going to scold or something? Ask her what she'd thought she'd been doing? Read her a lecture? She'd only told Sarah just before Anthea had come in, when Sarah had commented worriedly on the tardiness of her monthly courses. She'd been panicking that Tilda might be inconvenienced on her wedding night.

Instead she was probably going to have to tell her bridegroom that she was pregnant already.

And all her strict and upright maid could find to say was,

'Hmm. Be a spring baby, then. Dare say his Grace is tickled to death.'

'*Sarah!*' Tilda was so shocked that her toes tingled. 'Aren't you even going to ask me what I was doing?'

Sarah's grin was positively disgraceful. 'Be a main waste of breath, lass. I *know* what you was doing.' She looked thoughtful and added, for good measure, 'So did his Grace, I'd have to say.' She shrugged and said, 'Where's the problem? He's marrying you in two days and it ain't as if he only offered because of the child. An' like I said, I'll wager me best dress, he's as pleased as punch.'

Tilda didn't return an immediate answer. Her entire being swirled with confusing emotions. One moment she was elated, overjoyed to be bearing Crispin's child, exulting in the fact. The next instant she was shaking in fear at how close she had come to disaster.

'Ye *have* told him?' Sarah's voice broke in on her thoughts.

Biting her lip, Tilda flushed. 'N…no. Not yet.'

None of the etiquette manuals that she had ever read told a woman how to break this sort of news to her husband, even in the most proper of circumstances. Certainly none of them gave one the least notion of how to go on in this instance. She'd had enough trouble telling Jonathan that she was pregnant—and he'd been hoping for it. Crispin, pleased or not, was in for a shock. Besides, he'd withdrawn himself in the past week, since she had refused to share her bed with him. He made quite sure they were never alone and his goodnight kiss had become the merest peck on the cheek. He even called her *my lady*.

'Ah, well,' said Sarah prosaically. 'Be a nice wedding present, like.'

In the event, Tilda found it completely impossible to catch Crispin alone in the two days remaining before their wedding. The house overflowed with visitors, her aunt among them. Lady Pemberton made it perfectly plain that had she been able to chaperon Milly, the girl would certainly not be marrying Guy Malvern.

She took Tilda to task severely, finishing, 'And your uncle tells me that you *trapped* St Ormond into offering for you! It is all of a piece! A more scheming, ungrateful wench I never met! I hope your husband may not live to regret his foolish choice.'

Tilda smiled. 'I did warn you, ma'am. Obviously my fortune was too great a temptation for his Grace.' She saw no reason to inform her aunt that it was Lord Pemberton's interference that had prompted Crispin's offer of marriage. Nor that he had settled her own fortune back on her with no strings attached. Why he had done such a thing, she couldn't begin to imagine, but she was glad that he had. She could still go ahead with her orphanage and refuge for unmarried mothers.

By the night before the wedding she had given up trying to find a private moment with Crispin. She would be private with him tomorrow night. No doubt Sarah was right and he would be pleased. No doubt he wanted an heir, she told herself. And felt ashamed of her cynicism. No one who had seen him with Anthea could doubt that he liked children, would be a good father. He was not the man to resent it if she presented him with nothing but daughters.

She stood by the open window, staring out over the gardens in the faint starlight, unwilling to go to bed. She had finally sent Milly off to bed. Milly was in a complete daze of excitement and terror that at this time tomorrow night, she'd be in Guy's bed, giving herself and her love to a man who loved her. Tilda shut her heart against the stab of pain.

She had more than she had ever hoped for. And the taste was bitter.

This time tomorrow night…she would not be in this room. The Duchess's suite had been prepared for her. An enormous bedchamber with an equally enormous bed, a private sitting room opened off it; and beyond that, down a short private corridor, was Crispin's room. She'd peeped in when she'd been taken to approve her own rooms.

The sheer size of *his* bed had shocked her witless. She'd be lost in it—in more ways than one. Remembering the vigour of his lovemaking, she didn't doubt that the size of his bed would be a distinct advantage. Her senses reeled at the images that spun through her mind. Or would he simply come to her when he wanted her—as Jonathan had—returning to his own bed afterwards? He had been so formal and reserved the last ten days. Perhaps he had decided that a distant relationship would be best.

That might be easier, she told herself. If he didn't stay and hold her, pet her tenderly, love her with words as he had the first time, she might be able to conceal her love. She shut her eyes in despair at the thoughts.

Her bed would feel so cold, so lonely. So empty.

She stared at the bed that she would occupy tonight. Alone. And didn't know whether she wanted tonight to end swiftly or never.

Crispin stared out of the window of his bedchamber, wondering if he had made an appalling mistake, if he should have simply told Tilda the truth—that he loved her—because for the life of him he couldn't imagine how he was going to make love to her tomorrow night without telling her.

And how would she feel about that? She was putting a good face on it, but he had seen the sadness in her eyes whenever she saw Guy and Milly together, the half-hidden hunger. He had seen her weeping after Guy had kissed her in the library. How would she feel tomorrow night, knowing that the man she loved was making love to her cousin?

He swore. The last thing he wanted was to take her on

their wedding night knowing that she was breaking her heart for a man she could not have. He couldn't do that to her. And he didn't think he could explain it to her. Not without telling her that he loved her.

# Chapter Sixteen

'Dearly beloved, we are gathered here in the sight of God, and in the face of this congregation, to join together this man and this woman, and *this* man and *this* woman, in Holy Matrimony…'

Tilda stared straight ahead, not daring to glance to left or right. Crispin stood to her right and Milly and Guy to the left. She was shatteringly aware of her uncle and aunt behind her. She'd caught a glimpse of her aunt's face on the way past, and her uncle's face as he stepped back from Milly. If looks could have killed, she'd be lying dead at the chancel steps.

The Rector's gentle voice flowed on through the preface. She barely heard him and she was cold, so cold. At least she assumed that was why she was shaking. She trembled even more as Crispin's warm hand covered hers, anchoring it safely to his sleeve.

'…not by any to be enterprised, nor taken in hand, un-advisedly, lightly, or wantonly, to satisfy men's carnal lusts and appetites, like brute beasts that have no understanding…'

She whitened. Why was she here? Because of that very thing. Because she had given in to her desire and his…

'...the causes for which matrimony was ordained. First, it was ordained for the procreation of children...'

At this unwitting reminder, she flushed. They'd managed that bit easily enough. The seed of a new life grew within her. The new life she and Crispin had made. Surely that was a good thing?

'...for a remedy against sin...' Crispin's hand pressed on hers. Very unwisely she looked up. Only to encounter a wicked sideways glance. Hurriedly she dragged her eyes from his and concentrated on the Rector.

'Thirdly, it was ordained for the mutual society, help and comfort, that the one ought to have of the other...'

What help and comfort could she be to him? The question throbbed in her heart. She didn't know the answer, but she vowed in that moment that she would have to try. She'd done her best to be a good wife to Jonathan. She loved Crispin—even if he never loved her, she could still be a good wife. But there would have to be honesty between them—she needed to know why he'd married her.

Her trembling steadied as a measure of confidence returned, and the feeling that she was doing something dreadfully wrong receded. Crispin was so solid and reassuring beside her—they could at least be friends. They had much in common, therein would lie the *mutual society, help and comfort.*

She snapped her attention back to the Rector.

'Crispin Anthony. Wilt thou have this woman to thy wedded wife? Wilt thou love her, comfort her, honour and keep her, in sickness and in health; and forsaking all other, keep thee only unto her, so long as ye both shall live?'

'I will.' The two short words rang with utter sincerity, total conviction. They shook Tilda to the core. Did he mean it? Really mean it? There was no time for speculation, it was her turn.

'Matilda Frances. Wilt thou have this man to thy wedded husband to live together after God's ordinance in the holy estate of matrimony? Wilt thou obey him, serve him and love, honour and keep him, in sickness and in health; and forsaking all other, keep thee only unto him, so long as ye both shall live?'

She opened her mouth to give her assent. Nothing came out. Desperately she cleared her throat. Crispin had turned to her, startled query in his eyes.

'I will.' It came out hurriedly, hoarsely and far too softly, but the Rector was obviously satisfied, because he turned to Milly and Guy, both of whom spoke their responses without the least hesitation.

Then the Rector turned back to them.

'Who giveth this woman to be married to this man?'

Lord Winter stepped forward, and possessed himself of her hand. Firmly, protectively. Lovingly. He flashed her a proud smile as he placed her hand in the Rector's and stepped back. Her heart nearly burst with joy. This time she had been given with joy, with pride. She had been bestowed rather than disposed of—and the Rector was placing her hand in Crispin's.

Heat stole through her and she felt the clasp of his fingers tighten as he spoke after the Rector.

'I, Crispin Anthony, take thee, Matilda Frances, to my wedded wife...' sure and certain, his voice resonated through her as he repeated his vows '...to love, and to cherish...' his voice deepened on *love* and hope rippled through her '...till death do us part, according to God's holy ordinance; and thereto I plight thee my troth.'

Swallowing hard, she made her vows steadily, scarcely able to hear herself for the swirl of confused emotion. He'd spoken his vows as if he meant them—just what was she walking into here? Was it possible that he cared for her?

By the time she had pulled herself together, she had the ring on her finger and the Rector had pronounced them to be man and wife together. Dazed, she looked up at Crispin, whose large hand held hers firmly and protectively on his sleeve. His gaze met hers in searing intensity.

He spoke under the cover of Milly and Guy's vows. 'Mine,' he murmured. The deep, possessive growl shuddered through her. Golden eyes widened in shock. She shivered as he added softly, 'Always.'

The rest of the wedding and the wedding breakfast passed in a whirl. Half the county including Crispin's tenants seemed to have crowded into the church. Most of them came back to Ormsby Park where trestle tables had been set up on the south lawn to cater for the crowd.

After a repast in the State Dining Room, of which Tilda ate very little, Crispin escorted her out to the lawn to meet his tenants.

He had watched her through the meal very carefully and realised that she had eaten practically nothing. So he slipped his napkin into his coat pocket and led her firmly outside on to the terrace.

The catering had been generous and he had not the least difficulty in locating a pasty, still nicely hot. Wordlessly he wrapped it in his napkin and presented it to her.

'What...?'

'It's a pasty, ' he said blandly. 'Very filling, nourishing. Eat it.'

Unwillingly she took it from him. It did smell good. She took one bite and discovered that she was ravenous.

'That's better,' said Crispin cheerfully. 'Can't have the bride fainting dead away, after all.' He quizzed her gently with his eyes. 'Not for lack of food, anyway.'

Hot colour mantled her cheeks, as she thought of all the other reasons the new Duchess might find for being dizzy and short of breath.

Crispin was leading her out to be presented to his people as the Duchess. She must concentrate on them. Do her duty as his bride. And not think about the other duties of a bride—the ones on which she had already got a head start.

The last couple to be presented to her was the Marlowes. The keeper greeted her with pleasure and presented his wife with pride. 'We'll be celebratin' our twenty-fifth weddin' day in another month, your Grace. I'll take the liberty of wishin' you the same happiness. An' I hope I'll be here ter see it,' he said gallantly.

Twenty-five years, thought Tilda. Dear God, I'll be fifty! And Crispin would be in his sixties. She peered into the future. Anthea would be thirty—probably a mama herself. Dazedly her hand crept to her belly—and this little one— even this little one would be a man or woman grown. And there would be others, no doubt.

Smiling, she chatted to Mrs Marlowe, outwardly calm, as she spoke of stillrooms and preserves, and the best way to make beeswax polish.

'Aye. I did as you said and watched him.' Marlowe's voice came clearly to her ears. 'You were right, your Grace, though whatever made you reckon to *him* has me fair gapped.'

Crispin was nodding. 'Very well. Leave it. I'll have to deal with it now. Are there any left?'

What on earth were they talking about? mused Tilda. Whatever it was, Crispin looked as though he'd eaten something sour.

'Just the one, your Grace,' said Marlowe. 'Close by the right of way, near where the path from the gardens comes out. 'Tis back in the undergrowth a little.'

'You've sprung it?'

Traps. They were talking about traps. Tilda felt guilty. She'd given no thought to any of Crispin's concerns in the last weeks. And she'd known that this was bothering him.

'Are you quite well, Tilda?' Guy's voice was concerned. She looked up at him with a faint smile. 'I'm very well,

Guy. Just a trifle fagged. It is nothing to worry about. Besides, should you not be fussing over *your* wife?'

He grinned. 'I'll do that later, believe me.' For a moment his grin was just as devilish as his cousin's. Tilda had no trouble believing that for all his tender care and adoration of Milly, he had every intention of pleasuring his bride to the full.

As no doubt Crispin had. Her smile became rather fixed as she responded to Guy's banter. How on earth was she to conceal her feelings when they battered at the guard she had set on them, clamouring for their release?

As Lady Hollow came up, Guy took his leave of her and beat a hasty retreat to Milly's side. Even as she smiled at the old lady's cynical and scurrilous advice on how best to deal with the head of the Malverns, her eyes followed Guy and Milly surreptitiously. All very well for them, she thought despairingly. If Milly cried out words of love in the height of passion, her husband would be delighted. Determinedly she returned her attention to Lady Hollow and did not see Crispin watching her with a twisted smile.

Tilda waited with increasing nervousness for her husband. Sarah had long since been dismissed and still Crispin had not come to her. What on earth could be taking him so long? If he didn't come soon she'd be a gibbering mess. She'd never be able to say all that needed to be said.

Maybe he wasn't coming. The thought crept into her heart with chilly inevitability as time stretched on. She cast a glance at the branch of candles she'd left burning beside the bed. They danced and flickered mockingly. So easy to snuff out—had Crispin's passion died as easily? What did she have to offer him if it had?

Miserably she was about to blow out the candles and get into her lonely bed when she realised what she was doing; to wit, feeling sorry for herself. She straightened up and her eyes narrowed.

If she started feeling sorry for herself, that opened the way for others to feel sorry for her. Like her husband. Whatever else she wanted from him, pity wasn't part of it.

Damn it! It was their wedding night and if Crispin didn't want to mark the occasion in the usual way, then the least he could have done was come and tell her so. Her jaw tightened mulishly. He could tell her now. And his reasons had better be damned good ones!

Clutching her robe and temper around her, she stalked to the door that led to his room.

A single lamp burnt on the chimneypiece and she saw swiftly that the room was empty. A night shirt was laid out on the bed and his wedding clothes lay scattered over the floor. So where in the world *was* he?

Avoiding her obviously. Hurt fury shuddered through her. She might as well return to her own room. She could take a hint and she would not demean herself by waiting here for his Grace's pleasure.

Forcing back tears, she turned to go, and a large book on the window seat caught her eye. The last thing she wanted was a book, but reading all night would be better than crying herself to sleep.

She went over to the window, picked up the book and looked at the title. And blinked. What in God's name was Crispin doing reading the sermons of Doctor John Donne? Somehow she'd have thought the love poetry was more his style.

A light breeze from the open window fanned her cheek. The curtains fluttered. Still clutching the volume, she looked out, over the South Lawn towards the woods. Moonlight silvered the scene before her, casting black shadows, leaching the colour from everything.

Full moon, she thought. Nearly as bright as day. Bright enough to go for a walk...as her husband was doing.

Her jaw dropped and she stared in disbelief as her missing bridegroom stepped into view from the deep shadow cast by the house. Stunned, she watched as he strode across the lawn, in breeches, boots and his shooting jacket.

The conversation she'd heard between him and his keeper—Marlowe, wasn't it—came back to her in dizzying clarity. *I'll deal with that at the first convenient moment.* Did he consider their wedding night a convenient opportunity?

Then she spun around and ran to her room.

By the time she reached the side door, Crispin was nearly lost against the bulk of the woods. He wouldn't have had quite such a head start, but she'd had enough common sense to drag on her carriage dress, thick woollen stockings and a pair of list boots. Nothing else. Running fast enough to catch him would warm her quite satisfactorily.

She got within hailing distance just before he reached the trees. And discovered she was too out of breath. So she ran harder, her boots making no sound on the thick damp grass. She didn't dare let him get too far ahead in the trees, she didn't know the woods as he did. And then abruptly he stopped and looked around. And stared. She could feel his shock reaching her in waves.

Some instinct had warned Crispin that he was not alone. He swung around and wondered if he were dreaming. Tilda, her hair down, was tearing after him. She came up to him panting, her breasts heaving. He tried to ignore that, along with his body's all too predictable response.

'What…the…devil…do you think…you're doing?' she managed, stealing his line.

'Going for a walk,' he said shortly. 'Why don't you go back to the house and I'll tell you all about it later?'

'*Damn* you!' she exploded. 'You're chasing poachers on our wedding night? Don't you think that's taking your responsibilities a little too far? Or were you so eager to avoid me that you thought you'd go out and get shot?' She knew that was a trifle melodramatic, but by then she was too angry to care.

Judging by the look on Crispin's face, he thought she was being melodramatic as well. 'I can safely assure you that there's no danger to me. Go back to bed. If I'd thought you'd notice I was gone and worry, I'd have told you.'

'Notice? *Worry!*' She couldn't believe it. 'Just where did you think I'd expect you to be on our wedding night? And if there's no danger, then I dare say you won't mind if I accompany you!'

'No!' His refusal was peremptory.

'Hah! Then it is dangerous!' Her eyes glittered at him challengingly in the moonlight. 'Resign yourself to a companion, your Grace. Unless you plan on taking me back to the house and tying me to the bed.'

For a single searing moment Crispin considered doing just that. His blood roared. The images she'd conjured up were erotic in the extreme. Somehow he managed to control himself enough to say, 'An interesting notion, my dear. But my reasons for asking you to stay behind stem from discretion, not concern for your safety.'

'I'm not,' stated Tilda trenchantly, 'interested in discretion. Any more than I'm interested in safety. Try again.'

He swore. Tying her to the bed wouldn't work. He'd never make it out of the bedchamber. In fact, he probably wouldn't make it off the bed.

'Very well,' he grated as he started walking. 'But just remember later that it was your idea in the first place.'

Following him into the woods, she retorted icily, 'Naturally I acknowledge that you did not invite me to accompany you.'

'I meant when I tie you to the bed!' he ground out in savage frustration, painfully aware of the unbridled lust in his voice. And stalked on.

A pregnant silence followed as Tilda grappled with all the ramifications of this. To her absolute fury, the idea of

Crispin tying her to the bed did not cause a single flutter
of panic, let alone disgust. Shock was another matter. Delightful, anticipatory shock that rippled up and down her
spine in feathery excitement as she contemplated the
thought of being completely helpless and vulnerable before
him. At his mercy. Not that he'd need to tie her up to
achieve that.

Desperately she forced herself to think of something else,
before her knees gave out. Like the fact that if he wanted
to tie her to the bed, then maybe he hadn't come out tonight
because he didn't want her. Which meant that he must have
thought she didn't want him.

She stared at his back as he walked ahead of her. Large
and dark, positively unyielding. She'd thought she understood his motivation and reasons for marrying her. Quite
obviously she'd got things confused. Why on earth would
he think that she didn't want him? After the way she'd
behaved that night and every other time he'd touched her.

She cursed under her breath as she stumbled slightly.
And felt his fingers close like a vice on her wrist.

'Quiet now!' he ordered. 'We're getting close and I don't
want you to disturb him.'

As he spoke they stepped out of the narrow path into a
broad ride that Tilda recognised at once as the right of way
that ran straight through Crispin's lands. Considerably annoyed, she tugged at her wrist. It had absolutely no effect
at all. Except that he tightened his grip even further.

'There,' he breathed and gestured with the hand that held
the lamp.

At the side of the ride stood a tall horse. Even in this
light Tilda could see that it was not the sort of animal an
ordinary common poacher would ride. This horse belonged
to a gentleman. Or at least someone wealthy.

Releasing her, Crispin put the lamp down behind a bush.

'Wha—?'

'Shh. I'm listening.'

Tilda glared as she rubbed some life back into her wrist. Then she heard it too. Someone else moving about in the woods just beyond the horse. She couldn't think why she was surprised. After all, the horse hadn't come out here all saddled and bridled by itself.

A tall figure, carrying something, came into view between the trees.

'Stay here,' muttered Crispin and stepped out.

'Good evening, Sir Richard. Could I hold that trap while you mount?'

Tilda wondered if she were going mad. Sir Richard-all-poachers-should-be-hanged-Benton? Poaching? It didn't make sense.

There was a metallic crash and curse.

'*St Ormond?* What in the name of all that's holy are you doing out here tonight?'

Sir Richard, thought Tilda in confusion, sounded as though he'd nearly had a heart attack.

'Catching poachers,' he said calmly.

A snort greeted this. 'I'd have supposed you had something better to do with your time tonight of all nights! In *my* day we bedded our brides promptly!'

This was too much for Tilda. She stepped out of the shadows and said sweetly, 'I couldn't agree more. Perhaps, Sir Richard, you might explain just what you are about so that I can persuade my husband to attend to his duties.'

She ignored the outraged expression on her husband's face as she strolled up to them. Instead she concentrated on Sir Richard, who was goggling in disbelief.

Coolly she looked at the heap of metal at his feet. 'A trap, Sir Richard? I thought you disapproved of poaching. So, how do you explain this?'

'Tilda, please let me deal with this…' began Crispin.

'Oh, let be, lad,' said Sir Richard resignedly. 'No doubt you realised I'd take the chance, but I thought you'd be better off dealing with your wife.' He turned to Tilda and said, 'I beg your pardon, your Grace. I thought if I pushed St Ormond hard enough he'd crack down on the poaching on his lands. But I never intended Bull to get away and hurt anyone. Just a few traps to make him sit up and take notice. I've been removing them for the last couple of weeks.'

'Then I take it there'll be no more of it, Sir Richard,' said Crispin coldly. 'Because if there is…'

A harsh bark of laughter interrupted him. 'You must have a maggot in your head! My old bones are cursing me for what I've put them through, crawling about damp woods in the middle of the night at my age. Now if you'll pass that damn trap up to me, I'll be on my way.'

With that he mounted his horse, grunting audibly at the effort. He frowned down at Crispin. 'Well? Are you going to pass me that trap, boy?'

Crispin shook his head. 'Leave it, sir. I collect it's one of the old ones we got rid of when I inherited. Marlowe will collect it. Goodnight.'

The irascible old gentleman glared down at him. 'I'll wish you the same. Seems to me you'd better get that chit home and warm her up. Or maybe it's just my old bones.' With a final disgusted snort, he wheeled his horse and rode off.

Dazed, Tilda watched him go. Innumerable questions flashed through her head, but Crispin forestalled her.

'We're going home. Right now.' Determinedly he started walking. If he concentrated hard, he might just manage to get her home before he succumbed to temptation and took Benton's advice. Literally. Before he lifted her skirts and tumbled her right here in the woods like a village maiden on May Day.

## Chapter Seventeen

'How long have you known that Sir Richard was responsible?' Tilda was completely stunned by the denouement. Firmly she resisted the temptation to press close to Crispin's side as they made their way back through the woods. Small scurryings and an occasional squeal told her that they were not the only creatures in the dark woods. There could be nothing to harm her, she knew, but the darkness pressed in.

'For certain, only this morning, when Marlowe told me that he'd watched Sir Richard removing a steel trap. But I'd suspected, since after his dog attacked you.'

His voice was tight and clipped. Tilda sensed that he would prefer not to say any more, but she needed to know. Needed to know why he'd chosen to come out, tonight of all nights.

'Why did you suspect him?'

'The trapping stopped at once. And Marlowe mentioned to me that he'd noticed that most of the traps were set very close to that right of way. Sir Richard uses that path all the time, especially if he rides over to dine with old Whittlesea—which he does frequently. And he's a little old for crawling around in damp undergrowth.'

'Oh.'

'Of course Marlowe saw him, but never thought to watch him—of all people—until I suggested it. In fact, he tells me he'd generally say good evening to the old devil. He thought I'd run mad. But he watched. And saw Sir Richard removing the traps.'

Tilda understood. 'So you wanted to confront him privately—and by doing it this way, you didn't have to go to him and make an accusation. You could just ask him why.'

A short silence followed. 'That's it,' he said at last. 'You understand me very well. The last thing I wanted was to run the least risk of this getting out. If I'd called on him, there was always the chance of someone overhearing. And I certainly didn't wish to make a straight accusation.'

'But why tonight?' She still felt hurt. Surely he could at least have told her. Couldn't he? They were married. Did he not wish to share things with her? Did he want a fashionable marriage of the type he had intended with Milly? Had that note of sincerity as he took his vows really meant nothing?

His voice darkened. 'This, according to Marlowe, was the last trap. I thought he'd take the opportunity to remove it as quickly as possible. It was risky, being so close to the ride but, after today's celebrations, there was very little chance of being caught.' A note of irony crept into his voice. 'I somehow doubt that he expected either of us to be wandering around the woods tonight.'

That was only too probable, thought Tilda. She would be willing to wager a considerable sum that whatever Guy and Milly were doing right now, they were not out chasing poachers. Bitterly she faced the unpalatable knowledge that rather than bed his bride, her husband had elected to chase poachers. Tears stung her eyes, blurring the faint light cast by the lantern.

Plainly Crispin was in no hurry to consummate their marriage, which suggested that the night he had spent in her bed had not satisfied him in the least. No matter that she had died and shattered beneath him, that she had given herself and everything to their lovemaking—it had meant nothing to him. Certainly his comments about tying her up had been nothing more than a practical solution to keep her out of his way! Her wanton mind had imagined that note of lust in his voice.

Pain lanced through her as she fought to hold back a sob of despair. She should never have come after him. If she managed to get back to the house without crying it would be a miracle.

Stumbling over a tree root, she cursed under her breath and then gasped as she was caught up and held safely against Crispin's side. His powerful arm encircled her; she wriggled but his grip was inescapable. Fire shot through her, burning, melting. And her breathing hitched as her heart raced.

'I can manage.' She tried to sound calm, unconcerned. And succeeded only in sounding snippy.

'You'll be safer with me.'

Still his voice was tight, controlled. As if he'd prefer not to be holding her.

At that moment something snapped inside her. Something that had been gripping the reins of her self-control, holding her back. To the devil with *safe*! She didn't want him merely to look after her and protect her. She was sick of *safe*. She wanted him to love her. Right now she wanted him to ravish her—and all he could do was tell her she would be safe with him!

'I don't want to be safe!' She squirmed furiously. 'That wasn't why I married you!'

He let her go and she swung around to face him. 'Why not just tell me where you were going? How do you think I felt, when you didn't even come to me on our wedding night? When you weren't even in your own room? If you didn't want me, why marry me?' Fury and hurt split over. 'I'm sick of being protected! Of being rescued—looked after. Why can't you just see me as a woman? Why didn't you come to me tonight? What was the real reason?'

She was shaking with the effort not to cry, not to break down completely. Through her tears she stared at Crispin. His face was wreathed in shadows flung by the lantern. His expression was unreadable.

When he spoke it was in a flat, deadened voice. 'I thought, under the circumstances, you would prefer that I didn't force myself on you tonight of all nights. That was why I came out. It was the only way I could stay away from you.'

Tilda stared. 'Force yourself on me! What are you talking about? You're my husband!

She thought his mouth twisted bitterly. 'But not the husband you wanted. I was not prepared to bed you when you were, deep down, longing for another man. I didn't think it fair on either of us.'

*What other man? What was he talking about? Did he think she was mourning Jonathan?*

Tangled, confused skeins of thought robbed her of speech.

He went on. 'You needed time to recover from your disappointment. I intended to discuss the whole situation with you tomorrow. I should have done it long ago—but the time was never right, so—'

'What disappointment are you talking about?' An incredible suspicion was forming in her mind.

He groaned. 'Tilda, don't pretend with me. It's not necessary, my darling. I knew how hurt you were when Guy offered for Milly. I didn't intend to offer for you that morning—I was going to wait. I knew you'd think I'd offered out of obligation after what had happened—but your uncle was prepared to blackmail me into marriage with Milly by threatening to make public that you were my mistress. He saw me leave your room that morning. So I didn't dare delay.'

She pounced on the last sentence. 'You were going to offer for me anyway?' Shards of doubt, of confusion, stung her. Why had he wished to offer for her? 'You thought I was in love with Guy? But we never…I mean…we were just friends. He flirted with *me* to draw attention from his interest in Milly. I knew that. He never made any pretence otherwise and nor did I wish it.' Her eyes widened. Surely he didn't still think… 'I never slept with Guy…I…thought you knew that.'

'Of course I knew that!' he said roughly. He took a step towards her. She backed warily and he stopped. 'Tilda, are you saying that you weren't in love with Guy? Ever?'

'Never,' she avowed.

He swore. 'Damn it, Tilda, I was in the library that time you and Guy came in. He…he kissed you, and you kissed him back. Then you cried after he left. I…I assumed…'

Shock hit her. 'You were there?'

He nodded. 'On the gallery. I'm sorry. I didn't mean to eavesdrop, but by the time I realised you were there…'

'Guy was apologising for any embarrassment and hurt our flirtation might have caused me,' admitted Tilda. 'Milly and he both wondered if I had taken him seriously.'

'But you didn't.'

'No,' she said quietly. 'Why did you ask me to marry you, if you thought I was in love with him?' An unwelcome thought struck her. 'Or did you offer *because* you thought I was in love with Guy?' Marrying her because he believed it was his duty to protect her from a scandal he had in part created, she thought she could bear…but if…

He swore. 'Yes, damn it!'

A shudder ran through her. 'Not because *you* were in love?'

Tense, searing silence knifed between them. It quivered in the darkness, cold and deadly.

She was about to turn away when his answer came, as if it were ripped from him.

'Yes, that too. Very deeply.'

To hear him say it was worse than the silence. Worse than the prior knowing. This made it real. Gave it life.

'With Milly.' Her voice sounded as dead as his. She'd been mad to force the issue and lay bare his hurt. Believing her in love with Guy, he'd had the sensitivity to hold back from her tonight. She should have accorded him the same courtesy...

'With *Milly*?'

Dazedly Tilda wondered why every tree in the wood hadn't been flattened.

'But you knew I wasn't!'

Shock tore through him. How the hell could she have thought him in love with Milly? After all the cynical and hurtful things he'd said to her on the subject of marriage and his reasons for offering for Milly? And if she hadn't been in love with Guy, why had she been so upset? Realisation struck. She'd made the same mistake that he had. No—the same *mistakes*—plural. And one of those mistakes was not one he was prepared to make ever again.

'Let me get this straight,' he said very carefully. 'I offered for you thinking that you were nursing a broken heart over Guy; and you accepted, thinking that I was wearing the willow for your cousin? Is that it?'

'Well, sort of.' She sounded hunted.

'Sort of?' He couldn't help the edge in his voice. 'No more hedging, Tilda. What does *sort of* mean?'

'I never meant to accept an offer of marriage from you!' she burst out.

'Then what in Hades did you say *yes* for?' he demanded, justifiably incensed.

'I didn't realise you were offering marriage!' she shot back. 'I thought...I thought... *Oh, God!* You'd spent the whole *night* in my bed! I'd behaved like a...a wanton practically every time you touched me—I'd told you I had no intention of ever marrying again; that there was nothing marriage could give me that I couldn't have without it. And I'm as close to illegitimate as makes no difference. I thought you were asking me to be your mistress!'

'I beg your pardon?'

'I...I thought—'

*'And you accepted?'* Protective fury surged through him. How dare she hold herself so cheaply! How dare she accept such an offer! Even from himself? Come to think of it, how dare she even think that he would offer such a thing to her.

*'Why the hell did you accept?'*

And then he realised that she was crying. That tears were falling silently, spilling over in soundless pain. His own eyes felt hot as he saw her mouth trembling, saw her face crumple as she turned away.

Swearing, he took two strides and caught her. There had been enough distance between them. He enfolded her in his arms, cradling her against his body. And gloried in the way she surrendered and melted, soft curves moulding to his hard muscles. She clung to him, pressing herself closer, as though she wanted to be a part of him. And she would be. Very soon.

The surge of rampant desire he had been holding in check for weeks ripped through him. He knew a fierce satisfaction that he could give in to it now, seduce her to it. She had never loved Guy—she would be his and his only. Finally he thought he understood, thought he knew why she had held him at bay, why she had been so unhappy. But he wasn't taking any chances this time. He was going to make quite certain.

Tenderly he stroked her hair. 'It's all right...we're both idiots,' he whispered. 'We should have been more open with each other. But the main thing is that we understand now...and we're married. You're mine, Tilda. Always.' He rained kisses on her soft curls, threading his fingers through the silken strands, spreading them over her shoulders.

Gently he found her chin and teased her into lifting her tearstained face.

She could feel herself melting, but before he could kiss her, she put a hand over his mouth. She had to know the truth. 'Cris. You said before that you…that you were in love…' She gasped as he began kissing the palm of her hand, as he sucked gently at her fingers, taking them one by one into the wet heat of his mouth.

'I said…that…because I was…am,' he murmured between bites.

'Who…with?' Her knees were so jellified she could barely frame the question and a thousand darting fires had sprung up under her skin. And an aching, yearning hope that she dared not surrender to—that threatened to destroy her if it were denied.

'You mean, *with whom*?' His voice was unsteady. 'Haven't you understood that yet, my blind little love?'

He bent his head and took her lips in a kiss that was inexpressibly tender, his mouth moving on hers in passionate demand. And she yielded to it with a sob of joy, her lips parting under his in utter surrender as he gathered her closer. Fiery delight winged through her, scorching as she felt his arms tighten around her, felt the pressure of his lips deepen, felt his tongue plunge into the hot sweetness of her mouth in fierce possession.

Wildly she returned his kisses, tangling her tongue with his, exploring his mouth.

At last he lifted his head and breathed. 'Do you understand now, my darling?' With a groan he hauled her closer. 'But why? In God's name! *Why* did you accept my offer if you thought I wanted you as my mistress?'

'Because I loved you so much,' she whispered. 'I thought that it was all I'd ever have of you…and when I realised what you had offered, I was terrified…thinking that I'd never be able to hide how I felt in a marriage.'

She felt him stiffen. 'You loved me? You accepted what

you thought was a *carte blanche* because you loved me? And the night we made love—it was me you wanted? Not comfort?'

'Just you,' she murmured against his cheek. 'Only ever you. I couldn't bear to hurt you—insult you—by telling you what I'd thought. Especially as I thought you'd been hurt by Milly.'

A moment's silence ensued.

'I think,' said Crispin in a very careful voice, 'that we had better keep moving. We definitely need to be somewhere more private.'

'We…we do?' Her voice was breathless. 'Where?'

'Bed,' came the uncompromising answer.

'I thought you wanted to keep moving.' Tilda was puzzled at the detour. They were deep in the darkness under the willow tree by the lake and Crispin had drawn her into his arms.

'I said we needed to be somewhere more private,' he murmured, feathering a kiss over her trembling lips, biting softly at the tender lower lip and stroking it with his tongue.

Tilda gasped and he filled her mouth—a slow, purposeful penetration, a promise of things to come. She sank against him, into him, her body melting in surrender to his strength. She moaned and sobbed as he traced the line of her jaw with his lips, found the wildly beating pulse at the base of her throat and laved it with a hot sweep of his tongue. Fire streaked from her aching breasts to her belly and lower so that she shifted her thighs against him in frantic need. One corner of her dazed mind knew that she'd never be able to walk to the house if he kept this up.

He was nipping at one ear lobe, his warm breath driving her wild but she somehow managed to say, 'You…you said you wanted to take me to bed…' She sucked in a startled breath as his hand shifted to her bodice and began undoing buttons.

'I'll settle for just taking you.' His voice was a possessive, predatory growl, drifting down to her out of the dark.

For a moment she didn't understand. And then, 'Here?' A shock of wickedly knowing delight lanced through her at the thought that he was going to tumble her right here by the lake.

'Right here,' he affirmed. 'And now.' She could hear the devilish smile in his husky voice and the barely leashed desire.

Deft fingers had reached the buttons at her waist and he paused to slip one hand inside, to caress soft warm curves that heated and melted. His fingers teased and cupped the sweet mounds of her breasts.

'No chemise,' he observed. 'How very convenient.' On the word he bent his head and drew one puckered and aching nipple into the heat of his mouth. Tantalisingly he licked and teased until she cried out and arched against him, begging for more. She felt his lips curve in triumph and then he suckled, hard. She screamed softly, her knees buckling, and felt his arms tighten.

He released that breast, but only to treat its burning twin to the same sweet torture. This time she tried to control her scream, but he suckled harder until she sobbed her pleasure. Only then did he raise his head to say, 'No one will hear you out here. ' Undoing a few more buttons, he added, 'Except me.' His tone suggested that he didn't mind in the least if she screamed.

Wild with need, her fingers flickered over the buttons of his shirt, then gripped it, pulling it free of his breeches. His teeth flashed in a delighted smile as he stepped back and shrugged out of his shooting jacket.

She blinked as he flung it around her shoulders, sliding first one and then her other arm into it.

'Wha—?'

'You'll need it,' he growled.

She stared up at him in confusion, scarcely able to think

for the desire scorching through her veins. He was pressing her backward even as she wondered what he was doing.

'The ground's damp,' he said, with a wicked grin, as she brought up against the hard trunk of the willow. Her hands pressed against his chest; she wondered dazedly which was the harder, his body or the tree. She thought the tree might—just—have the advantage. His weight held her trapped as he took her mouth again, plundering, devouring.

He groaned in delight as he felt her soaring response, the wild sweetness of her kisses as her tongue danced with his, as her body clung and moulded. A shudder ran through him as he felt small hands slip under his shirt, stroking, exploring. One slid up over the hair-roughened muscles of his chest, found a nipple and circled it curiously. He felt his whole body tighten, shift from hard to harder; and then, as she found his other nipple, to sheer agony.

He lifted his head and through the haze of heat clouding his mind, concentrated on the buttons at the front of her gown.

'How far do these go?' he rasped.

'Hmm?' Plainly she was as dazed as he.

'Do they go all the way to the hem?' he ground out.

'Uh…yes.'

Every instinct howled with triumph. That, he thought, was a great deal more than convenient. It was inspired. He fastened his lips to her throat and slid down, tasting, feasting all the way into the creamy vale between her breasts and over the gentle swell of her soft belly until he knelt before her to deal with the last few buttons. So that she stood fully bared to his gaze, to his hands. And to his mouth.

She was tugging at his shirt and he raised his arms to allow her to pull it off. He felt her fingers sink into the muscles of his shoulders, entwine themselves in his hair. Felt her stooping to join him.

Instantly his hands gripped her bottom. Hard. Holding her upright.

'I told you,' he growled. 'The ground's damp.'

'But…' The protest strangled in her throat as she realised just what he intended. That the extra padding of his coat was not to protect her from the ground, but from the tree. Sheer wanton excitement speared through her at the mere thought.

Shudders of need rippled downward as he surged to his feet and lifted her against him. She was frantic with need, her body arching wildly as he gripped her bottom. Instinctively she wrapped her legs around his waist, opening herself to him.

'Please…oh please…' She sought his mouth with hers. He took it fiercely as he let her slide down on to him, as his loins surged, thrusting deeply into the heated, silken sheath that welcomed him.

They were one. His weight pinning her to the tree was hers, his hands beneath her bottom kneaded and supported her. And his mouth melded to hers, swallowing her cries of pleasure as he moved powerfully against her, inside her, his hair-brushed chest shifting against her swollen breasts even as he surged deep within her body so that she no longer knew where she ended and he began.

She broke and shattered in his arms, helpless and blind in the storm that tore them apart and left them clinging to each other in its wake. Tilda was barely aware of him lowering her to the ground and wrapping her safely in his arms. Warm hands caressed and soothed, a husky voice murmured words of passion, of love. And she floated, sated and content.

'I hope, lady mine, that you intend to let us get back to the house now.' His teasing question breathed into her ear as she drifted in a pleasurable golden void, bounded only by his arms and chest as he held her tenderly. They sat leaning against the tree.

'Hmm.' Her mind wouldn't focus. She didn't even want it to.

'The house,' he growled insistently.

Part of her mind revived. 'Why?'

His body shifted restlessly against her. 'So I can get on with my husbandly duties, of course.'

'Oh.' Now why hadn't that occurred to her? Possibly his style hadn't been in the least cramped by their present location. But he'd said something earlier, about the ground being damp. She wouldn't want him to catch a chill.

'Again?' There was no hint in her voice that she found the idea of carrying out her wifely duties again in the least distasteful. Quite the opposite, thought her gratified husband.

'Of course again,' he said. 'I can assure you that the last month has been hell on earth. And I have every intention of reaping my just rewards.' He dropped a kiss on her hair. 'Besides, we'd better get started on all those brothers and sisters Anthea requested. These things take a little effort as I'm sure you know.'

'Do they?' She couldn't help the mischief and sheer smug triumph in her voice.

Warily he asked, 'Don't they?'

'Not as much as you might have thought,' she whispered, sitting up so that she could see his face. Stunned shock followed by a strangely intense glitter blazed in his eyes. Then they were hooded as he looked down.

Slowly his hand shifted down from her breast to curve wonderingly, possessively, over her belly. Fingers traced and marvelled at the soft swell. She saw him swallow, then his eyes were back on hers.

'You're having my baby?' His voice was molten. 'Then that night...?'

Breathlessly she nodded.

'When…when did you know?' he whispered. His fingers still caressed and stroked her belly, as though he had to touch to believe.

She trembled at the loving awe in his touch. 'A week ago…I should have told you earlier…'

Dazed silence hung between them. At last he said, 'Thank God for your uncle, then.' And pulled her back into his arms, cradling her against him.

'My uncle?' Tilda couldn't see any reason to be grateful to Lord Pemberton.

'Oh, yes,' said Crispin. 'If he hadn't tried to blackmail me that morning, I wouldn't have offered for you. Not then. I was going to wait, give you time since I thought you were in love with Guy.' He groaned. 'Fool that I was! But I knew if your uncle saw you first, you'd never accept my offer. You'd think I'd only offered out of obligation… And if I'd waited—then found you were increasing…' His arms tightened, his voice became muffled against her hair. 'You might never have quite believed that I married you for love. It's been hard enough. Did Pemberton tell you he'd seen me? What he'd tried to do?'

'Yes,' she whispered. 'I was so confused, I couldn't think straight. I'd thought you were hurt about Milly, but then I did wonder if you were offering for me to protect me…and I just couldn't ask…'

'You didn't trust me?'

She clung, realising his hurt. 'It wasn't that. After that night, I knew if we were alone together, if I tried to speak to you about why you really offered for me, I'd probably give myself away. I didn't want you to know I loved you, I didn't want you to feel sorry for me. And then you seemed to withdraw…so I decided to wait until tonight to tell you I was having your baby and try to find out why you married me…' She pressed closer. 'When you weren't in your room…'

'This reticence of yours is going to be a problem,' he

observed drily. 'I'll have to do something about it. Because I like hearing you say that you love me, and pity hasn't got a chance with all the other things I feel for you. So get rid of that idea.'

'Very well,' said Tilda dutifully. Then, curiously, 'Just what do you intend to do about my reticence?'

His lips curved wickedly and a matching gleam sprang to his eyes. 'Oh, I think I'll just encourage you to tell me what you're feeling.'

One hand slid over her hip, teasing, heating her.

She gasped and wriggled in sudden excitement.

'Not good enough, my sweet.' His voice was low and hungry. His fingers explored further and she cried out in pleasure, her fingers sinking into his shoulders as he stroked and probed, releasing a flood of searing desire. He could feel it flowing through her.

'Better,' he murmured as she twisted against him. 'But I can see you need lots of practice.' He drew a deep breath. 'In bed!' Determinedly ignoring her outraged protests and his own inclinations, he hauled her to her feet and started to do up the buttons of her dress. And realised that wasn't a sensible move.

It was far too tempting to undo them again.

'You do them up,' he said firmly, looking around for his shirt. He pulled it on over his head. It smelt of damp grass. God only knew what Stubbs would think. Or of the inevitable grass stains on his leathers, he thought as he buttoned them up. He could only hope the truth wouldn't occur to him. Not that Stubbs wasn't discreet. He just didn't think that he could deal with the pokered-up face his valet used to conceal amusement.

And he definitely didn't relish the idea of any of his staff catching them sneaking back into the house at dawn. No. Returning to the house now was the best option. Before things got out of hand. Once in his bedchamber he had every intention of making sure that things got thoroughly out of hand.

Crispin awakened in the grey light of dawn with his exhausted, sated bride settled safely where she belonged. In his arms, in the ducal bed. He'd finally got past Tilda's reserve to the achingly sweet, loving woman it had hidden. The wildly passionate wanton. To discover that she was his, body, heart and soul. She'd given him the two most precious gifts she had to offer; herself—completely and unconditionally. And she was carrying his child. Boy or girl— he didn't give a damn. The knowledge sent his heart soaring.

'Crispin?' It was the softest of murmurs.

'Mmm?'

She wriggled even closer, snuggling her cheek into the curve of his shoulder, his arm tightened possessively.

'Did I mention that I love you?'

'The subject did come up,' he said with a throaty chuckle. 'But I'm quite happy to be reminded.' A short, considering pause as he slid his hand lovingly over her curves. 'Frequently. I take my vows seriously—there was something in there about being fruitful in the procreation of children.'

A deliciously voluptuous, sleepy chuckle greeted this. 'You've already dealt with that, your Grace.'

'Practice,' asserted his Grace virtuously, 'makes perfect. Besides, I said I'd worship you with my body, my darling, and I intend to do just that.' And he suited the action to the word.

\* \* \* \* \*

## Harlequin Historicals®
### Historical Romantic Adventure!

# ESCAPE TO A LAND LONG AGO AND FAR AWAY IN THE PAGES OF HARLEQUIN HISTORICALS

## ON SALE APRIL 2005

## THE VISCOUNT
### by Lyn Stone

Lily Bradshaw finds herself in a dire situation after her husband's death and seeks out the only person she knows in London: Viscount Duquesne. Guy agrees to marry Lily to protect her and her young son from harm's way. Will their marriage of convenience turn to one of true happiness and love?

## THE BETROTHAL
### by Terri Brisbin, Joanne Rock and Miranda Jarrett

Love is in the air this spring, when Harlequin Historicals brings you three tales of romance in the British Isles. *The Claiming of Lady Joanna* features a beautiful runaway bride and the man who is determined to claim her for his wife. In *Highland Handfast,* a Scottish lord agrees to a temporary marriage with an old childhood love, but plans on convincing her to make it permanent! And in *A Marriage in Three Acts,* a noble lord finds himself enchanted by a beautiful actress when her troupe of traveling players arrive at the lord's estate.

# Harlequin Historicals®
## Historical Romantic Adventure!

## FOR RIVETING TALES OF RUGGED MEN AND THE WOMEN WHO LOVE THEM CHECK OUT HARLEQUIN HISTORICALS!

### ON SALE MARCH 2005

### THE BACHELOR
### by Kate Bridges

At the town harvest festival, dashing bachelor Mitchell Reid is raffled off for charity—and lands in the unlikely arms of no-nonsense, hardworking Diana Campbell. Ever since the Canadian Mountie mistakenly tried to arrest her brothers, she's attempted to deny her attraction to the roguish Mitch. Twenty-four hours spent in his company just might change her mind....

### TURNER'S WOMAN
### by Jenna Kernan

Rugged mountain man Jake Turner rescues Emma Lancing, the sole survivor of an Indian massacre. Burned by love in the past, he's vowed to steer clear of women. But the young woman in his care is strong and capable—and oh, so beautiful. Can this lonely trapper survive a journey west with his heart intact?

**www.eHarlequin.com**

HHWEST36

# Harlequin Historicals®
## Historical Romantic Adventure!

## SAVOR THESE STIRRING TALES OF LOVE IN REGENCY ENGLAND FROM HARLEQUIN HISTORICALS

### ON SALE MAY 2005

### THE DUCHESS'S NEXT HUSBAND
#### by Terri Brisbin

The Duke of Windmere receives word that he's going to die, and tries to get his affairs in order—which includes finding his wife a new husband! But as the duke's efforts go awry and he starts to fall in love with the duchess again, dare he hope they will find true happiness together—before it's too late?

### THE MISSING HEIR
#### by Gail Ranstrom

Presumed dead, Adam Hawthorne returns to London after four years to discover his uncle passed away and the young widow is in possession of his inheritance. Adam is determined to uncover the truth, but the closer he gets to Grace Forbush, the more he desires his beautiful aunt-by-marriage—in his arms!

If you enjoyed what you just read,
then we've got an offer you can't resist!

# Take 2 bestselling
# love stories FREE!
# Plus get a FREE surprise gift!